Urgent
Care

HANNAH ALEXANDER

THE HEALING TOUCH BOOK THREE

Urgent Care

BETHANYHOUSE
MINNEAPOLIS, MINNESOTA

Published by Bethany House Publishers
11400 Hampshire Avenue South
Bloomington, Minnesota 55438
www.bethanyhouse.com

Bethany House Publishers is a Division of
Baker Book House Company, Grand Rapids, Michigan.

Printed in the United States of America

Library of Congress Cataloging-in-Publication Data

Alexander, Hannah.
    Urgent care / by Hannah Alexander.
        p.   cm. — (The healing touch ; Bk. 3)
    ISBN 0-7642-2530-8 (pbk.)
    1. Clergy—Fiction. 2. Storms—Fiction. 3. Physicians—Fiction. I. Title.
PS3551.L35558U74   2003
813'.54—dc21

                                                                                        2003000975

"When you pass through the waters,
I will be with you;
and when you pass through the rivers,
they will not sweep over you."
ISAIAH 43:2a

In loving memory of

Cecil Louise Robinson,

June 3, 1909—August 5, 2002,
a beloved neighbor and friend,
who inhabited our hearts through
the character of Mrs. Cecile Piedmont.
Your children rise up
and call you blessed.

Books by

Hannah Alexander

FROM BETHANY HOUSE PUBLISHERS

Sacred Trust

Solemn Oath

Silent Pledge

THE HEALING TOUCH

Second Opinion

Necessary Measures

Urgent Care

Web site for Hannah Alexander:
www.hannahalexander.com

HANNAH ALEXANDER is the pen name for the writing collaboration of Cheryl and Melvin Hodde. They have eight previous books to their credit and currently make their home in Missouri, where Melvin practices emergency medicine.

CHAPTER 1

Ernest Mourglia slid his stringer of fish into the shallow water along the shore of the Black Oak River, loving the smell of the water, the squeak of his chest-high rubber waders, the chatter of the rapids downstream. He loved Missouri in April, especially when he managed to lure Dutch Rosewitz, his favorite fishing rival, away from the barbershop on an unseasonably warm Friday evening.

Even better, he enjoyed the fact that his nearly eighty years of fishing experience almost always guaranteed that he would fill his stringer before Rosewitz—a youngster in his sixties.

Ernest baited his hook and drew his fishing pole back for another cast.

"Gettin' late," Rosewitz said.

Ernest halted, midswing, and gave his buddy an irritated glance. Disturbing an expert fisherman midcast was like trying to distract a champion checkers player from a winning move.

Again, Ernest drew his pole back, and with a long-practiced flick of his wrists he released the line.

"Storm's brewing, too," Rosewitz said.

The hook snagged a limb of the sycamore above them and plopped barely ten feet from shore. Ernest glared at Rosewitz as he reeled the line back in. "You did that on purpose."

The barber raised eyebrows that grew with the same abandon as the kudzu vine that was trying to take over the forest across the river. "Just telling it like it is. Look at that sky. Fish'll stop biting. We might as well go home."

"They might've stopped biting for *you,* but I plan to have my limit in just a few minutes." A low rumble of thunder echoed Ernest's final cast, and this time the line flew in a perfect arc across the water.

Rosewitz reeled in his own line. "Showoff," he muttered, scrambling along the rocky shore toward the cliffs downriver.

Ernest chuckled and stepped deeper into the water. "Not my fault you don't like to wear waders." A fella had to be willing to get a little wet sometimes if he wanted to catch anything edible. Not that Rosewitz would care, since he didn't even like to *eat* the fish he caught. To him, it was all just a contest.

Something tugged on the line. Satisfied that this would complete tonight's collection, Ernest set the hook and stepped backward. The sole of his left boot slipped across a flat rock. Before he could catch himself he'd stepped off a ledge into hip-deep water. The river shoved him forward as he dug his heels into the gravel. He turned and automatically leaned against the flow.

Too late, he felt the cold water invade his waders, sloshing all the way to his toes as the current shoved him backward. Hard.

"Dropped your pole!" Rosewitz crowed.

Ernest's feet dug a trench in the river gravel. The icy coldness froze him. He opened his mouth to holler out, and his head went under. Water rushed into his ears and nose, and it tried for his throat, but he closed his mouth and shoved upward with all the force his legs could muster.

He broke surface and gasped, choking. "Help me—"

The river grabbed him and dragged him under again. His body thunked against a boulder, turning him into human sandwich meat caught between rock and water.

He needed to breathe. He *had* to breathe, but he couldn't reach the surface. He felt the darkness creep around him, felt his mouth open like a fish on a hook, but before he could inhale the river into his lungs something jerked at the shoulder strap of his waders. He felt his face break surface; he gasped again, caught the blurry image of Rosewitz's ugly face just before the Black Oak tugged him back under.

Rosewitz wouldn't let go. The strap tightened again. Ernest followed it up and out, caught a deep breath, shoved against the boulder, and reached for Rosewitz with his free right hand. One loud growling grunt later Ernest sloshed to the shore, gasping and choking, stumbling atop his good friend as gallons of river water poured over them both from the deepest parts of his waders.

Thunder rumbled overhead with intensified force. Ernest coughed up more water, gagged, choked.

"Buddy!" Rosewitz shouted. He grabbed Ernest's shoulders and eased him over onto his stomach, face down, smack dab into the sand. "You okay?"

———

Kent Eckard shut the driver door of his mom's car to the sound of rumbling thunder and the bright flash of lightning. He ran to the front porch, stopped at the door, braced himself before stepping inside.

Mom would grill him again. She'd be lurking in her easy chair in the sitting room to the right of the hallway, where she'd been parked for the past three weeks, trying hard to carry his unborn half brother to term. That kid was making Mom crankier every day.

Wouldn't his friends laugh at him now, living with his pregnant mother, working a full-time job, staying home weekends.

Not that he had any friends left in town. Too bad he hadn't realized earlier that those people hadn't really been friends at all.

He shoved open the unlocked front door and then jerked backward as a crack of thunder seemed to shake the whole house. Wind blew splatters of rain onto the porch. He accidentally kicked the threshold as he rushed inside. Sure enough, the famous Joanne Bonus war cry bombarded the hallway from the sitting room.

"Kent! That you?"

"Yeah, Mom." The wind blew the door shut behind him.

"Quit banging around like that!"

Yep, she was feeling bad again. "Sorry, I didn't mean to—"

"What're you doing home so early?"

Early? That was new. Usually she hollered at him for being late. "Things were slow at work." He stepped into the small sitting room where she sat in the recliner with her legs up. "Storm's brewing." A couple of days ago, when he'd just happened to catch her in a good mood, she'd showed him how she could press her fingers into her thigh, and the flesh stayed that way, like Play-Doh without the play. Pretty awful.

"You okay, Mom?"

"Head hurts." She fluttered her fingers in front of her chest. "Feels like my heart's beating wrong."

"Think you need to see the doctor?"

"In that storm?" She dismissed the idea with a wave of her hand. "Nope. Serves me right, anyway, having another baby at my age."

She'd said that at least twice a day for the past three months. She was thirty-eight. Kent's ex-friends would have teased him about it—his twice-divorced mom getting pregnant again, and him already eighteen years old. At least he didn't have to worry about being teased at work. He barely spoke to anyone there.

Mom folded her hands over her huge stomach and leaned her head back against the chair cushion. Her eyes were almost closed when Kent turned to quietly leave the room.

She groaned, raising her hand to her face, as if the light from the hallway bothered her. "You clean?"

He gave a silent sigh. Here it came. "Yeah, Mom."

She raised her head and narrowed her eyes at him. "You sure?"

"Mom." He hated the whine in his voice. "I've been off the stuff for months, okay?" Even if he *did* want a hit, where was he going to get it? Meth was scarce in Dogwood Springs these days. Besides, he didn't want the stuff. It was nothing but trouble.

She rubbed her face with puffy fingers. "Come here."

He clumped toward her, his heavy work boots loud on the wood floor. Feeling like a prisoner being interrogated, he stood beside his mother's chair.

"Bend over and let me look in your eyes."

He did as he was told, reminding himself that at least she had let him move in with her when Dad kicked him out. If not for her, he'd probably be in the state pen, putting up with a lot of people a whole lot grumpier than she ever was.

She gave a quick sniff, studied his face, then aimed a slight smile his way and patted him on the arm. "That's my guy. You stay clear of that stuff."

"I am. They're tellin' people over the radio to take cover down in Carroll County. Think we should go downstairs?"

"Take cover? For what? A tornado warning all the way down in another state?"

"I don't think the state-line signs are going to affect the weather." Especially since they lived so close to the border between Missouri and Arkansas.

He gestured toward the window, where the shadow of wildly waving branches created a creepy outline against the streetlights. "Wouldn't hurt to be careful, what with the baby and all."

"Waste of time," she muttered, closing her eyes again. "Nothing like that ever happens here, and I couldn't get down those steep stairs, anyway."

He hesitated. Maybe she wasn't thinking straight. She'd been acting weird the past couple days. Should he just try to pick her up and carry her to the basement? He could do it, even if she had gained nearly sixty pounds in the past few months.

Another round of thunder rattled the candy dish on the coffee table. He glanced out the window at the sound of raindrops hitting the pane. Maybe she was right. Dogwood Springs had never been hit by a tornado. Besides, he was hungry.

Instead of arguing, he went to the kitchen and pulled open the fridge door. He was reaching for the salami when he heard another crash of thunder and nearly dove for cover. The crash was followed by the all-too-familiar sound of his mother's voice.

"K-Kent . . . help . . . Kent!" she cried.

He shoved the door shut and ran back down the hallway. He stormed into the sitting room to find her sprawled sideways in the chair, her left arm hanging over the side of the armrest.

"Mom?"

Her whole body jerked spasmodically. Her eyes were at half-mast. Her mouth moved, but no sound came out.

"Mom! I'm getting help." He jerked up the telephone beside her chair and dialed emergency.

"Told you I'm okay," Ernest Mourglia muttered as he sat dripping river water onto the vinyl chair and tile floor of the ER waiting room. He coughed hard and deep, and heard the rasping creak of inflamed windpipes—at least it sounded like that to him.

"I'm not taking you home until we get you checked out," Rosewitz griped back. "You could barely catch your breath there for a while. You could get pneumonia. You could still die, you know."

"Don't get your hopes up." Ernest hunkered forward, resting his elbows on his knees, prepared to wait awhile, but before he could get comfortable, the door beside the reception desk opened. The dark-haired, dark-eyed nurse in her fifties with the underbite of a pug stepped out, holding a clipboard. Handsome woman except for that underbite. A little stocky. Familiar.

He should know her. What was her name? She looked straight at him, smiled, and curled her forefinger at him.

Rosewitz reached for his arm, as if he had to help the poor elderly patient across the room. Ernest pulled away and stood up. He wasn't that decrepit yet.

He was stricken with a fit of coughing about the time he reached the nurse at the door.

"You okay, Mr. Mourglia?" The fifty-something nurse reached for his shoulder.

"I'm great," he rasped. Obviously, *she* knew who *he* was, but most folks in Dogwood Springs did. He'd endured the extra attention since Jade landed the job as mayor of the town. He'd learned real quick that the mayor's uncle couldn't do anything without the whole town knowing about it—good, bad, or indifferent. He didn't want to embarrass his favorite niece.

He coughed again as he followed the nurse through the door to where all the real ER action took place. He just hoped they didn't call Jade about this. Last time he'd landed here, she wouldn't leave him alone for weeks afterward.

The sound of a siren barely reached the interior of the department as the nurse escorted Ernest into exam room four. Nobody rushed to the window to see who was being brought in, the way they did down at City Hall. He figured most of the ER staff had long ago gotten used to the shrill peals of alarm that stopped cars and turned heads in the outside world.

"I guess you know you're dripping wet, Mr. Mourglia," the nurse said as she directed him to the bed.

He caught sight of her name badge. *Muriel Stark.* Of course, that was it. Where was his mind? She'd worked at this hospital for years. Jade had mentioned this nurse was dating Will Butler, the hospital administrator. "Rosewitz wouldn't take me home to change."

"Good for Mr. Rosewitz," Muriel said. "That water isn't going to hurt this exam room, but we need to get you out of those wet clothes and find you some warm blankets."

Ernest crossed his arms over his chest. He was *not* letting a young woman like her get him out of his clothes. He didn't care if she did have a license to do it. He coughed again. "Why don't you check me out real quick before you go to all that trouble?"

"That's an excellent idea." She patted his arm and smiled, and those dark eyes seemed to glow with glee at the prospect of peeling him to his skin. "Tell you what, I need your shirt off so I can hook you up to a monitor, take your blood pressure, things like that. You can keep your pants on for a few minutes."

He frowned. Sounded like a striptease to him. Maybe he oughta just slip out the back door when nobody was looking and *walk* home. Let Rosewitz spend the night in the waiting room if he liked this place so all-fired much.

"Work with me on this, okay?" Muriel said, reaching for the top button of his long-sleeved shirt. "It would be bad for business if word got out that our ER let the mayor's uncle get sick."

"Won't do any good to threaten me," he said. He could see it now— a picture of him in one of them skimpy, gownlike things, gaped open in the back from the neck to the knees.

Muriel had his shirt off, the dreaded gown on him, his blood pressure checked, and one of those clothespin-type apparatuses on his left forefinger before he could find the courage to protest again.

"Now," Muriel said as she jotted something on a clipboard, "I think you'd be more comfortable if we took off these cold, clammy pants. Don't worry, your numbers don't look too bad, so we can give you your privacy while you—"

Another nurse entered the exam room. "Muriel, we've got a hot one coming in. Late-term pregnancy, looks preeclamptic. About eight minutes out. Can you take it? You're more experienced with OB than I am." The nurse smiled and waved at Ernest. "Hi, Mr. Mourglia."

He grunted hoarsely and hunkered on the bed. *Privacy, huh?*

"Let me know when they bring her in." Muriel turned back to Ernest. "Now, let's get you hooked up to the monitor."

"Why don't you go check on your other patients," Ernest muttered. "I'm old enough to change my own clothes."

———

Kent slammed on the brakes and the tires squealed. The big boxy ambulance loomed in front of him, siren wailing. The lights atop the vehicle cast an eerie strobe of red-blue-orange through the deepening night, though he was too close to actually see the lights. He gripped the steering wheel so hard his hands went numb. He had run a stop sign and a red light in order to stay behind the ambulance, even though he knew that if the police caught him they could do all kinds of things to him, maybe even throw him in jail.

Rain pounded the windshield like a waterfall, whipping in all directions at once. Kent couldn't remember ever being so scared before—not even when he got mixed up with the town's most notorious drug kingpin, Simon Royce.

Right now, the only person in the world who cared anything about Kent was in that ambulance, and his baby half brother might not be born alive. Kent knew a big strong guy like him should be ashamed of being so scared, but he didn't care. He hadn't felt big or strong in a long time.

The ambulance fishtailed in the water on the road, and this time Kent put his brakes on before he got too close. Lights blurred, and he sniffed hard. They had to get her there in time. They *had* to!

———

Ernest Mourglia pulled the bed sheet up to his chin when Dr. Grant Sheldon strolled into the exam room with a stethoscope looped behind his neck and a clipboard in his hand.

"Ernest Mourglia, what brings you here on a stormy night?" The doctor had a genuine smile and a firm handshake.

"That ornery fishing buddy of mine, that's what," Ernest grumbled.

The doctor set the clipboard on the tray table beside the bed and removed the stethoscope from around his neck. "I heard the Black Oak tried to beat up on you a little."

"I'm doing better by the minute. In fact, if Muriel'd give me back my clothes I'd be glad to get out of your hair."

Grant placed the bell of his stethoscope on Ernest's chest. "I'm a little concerned about that cough."

"What cough?"

"The one I heard clear across the department a couple minutes ago." The doctor had a good bedside manner, and Ernest knew the guy was experienced—had to be, he was the director. Evidence of his years of experience showed in the lines of character that etched his face. He was single, too. A good prospect for Jade. At least he still had all his hair, not like the guy Jade was dating right now.

"Breathe for me, please," Dr. Sheldon said.

Ernest did as he was told, allowing the doctor to complete his exam. "Guess you know Muriel's already done all this."

"Bear with us, Ernest." Dr. Sheldon checked the vitals Muriel had written down. "You don't have a fever, and your heart looks good."

"Then what'm I doing here?"

Dr. Sheldon chuckled. "If you inhaled any of that water, you could develop aspiration pneumonia. We need to make sure that doesn't happen." A crack of loud thunder echoed the doctor's words.

Ernest shifted in the bed and gave the doc his most innocent feeble-elderly-patient smile. "Seen my niece lately, Dr. Sheldon?"

The doctor marked something on his chart. "Not lately."

"You could, you know. One word from you, and I bet she'd drop the fella she's dating like snake on a fishhook."

Dr. Sheldon sighed and shook his head.

"She admires you," Ernest continued. "Likes your kids. She even has time to eat dinner on occasion, if you were to invite her out."

"I would never dream of intruding on her relationship with Norville Webster. He's a good man. Have you found any new fishing spots?"

Ernest scowled. "None as good as the old place at Honey Creek."

"Sorry to hear that. Lauren McCaffrey's still searching, too."

Aha. So that's the way it's going to be. "Lauren, eh? Heard you two might be sweet on each other. That why you're not dating my niece?" Blast the luck.

The doctor nodded. "I'd get confused if I tried to spend time with two different women."

"Lauren's a good'un," Ernest admitted. Or at least she would be if she didn't have the nasty habit of catching all the biggest fish before her fellow fishermen could even get their lines wet. If she were a real lady, she'd leave a few for—

"Yes, she is," Dr. Sheldon said softly.

Ernest winced at another shot of thunder that sounded as if it had come directly from the barrel of a cannon. The lights flickered, and a child cried out.

There was a knock at the doorway, and the night secretary leaned into the exam room. "Mr. Mourglia, you walked in here under your own steam, didn't you?"

"Yes, and I can walk back out the same way."

She didn't even attempt a smile at his poor excuse for a joke. "I guess you heard the flash-flood warnings."

"Sure, but that's not likely to reach us here."

"Don't bet on it."

Ernest frowned at her.

"Dr. Sheldon," the secretary continued, "there's been a tornado sighted outside Eureka Springs. Mr. Butler just called, and he wants us to get all our ambulatory patients downstairs to the basement."

Ernest looked down at the flimsy gown he wore. This could turn out to be worse than he'd even imagined. "I didn't hear no public alert."

"Knowing your niece, that'll happen soon enough, but Mr. Butler's taking no chances. He wants us to begin evacuation now."

The automatic frosted-glass doors of the ambulance entrance slid open as the crew pushed Kent's mom inside on a gurney. Kent didn't ask permission to follow—he just stayed close behind Bill, the EMT. Wind-driven rain followed them inside, in spite of the awning that was supposed to protect them. The wind roared, and a small tree branch whacked the thick glass beside the door.

Mom cried out at the sound. "Where's my son?" She raised her left arm—the one attached to the IV tube.

"I'm right here," Kent said.

"He's right behind us, Mrs. Bonus." Christy, the paramedic, grabbed her arm and gently lowered it. "Just relax and let us take care of you, okay?"

"Where are we? What's going on? My head . . . oh, my head."

A nurse came rushing toward them from a large central counter. "Sorry, Christy, we've got a code black pending, and we're shuffling everyone we can downstairs."

"I didn't hear any alarm," Christy snapped. "This woman needs treatment *now*—right here in this department."

The nurse leaned closer to Christy. "Did you hear what I said? You *do* realize what a code black is?"

"Yes."

"I don't," Kent said. "What is it?"

"Tornado alert," Christy said. "Muriel, listen to me. She's thirty-eight years of age, thirty-six weeks pregnant, non-insulin-dependent diabetic, and her BP is 180 over 102. According to her son"—she jerked her head in Kent's direction—"she was shaking and unresponsive before we arrived on scene, and now she has a bad headache, groggy. What does that tell you?"

Muriel's chin came forward and she put her hands on her muscular hips. "It tells me we need to get her downstairs into the basement with the rest of the patients."

"You don't have the supplies you'll need downstairs," Christy argued. "Come on, Muriel, we need to treat her up here. She's eclamptic."

"And take a chance with a tornado?"

"That won't happen, and you know it. Besides, we can use one of the central rooms. Where's the doc—"

There was a loud pop and crackle, and the lights flickered out.

Someone cried out with fear. Mom started to cry. Kent tried to get to her side and tripped over something that clattered to the floor.

The overhead battery-pack lights came on, illuminating the department with a shadowed glow. Kent had knocked over a padded stool.

"*Now* can we take the rest of the patients downstairs?" Muriel checked Mom's IV site. "The emergency backup generator should've already kicked in. Hold on there for just a little longer, hon, and we'll get you settled out of the storm."

"No!" Kent didn't know he was going to blurt the word until it left his mouth. "My mom needs treatment now. She's sick, and she's having a baby."

"She's in *labor*?" Muriel exclaimed.

"Not yet," Christy said.

The overhead lights came on, the computer backup batteries beeped, and Christy turned to her EMT. "Bill, go get one of the crash carts from the trauma room. We may need it." She gave Muriel a challenging glare. "Somebody get us a flashlight. I don't trust the generator."

"Got one here." Muriel reached into her desk. "Let's get these people downstairs."

CHAPTER 2

D r. Mitchell Caine drove his GMC Envoy into the hospital parking lot, carefully watching as the power of the mid-April storm threatened to whip Dogwood Springs senseless. What he wouldn't give to possess a little of that power himself right now. Instead, he felt like one of those dead pin-oak leaves that always lingered through the winter on the trees that lent shade to this street. Ordinarily, pin-oak leaves didn't fall until pushed out by the new spring leaves. At this rate they could be history by morning. He often felt that way himself recently, due to circumstances beyond his understanding, if not beyond his control.

Multiple streaks of lightning seemed to rim the tree line above Dogwood Springs with fire, like magic from a giant's wand, followed immediately by an explosion of thunder. The clouds reflected the fire, massive billows of smoke from noisy explosions.

The wildly waving tree limbs didn't concern Mitchell—he loved a good storm to clear the air. What did concern him was his increasing reluctance to come to the hospital for patient rounds and his increasing antipathy toward his work.

He pulled beneath the long carport connected to the back of the hospital. Ordinarily, Mitchell parked as far away from other automobiles as he could get, but tonight he didn't feel like drowning. Besides that, he always placed his protective brush guard across the front grill when it looked like the weather might get interesting, so for tonight, at least, that section of his vehicle was protected from anyone who wanted to take their frustration out on one of the supposedly "rich docs" some of the patients resented so much.

In spite of overhead shielding, the rain attacked Mitchell as he stepped from the SUV and locked it. He rushed to the back hospital entrance, brushing the droplets from his shoulders, and used his passkey to get inside.

He glanced at his watch. Seven-thirty. Friday nights were usually quite busy, but judging by the dearth of cars in the lot, the storm had kept visitors to a minimum. Good. Maybe he could wade through the patients on his service without too many interruptions. Often, when it looked to be a busy night, he would wait until after visiting hours before he braved his hospital rounds. It cost him the least amount of time on repetitive questions.

He shivered as he entered the rear hallway. It got colder in this hospital every day—did the maintenance people *intend* to freeze the poor patients to death? Last year, when he was chief of staff, he'd said something about the temperature to the head of maintenance. The overstuffed bozo had the audacity to protest that he couldn't concentrate when he was too warm. Mitchell had then reminded the man how cold it got down at the poultry processing plant during the winter months. The twit had the brains of a gum-ball machine. No wonder nothing worked right in this hospital.

Two young women wearing scrubs came rushing around a corner in the hallway, their faces tense.

The one on the right—he thought her name was Lela—had worked in the emergency department for a few months last year, when Mitchell had been moonlighting quite a few shifts. She had been new and awkward. It had not been a good experience for either of them, and while he was still chief of staff he'd seen to it that she was transferred from the department. The ER was no place for a newcomer.

"Hi, Dr. Caine," she said.

"Hello, Lela." He pressed the elevator call button. He wanted to wade through his patients and drive home, swallow a much-needed dose of Tranquen—his prescription medication to calm his nerves and bring on sleep—enjoy a nightcap or two, and go to bed. It was Friday night, and he was due.

"You heard the overhead announcement, didn't you?" Lela asked, stopping beside him unexpectedly.

"Announcement? No, I'm afraid I didn't. I just arrived here for—"

"They called a code black," her friend blurted. "Come on, Lela, we've got to get upstairs and help with patient—"

"Attention all personnel," the overhead speaker blared, "code black. Attention all personnel, code black."

The two women rushed toward the stairs, leaving Mitchell alone in the hallway. For a few seconds he felt a frisson of alarm, but it didn't last. Dogwood Springs experienced these warnings at least a couple of times a year, and he knew for a fact that William Butler, the hospital administrator, often erred on the side of caution when it came to the safety of the patients. More than likely, a tornado had been spotted somewhere within a hundred-mile radius, and Butler was taking no chances.

Mitchell had never been caught at the hospital during an alert before, but he knew the drill. Roll bedridden patients out into the hall-way on the second floor, and then get all unnecessary personnel and ambulatory patients—as well as any ambulatory patients in the emergency department—to the basement.

He knew this place could withstand all but the worst nature had to offer, but he didn't care to test that theory just now.

He stepped into the elevator and was reaching to press the basement button on the panel when he heard the overhead announcement again. He had a right to go to the basement and avoid the storm. All unneeded personnel would go there immediately.

Nevertheless, he did not relish the prospect of being surrounded by the night hospital staff, enduring the curious stares, hearing the whispers. . . .

He pressed the button for the second floor. It wouldn't hurt him to shuttle a few patients to the hallway. After all, he had patients up there, and he could imagine the fear they must be feeling as word swept through the floor about impending danger. It wouldn't hurt him to improve his public relations a little, either.

Besides, old Mr. Horner in room 232 was afraid of storms. A tornado warning would terrify him. He could use some reassurance.

Jessica Lane Pierce took the final curve of the tortuous drive between Branson and Dogwood Springs to the fanfare of a brilliant spring storm that sent a cascade of rain across her windshield in circular waves, like a giant intermittent sprinkler system. Rain washed the state highway to an ebony sheen, and she could feel even her all-wheel-drive Subaru hydroplaning on certain sections. The drive from the theater had taken her nearly an hour, as opposed to the typical thirty-five minutes in good weather. Branson traffic had been snarled even more than usual because of the deluge that had split the sky a few minutes after her show ended. It had cut her usual greet-the-star time in half due to the urgency of the bus drivers and senior citizens to beat the storm.

Another flash of chain lightning gave her a fascinating view of her new hometown, set on the peninsula of a gently sloped hill overlooking the Black Oak River, which would most likely tumble out of its banks before morning if this rain continued.

Tonight, Dogwood Springs didn't hold its usual appearance of comfortable safety. The waving branches tossed sticks and leaves—highlighted to bone white, then darkened to a menace of fleshless arms and fingers—as if they were reaching out, trying to grab her car or thrust her from the road.

Jessica couldn't wait to get home, remove her stage makeup, and fall into her loving husband's arms—not that the last part was likely to happen soon. If she knew Archer, he wouldn't be home yet. He was the on-call chaplain at the hospital tonight.

She pulled to a stop at the first traffic signal, which swung like the Sword of Damocles in the wind, threatening to topple onto her hood at any moment. She turned right to bypass the commercial section of town with its quaint shops and tourist-trap junk marts.

Three blocks farther, she hit the brakes with a gasp at the sight of the cascade rushing over the low-water bridge in front of her. Headlights flashed as a car pulled up behind her—too close behind. She lowered her window, getting drenched in seconds, and stuck an arm out to wave the other driver back.

The other driver made a U-turn and drove back the way he had come. Obviously, he was aware that this little bridge often flooded, leaving the residents on the hillside beyond it with only one other access to their homes.

Jessica had no intention of trying to cross, either. She followed the other car toward the Black Oak River bridge, grimacing at the thunder that cracked overhead. She breathed a quiet prayer that, for once, Archer would be at home when she arrived.

A fresh flood of rain bashed the windshield of the Subaru, and water glistened from the black street. Set as it was on this tree-covered hillside, the town of Dogwood Springs seldom had trouble with flooding, but this storm seemed to be attacking from all sides at once.

The blare of a nearby horn startled her. She jerked around to see who was honking but only saw an empty street. The blare rode up to a deafening scale and back down again, and then she recognized the public alert system. Storm warning? Big surprise. What took them so—

Her cell phone chirped from the seat beside her, further stealing her breath. She stopped in the middle of the deserted street and answered it.

"Jessica, where are you?" The tense, frightened voice, accompanied by generous static, belonged to her husband.

"I just got into town, honey. I'll be home in a few—"

"Do you have the keys to the church?"

"Of course, I keep them on—"

"Get there now!"

She stiffened at the sound of urgency in his voice. The siren took on a new significance.

"Jessica, *now,*" he repeated. "There's a tornado warning—one's been sighted on the ground near Eureka Springs, and that's too close for comfort. The storm system—"

"Where are you?"

"Hospital."

"Then I'm coming there."

"No, you're not. If you just got to town you're closer to the church, and we need it unlocked. It's a designated tornado shelter. Hurry, Jess."

"Okay. I will. Archer, be careful. I love you."

"Then get to the church basement." Jessica heard tense voices in the background over the telephone. "I love you, too," Archer said. "I'll see you soon."

———

Archer Pierce, pastor of Dogwood Springs Baptist Church and Friday night on-call chaplain, reluctantly broke the connection with his wife, shoved the cell phone into his pocket, and turned back to face the basement hallway. The place teemed with nervous patients and staff.

He heard Dr. Grant Sheldon's voice rise above the confusion of people who had congregated in a large conference room at the west end of the hallway. "We need you to stay in the corridors," he called. "Everyone, may I have your attention! The safest place to be is in the corridors."

The hallway filled with a mass exodus until it resembled an airport terminal at Christmas. Not everyone took the alert seriously, and many laughed and joked, chattered and complained, until Archer thought his eardrums might implode.

He was about to raise his hands and ask for silence when he heard a commotion from the other end of the main corridor, at the elevator door.

"Coming through! Excuse us, coming through! Where's a doctor?"

Christy, the ambulance paramedic on duty, threaded a gurney—complete with a patient—through the lively group of people. Bill, the EMT, helped guide the gurney from the other side.

"Oh my goodness, what happened to her?" a woman cried. "Was she injured in the storm?"

A shocked silence followed her words, and Archer took that opportunity to raise his hand and get Christy's attention. "Grant's down at the other end of the corridor trying to direct traffic. Everybody step back, please!" He used his pulpit voice. "Please stay calm and allow the attendants to do their jobs."

"What do you have?" Grant asked, making his way toward them against the tide of people.

"Looks like eclampsia," Christy said.

They met in the middle of the crowd, the automatic focus of everyone. The doctor grasped the rail of the gurney. "She's already seized?"

"Yes," Christy said. "Her son described activity typical of a seizure, which was why he called us in the first place. In the ambulance she was complaining of abdominal pain and severe headache. She was confused and disoriented. We brought a crash cart down from upstairs."

While Christy gave her report to Grant, Archer studied the patient's face, frowning as he ignored the press of people around him. She looked familiar—had probably visited church in the past few weeks—but he couldn't remember her name.

"Uh, Pastor Pierce . . ." a tentative male voice whispered from behind him.

Archer looked around. Recognizing one of the most notorious eighteen-year-olds in the county, he suddenly realized who the patient on the gurney must be. "Kent Eckard, isn't it?" He held his right hand out.

The young man looked at Archer's hand, narrowed his dark-shadowed eyes, and slowly reached out and shook it.

"The patient is your mother?" Archer asked gently.

Kent's overfirm grip tightened on Archer's, then he released it and nodded. He was muscular and broad-shouldered. Archer could see why some of the kids in the youth department got nervous when Kent and his mother, Joanne Bonus, attended services. They'd only been to the church about three times, and at those times, Archer had been dismayed by the lack of enthusiasm from the congregation—all except for the people who had the most reason to avoid him—Evan Webster and Grant's twin teenagers, Brooke and Beau Sheldon. Kent had been with the drug kingpin Simon Royce when Royce nearly killed Evan and Brooke in a rage last Christmas season.

"She's in good hands," Archer said.

"She's having a baby," Kent said, as if that weren't obvious.

"Dr. Sheldon will know what to do," Archer assured him.

For a moment, Kent didn't react, and it was obvious his attention focused only on his mother and the treatment she was receiving a few feet away. That focus changed, apparently as Archer's last statement registered.

"Sheldon," Kent murmured, frowning. His eyes widened. His mouth gaped open. He pointed toward Grant. "That's Dr. Sheldon?"

"That's right, and he's good."

"Yeah, but does he know he's treating *my* mother?" Kent's voice deepened, his brows lowering in suspicion.

Archer took Kent's arm and urged him closer to the gurney, where the others huddled over Joanne.

Grant leaned over the patient. "How are you feeling, Joanne?"

"Awful, Doctor." Tears dripped down the sides of Joanne's face. "I'm sorry. I can't stop shaking. I'm so scared. . . ."

He rested a hand on her arm. "It's okay. We're going to take care of you. Just relax and let us do the worrying." He straightened and looked around, then motioned for Muriel Stark to join them. "See if the mag sulfate is in the crash cart."

The stocky, experienced nurse nodded. "It is. I already checked."

"Good. Set it up for 6 grams over ten minutes. We need to stave off another seizure if we can. What about labetalol? We need to control the blood pressure."

"We've got it."

"Good. Give her 20 milligrams, IV push." Grant straightened and looked around at Kent. "We're going to take good care of her, son. Meanwhile, would you and Archer pray for her?"

Kent's face reddened. He pressed his lips together into a tight line, as if sealing his mouth shut would prevent him from expressing his fear. Archer touched his arm and gestured for him to go to the stairwell. They could pray there with some privacy.

———

Jessica studied the darkened three-story outline of the Dogwood Springs Baptist Church set deep into the hillside, occupying a very visible section of town. She pulled into the lower level of the church lot and parked as close as she could get to the building. To her surprise, a familiar gray Buick sedan pulled in beside her. As Jessica sprang from her car into the blowing rain, fumbling with her key chain, she recognized John and Helen Netz. She waved at them and tensed.

Apparently, at some time in the past, Jessica had inadvertently offended or disappointed Helen in some way. Theirs was not an easy camaraderie.

Tall John, with his craggy face and work-gnarled hands, stepped out of the car. He wore his customary gray winter cap with a matching gray raincoat. Through the car's rain-spattered window, Jessica could see that Helen had a plastic hood over her carefully sprayed helmet of gray-bronze hair.

Before Jessica could find the right key, John reached the double doors of the basement with his long, decisive strides and stuck his key in the lock. He pulled the right door open with a flourish and held it for Jessica, then hurried back to his wife, who was waiting patiently for him to open her door and help her out.

Not that she needed help. Helen was an able woman who held positions on half the committees in church and operated all kitchen activities with the authority of a police sergeant.

Jessica held the door for the older couple when they reached it, and droplets splashed across her face and arms as Helen drew the plastic from her head.

"Honey, don't you have a raincoat for weather like this?" Helen patted Jessica's arm as she passed, and her gaze rested a little too long on Jessica's face—at the heavy makeup—and wandered down to her glittery green dress.

"The sky was clear when I left this afternoon," Jessica said.

John took his hat off and perched it on a hook on the wall, then helped his wife with her coat. "We thought we'd come down and make sure the doors were unlocked," he told Jessica. "Archer's always so busy, and the custodian's out of town this week."

"Yes, Archer called me." Jessica flipped on the fluorescent lights. "He's at the hospital."

"Figures," John said. "He can't seem to stay away from that place."

Helen proceeded to the large kitchen area that took up the far back corner of the basement. It was nestled into the side of the stairwell for partial protection from flying basketballs or volleyballs when the rest of the large multipurpose basement was transformed into a sports arena.

She pulled open a cupboard door. "I thought we'd make some coffee and sandwiches. John, why don't you get out the big coffeepot. I can't reach it."

"You know, I don't think anyone expects us to feed them," Jessica said. "I doubt if any of the other tornado shelters in the area—"

"*What?*" The lady's eyebrows rose until they nearly met her helmet of hair. "I can't believe I'm actually hearing the daughter-in-law of Eileen Pierce say such a thing." Helen pulled a couple of packages of cookies out of the cupboard. "*She* was the one who thought we should start keeping food on hand for times like this."

"Food for *tornado* alerts?" It didn't make sense.

"Yes, and she was always one of the first to pitch in and help. And did anyone ever hear her complain? Not a peep."

"I'm not complaining," Jessica soothed. "I was taught to stay away from all things electrical during an electrical storm. It seems to me that operating a coffeepot and heating water for cocoa are tempting injury." And she still refused to believe her practical mother-in-law would condone this kind of thing.

"Well, nothing like that has ever happened here. Eileen believed the witness of this church to the community was the most important thing, and we wanted to give them something to remember us by when they went home." She pulled a serving plate from another cupboard. "She was an asset to her husband and to this church," Helen said more softly.

"I know she was," Jessica said. "And she still is." It was obvious Helen Netz still grieved the loss of a thirty-year friendship when Mom and Dad Pierce moved away from Dogwood Springs after their retirement. It was also obvious Helen didn't intend for anyone to take Mom Pierce's place. Jessica had no intention of trying.

"If I can find an apron, I'll kick off my shoes and help," Jessica said.

"Well, okay, if you feel like you want to do some work."

Silently chastising herself for being overly sensitive, Jessica pushed her stretchy sleeves up to her elbows and turned as John came from the freezer with two loaves of white bread and some lunch meat.

Jessica barely resisted the urge to roll her eyes. *Junk food for Jesus. For this I'm risking my life.*

Helen reached into the drawer for a spoon. "Why don't you dish out the condiments, Jessica? That won't be too difficult. You'll find some small bowls in the third cupboard down and some butter knives in the drawer below it. No, not that one, the next one. There you go."

Jessica ignored the woman's condescending tone and reminded herself of how generously this couple gave of their time to make sure the church functioned smoothly.

She was going to learn to appreciate this dedicated couple if it killed her.

"Do you think many will come?" Jessica asked as she worked.

"You'd better believe they'll come," John said. "This place is a life-saver for those poor people who don't have a basement. Literally."

And cookies are a necessary part of the rescue? "How often do we get tornado warnings in Dogwood Springs?" Jessica asked.

"Oh, I can remember quite a few times these past few years—can't you, John?" Helen pulled two aprons out of a drawer. She handed one to Jessica and kept the other one for herself.

"But has this town ever been hit by a tornado?" Jessica asked.

"Not yet," John said. "Not likely to, sheltered as we are. I reckon this one'll fizzle out any minute. Still, folks get scared, so they come to the church. My theory is God causes these tornado situations just to get some people into church who wouldn't otherwise darken the doors." He placed the meat in the microwave to defrost it. "How's a person sup-posed to meet God if he never visits where God lives?"

"But God doesn't live in this building; He lives where His people do," Jessica ventured. She was immediately sorry when she caught sharp looks from both directions.

"Well, His *people* should be *here*," Helen said. "That way there won't be any confusion about where *He* is."

Jessica turned away to spoon the condiments into the bowls just as the first set of headlights flashed through the basement windows. For the next few minutes she busied herself greeting strangers and church members alike, reassuring them, making them feel comfortable as she urged them toward the more protected part of the basement near the back. She received several enthusiastic greetings from church members as well as from fans who didn't attend the church but had seen her show. She received only a few strange looks from people who didn't know her. She wasn't exactly dressed for a casual tornado party.

Tornado party. Oh, Lord, forgive me. This is no party.

CHAPTER 3

Archer hovered beside Kent Eckard in the stairwell, several yards from the gurney where Grant and Muriel worked over Kent's mother. Ordinarily, at a time like this, Archer would be mingling with the others, reassuring those who needed comfort, asking people if they wanted him to pray for them, but right now he could almost feel Kent's tension. Apparently, the crowd, which had been so intrusive a few minutes ago, had picked up on Kent's tension, too, and had moved away a bit. Perhaps word had spread about who he was and that his emotions were rumored to be unstable. Joanne and the medical team working with her now had a modicum of privacy—but only a modicum.

"She doesn't look good," Kent muttered. "What're they doing to her?"

"Still trying to prevent another seizure," Archer said. "Don't worry, Kent, Dr. Sheldon will do all he can to help your mother."

The ambulance attendants, Christy and Bill, had remained in the basement assisting other hospital personnel with frightened patients.

"Dr. Sheldon, we're running low on mag sulfate." The warm tones of Muriel Stark's mature voice were strong enough to make a point but not loud enough to attract attention from the masses. "Her blood pressure's going back up. Let me just run upstairs to the department to get more—"

"No, I need you here," Grant said, "I don't want to risk it. Is the other crash cart restocked?"

Archer heard Kent's breathing deepen beside him.

"Yes, Lauren always keeps them in good supply," Muriel said. "Really, I don't think there's any danger for me up there. What do you want to bet they'll be calling the all clear any minute?"

Archer gave Kent's arm a pat, then crossed the few yards to Grant's side. "Why don't you let me go up and get the other crash cart, if you think it has what you need, Dr. Sheldon. It won't take that much time, and you don't need me here."

Grant hesitated for only a couple of seconds as he checked the blood-pressure reading. "Okay. Thanks, Archer."

"The cart in the trauma room will work fine," Muriel said.

Archer turned to find Kent hovering behind him.

"I can go with you."

Archer shook his head and put a gently restraining hand on Kent's muscular left shoulder. "Why don't you stay down here? That way you can be close to your mom if she calls for you."

Kent returned his attention to his mother. Archer took the stairs two at a time and stepped out into a preternaturally vacant corridor that connected the emergency department to the rest of the hospital. The rain still fell, and the wind continued to howl beneath the roof of the ambulance bay, whipping and breaking tree limbs with frightening violence. It was unusually dark outside with no streetlights, no glowing *Ambulance Entrance* sign. The hospital must still be running on auxiliary power.

Headlights flashed through the plate-glass windows in the waiting room as he rushed through on his way to the ER proper. He didn't look to see who was pulling in. He would catch them as he came back out of the ER.

He found the red crash cart—a waist-high contraption that looked like a tool chest with a defibrillator unit on top and an oxygen bottle on the side. He shoved it forward and guided it out of the department. As he passed through the waiting room, the seventeen-year-old Sheldon twins splashed through the doors into the waiting room, their shoes squeaking on the tile and Brooke's chatter mode in full working order.

"For once I wish you'd trust me, Beau. I mean, don't you think those spotters know what they're doing?" Her hair was dripping, her clothing drenched.

"Not with you distracting them." Beau was no drier than his sister.

"Evan will never forgive me when he gets back from his mom's and finds out I actually had the chance to get a real tornado on film." Brooke's voice echoed through the empty waiting room. "Do you know what he could do with something—"

"Hey, you two," Archer called, aiming the cart toward the central corridor that led to the elevators. "We're having a party downstairs. Why don't you join us?"

"In the *basement*?" Brooke protested, barely breaking stride as she turned in his direction. "How are we supposed to see anything down there?"

Beau grabbed her arm and urged her along the hall toward Archer. "Code black?"

"That's right," Archer said. "What are you two doing out on a night like this?"

"We were cruising the square when we heard the public alert," Brooke said.

"And Brooke decided this would be a great opportunity to risk her life and mine so she could observe the tornado spotters," Beau said. "Since she was driving at the time, it took me a few blocks to convince her to get to safety."

"And *then*," Brooke said, "when I turned around and started back, a tree had fallen across the road. Just that fast. I mean, the wind is awful."

Beau wiped the lenses of his glasses with the tail of his wet shirt. "Do they need help with patients? What're you doing with a crash cart? Is someone hurt?"

"We have a patient with eclampsia," Archer said. "Kent Eckard's mother. You two are back on speaking terms with Kent, aren't you?"

"Sure," Beau said. "I invited him to church the first time."

"Then why don't you go keep him occupied. He's pretty worried about his mom, and I'm not sure how he'll react if there's a bad outcome."

"I can do that," Brooke said. "If he acts up I'll sucker-punch him again."

Beau rolled his eyes. "Archer, want some help with the cart?"

"No, I can handle it. The guidelines are no unnecessary use of elevators during a code black. You two get downstairs so your father can see that you're safe."

They went, and he took the long way around to the elevator. The doors opened almost as soon as he touched the button and revealed another passenger standing in the far corner. It was Lela, one of the floor nurses. Her curly brown hair framed a face pale with fear.

"Oh, hurry! Come on in! Please hurry!" She reached for the cart and urged him inside, then pushed the basement button. "I know I'm not supposed to be in the elevator, but I was in a hurry to get downstairs, and I thought this would be faster." Her hands shook, and she pressed her fingers to her face. "This thing could stall. If lightning knocks out our power again we could get stuck in here, maybe even electrocuted, killed in an—"

"It's okay, Lela," he soothed. "We're almost there."

"But it could happen just like that." She snapped her fingers as the ball of her right foot tapped the floor, keeping time with her words. "I've heard too many stories about tornadoes ripping out whole towns from their foundation, killing everyone—"

"Lela, listen to me," he said as the elevator descended. "I don't think it would be a good idea to share this with the patients, okay?"

Before she could answer, the elevator stopped and the doors opened to a huddled crowd. With a dramatic sigh, Lela rushed out, then turned to Archer with an apologetic shrug. "Sorry." She reached for a corner of the cart. "Here, let me help you with that. Looks like the ER patients got redirected down here, didn't they? I guess they could use another nurse."

"Yes, and they have a critical patient, so they'll probably be happy to see you." He was not at all sure she would be capable of reassuring the patients in her state of agitation. "Did they get everyone moved into the hallways on the patient floor?" he asked her. "Maybe I could leave this with you and go on up to help."

"Dr. Caine was getting the last patient out into the hallway when I left," she said. "He's up there with two more nurses, an aide, and a couple of fire fighters who showed up a few minutes ago."

"Dr. Caine's in the hospital?"

"Yeah, I think he was getting ready for patient rounds when they announced the code black." Some color had returned to her face. "Kind of surprised me." She glanced around at the people hovering nearby.

"Surprised?"

"His going up to help us move the patients. It isn't like he's the kind of person who goes out of his way to help others."

Archer watched her in thoughtful silence, and she must have caught some hint of censure in his expression.

"Well, I mean, you know, there are some doctors you just know are in the profession to help people," she explained, "and the fact that they earn a good income is like a reward for their kindness. You know what I mean?"

Archer knew. "I think appearances, and personalities, can be deceiving."

She shrugged and fell silent, as if she disagreed.

Archer decided not to try to convince her, but it concerned him that so few people were willing to dig beneath the surface these days, to try to see what their friends, co-workers, or fellow citizens might be struggling with.

Mitchell Caine wasn't the bad guy so many believed him to be, but it was true that he had alienated quite a few patients and staff in past months.

Patients sat in chairs along the walls of the hallway, some in hospital gowns, some in robes, others in street clothes. No arrangements had been made to allow for patient privacy, but at this point, the only person who seemed to care was poor Mr. Mourglia, who sat huddled in a corner beside his fishing buddy, wearing a hospital gown, with a blanket wrapped over his shoulders like a shawl.

A nurse circulated among the patients, keeping track of vitals, reassuring the nervous and the irritable.

Lela knelt beside a young teenager who was doubled over, holding her stomach. Archer pushed his crash cart to the far end of the hallway, where Grant and Muriel hovered ever more closely to their patient.

Brooke and Beau stood with Kent in the far corner.

Grant looked up and reached for the cart. "Thanks, Archer. I'll put this against the wall over there. We still have enough supplies for now, but we're running low."

"How's Joanne?" Archer asked.

Grant stepped closer and lowered his voice. "She had another seizure in spite of the drugs we gave her. We were able to break it quickly enough, but if she starts to seize again, I don't know if we can break it again. If we can't, then the only thing left for us to do is take the baby."

"Take it? You mean induce labor?"

"I mean do a Cesarean section. At thirty-six weeks, the baby is full-term anyway, and prolonged seizure can endanger both mother and child."

Joanne's voice rose in a moan as if to emphasize Grant's point. Muriel murmured some soothing words and dabbed at the patient's forehead with some moist paper towels.

"Do you have what you need down here to do the C-section?" Archer asked Grant.

"No, we'd have to try to move her into Obstetrics, and we can't expect an OB doc or anesthetist to get here through this storm."

"Doesn't Mitchell Caine help in obstetrics sometimes?"

Grant shrugged. "He does, but the problem is the same. Even if he lives closer to the hospital, we can't—"

"He's upstairs on the patient floor," Archer said. "Lela just mentioned it when she came down with me."

Grant sighed and closed his eyes briefly, and Archer couldn't tell if he was relieved or alarmed. Grant and Mitchell had a stiff relationship at the best of times.

"Why don't I go get him," Archer suggested.

"Thanks. I'd appreciate it. At least alert him to our problem so he'll be prepared in case this continues. Also, he'll have a key to OB." Grant returned to his patient, and Archer went upstairs.

As soon as he entered the main corridor on the patient floor, he noticed the unusual silence, and he stopped. Several patients lay in their beds, lined up along both sides of the corridor, with blankets and pillows wedged between them and the bed railings. The doors to the rooms were all closed, and the hallway seemed oppressively dark in spite of the overhead lights.

One steady, rhythmic sound caught his attention from the far end of the corridor. He looked up and saw a pine branch caught in the glow of the hallway light. It slapped the window—the only one that hadn't been covered by a mattress—with increasing force.

"Pastor?" called an elderly woman several yards along the hallway. It was one of the members of the Episcopalian church down the road from his. She had fallen and broken a hip last week. "What are you doing up here?"

Archer stepped over to her. "Just checking things out. Are you okay?"

She nodded, her face pinched, hands clenched tightly on the bed rails. "I'm a little scared, I guess."

"I know, I'm nervous myself. Have you seen Dr. Caine?"

The lady pointed down the corridor. "He's down there with Mr. Horner. Poor old man's terrified of storms." She touched Archer's arm. "Would you please pray, Pastor?"

"Of course." He placed a hand on her arm and said a quick but heartfelt prayer for protection and healing and then left and made his way toward Mitchell.

The rhythmic slap of a pine branch against the window at the end of the hallway caused Mr. Horner to shudder beneath Mitchell's touch. The patient never cried out, but Mitchell knew he was frightened.

All of the patients had been moved out of their rooms, either into the hallway or downstairs. Two nurses, an aide, and two fire fighters checked to make sure everyone was out of harm's way—or as far removed as possible from the path that could be taken by flying debris. Archer Pierce, the pastor on call tonight, had evidently been unfortunate enough to be stuck here at the hospital, as well.

Mitchell watched him make slow progress down the corridor as patient after patient called to him. He had a word of encouragement and a smile for each one, but he glanced at Mitchell several times, and he seemed to be making his way in his direction.

It amazed Mitchell that one of the only people who continued to welcome him with kindness and respect these days was Archer Pierce, the one man from whom Mitchell expected the least consideration, in light of past conflicts. The only explanation he could think of was that the newlywed preacher was paid to be nice.

There was a loud crack of thunder, and then a high-pitched shriek echoed through the hallway. Mitchell cringed at the aide's voice. Why couldn't she go downstairs to the basement if she was so frightened?

"Would you listen to her?" Mitchell grumbled to the silent patient. "I don't understand why everyone is stirring up such a panic. Do you remember a single time when Dogwood Springs was hit by a tornado?"

Mr. Horner shook his head. It was all he could do. He'd lost his voice to throat cancer.

"Neither do I," Mitchell said, "and I grew up here. Some people say this town is naturally protected by the cliffs on the west side of the hill. No tornado can get past them, and since that's the direction most weather systems come from, we'll be safe unless something just drops out of the sky. Do you know the odds of that happening?"

Mr. Horner shuddered again, and Mitchell squeezed the man's shoulder. "Watch and see if we don't get the all clear any moment—after all the trouble we took to move the whole ward into the hallway. All I've ever seen damaged has been a few trees and some roofing." He continued to talk quietly and was glad to note that the patient had stopped shaking. Gratified that his uncharacteristic effort to keep up the conversation was being appreciated, he continued to recall tidbits of information that would reassure the frightened man.

Mitchell avoided eye contact with anyone else. All the other people on this floor could scream or cry or talk about what frightened them, and some of them did, at the tops of their voices. This man couldn't.

If Mitchell's father were still alive, he would be following in the wake of Archer Pierce, comforting patients, talking to staff, making himself useful. Mitchell was nothing like his father. What a joke. His dad had been the consummate family doctor who loved his patients more than he loved the money he made from his practice—more, even, than he loved his own family. He'd made enough to send Mitchell to university and medical school in the face of Mitchell's resistance.

And now in spite of all his father's heroic efforts, Mitchell's life had crumbled into an unrecognizable mess, which was affecting his health. He'd lost twenty pounds in the past few months. His own physician would diagnose him with clinical depression and stick him on medication if he mentioned the problems. He refused to even think about that. He was already too dependent on one drug; he couldn't afford to risk more.

He just needed to focus on keeping his private life private and stop bringing his problems to work with him. He couldn't afford to alienate any more colleagues or members of the hospital staff, especially since he was no longer chief of staff.

"Dr. Caine?"

He looked up to see Archer drawing near.

"Would you mind coming down to the basement?" When he reached Mitchell, he lowered his head and his voice. "Dr. Sheldon has an eclamptic patient, and he needs you to stand by for a possible emergency C-section."

"Eclamptic?" Mitchell said. "Is she seizing now?"

"Not when I left, but she apparently has had at least two seizures already."

"And Dr. Sheldon already wants to take the baby? Isn't he getting a little aggressive?"

"He's been attempting to control her symptoms with medication from the crash cart, but he seems concerned it may not last."

Mitchell balked. If he hadn't already been here at the hospital, would Grant have asked for his assistance? On the contrary, when Dr. Sheldon came here last year to take over as director of the emergency department he had cut Mitchell's moonlighting shifts.

Mitchell knew he had every right to refuse. "I doubt there's much I can do with a patient in the basement. Without supplies—"

"I'll stay up here with Mr. Horner," Archer said. "This is an emergency, Dr. Caine. I don't think Grant would have asked if he didn't think it was necessary." Gone was the usual conciliatory thread in Archer's voice.

Mitchell attempted to hide his irritation in front of the patients. He gave Mr. Horner a final squeeze on the shoulder, nodded to Archer, and headed for the stairs.

CHAPTER 4

The public warning system had gone silent, much to Jessica's relief. For several minutes it had blasted through the church basement with extra force every time the doors admitted a new arrival. Now, with seventy-some individuals in attendance, the flash of headlights against the windows promised more to follow unless they received an all clear before long.

Helen Netz had commandeered her husband to round up more food from the freezer and was in the process of opening another package of frozen cookies, clucking her tongue at the rowdy teenagers who had swarmed in upon them in the past few minutes.

"Listen to them," Helen muttered. "Laughing and acting up like this is some big joke. They've all been out cruising the streets."

Jessica smiled and nodded. "I did that a few times when I was a teenager."

"We'll have a mess to clean up when this is all over," Helen warned. "We'll have dishes to do."

"Didn't I see some paper plates up there somewhere?" Jessica asked. "Maybe we could use them instead, since this is an emergency situation."

Helen gave a warning glance that told Jessica, more clearly than words, that she was once again treading on sacred ground. "Eileen believed we should always offer our best to God, especially for the poor souls who've never seen His hospitality."

Headlights flashed again across the basement windows. Jessica thought she recognized the outline of a pickup truck. A flicker of lightning flashed a brief snapshot of the driver—Lauren McCaffrey, long blond hair, classically pretty features. She parked just about the time a strong blast of rain-soaked wind sent an arm-sized tree limb skittering across the parking lot.

Lauren shoved open the door of her truck and scrambled out of the way as the wind closed it for her. She turned and ran toward the church, eyes wide, her face a mask of fear.

The wind switched directions again, driving the rain against the church windows like an ocean tide. Jessica instinctively laid her spoon down and rushed to the entrance.

She pushed down the bar and tried to shove the door open, but it didn't budge. Through the reinforced window she saw Lauren grab the handle from the other side and pull. The wind changed. The door gave way, and the whirling wind caught it and jerked the bar from Jessica's grip. Lauren stumbled, and Jessica rushed out to help her as the door slammed against the outer brick wall. Thunder shot through the darkness, and Lauren froze as if paralyzed with terror.

"Come in. Get out of this!" Jessica put an arm around her and urged her through the wide-open threshold, then reached for the door to draw it shut. The wind jerked it from her grasp again with startling power.

Jessica stood breathless against the onslaught of water, then gave up and escaped back inside.

"What on earth?" came a shocked cry from behind them that mingled with the roar of the wind and the onslaught of rain.

Jessica turned to find Helen Netz and several others rushing toward them.

"What'd you do to the door?" the woman cried.

Jessica escaped the path of the incoming rain. "The wind caught—"

"We just *got* those doors this year."

John rushed to the entrance and nudged his wife aside. "For pete's sake, Helen, you can't shame the wind. Come on, everybody out of the rain. No use in catching pneumonia." He and two other men braved the storm and wrestled the door shut once again. "Better get out of line of the windows, folks," he shouted over the roar. "Never seen it do any-thing like this before."

"Think we oughta build us a barricade with the tables?" someone said.

"Sounds good to me," John said.

"Thanks" came a soft voice behind Jessica.

She turned to find Lauren hugging herself, shivering.

"You're welcome. Are you okay? We need to get you warmed up."

"I'll be fine. I'm just a coward when it comes to tornado warnings." Lauren gave one more glance over her shoulder toward the wall of rain. "Mind if we get away from the windows?" She turned to lead the way toward the back, in the direction of the kitchen. "I should have gone to the hospital to help with patients, but I was too scared to drive that far."

"Sounds to me as if coming here was the smart thing to do," Jessica said.

"Listen up, folks!" Mr. Netz called over the din of voices, "I heard over the radio that they extended the warning another thirty minutes. Better settle in and be prepared to wait awhile. The storm could get worse."

Lauren groaned and hugged herself more tightly.

―――――

As soon as Mitchell Caine reached the crowded main corridor of the basement, he was sorry he'd come to the hospital at all.

"Oh, Dr. Caine, thank goodness you're here!" The familiar face of one of his single-mom patients beamed at him from the small crowd huddling by the elevator doors, and she pushed her way past the others. Mitchell nearly groaned aloud. Since his separation from Darla, this woman had become a pest.

"Dr. Sheldon's busy with some other patient," she explained, "and Mark got his arm sprained or broke or something in track at school." She pulled her fourteen-year-old son from the crowd and nearly dragged him forward. "Can you look at it?"

Mitchell closed his eyes and sighed. Why did some patients think he could reach out and touch them and everything would be better? "I'm sorry. We would need to have an x-ray of his arm, and our x-ray equipment is upstairs. I'm sure this alert will end soon, and the personnel will take Mark to Radiology."

"But, Dr. Caine—"

"Excuse me, I've received word that there's an emergency down here. Where is Dr. Sheldon?" Without waiting for a reply, he threaded his way past the people toward the far end of the corridor, where he saw the white coat and dark hair of the ER director, who worked beside Beau and Muriel to lower their patient's gurney.

Mitchell swallowed the automatic rise of antipathy he always experienced when in Grant Sheldon's presence. This was no time for personal conflict. He could see before he reached them that the patient was having another seizure. Her whole body arched, and Sheldon's team hovered over her.

They might, indeed, have to do an emergency C-section on this woman.

———

Lauren's green sweat shirt and denim bib overalls dripped water, and her blond hair clung to her neck and shoulders in wet tendrils. Jessica searched through the kitchen drawers until she found the towels. Silently daring Helen to complain, she took out two and handed one to Lauren.

"Thanks. Sorry to be such a coward, but I've always been terrified of tornadoes." Lauren dabbed at her face and neck and then went to work on her hair.

"I don't know anyone who's too crazy about them," Jessica said as the two of them withdrew to a far corner of the cavernous room.

"I have nightmares about 'em." Lauren gave another dab at her hair. "Pretty dress, Jessica. Looks like you just got home from a show. Nasty weather for driving."

"It took me a while to get here from Branson."

"Bet you wish you'd stayed up there for the night."

"Ordinarily, I don't mind driving in the rain," Jessica said.

"Same here. Most times, I like a good thunderstorm," Lauren said. "I even like walking in the rain, but when I heard that alert go off tonight, I felt like someone had shot me with a dose of epinephrine. I didn't even take time to get my raincoat; I just grabbed my keys and ran out to the truck. Times like this I wish I'd bought a house with a basement."

Jessica noticed Lauren's slight Ozark accent, which ordinarily wasn't so obvious.

"Want to hear something funny?" Lauren asked. "It was a tornado that made me decide to become a nurse in the first place. I saw the effects of a bad one coming home from church camp one year, up by King's River."

"What was it like?"

"We heard about the warning when we were at camp," Lauren said, her mezzo-soprano voice softening with the memory. "We didn't think much about it. To us kids, it was just a good excuse to act silly and huddle together in the storm shelter, exchanging scary stories." She gestured toward some of the teenagers who were congregated together in the far back corner, who looked as if they were doing the same thing.

"The tornado didn't hit then?" Jessica asked.

"Nope, we just got a little rain at the camp." Lauren's expressive face reflected the sorrow and horror she must have experienced all those years ago. "But on the bus going home from camp, we drove past the town." Her green eyes widened, and she touched Jessica's arm for emphasis. "Practically eighty percent of the buildings had been destroyed, Jess, and seven people were killed. I cried the rest of the way home. It was right then that I decided I wanted to go into medicine."

"Particularly emergency medicine?" Jessica asked.

"That's right. I wanted to be able to help people like that if it ever happened again." She spread her hands. "And here I am, hiding out at church instead of seeing to the patients at the hospital."

"Well, I'm glad you're here," Jessica said, studying Lauren more closely. Even dripping wet in bib overalls she was a beautiful woman, with softly sculpted facial lines, well proportioned and wholesome.

To hear Archer tell it, Lauren had the faith to move mountains, the ability to charm teenagers into silence for hours at a time, and the gentle touch of Mother Teresa—although when Jessica asked him how he knew what her touch felt like, he blushed and explained that he didn't know about that personally, but several patients had commented on it.

Archer had known Lauren McCaffrey for nearly twenty-five years, since they were kids. He obviously admired her, and even though Jessica had battled jealousy in the past, she respected Archer's insight.

Lauren glanced toward the kitchen. "Uh-oh, Helen's looking our direction. You know, I don't think that woman knows how to sit down and take it easy. Sometimes I think if we were to sneak in here in the middle of the night, we'd find her in that kitchen, behind that counter."

"Even during a tornado alert." Jessica regretted the sarcasm as soon as the words left her mouth. "Did my mother-in-law really start this business of serving snacks during these storms?"

Lauren shrugged. "Eileen was the essence of hospitality, so it wouldn't surprise me, but I didn't grow up here. I went to church in Knolls until I moved here last year." She glanced at the kitchen and saw Helen making more sandwiches. "Guess we could go help Helen."

Jessica followed reluctantly.

Mitchell barely noticed the voices of the crowd or the occasional greeting from a patient or a staff member. His attention, along with that of Grant, Muriel, and Beau—as well as Joanne's brawny son, Kent—was focused on Joanne's swollen face, caught in a grotesque mask of seizure.

Mitchell nodded toward Grant. "What are you giving her?"

"Up to now I've given her labetalol and mag sulfate," Grant said. "Nothing seems to be helping this time, and I can't give her more mag sulfate. Her breathing was getting shallow before this seizure began, and it was fine when she arrived."

Mitchell hated to admit Grant was right about this one. They needed to do a C-section, and they needed to hurry. "We'll take the baby."

"We won't be able to get an anesthesiologist here in time," Grant said.

"You'll have to take care of the anesthesia. We have no choice."

"Let's go, then," Grant said. "Do you have the keys to OB?"

"In my pocket."

"We're out of labetalol," Muriel said.

Mitchell checked the patient himself, then pulled the keys from his pocket and turned to Grant. "Let's get her to OB. Quickly. Muriel, will you assist? You have OB experience."

"You'd better believe it," Muriel said. "I'm not leaving this patient's side until she's out of danger. Let's get her up the elevator while it's still working. Beau, you clear everybody back. Where's Lela? I saw her down here a few minutes ago. She can circulate—"

"Not on my watch, she can't," Mitchell said. "Beau, come with us. You can assist, can't you?"

"Yes, I think I can."

"You *think*?"

"I can do it."

Mitchell nodded. "Good." Although Grant's son was only a part-time tech here at the hospital, he had a passion for medicine and could be trusted to keep his cool and assist when needed, unlike Lela-the-Emotional, who cried when she got stressed. "Let's go."

"Wait a minute." The kid with the muscles who had hovered in the corner of the hallway came forward. "I want to go with my mother."

"I'm sorry, Kent," Grant said. "Not this time. Don't worry; we'll take good care of her."

Kent glowered at him.

"She'll probably be okay as soon as they deliver the baby," Beau said quietly as they wheeled the gurney past Kent. "Why don't you stay here with Brooke? That way we can locate you more easily when we're finished. C-sections don't take long."

———

"Hey, Jess," called one of the teenagers from the back of the room, "storm's letting up. Can we go now?"

"Not yet," she said. "We haven't gotten an all clear."

There was a general groan until Helen Netz filled a plate with cookies and handed it to Jessica to pass across the counter to the group of hungry teenagers. "That'll keep 'em occupied," she said. "Speaking of your mother-in-law, Jessica, now *there* was a church worker."

"Yes, that's what I've heard," Jessica said. *Over and over and over again.*

"That woman could cook, and she loved company. She could pick up on a person's troubles without anyone having to tell her. She fit the bill for this church. She knew just what a pastor's wife ought to be."

Lauren wadded a piece of used aluminum foil and made a perfect bank shot into the trash can against the wall. "I love Eileen, but every person has her own set of gifts, Helen. I don't think there's any *list* set in stone for a pastor's wife."

Helen shoved some sandwich material in Lauren's direction and ignored her comments. "You know, Jessica, when Aaron Pierce was pastor, Eileen had a spring brunch at the parsonage every year and invited all the women in the church. I know they'd love to do that again."

"Every year?" Lauren exclaimed. "How'd she fit everyone into the parsonage?"

"*She* didn't have any trouble." Helen poured hot cocoa into cups and shoved them toward the far side of the counter with a little extra force, nearly spilling the contents.

"I don't know how Jessica would ever find time to do that," Lauren said. "Eileen Pierce makes the best strawberry tarts I ever tasted, but no music ever touched my heart the way Jessica's does."

Jessica looked at Lauren in surprise. "Thank you."

"Still," Helen said, "a little hospitality goes a long way toward encouraging the church to have a sense of community. Just trying to make some helpful comments, dear." She patted Jessica's arm. "You've got some mighty fine shoes to fill."

"I'm all for hospitality," Lauren said. "But have you noticed how big our church has grown? We've got about two hundred more members than when Aaron Pierce was pastor."

"When Eileen lived in the parsonage, they always had company," Helen said. "Folks in the church knew they were always welcome there. Aaron and Eileen had a special relationship with our church. It's important for people to get to know their pastor and his family."

Jessica did not reply. In spite of her high-profile career choice—or perhaps because of it—she had a strong need for privacy when not on stage. It had been one of the reasons she'd hesitated to marry a pastor in the first place.

She hadn't been raised in church the way so many of their members had. She'd attended vacation Bible school a couple of times, and every so often a neighbor had taken her to Sunday school at the Methodist church in Kimberling City. That was when she'd first been told about the perfect love of a heavenly Father, which seemed much less real to her than the distracted, irritable love of her very earthly, overworked father.

She didn't come to understand the powerful concept of God's love until she joined the cast of *Two From Galilee* at the Promise Theater. It was then that He became real to her. It was then that she fell in love with the God of the universe. Her heart had been transformed by that love, and she poured out her worship when she sang before audiences consisting of tourists from all over the world.

"We could have a special church night at the theater when you're singing, Jessica," Lauren said. "Or maybe you could have a praise concert at our church."

"Oh, Lauren. Be serious, dear," Helen said.

"I am serious. I betcha it wouldn't take much convincing to get my old church in Knolls to come and join us. We could pass the collection plate and forward the proceeds to help some local families with groceries. There you'd have your hospitality."

"How is that going to help Jessica get acquainted with the women in the church?" Helen asked.

"Once they've seen and heard her, they'll definitely understand her better through the music God gives her to sing. I say give people in the church a chance to worship with the real Jessica Pierce."

Jessica felt a silly grin spread across her face. No wonder Archer liked Lauren McCaffrey so much. What wasn't there to like?

Helen frowned at Lauren. "Don't you think it would be a little ostentatious to—"

"Nope," Lauren said. Was that an edge in her voice? "I don't think so, not at all. Why, Jessica's music is a ministry all in itself. We'd have a great worship service. Have *you* ever been to one of Jessica's shows, Helen?"

"No, I can't say I've had the pleasure, but I've heard her sing in church several times."

The public alert siren went off again, intruding over the laughter and chatter in the basement. Jessica felt a little shock course through her whole body. She saw Lauren's face freeze, her right hand held suspended in midair for several seconds as the raucous sound filled the basement.

Jessica took her hand and squeezed. "Maybe we should do some praying. What do you say?"

Lauren relaxed only slightly. "I think that's a great idea."

———

Mitchell ignored the muted sound of the siren, suppressing his fear. There were no windows in this room, and this hospital was solidly built. Besides, they had no choice. Joanne Bonus was still in seizure. If they took her back downstairs to escape possible storm damage, they would be risking her life and the life of her baby.

He used Valium in a partially successful attempt to control Joanne's seizure long enough to work on her abdomen. Muriel assisted in the sterile field with Beau circulating and keeping them supplied with what they needed. As Mitchell had expected, the kid knew what he was doing.

Grant stood by to help where he could and then tend to the baby after it was delivered.

Although the seizure indicated an altered level of consciousness, Mitchell used a local anesthetic just in case Joanne was able to feel pain when he made the incisions.

"Give the ketamine now," he said just before he made the final incision, and then quickly, before that drug could reach the infant through the mother, he lifted the slippery baby from his cozy spot, handed him to Grant, cut the cord. The healthy-looking baby boy was fully formed, good sized—perhaps a little over six pounds. Joanne's seizure ended almost immediately, and even as Mitchell examined her uterus, Joanne moaned in pain.

"She's starting to feel it," Muriel said.

"Grant, can you push the fentanyl?"

"Got it. She'll be okay soon."

"Blood pressure is dropping already," Muriel said.

Exactly as it should be. Mitchell reached for the suture supplies Muriel had prepared for him. In the past few years he had taken on fewer obstetric cases, and now he wondered if that had been the right choice. Yes, it was a high-risk occupation, and one bad outcome could wipe out the livelihood of a good doctor. And yet . . . there was something about bringing a new life into the world that could make all the middle-of-the-night calls worthwhile. Besides, his wife was doing a perfectly good job of wiping out his livelihood now, anyway.

How could he have forgotten the excitement?

He knew how. In the past two years, every time he delivered a baby he couldn't prevent the mental picture of his own tiny granddaughter, who had not been healthy—who had been poisoned by her own mother's habit.

The patient's moan was softer this time.

"We'll have you sutured up soon, Joanne," he said. "Dr. Sheldon, how's the baby?"

"Strong heart rate, pink, mild respiratory depression initially. Excellent five-minute Apgar test scores." Grant held the baby up for the others to see. "Beau, you've assisted with your first C-section. How does it feel?"

"Like I could do this for the rest of my life," his son replied.

Mitchell allowed himself a brief nod of satisfaction. Maybe it had been a good night to come to the hospital, after all.

CHAPTER 5

Archer noticed the branch outside the hallway window had gone still, the corridors silent.

Mr. Horner touched Archer's arm, then gestured to his ear.

Archer listened. At first it sounded like a locomotive was rumbling by on the train track downhill from the hospital, but the rumbling grew louder. Others heard it and called out in fear. Fiona Perkins screamed, and someone snapped at her to get downstairs.

Mr. Horner gave a great spasmodic shudder and gripped Archer's hand.

"It'll be okay." Archer pulled the blankets over Mr. Horner and stuffed the pillows more firmly against the railings of the bed, then climbed over the rails onto the bed to block the patient from any flying debris.

The raucous noise filled the corridors and blasted him with the sound of a dozen charging locomotives. Archer braced himself, praying hard.

"Look at the trees!" someone cried.

Two limbs at least ten feet long and as thick as a man's thigh whipped across the church parking lot on a destructive course, slamming from car to windshield to car. Thunder shook the building and roared like an angry T. rex.

"That isn't thunder!" Jessica cried. She reached for Lauren as the roar of a jet during takeoff blasted through the basement.

Two audacious teenagers rushed toward the windows and pointed. Norville Webster ran out from behind the table barricade after them. "Get back! Get to the back of the—"

The outer doors flew open as if a huge vacuum had sucked them outward. Darkness blanketed the basement. Jessica shoved Lauren behind the kitchen counter and dove after her as rocks and limbs and glass invaded their safe haven.

"Everybody get down!" Jessica cried, but the attack of sound blasted her words back at her. She and Lauren huddled against the wall.

Something smacked the cabinet beside them with the sound of a rifle shot, and Jessica cried out. Lauren put an arm around her and drew her closer.

The roar thrust at them with rage, closing in with increased force. Jessica said a final prayer and waited to die, unable to think, unable to grieve her own impending death, incapable of conscious thought as the sound of the diabolical storm invaded her mind.

Archer mouthed a continuous prayer as he endured the assault of the terrifying noise combined with the vibration of the bed. He heard a crack of shattering glass and another scream. Someone rushed past him with a mattress and shoved it against the broken window to block the wind.

Nothing flew at them, and nothing toppled onto them from above. The lights didn't even go out, because the hospital was already on auxiliary power.

Archer dared to raise his head and look down the hallway to see how the others were faring. He saw one of the nurses shielding a patient with her body, saw another patient attempting to climb from his bed in a panic. One of the fire fighters rushed to him and restrained him—barely preventing him from ripping the IV tube from his arm.

There was another scream, and Archer covered his ears.

Mitchell was placing his final layer of sutures when he heard the crash of breaking glass somewhere out in the hallway, felt the oppressive suction, heard the roar.

"Lower the bed," he told Muriel, trying not to break the sterile field. He turned to find that Grant had already sent his son with the baby to safety. "Grant, come help us shield this patient."

They covered Joanne's abdomen with a sterile cloth and lowered the bed almost to the floor, then knelt over her, locking arms to protect Joanne's body with their own.

———

"Lord, protect us," Archer whispered. "Protect this hospital and the people in it. Protect Jessica and the church." He felt unaccustomed moisture sting his eyes.

Jessica. What was happening to her? He'd insisted that she go to the church. What if he'd been wrong to send her there? *Please, Lord.*

The roar grew louder, more oppressive. Archer pressed his hands harder against his ears, waiting to be slammed with flying debris, waiting for the roof to be sucked up into the sky, and the inhabitants of this building along with it. At last, he thought to pray for those souls who didn't know God, who couldn't afford to lose their lives tonight. *Lord, spare them.*

Suddenly, like someone had flipped a switch, the horrible, oppressive sound geared downward. Archer heard the echo of a roar, like a lion on the prowl in the distance, and then silence. Just that fast.

Afraid to trust his own senses, he remained huddled for another few seconds.

Mr. Horner stirred at last. Voices skittered along the hallway, tentatively at first, as if afraid their words might trigger another attack, and then louder. Sighs of relief and exclamations of amazement reached them.

Archer eased himself from the bed and looked around. Chunky, black-haired Fiona Perkins sat in the far right corner of the hallway, sobbing. The fire fighter who had rushed past them with the mattress lowered it enough to look outside into the darkness. The wind continued to blow, but the rain had stopped. Lightning flashed in the distance, and Archer breathed a quick prayer for others who might be in the path of the storm.

This building had withstood the tornado. But what about his wife? What about the church?

———

The horrible roar departed. For a moment, as Jessica continued to huddle next to Lauren, she wondered if the monster might return. The first thing she heard was the rhythmic drip of water from the eaves outside, then the cry of a frightened child somewhere at the far end of the basement.

She opened her eyes to find Lauren watching her.

"You okay, Jess?" Lauren's breath smelled of peppermint.

"Yeah, I'm fine. You?"

"No damage I can tell." She raised her head. "Mrs. Netz? You all right?"

There was a low moan from the end of the counter, just out of their sight. "I think so. You girls hurt?"

"We're okay," Jessica said.

Other voices reached her.

"Anybody hurt?"

"Was that really a tornado?"

"You guys okay?"

"Where'd the lights come from? I thought they got knocked out."

"We got battery packs, remember?"

Jessica cautiously stood to her feet beside Lauren, peering over the counter into the recesses of the basement. The battery-pack lights left too many shadows, and she saw John Netz and two other men mingling through the frightened crowd with flashlights to check for injuries.

"Nobody go outside yet," John said in his booming voice. "We haven't heard an all clear. Anybody hurt?"

"Here! We got someone hurt over here!" came a cry from one of the church kids on the other side of the basement. "Glass cut her."

"I need to get over to them." Lauren opened the kitchen drawer containing the towels. She took an armful of them and rushed across the debris-laden floor without waiting for an all clear. Norville Webster limped out to meet her.

Jessica followed, nearly tripping over a limb that had blown into the church with the wind. "Be careful where you step," she called. "There's glass all over the place." The smell of ozone hovered around them, and Jessica felt the grit of dirt and broken shards of glass beneath her shoes.

More people stood up from behind the tables that had served as a barricade against flying objects. She could only pray the tables had been effective.

"Okay, folks, help each other out," John said. "We got us a nurse here, so let's start doing some checking. Make sure your neighbors are okay. Norville? Norville Webster, where are you? Help me with this table, will you?"

There were moans and gasps of surprise, a few sobs, and then Helen Netz cried out from the front of the basement. "John, our car!"

Others rushed to join her and peer into the darkness. Continued flashes of retreating lightning outlined the damage in the parking lot. Jessica wasn't interested in checking the damage to her car just now. Still following Lauren, she pulled her cell phone from her pocket and punched Archer's number.

"Let him be there," she whispered. "Let him be safe."

When he answered, she could have wept.

"You're alive," she breathed.

"Jessica, thank God!" Archer said. "You're okay?"

"Yes. Any damage there?"

"Some broken windows. Nothing more that we've seen. A few stunned patients and a new baby, but no injuries from the wind. What's going on at the church?"

"We weren't quite so fortunate," she said, glancing toward Lauren, who was helping an older lady sit down on a chair that had been wiped clean of debris. "Look, Archer, I have to let you go. I need to help Lauren."

"Wait, what's happening? Has someone been hurt?"

"Yes, the windows were blown out, and there are some cuts. We're not sure how bad the injuries are yet—we're just now digging out."

"I'll get to you as soon as I can."

Mitchell Caine stepped out of OB and threaded his way along the crowded corridor feeling more energized than he'd been in months. He'd received word that the only damage the hospital had suffered was broken windows and some wet floors. When he went downstairs to the ER to help with incoming patients, the maintenance men were pulling a twelve-foot-long tree limb from the middle of the waiting room—it had crashed through the plate-glass window on the north side. A hastily scrawled sign directed new patients down the hallway to the outpatient Lab and Radiology waiting room.

The staff had already assisted patients back into their rooms upstairs. Mitchell would check on his own as soon as he assured himself he wasn't needed for emergencies.

Sure enough, the ER teemed with patients. Every room but one was occupied. As he made his way to the central control desk, he heard the secretary talking to Grant.

"Dr. Sheldon, we got word from Jessica that there are some injuries at the church, and they can't get a car out of the lot to bring them in. They apparently have some fallen trees. The ambulances are all busy. Archer's on his way there."

"Did she say how many patients?"

"Four at last count, but she hasn't checked everyone yet."

"Have you heard anything from Lauren?"

"Nothing. Sorry."

"Keep me posted. Have you called for backup staff?"

"Gina Drake from Respiratory is coming, and Eugene said he'd be here. I can't find Lester."

"Keep trying."

"I will."

Grant looked up and caught sight of Mitchell. "Good, you're still here. Can you stay? We've got two ambulances coming in, two more injured coming by private car, and as you can see"—he gestured around the department—"we're—"

"I'll stay." Mitchell mentally switched gears again. In this department, Dr. Grant Sheldon reigned supreme, but Mitchell didn't have to like it.

"Thanks." Grant handed him a chart. "Bad laceration, possibly a cracked skull. A limb hit his windshield. He's in two."

Mitchell took the chart, nodded, crossed the floor to see his patient.

———

Archer parked on the street with his headlights aimed across the lower parking lot of the church. He caught his breath at first sight of the damage. Two ancient oak trees had been torn from the ground, roots and all, and one of them lay sprawled across seven cars. The windshields had all been broken, roofs caved in, hoods dented. Debris had damaged other automobiles in the lot. The Netz car had taken a hit from a limb. Jessica's car, directly beside it, appeared unscathed, although he couldn't see well enough to know for sure. Lauren's gray pickup had a cracked windshield and a dented fender.

Just as Jess had said, the basement doors and windows had been blown outward, and as Archer got out of his car he saw Lauren and Mr. Netz helping an older lady through the gaping threshold of the basement.

"Archer!" Lauren called when she spotted him. "Am I ever glad to see you! Mind if we commandeer your car? We've got a few injuries—some cuts from flying glass. I'd like to get some of these people to the hospital and see if Dr. Sheldon thinks they need sutures."

"It's unlocked, so just load 'em in there. Have you seen—"

Slender arms grabbed him from behind in a death grip. He disentangled himself long enough to turn and assure himself that it was, indeed, his wife who held him.

She pulled him back into an enthusiastic embrace. "I never want to go through that again!" came her muffled voice from his shoulder.

He tried to gently draw her back so he could look into her face, smile into her eyes, convince her that everything was okay—but she wouldn't budge. He looked up and encountered several smiles aimed in his direction from the people behind her.

"Sweetheart," he murmured in Jessica's ear, "come to the hospital with me."

"You won't have room in your car. I'll try to get mine out of the tangle and follow you."

He heard her sniff and felt her shoulders shake. "It's going to be okay, Jess. Look, I desperately want some time alone with you right now, but I think you should drive my car, take those with the worst injuries. I'll stay here and help dig out, and I'll meet you in the ER as soon as I can."

Her arms tightened for a few exquisite seconds, and then she released him and drew back. Her face was appealingly flushed, her eyes moist. "I'll come back here in case you can't get the other cars out."

"Okay, let's get going." He kissed her again, and then he and Jessica and Lauren helped the injured into his car.

Jessica was driving away when someone shouted from the building. "Lauren! Help, over here! It's Norville Webster."

Archer followed Lauren back inside as the siren of an emergency vehicle reached them through the night. Good, maybe help was on the way.

He heard Lauren gasp, and his relief dissipated with the wind.

Norville Webster lay in a corner that the backup lights did not reach. John Netz raised his flashlight to reveal a streak of blood framing the right side of Norville's bald head. Norville moaned.

One of the women cried out, and others crowded around.

"He was walking around just a minute ago," John said. "I knew he'd had a cut or two, but—"

Lauren fell to her knees beside the balding man. "Norville?" She squeezed his right shoulder. "Norville!"

No answer.

CHAPTER 6

Norville!" Lauren kept her voice calm, in direct contrast to her racing heart. What was wrong with her? She never panicked in the ER.

But this was different. She knew this man, went to church with him. The pallor of his skin alarmed her, as did the amount of blood on the floor. She heard his labored breathing. The hemorrhaging seemed to come from a couple of scalp lacerations, likely caused by flying shards of glass.

As Mr. Netz tried to clear the crowd away, Archer held a flashlight for Lauren to see better.

She checked for glass in the cuts, found none, pressed a towel to the worst cut, behind his right ear. "Archer, hold this for me, will you? Keep pressure on it."

"Got it," he said. "John, would you hold this light for me? Have you called for an ambulance?"

"Can't get through right now," John said.

"I thought we heard a siren a minute ago," Lauren said.

"It didn't come here," John said. "I bet they're piled up with calls."

"We need to get this man to the hospital," Archer said. "Quickly."

"We can't wait for them." Lauren focused on the simple ABCs of trauma management. Airway. "Norville! Can you hear me?"

He moaned again. His lips moved, but she couldn't hear his voice above the chatter of the curious crowd that hovered around them.

"Everybody *quiet*," she said in her most authoritative voice. "John, *please*."

"Okay, everybody out of this area—now!" John's voice boomed through the basement. "Can't endanger a person just to satisfy our curiosity, now, can we?" he said more gently.

As the voices around her gradually drifted away, Lauren leaned close to Norville's mouth. "Please say something, Norville."

"Yes," he grunted.

Okay, his airway wasn't closed off, even though he didn't sound quite right. ABCs. Breathing. She unzipped his jacket and checked the rise and fall of his chest. His respirations were deep and even. She caught sight of the towel Archer held to Norville's head. It looked as if the bleeding had slowed or stopped.

Why hadn't she thought to bring her stethoscope? She couldn't even listen to breath sounds. She felt helpless.

"Is he going to be all right?" John asked, returning from his crowd-control duties.

"I don't know. Try again to call an ambulance." She felt at Norville's right wrist for the radial artery. Pulse fast but strong. Circulation good for now. The ABCs were covered. "Norville, can you still hear me?"

This time his voice was louder but high and strained. "Help me."

Stridor—upper airway obstruction?

She tried to recall the different causes of stridor. Spasm? Aspirated foreign body?

No. Think trauma.

Laryngeal fracture? *What am I missing?*

She unbuttoned Norville's shirt. "Shine the light here, Archer."

She caught her breath at the sight of swelling on the right, below his ear. *Oh, dear Lord, help us.* "He's got a neck hematoma." Blood was swelling his airway shut. "Ice, I need ice, quickly! We've got to get the swelling down. John, any response with the ambulance? We need to get him out of here."

"They're out on calls. No telling when we'll get one." He squatted. "Helen's bringing the ice. Looks like this one's up to you, Lauren."

Grant Sheldon placed a chart in its slot beside the desk and gestured to the secretary. "Becky, we need to redirect everyone who isn't injured into the designated waiting room."

She looked up at him, shaking her head and pointing to her headset. "Yes, I understand, Mrs. Harris," she said softly, turning back to her computer screen. "If you can get a neighbor to bring you in, that'll be your best bet. The ambulances are all tied up right now."

"Dad?" Beau sidled up beside Grant at the counter, drying his hands on a paper towel. He'd been doing triage and cleaning exam rooms as soon as they were emptied. "Brooke's in the break room complaining that she doesn't have anything to do. I won't let her close to the patients, but she'd love to do crowd control."

"Good. Get her. We need to clear this place of all unnecessary personnel. Have you heard anything from the church? Lauren hasn't come in, has she?"

"I haven't heard from her. You think she's okay?"

"I'm sure she's . . . I'm sure she'll be fine." *Liar*. He wasn't sure of anything. He couldn't stop worrying about her, couldn't get her out of his mind, especially knowing she would be here by now if she could.

Maybe she'd driven to Knolls to see her parents this evening. But she would've told him if she'd planned to do that. Besides, they were all going to her parents' place Sunday to celebrate Lauren's birthday. She wouldn't make the hour-long drive tonight.

Muriel shoved another chart in front of him. "Bad one in three, Dr. Sheldon. Looks like a concussion, maybe a serious one."

He glanced at the chart, then looked out the glass doors of the ambulance entrance. "Okay, I'll be right there."

———

The ice wasn't working. Norville's high-pitched stridor filled the basement with its sound of desperation as his agitated movements—shoulders flexing, head jerking—resembled those of a drunk.

Lauren removed the pack from his neck. The swelling had increased, and now Norville's Adam's apple edged slightly left of center.

Tracheal deviation.

She looked around at John Netz, who stood watching helplessly a few feet away. "The ambulance?" she asked.

He shook his head.

"Can we get a car?"

"Trees are blocking everybody."

"Okay." She forced herself to breathe deeply. She must not panic. "Okay, have Helen find the sharpest paring knife in the kitchen." *And then pray I don't have to use it!* "Have her sterilize it the best she can. If anybody has a lighter, she can hold it over the flame. And have her bring me some of those disposable kitchen gloves from the cabinet below the kitchen sink. And some towels. Quickly, John, please!"

What am I doing? Even Grant wouldn't try to decompress a neck hematoma. He would do an emergency intubation to protect the airway until a surgeon could get there.

But then, Grant didn't make a habit of practicing medicine in a half-ruined church basement in the wake of a tornado. All Lauren knew was that if she didn't alleviate the swelling soon, Norville would lose his airway. The carbon dioxide levels in his body would continue to rise until he went to sleep. Maybe forever.

Lauren had no intubation equipment.

She gently placed the fingers of her right hand against the Adam's apple, then slid them to the right side of his neck, searching for the carotid artery. There. She felt it. Barely. She had to avoid that. And stay away from the external jugular. That would be the most superficial and the easiest to avoid since it was now so prominent with the swelling.

"Norville, you still with me?"

He moaned.

"Norville, please listen to me. We may not be able to wait for the ambulance, and I might have to do a procedure on you to ease the swelling."

Even as she spoke, his agitation decreased slightly. His head lolled sideways. There wasn't time to get him to the hospital even if the ambulance was on its way—which it wasn't.

"Helen, where's that knife?" Lauren called over her shoulder.

"Right here," the older woman said. "Here you go. Be careful; it's sharp."

"Good, I need sharp." Lauren pulled the gloves on, then took the knife from Helen. Once again, she surveyed her landmarks, then closed her eyes, taking a deep breath. *Lord, I can't do this!*

She felt a hand on her shoulder and looked up to see Archer hovering over her. "I'll be right here to help; just let me know what you need."

"Straddle his chest and hold his hands so he can't fight me. John, I need you to hold his head perfectly still. And pray, Archer. We need lots of prayer."

"You've already got that."

She nodded. Norville's movements had slowed considerably. She had to do this *now*.

She pressed the knife to Norville's throat, rechecking her landmarks. She held her breath and made a short vertical incision.

A little blood dribbled down his neck, but nothing major. She would have to cut deeper.

"Jessica's back with the car!" someone shouted from the doorway.

Lauren withdrew, her hands trembling.

"Don't stop now," Archer said. "You can do this. Come on, Lauren."

She swallowed hard, steadied herself, and extended the incision, pressing a little more deeply.

Blood spurted. Archer pressed a towel against it, and Lauren took it from him. She handed him her knife and checked the wound. Blood continued to spurt. Dark, clotted blood.

"Got it!" Lauren cried.

A siren echoed in the distance as the swelling eased in Norville's neck. His breathing returned to normal with encouraging rapidity.

"I need more ice," Lauren called over her shoulder. "And another towel, please." *Thank you, Lord!*

She leaned over Norville. "You're going to be okay."

"Norville Webster's a lucky guy," Becky said softly as they listened to the ambulance report at the central desk. "Thanks to Lauren." She turned and grinned at Grant. "Have you been teaching her the tricks of the trade?"

"Not me. Don't forget, she's been in the ER for a lot of years." Grant couldn't have been more proud—or relieved.

He gestured to Eugene, the night RN who had arrived to help out barely five minutes ago. "Let's set up for our incoming patient in Trauma Two. I may have to intubate. Also, the patient in eight is ready for discharge."

"I'm already on it, Dr. Sheldon," Eugene said. "Lester's setting up the intubation equipment. Will you have time to see the guy with the swollen ankle in six? He needs an x-ray."

"Yes, I'll check in on him." He took the chart from Eugene, then turned and nearly collided with his daughter.

"They're out, Dad." She brushed the long dark bangs out of eyes that glowed with excitement. "There's nobody back here now that doesn't have a good reason. I'd make a good bouncer, don't you think? Got anything else for me to do? I can't leave—Beau won't let me take the car, and—" She glanced toward the door. "Oh, great, what's *she* coming in for?"

Grant followed Brooke's line of vision and saw Jade Myers entering the ER from the reception office. "She came to see about her uncle."

"Oh, sure, and she'll find some reason to corner you and—"

"Retract your claws, Brooke. She's a nice lady and a good—"

"She's after you, Dad."

"She's dating Norville."

"So? That doesn't—"

"Brooke, settle down. I don't have time to argue with you. Go back to my call room and get a set of scrubs from the cabinet. Take them to room five. I'm releasing Mr. Mourglia, and he needs something to wear home."

"Got it, Dad." She rushed off like an eager puppy, obviously pleased to be in the thick of the excitement.

"Heads up!" Becky called from the central desk. "Incoming. They're here with Norville."

Lauren helped Christy and Bill unload Norville from the ambulance and turned to find Grant walking out to meet them. Some of Lauren's tension dissipated. She saw Beau rushing past the desk and then caught sight of Brooke carrying a pair of green scrubs down the far hallway.

Safe. They were safe. Thank God.

As Christy gave report, Lauren followed the retinue. The place was packed, and more were coming. She'd be busy here for a while.

"There you are, Lauren McCaffrey. I've been looking for you!" Gina Drake caught her as soon as she entered the department. Gina's bright hair, the color of a new penny, fell in disheveled curls to her shoulders— she'd been growing it out. She touched Lauren's arm, tugged at her shirt. "Where's your Superwoman outfit? Everybody's already heard about the emergency surgery you performed. Way to go, girl!"

"Thanks, but—"

"No time to talk, we've got patients to see. I volunteered to help out here for a few hours, and I'm going to follow you around for a while to orient. You *did* come here to work, didn't you?"

"Of course, but—"

"Come this way, then. The triage area is now a regular exam room, and they're setting up for triage in the conference room. Got it?"

Lauren tried to keep up with her firebrand friend, the respiratory therapist turned ER aide. "Who's following whom around?" she teased. "How are the boys?"

"Oh, they're loving the excitement. They're at the neighbor's, where we rode out the tornado in the basement. Levi's disappointed that nothing happened on our street except one tree got uprooted."

Lauren heard a sudden gasp behind them. She turned to see the town mayor, Jade Myers, approaching the entranceway to Trauma Two, her intense dark eyes filled with shock, the slender fingers of her right hand covering her lips as she watched Grant and the others working over Norville.

"Uh-oh," Gina murmured. "Guess she just found out about Norville the hard way."

Lauren squeezed her friend's shoulder. "Why don't you go on to the triage area and start taking vitals. I'll be right there."

"Okay, but be warned, we're doing lots of urgent care tonight. Lots of cuts and bruises, scrapes and panic attacks, and we only have two docs. You're going to have to play nurse practitioner."

Lauren nodded, still watching Jade. Obviously, the woman cared a great deal about Norville. "It can't be any worse than what I've already had to do," she said softly. "I'll just check on Jade and be right there."

Gina went on without her, and Lauren stepped to Jade's side. "He'll be okay," she said softly. "They'll take good care of him."

Jade looked at her. "I didn't know. . . . I came to see about Uncle Ernest, and then this . . . What happened?" The woman's customarily deep, commanding voice trembled. "I tried calling him at home and couldn't reach him."

"He came to the church," Lauren explained. "When the tornado hit, two kids ran toward the windows, and Norville ran after them. It looks like a sliver of glass shot into his neck, almost like a bullet. It hit a vein, and the blood built up in his neck, cutting off his airway."

To Lauren's surprise, moisture filmed Jade's eyes. "But he's breathing now."

"We had to do an emergency procedure to relieve the blood. Don't worry, it looks worse than it is now. Dr. Sheldon will call a surgeon in, and they'll be able to take care of it."

"He's going to be okay?"

"I think he'll be fine."

Jade nodded, straightened her shoulders. "Then I'll stay out of the way and let them work. I need to see about Uncle Ernest." She patted Lauren's arm as she turned to walk away, all business once again. "Thank you."

CHAPTER 7

At one in the morning Grant Sheldon signed a final chart and placed it in the slot where it belonged. Muriel or Lauren would take it from there. Eugene had gone home over an hour ago, as had Mitchell Caine. Between Mitchell and Grant, they had ordered enough x-rays and sutured enough flesh to match a typical full week at this ER. They'd used the last suture tray in the department at eleven-thirty, and they'd been forced to borrow two from Surgery.

Grant leaned back in the chair and sighed, rubbing his eyes. Except for the sound of Muriel's voice as she discharged the only remaining patient, there was no other activity. He looked around the department for Lauren and was disappointed to find that she had apparently left without telling him good-bye.

That stung.

They had received word well before midnight that Norville Webster's surgery had gone well. The surgeon had identified and ligated the bleeding vessel and removed the glass. Except for the vessel no other vital structures of the neck had been damaged.

Grant yawned. Should he take a stroll upstairs to Recovery and see about Norville? The poor guy was probably getting some much-needed rest.

Not now. Maybe he'd make a quick visit later in the morning, after he completed this shift. Meanwhile . . . food. Grant was starving.

Archer found his wife slumped in a chair in the main hospital wait-ing room at one-fifteen. She had spent a hectic few hours shuttling peo-ple from church to their homes in Archer's car. Her car was just trapped, but quite a few others were still in the lot, some slightly damaged and others crushed under the oak tree.

He sat down beside her. "Need a ride home?"

She straightened, stretching her arms in a wide, lazy arc. She brought them around his neck with a sleepy smile. "Food first? I'm starved."

He buried his fingers in her thick, tousled hair. "Jessica Lane Pierce, how many times have I told you I love you?"

"Dozens." Her jeweled hazel eyes held traces of characteristic humor.

"Only dozens? I'm going to remedy that."

She giggled. "How are you—"

"Until tonight, I never realized how I've come to depend on you, how much a part of each other we are." He brushed several stray waves of light brown hair from her cheek. "Sometimes when we're together I almost feel as if I can see the world through your eyes. I know what you're going to say next, what you'll do."

"I hope I still manage to surprise you *some* of the time."

"You often surprise me," he agreed, "but still there's the feeling of being connected in a way I never dreamed possible." He took her hand and pulled her from her chair. They strolled down the silent hallway to the equally silent cafeteria. At this time of night only the vending machines offered sustenance of any kind.

Archer purchased two sandwiches and two cans of juice, then led the way past the empty food bar to a booth at the far end of the cafe-teria.

"Tonight," he said, sliding into the booth, "up on the patient floor, with the tornado screaming through the building, I prayed harder than I've ever prayed in my life. I couldn't help wondering if I would see you alive again—or if you would see me alive. All I could think about was you. I was desperate for you to be safe, desperate to tell you one more time how much you mean to me."

She was silent for a moment, then said softly, "That helps."

He stared out the window at the lights of Dogwood Springs. They had not been without power for long. The city lights revealed broken limbs, fallen trees, flooded streets that were already clearing. They'd had trouble finding a passable street between the hospital and the church, but things would soon be back to normal. This hillside town didn't hold water very—

He frowned as Jessica's words seeped through his preoccupied mind at last. He looked at her. "Helps what?"

She squeezed his hand, then released it and leaned closer to the window. "My resentment over the time we spend apart." Her voice was soft with apology.

Resentment? "Sweetheart, I'm sorry. I know I've been out far too much lately. We haven't discussed it in a while, and I just took for granted that you were getting accustomed to—"

"I've tried not to nag you," she said. "I kept thinking it would get better." She continued looking out the window, studying the view through the filter of night, as if afraid to face him. "We've only been married a few months, and everyone keeps reminding me that it takes time to learn how to be an effective pastor's wife."

"Effective pastor's wife?" Archer couldn't deflect the sharpness from his voice in time, and he saw Jessica slump. "Sorry, Jess, but that's a line of ridiculous . . . Wait a minute, you were with the Netzes at the church tonight."

"That's right." The dry sarcasm said it all.

Archer resisted the angry frustration that billowed around him like an evil spirit. Good, earnest Christian people could be real troublemakers when they jumped on their own personal crusades. If the Netzes meddled in his marriage one more time he was going to—

"She has a point," Jessica said.

"Helen this time, is it? Oh, she always has a point, and it's right on the tip of her tongue, sharp enough to slice a human—"

Jessica gasped, then giggled again. "Shh! Archer, someone'll hear you."

"There's no one around to hear, except you, and I *want* you to hear me."

She placed her hands over Archer's. "I thought Helen was best friends with your mother."

"My mother has a lot of friends. Helen was one of them, but she always had a sharp tongue and a critical spirit."

"Always?"

"As long as I can remember. Helen and John lost two children years ago, and I don't think they ever really recovered."

"Oh, Archer, I didn't know."

"They had a son who died of cancer at the age of twelve, and their daughter was killed in an automobile accident a couple years later. Because of that I give Helen the benefit of the doubt, but I still find myself avoiding her when I'm in a bad mood."

Jessica smiled up at him. "You? In a bad mood? I've never seen it. Anyway, Lauren has volunteered me to be the hostess of a spring fling."

"*Lauren?* I can't believe she would do that to you. Jessica, you don't have time. We both agreed we wouldn't allow the church to overwhelm you with responsibility."

"I'm on one committee—for the sake of appearances only—and they haven't even had a meeting since I joined. I sing in choir when I'm home on Sunday. I help out when they have a food drive. If taking on more responsibility would get you home more often, I'd be willing."

Archer sighed. He knew he spent more time than he should visiting sick members at home, visiting people in the hospital and following up on their recuperation, helping with the youth, getting involved in a wild array of counseling sessions with—

"I'm right and you know it," Jessica said.

"No, you're only partially right. You don't need to shoulder my load."

"Do you *want* to just keep passing each other at the front door?"

"No."

"Then what are you going to do about it?"

"Something I've put off far too long because I'm a coward who hates conflict."

"It offends me that there will even *be* conflict, Archer. Everyone should be able to see how much you do."

Archer watched her, hoping she would think about what he'd just said to her.

Finally, she must have caught the pleading expression in his eyes. She laughed. "You're not a coward, you're a peacemaker, and stop fishing for compliments. You would hate to see your own needs take precedence for once, but—"

"I'll have a little talk with the deacons and see if I can get some help—maybe a day off a week to start with, and maybe a full-time youth minister."

"You already have a designated day off," Jessica said. "It's called Friday, in case you'd forgotten. You never take it."

He opened her sandwich package and held it out to her. "Things are going to change." He would see to it. He had a better relationship with the deacons now; maybe they would finally listen to him the way they'd listened to Dad when he was pastor. Dad had always been adamant about carving out time to be with his family during the week.

That didn't seem like too monumental a request.

"Can we talk about something besides work?" he asked.

"Okay, but one more thing. The spring fling isn't what you think. Lauren suggested we have a church night at the theater or a concert at the church and donate any proceeds to hungry families in the area."

"Sounds good if you have the time, but—"

"This is something I *can* do. And maybe we can work on it together. It's one way to be able to spend more time with my husband."

It was wonderful having a wife who wanted to spend more time with him.

Two late refugees from the storm entered the cafeteria and conferred with each other about the selections in the vending machines.

Jessica folded the wrapper back over her food. "Why don't we take the food home with us? I could use some time with you right now." She gave him a warm smile. *"Alone."*

After a quick sandwich, Grant stretched out atop the covers on the call-room bed and closed his eyes. If he could take a quick nap he knew he'd feel better. . . .

For some reason, however, he couldn't settle down. Every buzzing telephone out at the desk, every car passing by outside sent his eyelids back to full alert. And every time he opened his eyes he thought about Norville.

It wouldn't hurt to go upstairs, pay a visit, make sure Norville was resting comfortably.

Grant told Muriel where he would be and took the stairs to the second floor, where two maintenance men were replacing the window at the far end of the hallway. They nodded to him as he passed.

In Recovery a nurse hovered at Norville's bedside, charting vitals. Grant nodded to her.

She held the chart up for him to see. Everything looked good. Before long they would be transferring the patient to a regular room. He smiled at her, studied Norville's relaxed face for another moment, and turned to leave, giving Norville's right leg a gentle parting squeeze.

Norville moaned in his sleep.

Grant turned back, frowning.

The nurse looked up. "Is something wrong, Dr. Sheldon?"

"Has he been moaning like that since the surgery?"

"I haven't heard a peep out of him until just now."

Grant touched Norville's right lower leg again, palpated the outer calf. Again, Norville moaned.

The leg felt as hard as stone. Grant pulled back the covers.

"Dr. Sheldon? What are—"

Grant gestured to Norville's leg, which was swollen very tight and mottled blue-purple—one giant bruise. Grant pushed the toes downward, which elicited another moan, more emphatic. A quick check revealed that the pedal pulse and capillary refill were within normal range. Thank goodness.

While Grant put in a call to the orthopedic surgeon, he prayed that his own oversight would not cost Norville the use of his right leg.

At one-thirty Saturday morning, Lauren walked her friend out to the employee parking lot. "Thanks for helping out tonight, Gina. You'll be a great nurse if you ever decide to leave respiratory therapy."

"Like that'll happen." Gina unlocked her car door and opened it. "Speaking of which, you'd make a great nurse practitioner. Urgent care centers use them all the time to fill the gap caused by the doctor shortage, and they make better money than nurses."

"They also have more responsibility. No thanks."

Gina waved a hand in front of Lauren's face. "Hello? Anybody home? If you can slice into a guy's throat in the wake of a tornado you can handle any responsibility that comes your way."

"Not willingly. God was guiding my hands—that's all I can say. I've had enough of that to last me awhile."

Gina shrugged and got into her car. "Did you ever get a chance to talk to Grant?"

"I said hello, and that was about it."

Gina gave a helpless shake of her head. "Lauren McCaffrey, for someone who's practically engaged, you're far too independent."

"I'm not practically—"

"And you're not very receptive. I've seen the way he looks at you—and the way you look at him. Get back in there and reassure Grant that you're okay."

"He knows I'm okay. He saw me with his own eyes." She chuckled at Gina's obvious exasperation. "Okay, fine, I'll take care of that right away, oh wise one. Give Levi and Cody hugs for me."

Grant didn't return downstairs until Norville had been taken back into surgery for the second time in less than five hours. He walked into his office, closed the door behind him, slumped into his chair. He had failed a patient.

He picked up the telephone and punched the cell phone number Jade Myers had given him several months ago—before she and Norville began dating, when Jade had made it clear that she wouldn't mind Grant's company for dinner or a show in Branson. Tonight it had been obvious to everyone that Jade had begun to take great personal interest in Norville's welfare.

She answered on the first ring, her voice as brisk and alert as high noon.

"Jade, it's Grant. I'm afraid I have some disappointing news."

It wasn't until Lauren was back inside the hospital that she realized she didn't have a way to get home. Her truck sat stranded at the church with a broken windshield and a dented fender. It looked as if she was the last of the call-in staff on the premises. One glance out the ambulance entrance revealed that Archer's car was gone. Jade Myers had taken her uncle home well over an hour and a half ago.

Lauren smiled to herself when she recalled Ernest's complaint as he walked out the door beside Jade. *"Fella can't even catch a full stringer of fish without some blasted tornado ripping it away from him."* The codger probably wouldn't even develop a cold from his experience in the river.

As she approached the emergency-staff break room, a familiar female voice drifted through the open doorway into the hall.

"Just because we're all buddy-buddy now doesn't mean I'm going to apologize for beating you up last year." It was Brooke Sheldon, and for a moment Lauren was so glad to hear the seventeen-year-old's voice that she didn't consider the words spoken.

"Anybody needs to apologize, it'd be me" came a gruff unfamiliar male voice.

"That's a good start."

"Brooke, be nice" came Beau's quiet voice. He sounded so much like Grant these days.

Lauren stepped around the corner and discovered that the other person was Kent Eckard. At eighteen, Kent had the physique of one of those all-star wrestling actors, and in the past year he had displayed the mind-set to match, picking fights and getting involved with the drug underworld.

As incongruous as it seemed, Brooke, Beau, and their friend Evan Webster had gone out of their way to be friendly to Kent in the past two months—incongruous, because Kent had inadvertently accompanied a crazed drug kingpin to the school, where Brooke, Beau, and Evan had been held at gunpoint until the police arrived.

"Kent was just getting ready to tell us how he avoided prison at

Christmastime," Brooke informed Lauren. "Have a seat; this should be good."

"Brooke," Beau warned.

"Nah, that's okay," Kent said. "I'm getting used to your sister's mouth."

Brooke gave her brother a cheesy grin. "In other words, I'm right."

"I been talking to your preacher about helping out in his drug awareness classes on Tuesday nights," Kent said. "You know, telling kids not to do what I did. That meth really got to my mind, you know?"

"Well, duh," Brooke said.

"Brooke."

"Shut up, Beau. So, Kent, why *didn't* they lock you up?"

"They decided I hadn't done nothing worth sticking me in prison. I was just with the wrong person at the wrong time."

"So what were you *really* doing with him at the school that night?" Brooke asked.

"He wanted to make some meth, but he didn't have the supplies because all his friends had been busted in that drug raid the week before. He knew I still had a key to the chemistry lab at school, so he made me go with him to get him in. He had this gun, you know? It was huge."

"We saw it," Beau said dryly.

"So I'm gonna tell your preacher's class that now I've gotta go get my GED because they don't want me back in school."

"Because you did drugs," Brooke said, counting off his offenses on her fingers. "And introduced your pusher friend to minors, and encouraged other kids to take drugs, and attacked Evan in the hallway."

"I wouldn't do it again," Kent said. "I mean it, I wouldn't. I learned my lesson. I don't want to end up like Royce."

A solemn silence.

Lauren was about to ask for a ride home when Kent spoke up again. "Ever hear that rumor about Dr. Caine?"

Another round of silence. Beau shifted uncomfortably.

"You know, he was the one that took care of Royce when the ambulance brought him in?" Kent said. "Some people think Caine killed him somehow."

"Killed Simon Royce?" Beau exclaimed. "Dr. Caine wouldn't do that."

"He had a good reason," Kent said. "Guess you've only been here about a year, so you didn't know Simon got his way with Caine's daughter about four years ago."

"His daughter? I didn't know he had a daughter," Brooke said. "How old is she?"

"Probably about twenty now."

"Which would mean she was sixteen when it happened?" Beau said. "Isn't that statutory rape?"

"Couldn't prove anything, and Trisha wasn't talking. She ran away with him, and Dr. Caine and his wife went nuts trying to find her. When they finally did, she was living with Royce in Springfield. They brought her back, but she just left again, and she's never moved back home."

Lauren had heard rumors, but she didn't pay attention to them, and she didn't intend to do so now. Still, Mitchell Caine's past could have a lot to do with his impending divorce.

"Yep," Kent said, "I guess if Caine did do something to kill Royce that night, he did everybody a favor."

"But he did *not* kill Royce," Beau said.

"Beau," Lauren interrupted, "would you and Brooke mind giving me a ride home?"

Beau got up quickly, as if he, too, felt uncomfortable about the topic of conversation. "Sure, Lauren. I just want to go upstairs one more time and check on Joanne and the baby, and on Norville, to make sure they're still okay."

"I'm going with you," Kent said. "Guess I'll sleep in the waiting room."

"I'll meet you in the ER in a few minutes, then," Lauren said. Meanwhile she would follow Gina's orders and see Grant before she went home.

———

Grant was slumped in his chair, brooding over a blank computer screen, when he heard a knock. He looked up to the very welcome sight of Lauren framed in the small oblong window of his office door.

She entered and closed the door behind her. "I thought for sure you'd be in the call room trying to sleep, quiet as it is out there right now."

He circled the desk and went to her, reaching for her, not caring that they were in full view of the window. He caught her against him and buried his face in her hair, amazed by the sudden comfort that flowed through him.

He held her that way for a long moment.

Lauren stirred. "What happened?"

For another moment he held her.

"It wouldn't have hurt you to call me, would it?" he said at last, drawing away to look down at her. "You do have a cell phone."

"In my truck, and by the time we got outside I was helping transport patients." She smiled at him. "So you were worried about me?"

"You know I was. Have you heard about all the damage around town?"

"Honey Creek's over its banks again, and so's Black Oak River. I've been talking to some of the locals, and they say this is the worst spring we've had in a while." She ambled to the chair in front of his desk and eased down into it. "The water level's way above normal. I hope no one tries to go swimming in the creek for the next few days or we might see 'em here in the ER. I didn't notice a whole lot of damage between here and church. Someone said the church bore the brunt of the storm. From what I could see, that wasn't nearly as bad as it could have been."

He leaned over her and kissed her gently on the forehead. "It must have been terrifying for you. I know how you hate tornado warnings."

"Oh, don't worry, Jessica was there. She and Helen Netz kept me occupied. I heard all kinds of stories about the *last* time they had a bad storm, and they didn't have a working sewer system for three days after the storm, and they had to build their own outhouse or use the convenience store up the road. Now they'll all have something new to talk about for a few years."

He pulled his chair around the desk and sank down next to her. He wanted the telephone to ring with news of Norville. He wanted to go back upstairs and hover in the surgery lounge.

Lauren held his gaze for a few seconds, and then her green eyes narrowed. "What else happened?"

There it was. The same sense of connection he once experienced with Annette—something he had never expected to find again after her death.

"Grant," Lauren said gently. "What else?"

"Norville Webster is back in surgery. I missed a compartment syndrome."

She caught her breath, then exhaled softly. "Oh, Grant, no. Have you heard if he's going to be okay?"

"Not yet."

"Has anyone called Evan?" Norville's sixteen-year-old son was spending the weekend with his mother and stepdad in Springfield.

"Becky called him earlier," Grant said. "His mother's bringing him back tomorrow." He sighed, closing his eyes. "If Norville's lost the use of his leg because of my oversight . . ."

He felt a gentle touch on his shoulder and opened his eyes to see Lauren leaning toward him intently.

"If anyone's to blame it would be me," she said. "I was first on scene; I should have given him a thorough exam. I even saw him limping right after the tornado hit, and—"

"Lauren, you did all you could to save his life."

"Exactly. Are you trying to tell me you should have taken the time to do an exhaustive head-to-toe evaluation to make sure you didn't miss some other injury that *might* also present itself? And what would have happened to the other incoming patients in the meantime? Let up on yourself a little, okay?"

He allowed the comforting words to settle. "Do you have any idea how much I value our friendship?"

She smiled. "Yeah, I do."

There was another knock at the door. They both looked up to see Brooke and Beau grinning at them through the oblong pane. Beau opened the door and led the way in. "Good news. Norville's leg'll be okay. He's in recovery again, and Jade's decided to camp out in the surgery waiting room just in case something else happens here tonight."

Grant saw his relief mirrored in Lauren's eyes. How he loved this woman.

CHAPTER 8

B y late Monday afternoon the sounds of reconstruction ended in the ER waiting room, for which Dr. Grant Sheldon was very thankful. Though he didn't have time to step out and inspect the handiwork of the maintenance people, rumor had it they had a new plate-glass window, impact resistant.

Grant entered exam room four to find Mimi Peterson sitting on the side of the exam bed, breathing fast and shallow as she held her hands over her abdomen, shoulders hunched forward. Her long face and pale features were drawn together in the typical mask of suffering that haunted this department so often. The lines of the grimace aged her far past the forty-five years noted on the chart Lauren had given him.

"Mrs. Peterson?"

Her gaze focused on him, eyes narrowing.

He stepped to the bedside. "I'm Dr. Grant Sheldon. I understand you're having some abdominal pain."

"I thought it was my spastic colon, but it kept getting worse." Her voice cracked. She cleared her throat, still watching him with that disconcerting focus.

"Does the pain feel the same as your spastic colon has felt in the past?"

She shook her head. "It isn't acting the same at all. I don't have diarrhea or anything like that."

Lauren entered the room behind him and stepped to the other side of the bed.

"When did you start having these symptoms, Mrs. Peterson?" Grant continued.

"Mimi. I'm Mimi. Not quite a week ago, and they just keep getting worse."

"Continual?"

"No, it comes and goes."

"Any nausea, loss of appetite?"

"Some, but not always."

He listened to her heart and lungs with his stethoscope, then suggested that she lie back so he could listen to her stomach and inspect her abdomen for any visual signs of a problem.

She hesitated. "Can't you just call my own doctor? He knows how to treat it."

Grant looked at the chart. "According to your records Dr. Caine is your family physician?"

Mimi nodded and grimaced at another apparent spasm. "He knows me. He'll come and treat me here."

"I'll be glad to have him notified that you're here, Mimi, but he has patients at his clinic today, and—"

She raised a preemptive hand. "Dr. Sheldon, I've been through this whole thing before. Maybe *you* don't recognize my name, but Dr. Caine will."

"I'm sure he will as soon as—"

"If you don't think I know what I'm talking about, why don't you give my friend the mayor a call? My husband was transferred here last fall from Little Rock. He's the general manager of—" She grimaced again.

"I don't intend to ignore your request," Grant said. "But meanwhile, why don't we check this out and see if we can discover what's going on."

At Lauren's urging, Mimi lay down at last, but when Grant palpated the right lower quadrant of her abdomen she shoved his arm away.

"That hurts! I told you I've been in pain. Don't you believe me?"

"I'm sorry, Mimi, but I have to be able to find what is causing your problem. From what I can see, you have rebound pain, which could mean you have an inflamed appendix."

"It wasn't my appendix last time."

"I thought you said you had a spastic colon last time."

"No, that isn't . . . I've had this before, too. It goes away with Percocet."

Grant straightened and stepped back, enlightened at last. "Percocet." He glanced at Lauren.

"I told you," Mimi said. "Dr. Caine knows what to do about it. If you'd just call him he'd come and see me here."

Grant doubted Mitchell would do anything of the sort, especially with someone who had all the symptoms of a drug seeker—she already knew what drug she wanted, her symptoms were not typical of anything in particular, and she didn't want close scrutiny. How many times in the past week had he heard some of these same lines?

"It's your option," he said. "I'll be happy to take care of you, get the tests started—"

"Tests?" She rubbed her neck. "What kind of tests? I've already had every test imaginable."

"Does Dr. Caine have the results?"

"I'm sure he does, but they were all negative."

"You had blood drawn?"

"Yes, and I don't want to do that again. Dr. Caine knows I hate needles."

"I understand, Mimi," Grant said, "but your temperature and other vitals are normal. We have a phlebotomist who is excellent at drawing blood, and I think you'll feel better if we can get a little more information about the culprit that's—"

"Would you just *call* Dr. Caine?" she snapped.

Controlling his own irritation, Grant turned to Lauren. "Have the secretary get Dr. Caine on the line if she can."

Lauren nodded and left the room. Grant turned to follow her out.

"Wait a minute, you're just leaving me here?" Mimi cried. "I'm in pain! What if something happens to me?"

Grant willed himself to remain pleasant. "We'll leave the door open, of course, Mimi." He indicated the central desk, in sight of her bed. "We'll never be far away."

"You're going to leave me just sitting here in plain view of anyone who wants to walk by and see me? I thought patients had a right to their privacy."

"I'm sorry, but if you're truly ill you need to be—"

"What do you mean *if* I'm truly ill? You think I'm lying?"

Grant paused, took a slow, steady breath. He exhaled softly. Her strident voice had most likely carried all the way out to the waiting room. "Is there someone you would like us to call? Your husband, perhaps? Or a friend."

"I *told* you what I wanted."

"Dr. Sheldon?" called the secretary from her switchboard at the central desk, "I have Dr. Caine on the line."

"If you'll excuse me for a moment, Mimi," he told the patient, "I'll take this call."

"Tell him I need to see him," she ordered as he left the room.

By the time he picked up the receiver in his office he was more than willing to turn Mitchell's patient over to him. "Dr. Caine, I'm sorry to bother you. I know you're busy. I have one of your patients, Mimi Peterson, in the department with severe abdominal pain."

"Oh, no. Spare me from that woman if you have any compassion in you."

"So she isn't your patient?"

"Unfortunately, she is."

"She insists on seeing you, and she refuses further testing."

"So you haven't even completed an exam?" Mitchell asked.

"Only a partial one. She shows some questionable rebound tenderness in the right lower quadrant, no nausea or vomiting, no diarrhea. So far I have failed to convince her to allow a blood test."

There was a pause, then a sigh of irritation. "Dr. Sheldon, if you think it's a surgical appendix, contact the surgeon on call. I can't get away to hold her hand right now. I have other patients in my waiting room."

"She told me you've treated her for her pain in the past and you know exactly what she needs. She requested Percocet."

"Of course she did. It's what she always requests, and I've given it to her, a day at a time. I refuse to fuel her addictions. It is my opinion that she generates these symptoms from one organ of her body, and that is her brain."

"I can't give her pain medication until I have an etiology for the source of that pain," Grant said.

There was a dramatic, long-suffering sigh. "Fine, I'll see her when I do my rounds tonight. Meanwhile, the queen can wait. Tell her I insist that she have a blood test taken before I get there."

"Thank you, Dr. Caine. How long should I tell her to expect to wait?"

"At least thirty minutes, maybe forty-five." He hung up.

Grant shook his head and sat back. He could only hope Mitchell's final few patients were cooperative.

————

At five-fifteen Monday evening, Mitchell Caine glowered at the chart of his final patient of the day. Clyde Buckman, a sixty-seven-year-old farmer, sat on the exam table. He stunk of cattle manure, though his clothing didn't look soiled. Most likely he'd stepped in something, and his senses were so accustomed to the smell of the barnyard that he didn't even notice. He had been kicked by a steer when he and his wife were herding cattle into a truck to take them to market early this morning. This morning!

"Why didn't you go to the emergency department when it happened?" Mitchell asked as he examined Clyde's bruised shoulder.

The patient grunted when Mitchell pressed the affected area. "Didn't think it was that bad, Dr. Caine, and I couldn't afford to miss sale day. I heard prices would drop before the next sale—"

"Sit up." When the man did so, Mitchell checked range of motion, and Clyde couldn't complete the process. "As I said, you need to go to the ER, Clyde. You should have gone there in the first place, this morning, as soon as it happened." *When are people going to realize they can't abuse their bodies time after time and then blame the physicians when they don't heal right away?* "They'll have to x-ray your shoulder."

"But do I have to check into the ER to do it? That'll cost a lot of money, and all I've got's Medicare."

"You can work that out with them." Mitchell was tired. He'd seen more than his share of complaining patients today, and he didn't get paid overtime wages when a patient decided, several hours after an accident, that he felt bad enough to come in to see the doctor.

"Couldn't you just give me something for the pain like you did last time?" Clyde asked. "Then if there's a problem it'll show up in a couple of days."

Mitchell rolled his chair away from the patient-room computer keyboard. *Do I look like a drug pusher today?* "I'll be the one to make a diagnosis, and I'll be the one to decide your treatment, or you can find another doctor." He reached for his prescription pad and jotted orders, dated it, signed it. He ripped the sheet off and gave it to Clyde. "That is for an outpatient x-ray. You won't have to check into the ER for that."

"Well, thanks, Dr. Caine. This x-ray gonna help me with the pain?"

Irritably, Mitchell jotted another script for Percocet and slapped it down on the table beside the patient. "Do *not* use these pills as a treatment for your shoulder, Clyde. Understand? If you do, I won't be responsible for the consequences. You could lose the use of that shoulder for good."

The farmer eyed Mitchell, then hesitantly reached for the prescription, as if afraid Mitchell might snap at him again before he could get it into his pocket.

Mitchell felt ashamed. He had grown up among these country hicks, and still he didn't understand them. They would rather make sure a field was plowed and ready for planting than take care of a physical ailment. And they were the least likely people to sue a doctor for a bad medical outcome. At least he had that in his favor. Lately, there didn't seem to be much else.

So why take my frustration out on Clyde? And where had all those good feelings gone from the delivery Friday night?

"As soon as you get the x-ray," he said more gently, "make sure I get a copy of it. If it doesn't need surgery, I'll treat it here in the office."

"Oh, thanks, Doc. You don't know how much that—"

"But you have to stay on top of this," Mitchell said. "I want to see you back in here as soon as your x-ray is read. If I can't treat it, I'll have to refer you to an orthopedist."

"That guy who treated me when I broke my arm?"

"That's the one."

Clyde looked disappointed, but he didn't complain. The crusty old farmer had as little to do with doctors as possible, and the only reason he came to Mitchell was because he had been the elder Dr. Caine's patient years ago. That was where half the patients in this practice had come from. Good old Dad.

Mitchell saw Clyde out the door, then reached into the pocket of his lab coat for the small vial of pills he had come to rely on lately. Tranquen—a benzodiazepine derivative with wonderfully soothing properties. The only drawback was the amnesia the drug caused. He snapped the kid-friendly lid and shook one of the small rectangular pills into his mouth. He swallowed the tiny piece of salvation, then walked down the hallway to his office and closed the door behind him. This was the second dose tonight, but the first didn't seem to be doing much good. Most likely, his stomach acid had converted it before it even had a chance to take effect.

He unscrewed the cap from the ever-present bottle of Evian on his desk and emptied it. Before long, he would be relaxed enough to drive home. Once he got there he could turn off the telephone ringer and let the machine fend for him the rest of the night.

He snatched a stack of files from the corner of his desk. He wanted to dump them in the trash. He wanted to light a match to the whole office and watch it flame. What would Darla say about that? She wouldn't be able to milk any more support from him then, would she? Maybe he should just retire now and dip into the offshore account he'd managed to conceal from her and her expensive divorce attorney.

Hmm. Skip the country and let them play hide-and-seek.

As for his daughter, Trisha-the-junkie, he hadn't heard from her in months, hadn't actually laid eyes on her in years. If his soon-to-be-ex was still in contact with Trisha she certainly wouldn't tell *him* about it. She would let him suffer in solitude. When he'd cut off Trisha's drug money, he'd realized he would probably never hear from her again. What he hadn't realized was that Darla would leave him over it.

For a few moments he stared out into the private garden, waiting for the initial effects of the drug to soothe the tight band of chronic anxiety that had overwhelmed his life for the past few months. If it continued, he would have to check into other options—a vacation, perhaps, or another medication he could take that wouldn't affect his medical judgment when treating patients.

At last the pills on board began to work their magic. He felt himself relax, and the sharp edge of anger that seemed to stalk him every waking moment dissipated. He knew it would be back tomorrow, but at least he could escape it for tonight. He'd better head out quickly, while he could still concentrate enough to drive home.

When he first started having trouble sleeping, soon after Darla left last December, he had resorted to the samples of Tranquen the drug rep left at the clinic. For the first few weeks, he had divided the tiny 5-milligram tablets into four separate sections with a pill cutter—one little quarter of the potent pill had been enough.

Then Darla and her attorney had become greedy. Darla claimed she needed psychiatric care for the pain and suffering she had endured in their marriage.

Mitchell shook his head and stood. Time to move before the brooding thoughts dragged him back down. He was now taking twice the highest recommended dosage of the drug, and still the memories haunted him from time to time.

He locked his office and left the clinic through the back entrance and headed for the detached garage that was reserved for his personal use. He'd learned from experience that if he wanted to get out on time, he had to move quickly and give no one occasion, or encouragement, to slow him down. After just one day of heavy patient volume, he desperately needed another weekend off.

He hesitated briefly as he climbed into the Envoy and pushed the garage door remote. Was there something else he'd intended to do before he went home tonight?

He glanced in the rearview mirror, and his vision blurred momentarily. Whatever it was, it would have to wait until tomorrow. He needed to get home while he could still drive.

"I'm sorry, Dr. Caine is unavailable at this time" came a resonant female voice over the telephone receiver. "If you have a medical emergency, please visit the Dogwood Springs Hospital Emergency Department. Dr. Caine's office hours are—"

Lauren hung up with a little more force than was necessary. "The man took off. I don't believe it. Just left a patient waiting for him in the ER," she muttered at the phone.

The secretary chuckled behind her. "Don't worry, you're not the only one he's stood up lately."

Lauren glanced around the ER. It was ten till seven. Eight exam rooms were occupied. The night staff had come in, and Lauren and Grant were tidying up so the takeover staff could get a jump on the situation.

"Our patient doesn't appreciate being stood up," Lauren said.

"Yeah?" Becky leaned toward Lauren and lowered her voice. "Well, I don't like being reminded every fifteen minutes that she's married to the president of the world, and that her best buddy is mayor of this town, and that if we don't start treating her with some respect she's going to write a letter to the editor of *The Dogwood*, and we'll all be in deep doo-doo."

Lauren grinned. "Mimi isn't that bad. She's just in pain."

"She's always that bad. I've heard about her. Just because she's married to some poor dupe who runs Jasper Corporation, she thinks she can run the town and cajole drugs from the docs whenever she wants them. Does she think she's the only patient in this department?"

"She's scared. I remember what it feels like to be a patient," Lauren said. "In a hospital, lying in bed, at the mercy of strangers, you feel exposed and vulnerable. She's just trying her best to regain some of the dignity she feels she's lost by coming in here."

"Lauren, you're a dupe, too." Becky chuckled to take the sting from her words as she turned back to her computer. "Every time you've walked past her door for the past hour and a half, she's called out to you, and you've run her errands, either to get her a cup of ice, or take her another pillow, or let her call a friend. Want to know what I think? I think it's just gas. You know . . . as in full of hot air."

Lauren gave Becky a playful tap on the shoulder and turned to give

Muriel information about another patient. If Mimi Peterson hadn't insisted on seeing Dr. Caine, she'd be out of the hospital by now, or she would be upstairs in a room awaiting surgery in the morning—although that wasn't likely. Her blood test results had been normal, and for the past hour she hadn't complained of pain.

After completing the shift-change report with Muriel, Lauren saw Grant walk once again into exam room four. She braced herself and followed him.

"We've called Dr. Caine, or attempted to call him, several times, Mimi," Grant was saying as Lauren entered behind him.

"I just tried again," Lauren added.

Mimi closed her eyes and held her wrist up to her forehead in an uncanny imitation of a silent movie heroine lying on a train track after the evil villain tied her to the rails. "Then I'm leaving," she said at last. "I have more important things to do with my time than—"

"I wouldn't advise you to leave before we've had an opportunity to do a more complete work-up to make sure there isn't something serious going on," Grant said.

He had made the same observation several times over the past two hours. Lauren knew what the reply would be.

"You said my blood test showed nothing of significance." Mimi checked her watch and sat up on the bed and gestured toward Lauren. "Where did you put my purse? I have an important meeting in forty-five minutes, and I refuse to sit here like a dunce when people need me. I'll see Dr. Caine tomorrow." It sounded almost like a threat. "I'll also be talking to the mayor to see if something can be done to keep this from happening again."

"That's fine." The ragged edges of Grant's reply were faint, and Lauren was probably the only one who detected his irritation. "I'm glad you're feeling better. I'll have our secretary bring an AMA form for you to sign."

Mimi resisted Lauren's attempts to help her from the bed. "What are you talking about? I'm not signing any—"

"The form simply states that you left this hospital against medical advice," Grant said.

"In other words, you're covering your backside." Mimi reached for the sweater that had been draped across the end of the bed. "I'm not signing anything for some glorified orderly who keeps me isolated back here in this cubicle without even a magazine to read to pass the time. Dr. Caine would never treat me like this, and he would never refuse to give me the medication I need."

Lauren resisted the urge to point out that Dr. Caine had done exactly that.

Grant sighed and shook his head and walked out of the room without another word. Lauren couldn't tell if he was more irritated by the patient's attitude or Mitchell Caine's failure to show up as promised.

"Here's your purse, Mrs. Peterson."

Mimi took it and stalked to the doorway, obviously recovered from her malady. She paused in the threshold and turned back. "I know what you're thinking. You don't fool me."

"What am I thinking?"

"You think I'm some kind of loon with a mental problem or a drug addict looking for narcotics. You're wrong. When I came into this hospital this evening, I was in pain, and that pain was real, and it *wasn't* just gas." She scowled. "You people also must think I'm deaf."

"I think none of those things," Lauren said. "But I do wish you would have allowed us to test you a little more thoroughly so we might be able to figure out what *is* causing the problem."

"No more tests." She draped the strap of her purse over her shoulder. "All any of those tests have done for me so far is convince people it's all in my mind. I know better." She left the hospital without signing the AMA form and without receiving help.

Mitchell awoke to the sound of a faint click and a beep in the background, and he straightened in his recliner. Answering machine.

He wasn't in the mood to take telephone calls. All he wanted to do was sleep . . . forever.

Darkness filled every corner of the den. He pulled the lever to lower the footrest, then unsteadily got to his feet. He switched on the lamp on the end table. The ornate clock above the bookcase said it was eight forty-five. He glanced toward the window. That must be P.M. If it were already morning, even if it were stormy outside, the room wouldn't be dark.

He left the lamp on and walked with slow deliberation toward the hallway. He took a step toward his bedroom, hesitated. Might as well go to bed, couldn't concentrate on a book anyway. Television was a waste of time these days, and there was something depressing about watching a movie alone.

When he entered the bedroom he hesitated again. The answering machine . . . someone called him? Had he forgotten something? Did he have a staff meeting tonight?

For a moment he considered checking the calendar he kept in his home office, but he was too tired. If he had a meeting, someone could fill him in on the specifics tomorrow. Right now he just wanted to crawl into bed and close his eyes.

CHAPTER 9

On Tuesday, April 16—while accountants all over America dug out from under the madness created by tax deadline—Grant sat down with his family for a Sheldon white-hot chili dinner to celebrate Lauren's thirty-sixth birthday. He and Lauren had spent the day in Branson, but at her request they were spending the evening with Brooke and Beau.

The smoky aroma of the chili added some confusion to the atmosphere for Grant. How did the kids feel about sharing their mother's special family recipe with the new love of their father's life?

They didn't seem to mind. In fact, Brooke had been nagging him about making the relationship more permanent. She adored Lauren, and he hoped, for her sake as well as his, that things worked out the way she obviously hoped they would. Though Brooke exhibited a tough exterior, she had a heart like her mother's, tender and easily broken.

Annette had been gone for nearly three years. They still missed her and always would, but she would have wanted them to allow someone else into their lives. She would have approved of Lauren.

Grant basked in the presence of the people he loved most in the entire world. He suppressed a grin at his daughter's unceasing—and probably unthinking—chatter about her school day.

" . . . Evan's impossible to live with anymore. I mean, Dad, did I tell you he got that commendation from the mayor in *The Dogwood*?"

"Yes."

"What commendation?" Lauren asked. "I don't get the paper."

"Praising him for the series of articles during this past Christmas season." She cast a long-suffering gaze toward the ceiling.

"You're jealous," Beau said.

"I'm not jealous."

"Are too. He tried to share the by-line with you and you wouldn't let him, so stop whining."

"I'm not whin—"

"Why did he get the commendation for the articles?" Lauren interrupted.

Brooke waved her spoon in the air and sighed. "Because it 'heightened public awareness about the blight of illegal drugs in our fair community.' Brother. It's like he saved the town with his purple prose. I mean, everybody knows the mayor's dating his dad. I'd be humiliated if I were him."

"You *are* jealous." Beau pushed his glasses back up his nose, and a half smile touched his lips.

Grant would never grow tired of looking at that smile. Last year at this time he had been so sure he would never see that smile again—not after the damage that his facial nerves had received in the same wreck that had killed Annette. The regeneration of those nerves had been gradual over the past few months.

"So, Lauren, what shows did you see in Branson?" Brooke pointedly ignored her twin.

Lauren didn't appear fazed by Brooke's sudden topic change. "None."

Brooke gave a dramatic gasp. "You went to Branson and didn't see a show? Isn't that illegal or something?"

"Not if you've already seen most of them, and no, we didn't go to Silver Dollar City."

Brooke leaned forward, narrowing her eyes. "If you two slipped off and got mar—"

"Dad, have you ever heard a death scream?" Beau asked suddenly.

Brooke dropped her fork in her plate with a hiss of disgust. "Beau! We're trying to eat."

"Sorry, but your line of questioning wasn't much better," Beau said. "They went shopping, okay?"

They nibbled in silence for a few moments. Grant watched Brooke give Beau a few curious glances, which Beau ignored.

Finally Brooke put her fork down. "Okay, what's a death scream?"

"Hush," Beau said. "Lauren's trying to eat."

"She has a strong stomach. She tortures worms with fishhooks for entertainment."

"Watch your mouth, young lady," Lauren said. "Fishing is a socially acceptable method of securing edible protein for a complete, healthy diet. I see nothing wrong—"

"Sure, fine, whatever." Brooke fluttered her fingers at Lauren. "I just wish you wouldn't do it in front of me."

Lauren grinned at her, and Grant felt a surge of satisfaction. In the past couple of months, Brooke had gone fishing with Lauren at least three times. According to Lauren's reports, Brooke still refused to use live bait and would not clean the fish, but she never turned down an invitation to go along. Even Beau had gone a couple of times, although he usually hung out in the emergency department when he wasn't in school.

"So, Beau, what's a death scream?" Brooke asked again.

Beau took another bite of chili, ignoring her.

Brooke's impatience flickered across the formerly serene atmosphere at the table, her dark gray eyes promising revenge. "Speaking of death . . ."

"It's a scream." Beau took a sip of his lemonade and swallowed, caught and held Grant's gaze for a moment. "Have you heard it, Dad?"

"I've heard the urban legends. I think that's all it is."

Lauren straightened, cleared her throat.

"Would somebody please explain what a death scream is *supposed* to be?" Brooke demanded.

"Well." Beau set his glass on the table. "Some people say that when a dying person's spirit takes a step into the next world, she takes one—"

"What do you mean 'she'?"

"Do you want to hear this or not?"

Brooke crossed her arms over her chest. "Go ahead."

"Anyway," he said, his voice a theatrical whisper, "that patient's physical body shrieks out this unearthly sound. It isn't loud, and it rarely happens, but it is said that when someone hears that scream, she will never be the same."

"Sounds like you've been talking to Evan again," Brooke said.

"I heard about it at work."

"Where at work?"

"One of the nurses at the hospital was talking about it during break one day, and I just happened to be there. They say Simon Royce gave a death scream the night he died."

Brooke raised a shapely dark brow and looked at Lauren, who seemed to have developed an unusual amount of interest in the wood grain of the table. "Have you heard it, Lauren?"

There was a short pause, then, "Yep." The reply was spoken a little too casually.

The whole family stopped eating.

Lauren didn't smile. She didn't even look up from her bowl of Sheldon white-hot chili.

Grant could tell from the slight flush that crept over her cheeks that she wasn't kidding. She continued to eat.

"It's that bad?" Beau asked.

Lauren looked up. No teasing smile touched her lips. No glint of laughter danced in her clear green eyes.

"When did you hear it?" Grant asked softly.

"Several years ago." She put down her spoon, pushed her bowl away, and leaned back in her chair, as if pushing away from an uncomfortable memory.

"And?" Brooke prompted.

"It was . . . pretty scary."

"You don't have to tell us about it," Grant said.

"But you can if you want to," Brooke urged.

Lauren grinned at Brooke's impudence, but Grant couldn't help noticing the lack of humor behind that grin. "Even if it could give you nightmares?"

"I have Beau for a brother. I can handle a nightmare or two."

There was a thump beneath the table, and Brooke grunted.

"I was working as an ER nurse at Knolls Community Hospital about six and a half years ago," Lauren said. "The ambulance brought a man in with cirrhosis of the liver, terminally advanced. It especially upset us because our staff knew the man well. He was a physician."

"An ER doc?" Beau asked.

"Family practice, with a clinic in the hospital."

"He had cirrhosis?" Grant asked. "He was an alcoholic?"

Lauren nodded. "For years. His wife had begun attending a small local church. He stormed into the church during a service one day reeking of booze and threatened to drag her out. When some of the men in the service challenged him, he screamed curses at them and at God."

"So it's safe to say he believed there was a god of some kind," Brooke remarked.

Lauren shrugged. "Anyway, when they brought him into the ER, he'd filled out a DNR form and made sure everyone knew about it. He did not want resuscitation, so we didn't call a code when his vital signs deteriorated."

"So you didn't intubate," Beau guessed. "Nothing to block his voice."

Lauren nodded. "I was in the room when he died. So were his daughter and his wife, and that was what made it so hard. He was on heavy doses of pain-killer and was unconscious most of the time, but just as his heart failed he opened his eyes, and it seemed as if he was staring straight at me." Her voice cracked. She swallowed and took a deep breath. "I've never seen such horror in a person's gaze. His lips parted, and he emitted the most awful, haunting sound of anguish I'd ever heard. It wasn't loud, but it was as if it had the power to reach into a person's soul."

There was silence at the table for a moment.

"What did it sound like?" Brooke's voice was hushed.

"Not a human scream."

"Then what?"

"I heard at work that it was kind of a combination of the cry of a screech owl and the bleat of a sheep," Beau said.

Lauren looked at Grant. "Like the cry of someone who had glimpsed hell for the first time."

The twins finished their chili in silence.

This wasn't exactly the birthday dinner Grant had anticipated when he first planned it, but it promised to sweeten momentarily. And the cake was just the beginning.

Mitchell Caine stepped to the doorway of exam room three in the ER. He hesitated at the sight of Mimi Peterson sitting on the side of the bed, hunched forward, arms crossed over her stomach protectively.

"Well, Dr. Caine, nice of you to stop by." Sarcasm laced her voice. "But I didn't even ask to see you this time."

"I'm the physician on shift. The nurse says you're having some pain."

"Oh, really? Did she also tell you it was probably just gas again?" Mimi leaned back on the pillow and swung her feet up to the mattress. She stiffened and groaned, eyes closing tightly.

He helped her position her legs. "Gas? I'm sorry, I don't understand what you mean."

"Sure you don't. Haven't you even read my chart?"

He knew she'd come to his office a number of times in the past few months. He had determined it wasn't anything life threatening, and he'd given her a pain pill and sent her on her way.

Lately it seemed as if all he ever did was give pain pills and write scripts for narcotics.

"You didn't even bother to come in to see me last night," she said. "Why now?"

"I'm sorry, but what happened last night?"

She gave an exasperated sigh. "You never showed up—*that's* what happened. I was here, remember? They said they called you, but you never came in to see me."

Hiding his confusion, Mitchell stepped to the hallway to signal for a nurse to assist him, then did a focused exam. When he finished he walked out to the central desk and asked for any records on Mimi's chart from the night before.

Sure enough, there was a notation that Grant Sheldon had called him once, and Lauren McCaffrey had attempted to contact him three times after that.

He didn't even remember receiving the initial call . . . or did he?

He picked up the telephone and hit the speed dial for Grant's home number. He recognized Beau's voice when he answered, and he suddenly felt disarmed. Someday the kid would make a great doctor, if Mitchell couldn't manage to warn him away in time.

"Hello, Beau, this is Dr. Caine. May I speak with your father for a moment?"

The kid was too idealistic and pure hearted to practice medicine. For that matter, Mitchell was beginning to think the father had those same tendencies, although in him, for some reason, they proved to be more irritating.

When Grant came to the phone, Mitchell said, "I have a return patient from last night, Dr. Sheldon. Do you remember Mimi Peterson?"

"There's no way I could forget her, Mitchell. What happened last night?"

"I beg your pardon?"

"You didn't come in to see her, and she was extremely upset when she left."

"The report says you spoke with me about her."

"The *report*?" There was an uncomfortably long silence. "Mitchell, you do remember last night's call, don't you?"

Mitchell struggled with a growing sense of alarm. "No."

"Okay," Grant said. "How is she now?"

For the first time, Mitchell had to admit to himself that he truly had forgotten the call. In spite of his past conflicts with Grant over the shift schedules, Grant was a painfully honest person.

The sleeping pill . . . Mitchell remembered taking one before his final patient of the day, knowing it would take a few moments to feel the effects. Obviously, his timing had been off.

"She's experiencing pain again," he told Grant. "My apologies for the oversight. I should get back to my patient."

"Any ideas about the etiology?"

"None yet. Good night." He hung up and checked the chart again. He had to stop taking those pills. He would do so as soon as the divorce was final and his stress level became more manageable.

Still, maybe he should switch to something less potent right away. He had patients depending on him, and he would be risking lives if he treated a dangerous case under the influence.

He had to get this thing under control.

CHAPTER 10

Beau jumped up from the table as soon as Grant returned from the confusing telephone conversation with Mitchell Caine. "Dad, why don't you and Lauren go on into the den and relax. There's a fire in the fireplace. Brooke and I will clean this up since you cooked."

"Beau," Brooke muttered, "you volunteer me for any more work tonight and you'll hear your own death scream."

"That's okay, just sing for me and I'll get the idea."

"Dad!"

"Shut up and stack dishes," Beau said. "It's Lauren's birthday, and Dad needs a night off."

Grant smiled at the typical exchange and strolled behind Lauren through the living room into the den-office, where a fire flickered, low and romantic, in the corner hearth. The flat slabs of Arkansas rock had caught Grant's attention the first time he'd entered this room and had ultimately led to the purchase.

Lauren held her hands out to the warmth of the flame. Her thick blond hair seemed to shimmer in the firelit room, and the muted glow outlined her feminine figure. Grant had trouble controlling his gaze.

"Happy birthday." He sank down onto the raised stone that stretched past the length of the hearth.

"Thank you," she said. "For everything. Dinner was delicious."

"Not as good as your mom's fried catfish and chocolate birthday cake Sunday afternoon."

"Mom's a great cook, but I like hot stuff. There's enough habaneros in your chili to melt the state of Alaska." She sank into the love seat that someone—most likely Beau—had pulled close to the hearth, and held her hands once more to the fire. For several moments she didn't say anything. Unusual for Lauren.

Grant frowned. "I'm sorry if the kids brought up an uncomfortable subject for you."

"Uncomfortable?" Her attention didn't waver from the flames.

"Death scream. I don't know where they get their interest in the macabre. Certainly not from me."

"I'm fine."

He eyed the cushion beside her. It looked more inviting than this rock hearth, but something about her expression held him back. Her eyes, which changed shades with her moods, appeared more gray than green in this light. That could mean she wasn't feeling well, or that, perhaps, she was grieving.

This was her first birthday since her brother's death. Grant understood. He missed Annette with more painful clarity on holidays and birthdays.

He heard the kids in the kitchen, laughter mixed with chatter mixed with the arguments that had graced their relationship since they first began to communicate with one another in their "twin language" when they were a year old.

"For some reason I get the impression this hasn't been the happiest of birthdays for you," Grant said at last.

Finally, Lauren looked at him. "Sorry. I don't mean to seem ungrateful for the dinner. It really was good. I enjoyed . . . I liked spending time with you and the kids."

"But you're thinking about Hardy?"

She nodded. "Partially. I miss him. I even miss whatever practical joke he would've played on me today." She leaned back in the cushions of the love seat and sighed. "And the usual birthday doldrums are knocking around inside my head."

"Ouch. That must hurt."

Her forced grin didn't draw the gray from her eyes. "I'm thirty-six, Grant. I have friends who are just a few years older than me and they're already grandmothers."

Discovery dawned. Grant understood. "You're not elderly yet, Lauren. Trust me, there's time for children."

Her eyes widened slightly. He cleared his throat and leaned forward, hovering on the brink of the question that had nagged him for the past four . . . five . . . six months and that had been left unsaid because he didn't think she would accept it with as much ease as he wanted to give it.

"Grant, I think . . . This is a drastic change of subject, but it's been on my . . ." She closed her eyes and sighed, eased forward and looked at him. "You know how much I care about Brooke and Beau."

"You make that obvious."

"And you know I care about you." A slight flush spread across her face and neck, and she returned her attention to the fire. "I can't say I haven't thought about . . . about the possibility of . . . Oh, brother, where am I going with this. . . ."

"I hope you're getting ready to tell me that you might possibly love me, not just as a good friend loves a good friend, but—"

"Exactly." She took a deep breath. "And yet I suspect my motivation."

"Motivation?"

She spread her hands out to her sides. "I want a family. I always have. How much does my biological drive affect my emotions? How much—"

"Aren't you getting overly analytical? I thought you'd already dealt with that last year."

"Get real, Grant. A woman doesn't bury her God-made biological drive with one little prayer. Or even a hundred prayers."

"I've never known you to be anything but honest about—"

"Okay, fine, you want me to tell you what I think?" She looked down at her entwined fingers. "I think I love you—I mean truly love you—and it doesn't feel like anything I've ever felt before."

Grant felt the sudden flush of joyful warmth travel from his feet to his scalp in less than a second. *Yes!*

"And I'm old enough to know better than to rely on emotions," she continued. "And if this is what love is, then I've never experienced true love before."

Ah, the nervous chatter. A good sign. Grant moved from the hearth to the love seat and took her hand. She had the most awesome hands. He loved the feel of them.

"Let me make it easier on you. I *do* love you, Lauren, and I *have* been in love before. I know what it feels like. I also know what it looks like and that those first feelings can mature into something more solid and permanent with time. I do think you love me. I know you love Brooke and Beau. I've watched you with them. I believe we could make a wonderful family."

She quietly caught her breath. Judging by the look on her face, he'd taken it a little far. Her nervous chatterbox mode was contagious.

"But, Grant—"

"And I'm sure you've already heard Brooke hint she wants a little baby brother or sister."

Her face flushed nicely. "Grant—"

"And I'm not so ancient that I—"

"Grant!" Lauren laughed, and some of the gray disappeared from her eyes. The color contrasted well with the glow in her cheeks. "Would you slow down?" She fanned her fingers across her face. "Man, when you get started you turn into a steamroller."

"Of course there would be problems we'd have to work out."

"Problems?"

"Mom still has Alzheimer's. She refuses to move here from St. Louis, but some day we may have to bring her here in spite of her protests, depending on the progression of the disease. I would want to keep her here with us as long as possible."

"Of course you would."

"She isn't always the easiest person to get along with."

"Neither am I."

Grant hesitated. "So in spite of the complications, will you marry me?" As soon as he blurted the words he realized how terribly unromantic they sounded.

"Time for presents!" came a bright voice from behind them.

Grant and Lauren turned simultaneously to see Brooke and Beau stepping into the room, arms filled with brightly wrapped packages—the largest, in the shape of a fishing pole, bumped the side of a lamp as Beau stepped around the end of the love seat.

Grant caught the lamp before it hit the floor. Lauren laughed.

Brooke plopped her packages down on the table beside Lauren. "Notice not one of these packages is black, but watch out when you turn forty."

Grant continued to watch Lauren. She didn't crack a smile. She thanked the kids with genuine excitement and reached for the present that Brooke handed to her.

Like an excited child, she shook the present, sniffed it, then ripped the paper away.

"It's perfume," she guessed.

"Nope. It doesn't smell."

"No smell? Does it have a sound? You know, like *woof-woof* or *meow-meow*. I'm allergic to cats, you know."

"Are you allergic to fish?" Brooke asked.

"Nope. Never. You got me fish? How romantic."

"Beau and I pooled our money and got you a new tackle box and fishing pole, with tackle stuff to fill it."

"Brooke," Beau complained. "Why did we go to all the trouble of wrapping the packages?"

Lauren ripped the box open and pulled out a jar of salmon eggs. "Fish bait that doesn't wiggle. How thoughtful of you, Brooke. Something for *you* to use when we go fishing."

"I thought you might give it a try. I know it's a little too dead for you, but hey, we're going fishing soon, right? As Evan would say, I'm just covering my bases."

Lauren unwrapped the next package, which turned out to be a state-of-the-art fishing pole. "Don't tell me," she said. "I'm expected to know how this thing works."

"It won't take long," Beau said.

"You'll have to show me how it's done."

Brooke stood up. "We've got something else. Beau, you have to help me carry it. Come on."

The kids disappeared into the other room, and Grant placed a small, exquisitely wrapped package in Lauren's hand.

Lauren turned the package over, then raised it to her ear and gently shook it. "I don't hear a sound. So it isn't a rattlesnake rattle or anything, right?"

"Right."

"That's what Hardy would have done. Okay, so it isn't a necklace, or the chain would have made a sound. What is it?"

"What does it look like?"

"Like a box from the jewelers."

"You'll have to open it and see."

She hesitated a moment too long. By the time she had the package unwrapped to reveal the leather jewelry case inside, the kids had returned with a large cardboard box.

"It's a porch swing," Brooke said. "Wood. You can hang it up at your house, or"—she winked at Beau—"you could hang it up on our deck out back."

"Oh, Brooke, thank you. I've always wanted a porch swing."

"I know. Dad and Beau are going to help you put it up wherever you want." Brooke's attention focused on the case in Lauren's hand. "So did you open that yet?"

"No."

"Well?"

Lauren raised the lid and caught her breath.

Grant imagined that he saw a brief flash of relief in her expression as she touched the emerald lapel pin in the shape of a fish.

"Oh, Grant, it's beautiful."

"And appropriate," Brooke said. "You can wear it on your scrubs at work. So are you going to marry Dad?"

"Brooke," Grant said.

"Okay, okay, but I just want to know one thing."

Another hesitation. "What's that?"

"What will we call you if you do become our stepmom?"

No answer.

"How about Martha?" Beau suggested dryly. "What do you mean what will we call her? She's Lauren."

Brooke cast her gaze toward the cathedral ceiling and shook her head sadly. "She won't be just Lauren anymore, she'll be—"

"I'll always be Lauren, you know."

"Do you think if she becomes our stepmom she'll get to boss us around?" Beau asked.

"Okay, you two," Grant said.

"But really, Dad." Brooke sat forward on the sofa. "Lauren would respond to a mother name if you two had a baby, and it just doesn't seem right that our little brother or sister would get to call her Mama and we wouldn't."

"Brooke," Beau said, "Maybe we should back off a little."

"Okay, but this is import—"

"Brooke, stop it," Lauren said firmly. "*Now*. How's that for bossy?"

Brooke blinked at her. "Okay," she said slowly. "But you *are* going to marry Dad, aren't you?"

Lauren sighed. "Would you give me some time, please?"

Brooke poked her brother in the ribs with her elbow. "Told you he would propose tonight."

Grant watched Lauren's face. The smile in her eyes had died long ago. The truth hung in the air for everyone to notice. Yes, he had proposed, but she had not accepted.

CHAPTER | 11

Wednesday morning, in response to a call from the administrator, Grant took the elevator upstairs to the east wing of the second floor of the hospital. All was business as usual in this wing. The only indication he saw of tornado damage was fresh paint around a window casing. The maintenance personnel in this hospital were every bit as efficient as those in Grant's old place of employment in St. Louis.

The only complaint he ever had was they kept the temperature below seventy degrees at all times.

The administrative assistant, Doreen, sat at her desk in the outer office, leaning over a chart. She looked up and nodded. "Hi, Grant." The forty-eight-year-old woman's voice was cigarette gruff. She gestured over her shoulder with her thumb toward a door that stood half open behind her. "He's in there, waiting to see you, multitasking, as usual." She peered over the top of her reading glasses. "Know what I think? You need to send him on another forced vacation before he wears himself to a bare nubbin again."

"I've tried. He won't let me."

There was the sound of a carefully cleared throat from the depths of the office in question. "I still have ears" came William Butler's calm baritone.

Doreen chuckled. "Go on in, Grant. He isn't doing anything in there except working on his first heart attack. If he gets too intense, just mention Muriel. That'll bring a smile to his face."

"Mind your own business," William instructed his assistant.

Doreen winked at Grant. "He's deluded," she said in a stage whisper. "He thinks no one knows he's madly in—"

"Doreen." The baritone deepened.

She waved Grant toward the open door. "Get on in there and see what you can do with him. He's been a grump all morning."

Grant knew Will and Muriel Stark had been close friends for several months—in a town of seven thousand, that information was unavoidable—but he also knew they preferred to keep the talk to a minimum.

"Oh, and tell your daughter I could use more help with the filing when she gets a chance," Doreen called after him. "I know how badly she and Beau want to get that car paid off."

"Thanks, Doreen, I'll tell her when I get home tonight." Grant entered William Butler's office to find the sixty-one-year-old administrator hunched over a laptop behind a worn oak desk that looked as if it might be almost as old as he was.

William's gray hair shone with more white than it had when Grant started working at the hospital last year. His bushy salt-and-pepper eyebrows had a will of their own, and the skin around his eyes crinkled with new creases from a frown that had taken up residence in his expression these past few months.

"Close the door behind you, Grant." William leaned back in his chair and turned for a moment to look out the window onto the broad lawn in front of the hospital. "We've got something to discuss."

Grant took one of the chairs in a grouping beside the window while William joined him with a cup of coffee and a patient file.

"That's decaf, right?" Grant asked.

William sank into the chair next to him. "It's all my nerves can take lately. Want a cup?"

"No, thanks. Doreen's right, Will, you could use another vacation." An avid hunter who spent much of his limited leisure time in the woods, William had been diagnosed with Lyme disease last winter. To add to that madness he continued to battle a paper work nightmare after a third of the town's water supply had been contaminated with mercury from the offal of methamphetamine production. After nearly a year, the financial impact of that catastrophe still threatened the operation of the hospital.

"I received a call from our mayor first thing this morning." William tapped the corner of the file balanced on his knee. "Did you realize one of your ER patients Monday evening is a close friend of Jade's?"

"We couldn't have avoided the information if we'd tried," Grant drawled. "Mrs. Peterson, I presume."

"She wasn't impressed with the treatment she received."

"I'm sorry she was disappointed, but I haven't heard anything about a bad outcome."

Will shrugged. "Jade admits her friend has a tendency to . . . let's say . . . exaggerate."

"I think she has other tendencies that aren't so benign. I might have been a little stubborn about refusing the requested narcotic, but I wanted to find the reason for her pain before—"

"I didn't call you in here to interrogate you about the case," Will said. "I think I have a good idea about what happened. I understand Mrs. Peterson wouldn't sign the AMA form."

"She was a little emotional. Lauren saw what happened."

"And Mitchell Caine never showed up to see her after you called him?"

Obviously, Will had read the documentation. "That's right. We continued to check Mrs. Peterson while we waited for Dr. Caine to arrive. She refused a surgical consult. She said Dr. Caine had treated her pain with medication before, and she thought he could do so again. When he was delayed, for whatever reason, I asked Mrs. Peterson again about calling a surgeon. She refused."

"And you tried to call Mitchell repeatedly?"

"That's right. We couldn't reach him at home or at his office."

"Did he actually refuse to come to see his patient when you spoke with him?"

"No. He wasn't thrilled about the prospect, but he said he would be there. When we spoke about it, he indicated that he had forgotten. It sounds as if he might have been distracted for some reason."

"Have you noticed any problems with his treatment of patients in the emergency department lately, other than with Mrs. Peterson?" William asked.

Grant hesitated. "There have been other . . . instances," he said slowly.

William didn't ask for specifics—perhaps because he was already aware of other incidents.

"Addiction problem of some kind?" William suggested.

"There might be some red flags."

"He's becoming more and more difficult to communicate with," William said. "Not only for me, but for his patients. I've received other complaints. Have you ever smelled alcohol on his breath when he's been called to come in at night?"

"Once. Never when he was on duty."

"Drugs, then?"

Grant had heard one of the ER secretaries remark casually that she'd seen Dr. Caine take a pill from a prescription bottle a couple of times recently, but that could have been anything, and he didn't want to risk a guess about the contents of the bottle. "I don't know, William. Do you want me to talk to him?"

Will leaned back, rubbing his neck, staring out the window again, as if he received strength from the view. "I know the two of you aren't exactly friends, but for what it's worth, Mitchell Caine doesn't have many friends, especially since Darla left him. He has a lot of conflicts in his life right now, and the divorce battle can't be pretty. Maybe if we relieved him of some responsibilities here at the hospital, if you would reduce his hours in the ER, he could work through his own problems."

"Believe me, there will be a battle if I try to cut his hours in the department," Grant said. "There always has been in the past."

"I'm sure you'll keep the shouting to a minimum." William smiled for the first time since Grant had stepped into the office—unusual for Will.

The older man set his empty cup on the coffee table and slapped his hands on his knees, a characteristic indication that this conversation was over. "I have a week's worth of paper work to complete in the next few hours of daylight. You have a way with people, Grant. I hope you don't feel like I'm throwing you to the wolves, but you're the best one to handle this, in spite of Mitchell's antipathy. If you and I were to both hold a conference with him right now, I think it would be a painful blow to him."

In response to Grant's recent medical advice to William, the administrator had just delegated one of his responsibilities. Grant was the lucky recipient.

He'd better gear up for conflict.

———

Late Wednesday morning Archer Pierce arrived home from a hospital visit to find his wife waiting for him at the front door in a floor-length robe of burgundy velvet. Her hair was pulled up in one of those wicked plastic claw things, and wisps of luxuriant golden brown curls framed a face still groggy with sleep.

"Morning, beautiful." He kissed her on the cheek as he entered. "Did you get my note? I left it on the kitchen table. I had a call from the hospital early, and I didn't have the heart to disturb you."

"I found it. Thanks for the sleep." She closed the door and stretched, and Archer watched appreciatively.

In the kitchen she poured them each a cup of coffee and carried them to the table, then sank into her chair with the natural grace of a dancer. "What a way to start the day, when you'd planned to be free until church time tonight."

He sat down across from her. "Uh, Jess, about that . . . I was a little too eager to make those plans."

She hesitated with her cup halfway to her lips. "You told me there wouldn't be any problem switching days off this week. I know there's church tonight, but—"

"Mrs. Boucher reminded me I've got a meeting at four this afternoon, and Cyrus Hall was admitted to the hospital in Harrison. Mrs. Hall wanted to know if I'd drive down . . ."

Jessica slumped. "Isn't there anybody else in the church who can visit today? Can you go down tomorrow?"

"Ordinarily I would, but they're really worried about his heart, and Mrs. Hall said he was begging to have me—"

Jessica raised a hand. "Okay, okay, I can probably guess the rest.

You've known Cyrus for thirty-four years, and he would be deeply hurt if you didn't make a personal appearance, because he's watched you grow up in this church and he—"

"Something like that." Archer battled irritation at the long-suffering tone of her voice. "Jessica, this poor man is probably afraid he's going to die."

"Yes, I'm sure you're right, and I will pray for him and for his wife. But, Archer, you know everyone in Dogwood Springs, and in case you hadn't noticed, the town, as well as our church, is growing. You can't carry everybody on your own shoulders. You told me you were going to get some help from the deacons until the personnel committee could hire someone."

"I plan to ask them, but the meeting isn't until Friday night, and—"

"Good, ask them Friday night. Either get some help from them—you promised you'd ask, you know—or I'm enrolling you in pre-med."

He took heart from the teasing tenor of her voice. "Jess, you can't expect everything to change overnight. You've got to give the church some time."

She frowned down at her hands, and then slowly her gaze traveled up to his face. Oh, boy, he'd said the wrong thing.

"Time." She shook her head. "Our *marriage* needs time, but are we getting it? What if the deacons refuse to give you the help you need?"

"I think they'll listen to reason."

"Reason? Are you kidding? Why should they listen to reason? They've got you jumping through their hoops, doing the jobs that, according to *my* Bible, the church members could easily be responsible for. Ha! Reason." She shoved away from the table. "Archer Pierce, you're the most reasonable person I know, and do you listen to reason about this subject? No."

"I *am* listening to reason, Jess, but you've got to understand that they need to be eased into change. A church as large as ours has a lot of needy members, and they tend to put the pastor on a pedestal. I know because I saw it happen with Dad a few times. It takes finesse to make—"

"You don't think anyone else can do the job? Are you the church pastor or the church *puppet?*"

Archer winced at her words as if he'd been slapped.

Jessica gasped out loud and covered her lips with her fingers.

"I can't believe you said that," Archer whispered.

"Neither can I." She stood up and walked to the kitchen sink to stare out across the back lawn. "I'm so sorry. Please forgive me. It's just that I'm lonely. Even when you're here, you're not really *here*, with *me*."

He swallowed his own annoyance, went to her, and put his arms around her, drawing her back against him. "Something does need to change, I know. I'll talk to the deacons."

"I've been doing some thinking, Archer." She took a slow, deep breath. "If I were to request a new contract, with fewer performances—"

"No. Out of the question."

"Then what?" She turned within the circle of his arms to look up at him. "You tell me. If we're going to have a marriage, one of us is going to have to give up something. Heather's sharing the stage with me now. If it works out she might even be able to take my place."

"We'll think of something else. You're talking out of desperation, and we would both blame ourselves later if you felt forced to sacrifice your career to my rotten time management." He drew her against him. "Sweetheart, a little longer. Give me a little more time. You've been so patient with me, and I know I've taken advantage of that. I'm sorry. I've done this to myself. . . ."

"And to me." She rested her forehead on his shoulder.

"Yes, and to you. I'm not handling the transition well, and it's all my fault, not yours."

"You're trying too hard to follow in your father's footsteps." Jessica's voice was suddenly gentle. "Archer, what would you do if you weren't a pastor?"

He didn't have to think about the answer, because it was one he'd considered several times in the past few months. "I'd be a full-time hospital chaplain."

She nodded.

"I've thought about it more and more often lately, Jess. Remember the night Peregrine died?"

"I'll never forget."

"I still believe I was supernaturally drawn to the hospital that night."

"You're always drawn to the hospital."

"But do you know who seemed to benefit the most from my presence? Mitchell Caine."

"Dr. Caine," she said dryly.

"Jess, I still feel as if I'm needed in that type of ministry."

"By whom? God or the church? And what does it mean? Does it mean you now have two callings in life?"

"I'm not sure. I just know that the call is too loud for me to ignore."

She was silent for a long moment, and then she looked at her watch. "Why don't I get dressed and ride down to Harrison with you? We can stop for an early lunch. It's the only way I'll get to spend any time with you today."

———

Grant closed his office door and returned to the desk. One of the more rewarding aspects of his job as ER director was working with the staff. He'd always felt that a person could read the character of the administrator of any hospital by the attitude of the employees.

There were always exceptions, of course. William Butler shouldn't have to answer for Dr. Mitchell Caine's behavior or his treatment of patients, but if this treatment was allowed to continue, the whole hospital would feel the effects.

Grant dialed Mitchell's office number and wasn't surprised when the secretary answered with a tight, harried voice.

When he asked for Mitchell, she transferred his call without another word. He'd heard via the hospital grapevine that two of Mitchell's office staff had quit in the past few months, and his nurse was on the verge. Mitchell had a bad habit of pointing out the faults of the people with whom he worked, whether at his own clinic or here at the hospital. Some of his comments had been particularly damaging last year, when Mitchell was chief of staff at the hospital. His attitude still wasn't winning him any popularity contests, but his complaints held less bite now that the title of office had rotated at the first of the year. Dr. Spiegel now held that powerful position.

The line was answered curtly. "This is Dr. Caine."

"Hello, Mitchell, this is Grant."

There was an impatient sigh. "I've already been castigated by the mayor about Mimi Peterson today. Do you have something else to add?"

"Only that I think you might be a little overwhelmed lately, because I don't think you would ordinarily have allowed a patient to slip your mind."

"And you called just to tell me that." Mitchell's sarcasm was typical.

"I called to—"

"Don't waste your breath," Mitchell said. "I wouldn't have expected you to pass up this golden opportunity to delete my name from the ER schedule for the next month."

"How about just cutting it in half?"

"How about leaving it as is?"

"I wouldn't be helping you if I did that, Mitchell. I'll send you a revised copy of the ER schedule. I think you're getting a break from the medical call, as well. I received a new copy a few minutes ago."

There was a heavy silence on the other end, and Grant couldn't read it. "I'm sorry, Mitchell. I know this must feel like a slap in the face, but from my perspective, it's just an attempt to ease your load a little."

"And how would you know anything about my *load*?"

"You're not the only doctor who's ever needed a break."

"If I need a break I'll take one."

"I'll send the revised schedules to your office."

"No." Another heavy silence. "Put them in my box at the hospital. I'm not in the mood to give my secretary a good laugh today."

Grant paused, hearing the defeat in Mitchell's voice. "If you want to talk about it I'm available."

"Thank you for your kind and generous offer." Again the sarcasm.

"Counseling is—"

"Not for me."

Grant ended the call feeling helpless.

CHAPTER 12

Repair crews worked quickly in Dogwood Springs, and within a week of the storm new windows and doors replaced the destroyed ones in the church basement. The damage caused by flying debris had been sanded, painted, repaired.

The monthly deacon's meeting of the Dogwood Springs Baptist Church began with a favorite Baptist pastime of physical indulgence on Friday evening, thanks to the appetite of the deacons and the spirit of competition among their wives. Heavy homemade artillery lined the basement kitchen counters in covered dishes, filling the whole room with scents of roasted beef, fried chicken, yeasty rolls.

While the wives hovered, watching Archer's selections with pretended nonchalance, he spooned a small serving of every offering onto his plate; it was a trick Dad had taught him years ago, one of the most effective methods known to ministers to keep peace in the congregation.

Tonight was a particularly important time to promote goodwill—happy wives meant happy deacons. Happy deacons meant a happy pastor. Or at least that was the idea. Archer secretly struggled with the niggling suspicion that he was stroking egos in order to get his way.

After joking with the ladies and enjoying a plate and a half of stick-to-your-arteries roast with gravy, potatoes, creamed green beans, seven-layer salad, and three-layer double-fudge devil's food cake, Archer was ready to dialogue.

Unfortunately, the deacons lingered over their coffee and dessert while their wives cleared the tables. Archer helped the women, trying not to look at his watch or at the wall clock too many times as the conversation droned on and on.

He was on call at the hospital tonight, and he needed to get this discussion under way before he received a distress signal and missed the opportunity until next month's meeting. If it came down to the necessity of requesting another meeting, he was willing to do so, but he hoped it wouldn't come to that.

On the off chance that the hospital didn't call, and if Jessica got out of the theater in good time, there was a slight possibility that they could spend some quality time together—alone—talking about her hopes for Heather to join the show on a more permanent basis, talking about what they would do with all the rest of the time they planned to spend together. If they got it.

" . . . guest this evening, and I'm sure he has something he wants to say to us. I've never known Archer to turn down an opportunity to preach if he . . ."

Archer redirected his attention when he heard John Netz make his first attempt to move the deacons into the other room where they would have privacy for their meeting. The men chuckled at the little barb at Archer's expense, then went back to their desserts, in no hurry. Archer's attention wandered again. There went another five to ten minutes down the drain.

———

A few miles south of Branson's famous Highway 76, the Lake Junction Country Music Complex snuggled into a forested mountainside overlooking Lake Taneycomo. The newly constructed theater had such great acoustics that Jessica knew their audience could hear clearly, even when her sister, Heather Rose Lane, shimmied too far away from the microphone.

These most recent shows, in which Jessica had given Heather equal billing, had proved to be a great success, and Jessica cheered inwardly for her "baby" sister. Tourists from all over the world packed this auditorium, listening in rapt silence as the ethereal quality of Heather's voice danced through the air with its magical beauty, in perfect contrast to Jessica's more throaty tones.

"He's not in the distance, and He's not in the sky;
He's inside my heart, my friend, and I can tell you why:
Jesus came a callin' not too long ago,
And I invited Him to live right here inside my soul."

Jessica knew these words by heart, because she had written them herself, five years ago, and Heather had written the music. She only wished Heather grasped the meaning of those words.

The sisters ended the song and bowed deeply to the sound of enthusiastic applause. As always, Jessica put an arm around Heather as they straightened. Heather had a unique stage presence—she embraced the audience with every smile, every movement. The audience loved her. Jessica had learned long ago that life was too short to allow herself to be jealous of other Branson performers, least of all her own sister.

The applause died and anticipation once more descended over the theater.

No Branson show would be complete without its down-home country humor, and Jessica and Heather had developed their own version. With guitars in hand, they launched into a short, silly duet about the pet pig named Wally they'd raised for the Cape Fair pig races when Heather was eight and Jessica, a teenager by then, was in the 4-H club. When they finished, they could see the desired effect in the faces near the front. One man was doubled over with laughter, and a woman wiped tears from her eyes, still chuckling.

The lights changed, the music segued, and Jessica's voice drifted from the speakers, resonant one moment, soft and tender the next, filling the huge hall again with the crossover hit that had gained her nationwide recognition, "Daddy's Story Time."

Heather harmonized with her on the chorus, the sequins on her dress sparkling like jewels in the rosy spotlight, and then she took the next verse. Jessica watched and listened, enthralled by the beautiful voice of her only sibling, by her overpowering charisma.

For a brief moment, Heather's voice paused at the transition of the song's story from their earthly father to their heavenly Father. A spotlight reflected against a large mirrored heart that hung overhead. It illuminated a sparkle of tears on Heather's face and the pain of longing in her eyes. It was a dramatic moment in the song, and Heather knew how to evoke the most emotion from it.

Heather seemed to hesitate. Her voice quivered for the first time that evening. It complemented this tender song perfectly, and Jessica wanted to reach out to her, to assure her that everything would be okay, that the words of the song were true, that she was loved by her earthly father and her heavenly Father.

Heather swung away and walked to the other side of the stage on cue, the way she always did. Sequined tassels of her red western-style dress shimmered in the bright lights as she belted out the words about a love that transcended life.

Stage smoke swirled around Heather's slender figure, floating above the audience with a rainbow of colors.

For as long as Jessica could remember, Heather had craved an audience; she was always seeking a spotlight. Would it be wrong to offer her that opportunity?

Is it wrong to let it all go? Jessica retained her appearance of loving attention while she allowed the questions that had become an endless loop in her thoughts to buffet her. *Archer wants me to continue singing, but what do you want, Lord?*

Of particular importance to her was the fact that she could spend more time with Archer when he *did* have time for her; she could help more with the church instead of running off for a performance every afternoon and evening. She could become a part of the Dogwood Springs community instead of someone who hovered at the edges of social activity for fear of drawing a crowd by her well-known presence. A few years ago she had realized that she was gifted to write songs and sing them, just as a preacher was gifted to preach, just as a teacher was gifted to teach.

The thought of leaving all this hurt too much to contemplate.

Heather turned and looked at her across the stage as she finished her verse, and together they sang the chorus, their voices blending with the perfection of familial likeness.

When Jessica took the final verse, which told of the love of the

Father and her love for Him, a gentle glow of light filtered across the audience in an unspoken invitation for them to join the musicians in the final chorus.

This was the part of the show Jessica loved the most—singing with the audience. They took part enthusiastically, and she loved looking into those faces and seeing the joy written there.

Oh, Lord, may this never end!

————

When Archer was in his early twenties, he'd asked his father why their church only used the older men in their membership on the board of deacons, especially since a couple of these men only came to church for the meetings. It had seemed to Archer at the time that there were a lot more willing, dedicated women in their congregation than men, and even back then they had several younger families join the congregation. The deacons were mostly older businessmen, a couple of farmers, many of them retired.

Dad's answer had frustrated him. He'd said, "Tradition, son. It's how things are done around here, and it's what people are comfortable with."

"Why don't you do something to change it?" Archer had asked.

"Because I've already got the work God gave me to do, and my hands are full with that. If you find, someday, that God's called you to challenge the tradition, then you go ahead and do what He's called you to. But remember to pick your fights carefully. There's a lot wrong in this world and a lot wrong in this church, but as long as we stay connected to the Holy Spirit, God will root out the problems one by one, not all in one fell swoop."

And so Dad had admitted, after a fashion, that he had seen the problems in the church all those years ago, and Archer saw little change as he looked around the room. He glanced at his watch again, this time less concerned about the pointedness of his action.

John Netz apparently noticed the gesture. He cleared his throat and turned his attention from his notes. "Archer, I know you're a busy man, and you've got a hospital to attend to."

"And a wife," Archer said quickly.

John gave him a teasing smile. "Yes, and a wife to keep happy—"

"I hear you there, Preacher," Bud Caesar said from the end of the table. "That's an impossible task."

"Watch your mouth, Bud," his wife snapped from her spot in front of the dishwasher. "I can make sure you eat leftovers for a month."

Everyone chuckled, including Archer, and he was gratified to see the men push back from the table at last. They adjourned upstairs into the classroom where John Netz taught Sunday school.

"We'd better get down to business," John said. "I hear there's another storm coming our way."

"That one last week sure was a doozy, wasn't it?" Bud remarked.

"Yes," Archer said. "So I'll hurry and get this over with. I would like some of you, who feel led, to think about taking some on-call shifts for the church."

The chatter ended. Archer felt the attention of every man in the room.

"What do you mean, Preacher?" Bud asked at last.

"I'm in over my head with church activities," Archer said. "I've tried to make it a point to attend most committee meetings and most Sunday school class meetings, direct the youth, direct the Sunday School, conduct funerals and weddings, plus keep up with my duties in my volunteer capacity in the hospital chaplain program. . . . The list is getting longer by the day."

"Well, except for the hospital stuff, your father kept up with most of those things pretty good," Bud said.

"We have a larger congregation now than we did when Dad retired," Archer said. "I've been studying some statistics about church growth, and with more than six hundred fifty members on the rolls, and an average Sunday attendance of well over five hundred, I'm surprised we're not already losing members."

"Don't know that it'd hurt if a few of 'em went elsewheres," Dwight muttered.

"Then what is our church here for?" Archer asked.

John Netz nodded, apparently not surprised by the conversation.

Archer continued. "Many of our new members are also new Christians, with a hunger for the truth and for individual nurturing support.

I'm already stretched to the limit. I no longer find it possible to take a day off during the week because I'm on call for the church 24/7. I can't continue the pace."

"Can't Jessica step in and help you some?" asked Bud Caesar.

Archer gave him a pointed look. "My wife couldn't possibly do more than she's doing right now. I want more time with her, and she wants more time with me. What I'm saying is that I need help. Other churches our size in the area have at least twice as many paid staff members."

"You're saying we need to hire more ministers?" Dwight's face tightened with that same resistance that was always apparent when the subject of money came up. "We're already looking for a youth minister. What more do you want?"

"I need to know if there are a few deacons, or any other members of our church, who would be willing to put their names and telephone numbers in the newsletter every few weeks and be on call for members," Archer said. "Meanwhile, yes, since you've mentioned it, I would like to consider not only hiring a new youth minister, but education, as well, and perhaps another secretary to help Mrs. Boucher. She needs a break, too." Why not pull out all the stops? If he asked for even more, maybe they would realize the scope of need they had.

"Maybe permanently," Dwight muttered. "Gettin' a little old to take—"

"Watch it, Hahnfeld," John Netz cautioned, "she's only a couple of years older than you."

Dwight cleared his throat and looked at Archer. "You saying you want a break from the church already? You haven't been here much more than a year."

"A year and a half. And during that time we've added nearly two hundred new members to the church," Archer said. "I receive calls not only from members in distress, but from those who have visited our church and are seeking prayer support or spiritual counsel."

"Got to serve your members first," Bud said.

"That's right," echoed Dwight. "We're the ones that pay the bills."

Archer flinched. They weren't getting it.

"Seems I remember, Pastor," Dwight said, "that your father tended to slack on his duties from time to—"

"My father *never* slacked on his duties, but he did make his family a high priority in his life."

"Do you have to sit in on all the committee meetings?" John asked.

Ah, finally a morsel of encouragement. "No, it's just a tradition Dad began a few years ago, and—"

"But you do have a wife to help you with all that now," Dwight said.

"No," Archer said. "I didn't marry Jessica so we could add her to the church staff. She has her own ministry, which requires all her emotional and spiritual energy. In fact, her church in Branson had a special group that gave her constant prayer support, kept up with her schedule, encouraged her, and met with her for Bible study at a time that worked best for her."

"You and Jessica would have more time together if she came to church with you more often," Dwight said.

Archer felt his whole body tense. If he went with his emotions right now, he and Jessica would have plenty of time together, because he would punch Dwight in the nose, the church would have to fire him, and he could relax. He flexed his fingers.

"Seems to me," John Netz said, his calm bass voice flowing over Archer's ruffled emotions like soothing oil, "that the preacher isn't the only one in the church who's supposed to be a servant. Aren't we all supposed to serve one another?"

Archer relaxed a little. *Okay. Not bad.* "A youth minister. That will take a great load off." He would forget the rest for now.

"Well, that might not be coming along as fast as you might think." Dwight fidgeted in his chair, patted his belly, leaned back. "We haven't been able to get the members together to meet for the past month."

Archer bit his lip. *Lord, you might paralyze my mouth for the next few minutes.* "I would appreciate some help." It was a simple request.

"Seems I read somewhere in the Old Testament lately about how a man who'd taken a bride was released from armed services for a year so's he could stay home and keep his wife happy," John Netz said. "I don't doubt that being the pastor of this church probably seems like being armed for a fight, and it's a sure bet he and Jessica haven't had the time they'd like to spend together. Maybe they'd like to take another vacation before long. What d'you think about that, Preacher?"

"You're talking Old Testament," Dwight said, only half kidding. "This here's a New Testament church."

"We're a Bible-believing church," Archer said. "But since you've mentioned it, the early New Testament churches met in homes, not three-story church buildings like this one. I doubt they could fit five hundred people into one of those houses for Sunday school, and those small groups helped one another, they didn't depend on one man to take care of them. It just wasn't possible."

"No need to take this before the church," Dwight said. "The deacons have always been able to work these things out before." He held his watch up and shook his head. "Would you look at the time. Guess we should get on with the rest of the meeting before we're hit with another storm."

Archer waited for others to protest. They didn't. He remembered Dad's words about picking his fights, and he realized this would be one of them.

As they began a discussion about plans for a golf tournament next month, he excused himself from the table and went downstairs and through the kitchen to thank the ladies for their wonderful cooking. He didn't slam any doors, and he didn't kick any chairs—though he felt like it. He'd been wrong about the deacons. They still didn't take him seriously.

"Every second, every step,
Let me keep my eyes on you.
No returning, no regrets,
Let me keep my eyes on you."

Heather knew how to involve the crowd, and Jessica stood back and listened to her sister take the first verse.

"Peter saw you on the water
And he stepped into the sea.
Though he faltered with distraction,

He had much more faith than me."

Jessica joined her on the chorus again. She knew this was one of Heather's favorite songs, with its lively style, energetic movements, nice bass drums. The crowd sang along, complete with clapping and stomping and shouting, strobe lights flashing.

Ever since they had sung "Daddy's Story Time," the enthusiasm of the audience had increased—always a confidence builder. At the end of this final song the crowd once again erupted into enthusiastic applause, and she and Heather applauded with them. The audience stood.

Jessica waved kisses at the crowd, then as the applause gradually died down, she thanked them for coming, took her sister's arm in a sisterly embrace, and walked with her from the stage.

Once out of the limelight, Heather grabbed her in a tight hug and continued to hold her, as if she couldn't let go. "Oh, Jess, this was what I was born for!"

Jessica nodded. "Isn't it wonderful?"

Heather released her and stepped back, ignoring the stagehands as they shuffled past with props. "It was like a powerful connection."

"Exactly." Jessica turned and led the way along a side hallway that led to the theater lobby. There, they would stand and greet the audience, shake hands, pose for pictures, talk.

"Jessica, Hammerstain called me this afternoon."

"Garth? What did he want?"

"He asked me if I'd be interested in having my own show on the *Country Lady*." Garth Hammerstain, the owner of this theater, also managed a paddle boat cruise on the Lake of the Ozarks aboard the *Country Lady* that rivaled the quality entertainment Jessica had seen on the *Branson Belle*.

Jessica turned to her in delight. "Your own show! Heather, that's what you've always wanted!"

Heather didn't smile. "It would mean leaving you."

"It would be an evening show?"

"The same time as this one. I couldn't do them both."

"Oh, honey, I never thought about . . . What did you tell him?"

"I asked for some time to consider it." Heather turned and continued walking down the hallway.

Jessica fell into step beside her, watching the play of light through the blond waves of hair that haloed over Heather's shoulders, studying the thoughtful frown that deepened the interesting features of her sister's face.

"Heather, it would be a great opportunity for you. I know we love working together, but as you said, this is something you've dreamed of doing ever since you saw your first Branson show."

"Oh, don't get your pantyhose all twisted." Heather reverted to her typical gruff Heather Rose jargon. "It isn't that big a deal. And besides, I know you would strongly disapprove of some of those outfits they'd want me to wear."

"Outfits?"

They stopped at the door that opened into the lobby, where many of the audience would be waiting for them to make an appearance.

Heather grabbed the door lever. "One of the things Garth mentioned was that I had an . . . um . . . let's see . . . His words were, 'Heather, you've got a beautiful name, a beautiful voice, a beautiful body. I want to see to it that every aspect of your personality is expressed.' "

Jessica forced herself not to react as Heather opened the door and smiled broadly, greeting the people who stood waiting for them.

Jessica stepped up beside her and said softly, "Want to talk about it over a late dinner?"

"Yeah, I would."

Good, because this whole thing could turn out to be a disaster.

CHAPTER 13

Archer strolled across the church parking lot toward his three-year-old Kia and raised his face to the soft drizzle. He saw a flash of lightning and counted to ten before he heard the resulting thunder.

He didn't hurry. He liked the feel of the moisture on his face. It cooled his heated, angry thoughts.

The deacons meant well. He just needed to learn how to make his point with more clarity and authority. Meanwhile he intended to take more time for Jessica no matter what anyone else thought about it. As Dad had said several times when Archer was growing up, God established the family before He established the church.

Archer had not yet reached his car when the clouds let loose another onslaught to the already waterlogged earth. He covered his head with his jacket and rushed to the car. As he folded himself into the seat, the lightning flared and thunder echoed around him—not loud, but enough to get his attention. He closed the door against the raindrops that fell in ever-increasing girth and velocity against the windshield.

He half expected to see the others step out of the basement doors at any moment—no one seemed comfortable there after the tornado hit last Friday.

He dialed home on his cell phone, but Jessica wasn't there yet. He even considered calling Dad in Arizona for a little moral support, but he remembered his parents were on a mission trip to rural Mexico at the moment. Though Archer didn't make a habit of running to his parents for advice about every little thing, he respected their wisdom. And at a time like this he could use all the wisdom that came his way.

He turned the ignition and noted the time on the dash clock. Jessica should be out of the theater by now if the crowd didn't linger after the show, if the storm chased them away as it had last week.

He pressed the speed dial for her cell phone. If she was anywhere near home he would meet her there. If not, he would make his usual detour toward the hospital.

If the deacons started to complain when he began to actually *take* his Fridays off, then maybe that would be an answer to some questions that had been floating around in his head for the past few weeks. Maybe those complaints and the set of rules by which he knew he was being judged as pastor of this church were not of God at all. If he became convinced of that, he would seek God's will about leaving the church, perhaps even searching for a much smaller congregation . . . or whatever God led him to.

He didn't know if these compulsions to leave were rebellion or promptings from the Holy Spirit. However, as he'd told Jessica during their argument Wednesday morning, he could not ignore the needs at the hospital when he was on call there. To him, the hours he spent praying and encouraging those most needy of people—the hurting and the sick—were the most precious hours of his ministry.

Jessica's phone was apparently still turned off, and he received the typical instructions to try again later. He turned toward the hospital, driving with caution.

He knew his imagination was working overtime, but he couldn't quite shake the fear that this storm posed a particularly dark threat to Dogwood Springs.

———

"All these years, all this time, I've dreamed of having a show of my own, of seeing my name alone on the marquee and . . . now I'm not sure, Jessie." The exquisite lines of Heather's mouth pursed in a thoughtful frown. Her face held lines of worry.

"What is it that makes you unsure?" Jessica sat across the table from her sister at the Barbeque Pit, down the road from the theater. Jessica wasn't hungry, but Heather wanted to talk.

"I'm not sure. Maybe fear about what I'd be getting myself into," Heather said. "And I love singing with you," she added softly.

They had ordered stew, and while they waited for their food to arrive they sat and watched the rain fall past the huge window that overlooked Lake Taneycomo.

Jessica didn't know how long she would be able to keep her opinions to herself, especially since Heather could read her so well.

"I don't know the industry the way you do, Jessie," Heather said. "I didn't haunt the theaters when I was a teenager the way you did. I was more interested in my friends and school sports and boys."

"In other words, you were a normal teenager," Jessica said. Jessica, on the other hand, had made music her life early on.

"But don't you see?" Heather touched Jessica's arm. "I didn't earn my own show. You did. You're the one who can play the piano, the guitar, and the fiddle."

"You play guitar."

"You're the one who writes the words to almost all the songs you sing."

"And you're the one who can hear a new tune in your head and sing it for me so we can get the music for those songs," Jessica reminded her. She wanted to beg her sister not to break up the team.

Jessica had loved music—and Branson—for as long as she could remember. Her first after-school job had been at a concession stand at the Roy Clark Theater.

When Jessica graduated from SMSU and moved to Branson to pursue a full-time career in the music industry, Heather moved in with her, leaving their father behind on the farm, a lonely recluse after the death of their mother.

He had never been a demonstrative father—he'd been too busy keeping up the farm while working a factory job. But there was one good thing the girls always remembered about their father—sometimes after supper in the evening, if their dad didn't have to go back outside to check on the pigs and cattle, he would sit in his chair at the head of the kitchen table and tell them a story. Sometimes it was about his own father's experiences during the Depression when he hopped a freight train to California looking for work, sometimes it was his own dreams for the future, but always, after a story, he tucked them into bed and kissed them goodnight. It almost seemed as if getting in touch with his dreams also allowed him to get in touch with his tender side.

Years later, Jessica wrote a song about the shy country farmer whose life of near poverty didn't hold a candle to the dreams he dared to dream, and how he shared those with his daughters the way a typical father would share his hugs and words of love. His dream? Just to support his family on their farm. To bring his children up with good memories.

Their dad still lived alone on their old farm outside Kimberling City. He still kept his small herd of cattle, a few pigs, and his old hound dogs for company. He barely left the farm these days, still didn't have much money, and refused help whenever Jessica tried to give it. He was proud of his daughters, but Jessica knew he worried about them.

"I love you, sis, you know that?" Heather grabbed Jessica's hand across the table and squeezed it. "You've always been there for me, no matter what."

"Love you back. You know that."

"But if I were to leave the show, I'd feel as if I were deserting you, after all you've done for me—loving me, supporting me, standing beside me even through my rebellion and my attempt at suicide. Oh, Jessie, you can't know how much you mean to me."

"It sounds to me as if you've decided to take Garth up on his offer."

Heather held her gaze, then frowned and looked out the window. "I don't know, Jessie. I just don't know. Standing on that stage and looking out at the audience, it's almost like . . . like I get a brief glimpse into heaven every time I do it."

Jessica felt another thrust of pain. Heather still didn't know what heaven was all about.

The server brought their stew to the table. Jessica pulled her cell phone from her purse and had just punched the number for home when a blast of wind and rain attacked the window.

Archer didn't answer. She left a message, then punched his cell phone number. Nothing.

She shrugged and placed the phone back in her purse. She didn't really expect him to be home, not yet, anyway. He was either still in the meeting with the deacons or he was at the hospital. He would get her message, and he would see her later tonight.

Another blast of rain made her flinch.

"Sis?" Heather said. "You okay?"

"I'm fine. I guess I'm still a little nervous about the weather after that tornado last week."

"You could stay at my place tonight."

Jessica considered the possibility, then shook her head. "I want to get home to Archer if I can." Besides, she wasn't really worried for herself. "It'll be okay." She watched the blowing tree limbs for another couple of seconds, then turned her attention back to her sister. Everything would be fine.

When Archer arrived at the hospital he found Grant busy but not frantic. Five exam rooms were occupied, and one more patient was being checked by one of the night nurses in the triage room. Glad he hadn't overdressed for the deacon dinner, Archer saw a familiar face in exam room four, and without stopping to disturb Grant, went straight to talk with Mrs. Cecile Piedmont. The elderly lady was a member of his church. To her extreme irritation she had developed heart trouble this past year and had been forced to curtail some of her much-loved gardening and yard work.

Before Archer could speak, he heard another familiar voice carry from the exam room next to Cecile's. It was Dr. Mitchell Caine, apparently called here for one of his patients, since Grant was on duty. Mitchell was lecturing some apparently malingering patient about the nasty results of drinking more than one glass of wine per day and about the dangers of obesity.

Archer ignored Mitchell's voice, kissed the delicately lined skin of Cecile's cheek, and looked at the monitor above her bed. "Chest pain again, Cecile?" He kept his voice low, aware of Mitchell's presence in the next room and heedful of the doctor's disdain for the chaplain program.

Cecile nodded and looked away. "No more outdoor activity until I'll let them stick a machine in my chest," she growled.

"*In* your chest?" He took her hand and sat down beside her. "Pacemaker?"

She gave another curt nod.

"And you're going to do it, right?"

She continued to stare at some imagined spot on the wall for another few seconds, and then she looked at him sadly. "I'm tired, Archer. I don't want to be hauled up to Springfield and let them cut on me."

"I tell you what, why don't you call a couple of our church members who've had the procedure done recently. I know of two in the past three months. My aunt had it done three years ago, and she's able to do all the things she did fifteen years ago. You'll be more independent, Cecile. I know how important that is to you."

She fingered one of the wires that connected her to the monitor. "Like I said, I'm tired."

"I know. It's because you don't feel well. This pacemaker procedure isn't like open-heart surgery. You would recover quickly."

Her eyes narrowed. "Did James call you about this?"

"Nope."

"Rebecca, then? Martha?"

He chuckled. Mrs. Piedmont's six children doted on her. "I haven't had a chance to talk to any of your kids lately. I'm speaking from my own experience." Once again, Archer regretted the busy state of his life, which prevented him from doing the things he most enjoyed, such as talking with Cecile's family about their concerns.

She laid her head back against the pillow as Mitchell Caine's voice droned on in the other room.

"Have you prayed about it?" Archer asked her.

"Of course I've prayed about it," she snapped, uncharacteristically irritable. Mitchell's drone stopped in the other room.

"Would you try it one more time with me?" Archer asked. "I won't push. I won't try to twist your arm."

She watched him suspiciously. "Or God's?"

He allowed the comment to slide away without protest. "I won't try to twist God's arm, either."

Was that what people thought he was doing here? Using God as the Cosmic Enforcer to make the patients listen to their doctors?

No, he wouldn't think that way. Cecile was understandably depressed and upset right now, and so was he. Patients in this hospital needed the power of prayer, and ordinarily they appreciated the presence of someone who could remind them that they weren't alone and that God was in control. Prayer soothed them and gave them genuine hope, but that was only the beginning of God's influence on the cases in which Archer became involved.

Archer prayed with his old friend, and then her son and granddaughter came rushing into the room in an apparent response to a summons from the hospital. He greeted them and stepped into the hallway just as an apparition stepped from the exam room next door—Dr. Mitchell Caine in his dress shirt and tie and long white lab coat.

"Hi, Mitchell." Archer nodded at him and passed.

"Let me guess," Mitchell said dryly. "Our super chaplain has finally discovered that it takes more than God to fix some hearts." He fell into step beside Archer.

"I'm afraid I don't—"

"God wasn't the only one who heard that prayer." Mitchell thumped his fingers on the hallway wall as he passed by. "Sound travels well from room to room. Tell me, Archer, what do you think you did for your patient just now?" His steps slowed, and for a moment it seemed as if he swayed sideways, out of balance.

"Are you okay?"

"I'm fine." Mitchell gestured to the empty alcove near the back entrance. He stepped to the window and indicated with a nod of his head for Archer to join him.

Archer hesitated. Mitchell Caine was not one for small talk.

"You haven't answered my question."

"I prayed with her."

"You offered her some practical advice."

It seemed, lately, that Mitchell went out of his way to engage Archer in debate about Christianity and the act of prayer in a medical setting. He even seemed to enjoy it at times. Ordinarily, Archer did, too, but tonight he wasn't up to intellectual or spiritual sparring.

"Besides offering prayer, what did you do for your patient tonight?" Mitchell flexed his fists and reached up to straighten the lapel of his white lab coat.

"Besides prayer? Very little. I only attempted to draw God into the medical equation."

"Just to comfort the patient?"

"Look, Mitchell, let's not get into this tonight, okay?"

The doctor looked at him, then turned away. The uncompromising line of his shoulders lost some of its definition. "A simple question, Archer."

"I believe it does comfort patients when I pray," Archer said at last, "but my main reason for prayer is to call on God's power of healing. I'm aware you disagree, Mitchell."

"You don't have any idea what I'm thinking at this moment," Mitchell said. His voice was soft, barely loud enough to carry into the hallway, and he continued to stare out into the darkness. He reached up to rub his neck, and Archer saw a tremor in his hand.

A streak of lightning flashed across the sky, followed several seconds later by a rumble of thunder. Archer turned from the hallway and stepped up beside Mitchell, joining him in fascination at the array outside, one more display of God's creativity and power. And yet, Mitchell was antagonistic toward that very same God.

"You're right," Archer said at last. "I have no way of knowing what's going through your mind right now. On the other hand, I would think that by now you would find me boringly predictable. You should be able to guess what I'm going to say before I say it."

"Why is that?" Mitchell didn't look at him.

"Because my faith hasn't changed. My security in God hasn't changed." He hesitated, still resisting a debate but unable to avoid the subject. "Am I to take it that you actually want to know more about that faith?"

"What I want is most likely impossible." Mitchell cleared his throat. "What I would like is an opportunity to ask questions of some . . . knowledgeable person, some person who truly believes he is acquainted with this God of yours, without taking the risk of being put on a visitation list or a Sunday school class membership list."

Archer chuckled. Coming from Mitchell Caine, this was powerful encouragement. "I think I can do that, but you need to remember that I'm just a mortal human being, with weaknesses and faults, so I may automatically try to jot down your name and address and telephone number out of force of habit."

Mitchell didn't acknowledge the lame joke.

"I'm sorry if you've been offended by Christians in the past," Archer said.

"I've come into contact with too many who behave as if they have all the answers to all of life's questions."

"You can count me out on that. I have far too many questions of my own." Archer stared out at the rain. "The more I read the Bible, the more I realize that most of my pat answers to life's questions have little to do with God's truth and a lot to do with what I want to be truth."

"Are you saying you think you're a hypocrite?" Mitchell asked with the characteristic edge of challenge in his voice.

"Not at all. I believe the truths of the Bible. I just think that all too often we Christians have a tendency to try to pick and choose what we want to remember so that we can put God into a box of our choosing. He won't fit. God works outside those artificial boxes of human design."

Mitchell nodded. "I'm not talking about other Christians; I'm talking about you. Patients listen to you when they won't even listen to me at times."

Archer resisted the urge to ask Mitchell, again, if he was feeling okay. "I'm a preacher. I'm not sure why, but that seems to carry authority for some people."

Mitchell waited.

"Okay, let me tell you what I've discovered for myself about God. He doesn't love us dispassionately, in a detached way, but with more passion, more desire, more longing than we can imagine, and with more generosity."

"My argument to that," Mitchell said, "would be to point out, once again, my daughter's drug addiction. How does that reflect God's love?"

"That reflects *her* choice. But her redemption has already been paid for, and there is a way out for her, for you, for all of us, if we'll take it."

"Yesh . . . Yes, I've heard it all from your father. It's the Christian chant, isn't it? I thought you weren't into those pat little answers."

Archer frowned at the slight slur in Mitchell's words. "It's the Christian hope. Our truth. But not just *our* truth, *the* truth. It's a mystery, not a pat answer. It's where we meet God."

"And then what?" Mitchell challenged. "What have you discovered about God since you first met Him?"

"I've discovered His mercy. There have been times in my life when I've tried to turn away, to block Him out and choose my own direction, but He never lets me go. It's like He's always there, and every time I seek Him out, He allows me to see more of himself."

"And that makes you invincible to the problems we *lesser mortals* experience." Mitchell said it like a judgment.

Again, Archer noticed the slight slur of Mitchell's speech. "I know I'm not invincible. For instance, right now I'm watching that storm, and thinking about last Friday night, and wondering if we'll have another tornado warning. My fear of it is very human."

Mitchell lowered his voice. "Tell something. . . ." He hesitated. Cleared his throat. "I was wondering . . ."

Archer waited, staring at the window as if mesmerized by the rain, when in fact he was watching Mitchell's reflection in the glass. What was wrong with him? Sick, perhaps? Sleep deprived?

"The night Simon Royce died," Mitchell said at last.

"Yes, I remember it."

"I told you . . . some things."

"Which will remain in my confidence."

"They say . . . Some people have suggested . . ."

Archer turned to Mitchell. The man seemed to be having some trouble collecting his thoughts. "Mitchell, I know you did all you could to save his life, in spite of the way you felt about him."

"I told you I wanted him to die."

"There were several times I felt the same way you did, considering the things Simon Royce did in this town."

There was a long pause. "Do you believe in hell?"

"I couldn't be a Baptist preacher and not believe there is a hell. Are you asking if I believe in divine retribution?"

"Yes . . . I suppose that's what I'm asking."

"Yes, I do, Mitchell, but I also believe that there's someone standing between me and the same retribution Simon Royce is receiving."

Mitchell scowled and fluttered his hand in annoyance. "Yes, yes, I know, Jesus Christ, Savior of the world. I don't buy it. You're not a drug pusher. You can't compare yourself to Simon."

"No, but I can't earn my way to heaven with good deeds. My faith in Christ is what gives my life meaning—it gives my eternity meaning—and if there's any good in me, it's because of Him."

Before Archer finished Mitchell was yawning. "Time for me to leave before we get into another one of your famous dissertations." He no longer slurred his words, but he seemed to be choosing them with care.

"If you ever want to ask me any questions, without the dreaded threat of an onslaught of witnessing tracts and pastoral calls, feel free to do so."

Mitchell nodded and thanked him, then turned and walked slowly down the hallway.

Archer watched him for a moment. He didn't stagger, but he didn't seem especially steady on his feet. When he reached the end of the hallway, he turned and looked back.

Archer returned to the ER proper.

Grant was standing at the central desk filling out a T-sheet. He looked up with a warm greeting when he saw Archer. "I didn't realize we'd called you tonight."

"You didn't. I just got out of a meeting and thought I'd drop by." Archer nodded toward the secretary.

"Hi, Archer." She smiled at him, pretending to inspect his wool jacket. "I don't see any damage. Wasn't that Dr. Caine I saw you talking to a minute ago?"

"That was him."

Grant put his pen down and turned to face Archer. "Forgive me for saying this, but you don't look overjoyed to be here. Bad meeting?"

"Disappointing. I need to ask your advice about something, but I see you're busy."

"Not too busy right now. I'm just waiting on test results, and Dr. Caine took care of his own patient."

"Dr. Sheldon." Eugene, the tall, quiet young man who was one of the night-shift nurses, came up to the central counter and placed an inhaler box on the Formica. "Mrs. Eddingly didn't take this with her when she left."

Grant sighed and shook his head. "She won't drive all the way back to town to get it tonight, especially not in the rain."

"Mrs. Eddingly?" Archer asked. "Mrs. Racine Eddingly? She's a member of my church. If she needs that tonight, I can take it to her before I go home." He looked at his watch. "If I leave soon."

"Do you know where she lives?" Grant asked.

"Sure. Down in the valley as deep in the woods as a person can get." Mrs. Eddingly was eighty-two. Her husband had died ten years ago, but she refused to move away from the farm she and her husband had tended together all their married lives. She suffered from asthma.

"She's as independent as ever," Grant said, "but she doesn't like driving after dark in that old rust bucket of hers. I don't blame her. Why don't I walk you to your car, and we'll talk about that advice you wanted."

"I just wondered if you would be willing to let any other local pastors volunteer for the chaplain program," Archer said as they strolled toward the employee entrance of the department. "I know of a couple of new guys in the ministerial alliance who might be interested."

Grant slowed his steps. "Please tell me you're not quitting."

"Just backing off a few hours a month."

"Do you need a different day?"

"Different day, fewer hours, more help at the church." Archer sighed when they reached the door and stepped out into the deserted hallway. "I'm tired, Grant. I tend to take on more than I can handle, and that's my fault entirely. The thing is, this chaplain program is one of the most rewarding things I've ever done, but I have a responsibility to the church. People already complain because I'm not there for them."

"What can I do to help? Do you need more help with the high schoolers? I can—"

"What I need is to learn how to say no. As it is, the only person who hears that from me is my wife, and that isn't a good thing."

"No."

"How about reducing my hours to alternating weeks, and have the call on another night besides Friday. That's my day off, and I'm going to start taking it."

"Good." Grant watched him. "You don't want to leave the program."

"No, I don't."

"You and Jessica do need more time together. That's one of the most important things in life." He sighed. "Time with family."

"My father was good about that. I haven't learned the balance yet." Archer looked at Grant. "How are things going between you and Lauren?"

Grant hesitated so long Archer thought he wasn't going to answer. "I would love for her to be my wife. Brooke and Beau would love for her to be their stepmom."

"Is she aware of this?"

"Yes."

Archer smiled. "I can't think of anything better for all of you."

"I hope she comes to the same conclusion before Brooke blows a gasket. She's almost too eager for it to happen, and she's showing a few signs of emotional stress."

They reached the door, and Archer hesitated as he watched the deluge through the window. He couldn't back out now. Mrs. Eddingly would need her inhaler.

Still, he couldn't prevent a memory of roaring wind, breaking glass, injured people. As he stepped out into the storm he offered up a silent prayer for protection.

CHAPTER 14

Mitchell accidentally kicked the doorframe of his Envoy as he pulled himself inside. He muttered a curse at the offending frame as he settled in the seat, carefully pulled on his seat belt, glanced in his rearview mirror, and slammed the door shut. The headlights of Archer's little sedan streaked through the rain as he drove out of the parking lot, followed by the repetitive flash of the red turn signal.

"Reverend Archer Pierce, savior of the world." Mitchell drawled the words, mimicking Archer's deep voice. "Why do you concern yourself with me when you're struggling to keep up with a church full of emotional dependents?"

How could one man keep up with the needs of all those people? And why even try? It wasn't as if he was being paid a doctor's salary—not that the pay for a family practice physician was even worth the effort these days, especially after the divorce attorneys took their cut.

Mitchell's attention was drawn to the lights of Archer's brakes as he slowed for the stop sign, and then he watched the red taillights disappear over a hill. With a strange numbness in his fingers, Mitchell started the motor and listened to the low throbbing hum of power before backing the SUV from its prized parking spot. The motor jerked, hesitated, and jerked again, until he forced the accelerator to the floor and nearly collided with a car that had sneaked up behind him.

A horn blared; he slammed on the brakes and cursed.

Get home. He let the car pass and let up on the brake again, attempting to focus on each action, careful not to make a wrong movement.

Why hadn't he waited to take that second pill until he got home? He forced himself to focus. He had a sudden impulse to make a detour—he wanted to follow those red lights that had disappeared over the hill into the dense rain. He needed to talk to the preacher again.

Now there was a hilarious thought. Dr. Mitchell Caine seeking counsel from a man of God.

Something about Archer had always confused Mitchell. He never tried to soft-soap him. He was honest about not knowing all the answers about God.

Mitchell had every reason to believe that Archer's God was a weakling—if He even existed—and yet . . . something about Archer Pierce caused Mitchell to doubt his own conviction.

"Your God never wanted me, Pierce," Mitchell muttered. "What is it about me that He hates?" That was the burning question. Why did God hate Mitchell Caine?

He put the gear into drive and pressed the accelerator again. The vehicle bucked forward. He glanced down and saw the red light that indicated his emergency brake was still engaged.

Irritated, he released the lever and stomped the gas. The Envoy leaped forward like an eager racehorse, and Mitchell slammed the brake. His seat belt held him tightly against the seat, and for some reason this made him mad. It made him furious! A stupid inanimate object like this piece of material shouldn't be able to force his body where it didn't want to be.

He unsnapped his seat belt and breathed away the anger—one of his most constant companions lately, and one he regretted every time it found its mark. That happened far too often these days.

Almost as if there were a tractor beam inside that dinky car of Archer's, Mitchell turned left instead of right and followed in the preacher's wake, over the hill and into the water-filled dip in the street.

Mitchell had once attended the church where Archer now ministered so faithfully. He had endured months of sermons—Archer's father, Aaron Pierce, had been the pastor then. Darla and Trisha had grumbled about it every Sunday morning, but they had gone. Eventually the effort became too onerous and they stopped going.

Mitchell flexed his slightly numb hands, still aware of himself enough to realize that the typical "Tranquen fog" was settling more heavily over him and that he needed to get home instead of following those beckoning taillights and brooding about some other man's weakness.

And yet . . . what if Archer really did have some great cosmic answer to all this?

The car ahead of Mitchell signaled left. He was certain it was Archer's car, but he had to get home—the fog was increasing. He pressed the brake, intending to make a U-turn to head home, but as if drawn by an invisible hand, he followed the taillights onto the state highway that led out of town—a twisting ribbon of drenched blacktop.

Something about the taillights of that little tan car mesmerized him, made him curious, made him long for something he didn't have. He continued in its wake.

Archer pressed the brake and slowed at another dip in the road, where a small stream raced across the blacktop. Headlights streaked to his eyes from the side mirror on the passenger door. He tapped the brake a couple of times, hoping the driver behind him would take the hint and back off. He hated being tailgated at any time, but in driving conditions like tonight it was criminally stupid.

The hulking SUV behind him slowed down for a few seconds, and Archer increased his speed. The headlights flashed in his eyes again. That driver was far too close. Didn't he have any common sense? What was it with drivers these days?

As he followed a curve out of town and passed beneath a street lamp, the light fell just right, and he saw the outline of the vehicle behind him, even the silhouette of the driver. It was a sizable SUV, about the same shape and bulk of Mitchell's GMC Envoy, which had been parked in the lot at the hospital. Why would he be coming out this way? He lived in the opposite direction.

The headlights glared again as the driver once more pulled too close. Far too close. For a moment it looked as if he might make impact, and

Archer tightened his grip on the steering wheel.

When the SUV finally did back off, Archer couldn't relax. This was Friday night. Was he being stalked by a drunk driver?

Mitchell pressed the brake and felt the Envoy slide a few inches before the tires met the surface of the road. It startled him, because this big, heavy 4X4 should be having no trouble. The water must be deeper on this road than it looked. He took a breath and tried to concentrate past the increasingly lethargic synapses of his brain.

The bright red of Archer's taillights flashed, and Mitchell used that to help him focus. Another flash, and he gripped the steering wheel more firmly. Archer was obviously a cautious driver. He was probably also a kind driver, one of those guys who stopped to let people turn out onto the street ahead of them—one of those guys who actually left an opening in front of them when traffic was backed up past a side street, so the people on those side streets could get out.

The cozy thoughts about the friendly, compassionate preacher helped Mitchell settle more deeply into his seat. Archer wouldn't turn him away if he wanted to talk.

Another flash of lights. Once more Mitchell pressed the brake. His arms tingled, and he flexed his fingers again. The Tranquen was not working its usual magic. Instead, a thick, hot ooze of anger coalesced deep inside him, partnering with the effects of the drug. His animosity did not dissipate, rather it found a darker focus—hatred for the man who had haunted his thoughts these past few months. Hatred for his daughter's seducer.

The car ahead of him fishtailed, spraying water from a low place in the road. Mitchell pressed his brake pedal gently and slid through the same depth of water with ease as his gaze fixated on those taillights ahead of him. Every time they flashed, he braked. Every time they swerved, he allowed his foot to raise from the accelerator long enough to avoid hydroplaning. The world blackened around him except for those twin red lights, like devil's eyes glaring at him ... mocking him ... taunting him. Like Peregrine's eyes.

The hatred rushed through him like a living organism.

At the last moment, they flashed again, and Mitchell blinked from his stupor. It wasn't Peregrine in that car ahead. It was Archer Pierce.

"Bed," Mitchell whispered to himself. "I need a bed."

"Back off!" Archer shouted the words on a surge of panic at the drunk behind him. He tapped the brakes once more, but this time instead of backing off, the headlights just grew brighter, as if to force him forward.

"Are you crazy?"

It couldn't be Mitchell Caine. There had been no alcohol smell on his breath twenty minutes ago, and Mitchell would never do anything like this.

Swallowing the spot of raw panic that tried to seize control of his reactions, Archer tapped the brake pedal several times. He saw the marker for County Road 22 up ahead, and he flicked his signal. He'd take 22 back to town and double around onto Z after he got this bozo off his tail.

Thankfully, he saw the lights behind him recede. He slowed and took the turn at a safe speed, then followed the curve back along the winding county road. He sat back and took a deep breath.

The breath caught in his throat when the beams of those headlights once more attacked him from the rearview mirror.

Even worse, due to the high, narrow shoulders that funneled water onto the asphalt surface instead of away from it, this old road was notorious for accidents during wet weather.

Archer pressed his brake again, enough to flash the lights in the eyes of the driver behind him, to relay the message as clearly as possible that he needed to be careful.

What was a drunk driver doing out here?

The headlights glared again, closer still, so close that Archer flinched, bracing for impact.

That didn't happen. He retained a firm grip on the steering wheel and studied the road he knew so well from a lifetime of living in Dogwood Springs.

A hairpin curve loomed at the edge of the glow from his headlights, and a streak of lightning showed him what he'd expected—that far below the Black Oak River had overflowed its banks once again.

Another flash revealed how far past the banks the river had spread. The valley looked more like a lake than a river. It hadn't taken so long this time, because the ground was already saturated with water from previous storms.

In his thirty-four years, Archer had never seen so many changing weather patterns—and never had he felt so many storms in his own life. Maybe that was why he felt so ill at ease tonight with the careless driver hugging his bumper and beaming his headlights straight into the side mirrors.

Archer leaned forward to avoid the glare, unwilling to remove his hands from the steering wheel long enough to adjust the side mirrors—he didn't want to get caught unprepared. He tapped his brake again to warn the big SUV behind him of his intention to slow down. To his annoyance the other driver flashed his bright lights and didn't dim them.

Momentarily blinded, Archer pressed the brake harder than he'd intended. The car glided sideways.

He held his breath.

The car came to a stop near the cliff's edge. He caught a vivid view of the treetops—dogwoods and cedars reaching for him from the roadside.

Lightning flashed again and continued in a startling chain reaction.

It wasn't lightning. It was the arc of the headlights behind him as the SUV hit the water and hydroplaned straight toward him.

"No!" The reflection in the side mirrors temporarily blinded him. The jolt of bumper against bumper shocked him as his car lurched forward and pivoted in the mud. For one instant his own headlights revealed the face of the driver.

Mitchell.

The SUV slid sideways and rammed him again with the front grill. Archer pumped his brakes with no results. The earth gave way beneath his back tires. For a moment the car teetered on the ledge.

Archer tried to shove his door open with his left hand while releasing his seat belt with his right. The car shifted backward.

He had to get out of this car or he would plunge with it into the flooded river. He grabbed the seat to lever himself from the car, but he wasn't fast enough. The car flipped into an arc over the ledge of the cliff.

His seat belt released as rain drenched and blinded him. He shoved away from the seat and felt himself falling.

The car splashed into the river as Archer felt himself somersaulting into black empty air. He hit something hard, heard his own scream, felt himself tumbling like a lifeless rag into thick, oozing mud.

All went silent and black.

CHAPTER 15

Jessica arrived home at ten forty-three, still thinking about her conversation with her sister, still praying that she would make the right career decision.

Heather was changing, maturing. She still had a lot of issues to resolve, a lot more maturing to do, but she was getting there. Her heart was softening.

No lights greeted Jessica in the house, and she hadn't expected them. She turned on the porch light for Archer. Before leaving the restaurant, she had listened to the messages on the answering machine and heard about his decision to go to the hospital after he left the church. No surprise there.

Archer usually called about the time he knew she would be home after a show. If she was there and he could get away from a meeting or from the hospital, he did. If she didn't answer, he would often stay in the ER a little longer. She understood that he did this in order to juggle as many commitments as he could without leaving anyone out.

Ironically, that made her feel as if she was just one more obligation to him, though if he knew she felt that way, he would be hurt. It had almost become a sort of dark game to her—to be the last one home for the night. It made her feel less like the lonely wife pining after a workaholic husband and more like a lady in control.

She felt a slight nudge of irritation that Archer had won tonight's round—of a game he didn't know he was playing. She chafed at the very fact that it mattered to her. This wasn't a night for resentment and frustration—she already had enough to think about. If Archer's discussion with the deacons had gone well, there might even be reason to celebrate.

She stared out the kitchen window past the scattered droplets of rain, listening to the rhythm of the departing storm. She'd heard no weather report, but it had been a dark drive home from the theater, and she'd splashed through several low spots on the state highway that had an inch or so of water over them. Dogwood Valley—which surrounded the town on three sides—might well be flooded again. She had taken the route along the ridge, avoiding the valley road.

She paced back through the house to the front door, where she peered out the small square pane onto the reflection of the street light on the drenched blacktop. She wouldn't call the hospital like a nagging wife. She wouldn't try to dial his cell phone just yet, either. She'd done that in January and had caught him in the middle of prayer with a patient. Instead, she would relax on the living room sofa and wind down from the day's activity.

Soon. Archer would be home soon.

The rumbling threat of danger intruded at the black edges of Archer's consciousness. He tried to shift and sit up, but a knife jabbed his spine and sliced between ribs on his left side. His head pounded with pain so intense it nauseated him with his movements. His body felt encased in hardening plaster.

The roar of the river engulfed all other sound.

Tentatively, he reached down and touched the surface upon which he lay. Mud. The pain in his back most likely came from a rock or a limb beneath him—he hoped it wasn't more than that. He slid his fingers beneath his back, gritting his teeth, feeling for any object that might be causing his pain.

There was nothing.

Again, he tried to shift his body, and he cried out in agony as fire shot down his spine.

He caught his breath, panting to control the nausea, struggling to control his panic.

His eyes gradually adjusted to the darkness, and he saw the contrast of mist against the blackness of trees above. Moonlight filtered between patches of cloud. The rain had stopped.

Archer didn't know if he could trust what he saw.

One more time, slowly, with great caution, he raised his head from its muddy pillow and tried to raise his shoulders. Agony monitored every millimeter, and he eased back again. He managed to turn his head toward the rushing water and found he was lying on a mucky ledge that dropped with sharp abruptness into the river, which seemed to be about fifteen feet below.

He remembered the wreck, the car tumbling from the road. He remembered the SUV that pushed him, and he jerked his head toward the cliff. Another angry stab of pain streaked up his neck with such force his eyes burned with reflexive tears. A beam of headlights sliced through the gloom, and the relief made him giddy. It wasn't moonlight he had seen but rather lights from a vehicle.

"Is someone up there?" he called, then winced. His voice was lost in the roar of the river. "Help me!" he cried again in spite of the pain.

The image of a familiar face flashed through his mind, but for the moment he couldn't put a name to the face. "I'm down . . ." He grimaced.

He waited, remembering more, strobes of sound and movement, the crash of breaking glass, the powerful puff of the air bag, the scramble to remove the seat belt.

What happened after that? He'd apparently been unconscious for some time. How long?

The pain in his head, the difficulty with memory, probably meant a concussion, but how bad?

He'd spent enough time in the ER to know his concussion probably wasn't too bad if he could remember the accident.

Unfortunately, the pain made it obvious that he had other injuries.

"Hello! Is someone there? I'm down here!" Again the cry of pain tailed his words and he closed his eyes, blinking away the tears.

"Oh, God, help me," he whispered.

The familiar *thrum-thrum-thrum* of a nearby engine inserted itself into the flash of Mitchell's nightmare. Why was it so close?

His uncomfortable position on the bed had put a kink in his neck, and he shifted.

With methodical insistence, the discomfort and the unfamiliar sound jogged him to consciousness. He forced his eyes open.

For a moment he thought he was still fighting the dream, but the movement of the vehicle . . . the steady *thrum-thrum-thrum* that matched the gentle motion of an idling engine . . . the stream of head-lights that revealed tree limbs ahead of him—he wasn't in bed.

What am I doing here? How did I get here?

A pink dogwood blossom fluttered in the beam of his left headlight. Trees blocked his view, as if he'd parked in the middle of a copse of cedars and dogwoods. The console lights glowed the digital numbers of the time—11:20 P.M.

His head ached. He reached up to touch his forehead, felt a lump the width of a half dollar. He didn't have his seat belt on.

He always wore his seat belt.

The airbags hung flaccid, the transmission was still in gear, and those trees had apparently kept him from plunging over the embank-ment into the river. But the airbags had deployed. . . .

He tried to force his mind to clear, but it was as if some giant hand had plucked his truck out of the hospital parking lot and slung him here.

Or maybe he was truly still dreaming. Those tiny pills packed a con-siderable punch, and his dreams were often too realistic for comfort, especially when he took more than one.

Right now, all he wanted to do was go to bed and sleep this off. Maybe in the morning he could focus more clearly, but for now he just needed to be able to concentrate well enough to maneuver his way back onto the road, figure out exactly where he was, and navigate his way home.

He gripped the gearshift and put it into reverse. *Concentrate. Have to concentrate.*

———

After a long prayer and a quick shower, Jessica fixed herself a cup of tea and finally picked up the phone. Archer still hadn't made it home.

This wasn't like him. She dialed his cell number. She didn't care if it *did* interrupt a conversation or a prayer. He couldn't have been praying nonstop this long, and if he'd had any break at all he should have called her. He *would* have called. She knew him too well. She couldn't shake an uncomfortable sensation that something was wrong.

He didn't answer. After three rings, a voice came on the line, "The wireless customer you are trying to reach is unavailable at this—"

She disconnected. "Great, Archer," she murmured, "either your phone is turned off or you forgot to charge it again."

She dialed the church number and reached the recording on the fourth ring.

Next, the hospital ER. It rang six times before an unfamiliar voice answered. The call had been diverted to the main hospital switchboard. After being informed that they were busy in the emergency department at this time, she asked about Archer.

"Oh, the chaplain?" the girl asked. "I saw him earlier tonight. Didn't talk to him—I had too many calls at the time. Busy as they are back in the department, he might still be around. Is this his wife? Jessica Lane?" She breathed Jessica's stage name on a note of awe.

"Yes, this is his wife. I go by Pierce here at home," she said gently, hearing the buzz in the background of more telephones waiting to be answered. "Look, I know you're busy, I just wanted—"

"You want me to run to the ER and see if he's there? I could bring him to the phone myself, Mrs. Pierce."

Again the insistent buzz of other callers trying to get through to the busy switchboard operator. "No, there's no need. I just wanted to make sure he was safe."

"If I see him I'll let him know you called."

Jessica thanked her and disconnected. He would be home when he could get away. She shouldn't have panicked. Archer had been known to stay at the hospital all night after a bad accident. He even went to Springfield sometimes if a patient was transferred there. It wasn't protocol, since the larger hospitals had their own chaplains, but people attached to him easily. She could understand that. She was pretty attached to him herself.

Woozy with fatigue, she slumped onto the couch, crossed her legs, and rested her feet on the coffee table. The hospital must be really busy.

"Oh, Archer, if you only had forty-eight hours in a day. . . . If only both of us did."

She closed her eyes and said a quick prayer for God's wisdom in whatever situation Archer found himself. Then she pictured her husband's endearing face in her mind and thought back to before she'd met him.

Four years ago she had moved to Branson from Springfield in order to be closer to the Promise Theater, where she'd been a member of the cast and understudy for the role of Mary in "Two From Galilee." She'd met him at church six months later, where he was a youth minister.

He'd been busy then, but nothing like this.

Archer had a knack for showing God's grace simply by his loving attitude, and people were drawn to him. He didn't have the heart to turn anyone away. It was one of the things she loved about him—and one of the things that caused them the most trouble.

He was probably out there right now, using that loving spirit with someone who was hurting or frightened or alone. She could never take that away from him.

"Oh, Archer, please hurry home," she whispered as she drifted to sleep.

Archer awakened to the sight of the moon bleeding through a haze of mist that drifted into the beckoning fingers of the tree branches above him.

He shivered, glad he'd worn his wool suit coat to the deacon's meeting, glad the weather was a little warmer than usual.

The glow from the moon provided enough light for Archer to focus on his surroundings—what surroundings he could see without moving too drastically.

The reflection of light played across the surface of water that had spread out into the floodplain of the river—many feet higher than normal. The pale liquid luminescence bounced across the ripples . . . endlessly. There was nothing more, no opposite shore. Just flood waters. He remembered seeing the washed-out bridge and the river that had become a lake just before he turned from the highway.

Have to get out . . . have to get help.

But the pain was too much. Archer couldn't force himself to get up. Even if he were willing to risk permanent damage to his back—if it wasn't already permanently damaged—just the effort of attempting to raise up on his elbows caused him to cry out in agony. He wiggled his toes, ankles, tried to lift his legs. He gasped with pain that once more focused in the center of his back.

He rested as another memory snapped open in his mind, this time of hitting something solid and hard . . . a boulder? How badly was he injured? If pain was any indication, he could be in big trouble.

His head throbbed. He turned it slightly and felt the cooling effects of mud at the base of his skull.

"Dear God," he muttered, "help."

A rush of nausea struck him, and he fought it until the blackness of the night overtook him and he passed out once again.

Jessica awakened with a start and found herself lying awkwardly across the arm of the sofa, feet still braced against the coffee table. She sat up and gave her eyes time to adjust to the glow of the lamplight, grimacing at the pain in her neck and shoulders from the uncomfortable position. It took a few seconds to focus the blurred numbers on her watch.

Four o'clock.

She groaned and pulled herself from the sofa. She'd been asleep for hours. "Archer?" Maybe he'd come home and seen her asleep, and decided not to wake her.

"Honey?" She stretched and walked barefoot through the house, down the hallway to the bedroom. The door stood open, and she stepped from the residual halo of light from the living room lamp into the comfortable darkness, automatically listening for the sound of his breathing.

"Archer?" she whispered.

No answer.

"Archer?" She whispered more loudly as she turned on the overhead light.

The pale mauve and burgundy comforter lay as it had been when she first came home—which was the same way it had been this morning when she tossed it casually over the pillows. There was no indentation where he might have rested his head.

"Archer?" She glanced into the bathroom. "Honey?"

She pivoted and hurried back through the house to the garage. His car wasn't there.

She fought back panic. "Archer Pierce, where are you? What's going on?"

She searched the other bedrooms, the office, the back porch, the other bathroom, calling his name over and over, receiving no reply.

She searched the kitchen table and the coffee table in the living room for a note of any kind that would tell her where he had gone. Nothing.

Again, panic threatened to seize control of her thoughts. Again, she fought back. "Oh, God, please, where is Archer? He would have called by now if he could."

She continued her prayer under her breath as she picked up the telephone and dialed the number of the hospital emergency department. As usual at this time of morning, the secretary answered on the first ring, her voice cracking with the typical fatigue of the night shift.

"Becky? Hi, this is Jessica Pierce." She hesitated. What would happen when word got out that Archer Pierce's wife was looking for him at four in the morning? "I wonder, have you seen my husband in the past few hours? I got home late from my show, and it looks as if he might have been called out on an emergency." It wasn't a lie; he could well have been called out.

"Not for quite a while, Jessica." Becky's voice quickened with concern. "I saw him walk through last night when we were busy, but I don't know where he went. You're telling me he hasn't called you to let you know where he is? I'd tie him up by his toenails if I were you and—"

"Right now I'd just be relieved to see him. How bad was the storm in town last night? We didn't get much in Branson." She felt the tension tighten in a vise around the base of her skull. Here she was talking about the weather when—

"It was wild here for a while, and we've heard reports of flooding all around the area. The valleys and hollers were hit hard, and the old north bridge over the Black Oak River finally washed out—I'd been warning people that was going to happen someday."

"Was anyone hurt?"

"Some idiot tried to drive over a low water bridge and got stranded, but the fire fighters got to him about three this morning. His car's a goner, though."

"But it wasn't—"

"Nope, not Archer. He'd never do anything like that. That's all the emergencies so far. Some of the folks down on Ford Street are sandbagging around their houses. They didn't name that place Ford Street for nothing—you'd have to ford a lake to drive on it right now. Knowing Archer, he'd be down there helping if he could."

"You're probably right." That was exactly something Archer would be doing. So all this panic was probably for nothing. She would have a few words to say to *him* when he got home . . . after she smothered him with kisses, and told him how much she loved and admired him, and threatened him with bodily harm if he ever did anything like this to her again.

"Say, Dr. Sheldon just finished up with a patient. You want to talk to him?" Becky asked. "I can send your call to his office. He might know something I don't."

"Thanks, Becky, I'd appreciate it." Grant often worked the Friday night shift, and if anyone would know Archer's whereabouts, he would.

He, too, picked up on the first ring and listened as Jessica explained the situation.

"And you say he didn't leave a note or anything?" he asked.

"There was a message on the machine when I accessed it from Branson, but nothing informative. He just told me he was on his way to the hospital."

"Well, I sent him out into the country on an errand. Do you know where Mrs. Eddingly lives? She's down in the valley. If I'd known about the flooding problems I wouldn't have been so quick to let him go, but—"

"He went to her house?" Jessica knew the elderly lady. She lived so far out in the country that it took her thirty minutes to drive to church over the rough dirt roads, and when it rained a local creek sometimes cut her off from civilization.

"He could have gotten stranded out there," Grant said. "I think I heard her complain once that her phone line goes down every time it storms. Believe me, if he's out there he's as anxious to get ahold of you as you are to find him."

Okay, it was a reasonable supposition. Jessica silently blessed Grant Sheldon and his common sense. "Becky said the old bridge was out, but I know Archer is too sensible to try to cross it if there was water over it."

"If it would make you feel better, I'll call the police and see if there've been any updates on the storm damage, or a wreck or something."

"Thanks," she said, "but I'll call them myself. I'm sure he's just out helping the rescue people or something. You know he's an adrenaline junkie at heart."

Grant chuckled. "He'd have to be, or he wouldn't hang out here so often."

Jessica said good-bye and hung up, then immediately called the police. There was no further word about the flooding, but several residents down in the valley had been evacuated, and volunteers were helping sandbag some homes near the river. Since a major portion of Dogwood Springs occupied a hillside and ridge well above the flood lines, the problem mostly affected rural areas.

She paced through the house once more, then changed the announcement on their telephone recorder so that Archer would hear it if he called for her. Yes, with the flooding in the valley, he would be there to help. It was a waste of time and energy to pace and worry and fret about his safety while he was seeing to the safety of others. So she wouldn't pace; she would drive. She was going to search for her husband.

CHAPTER | 16

A chime of sound slid through the darkness of unconsciousness until Mitchell Caine slowly became aware of the disturbance. He didn't open his eyes immediately—the softness of the bed drew him back toward the comfort of oblivion. He hated mornings, and if he remembered correctly, this was Saturday. No clinic. No hospital rounds. His only in-hospital patient had been released yesterday afternoon.

As always, a fog hovered over his memory of the previous night. It had faded out somewhere in the middle of an interesting conversation with Archer Pierce, and he wondered what he might have said to the preacher this time. Eventually, some memories might return to him, but his drug of choice—though it served as a powerful sleep aid—had the unfortunate side effect of amnesia. A small price to—

The chime drifted to him again, and he frowned. Surely the drug wasn't playing havoc with his auditory sense. He occasionally dreamed musical notes, however, and his dreams were becoming more and more vivid in the past few—

The chime came once again, and this time he recognized it. The doorbell.

He forced his lids open and focused with difficulty on the lighted face of the clock. "Five-forty-five," he muttered. Why would anyone disturb him at this time of the morning?

A soft knock followed the chime, signaling that the visitor would not give up easily.

He dragged his body out of bed and retrieved his satin robe from his dressing chair.

Murky dreams—or were they memories?—hovered just past the edge of consciousness as he put on his slippers. Tranquen often caused nightmares, and he vaguely remembered a vivid one about red eyes blinking at him in the darkness.

He shook his head, winced at the pain, touched his forehead, felt the shock all the way up his arm. A goose egg? Had he stumbled and fallen during the night?

The doorbell chimed once more, and he walked down the silent hallway to answer it. He stepped into the marble foyer and touched the cold brass knob.

He drew back with a chill when another memory of the nightmare accosted him. Those flickering red eyes . . .

Impatient with himself, he opened the door, then gasped aloud at the sight of an emaciated young woman in dirty jeans and a wet T-shirt, dark hair plastered to her face and neck. Her pale blue eyes had dark circles beneath them that seemed to bruise her bony face with grief.

"Trisha?"

"Hi, Dad." She held up a torn plastic grocery bag, stretched to bursting with tattered clothing and toiletries. "I got kicked out of my apartment."

The sight and sound of her were so incongruous, he waited for her image to dissolve into the air.

She scowled at him. "Look, if you don't want me here just say so, but could I at least talk to Mom before I go?"

"Your mother?" Hadn't she been in touch with Darla, either? Was it possible she didn't know?

"Look, I'm sorry I woke you up, but—"

"I'm sorry, I wasn't thinking." It wasn't a dream—she wasn't an apparition. He stood back for her to enter. "Please, come in. I'm just so surprised to see you, Trisha."

She took a tentative step toward the open doorway, hesitated, then apparently decided he wasn't going to close it in her face. She moved as if she was almost too weary to take another step. He noted a smell not unlike a rat's nest as she pressed past him.

"How long since you left your apartment?" he asked.

"A few days." She dropped her bag on the marble entryway floor, crossed her arms over her nearly concave chest, and looked around the room like a starving child who had just stepped up to a buffet. "Wow," she whispered. "I missed this place. I can't believe it." She turned back to him. "Is Mom still asleep?"

"I . . . wouldn't know, Trisha. Your mother left months ago."

He expected her to be surprised by his words, but he wasn't prepared for the horror that cracked open across her face.

"I'm sorry. I thought you would know. I thought she would contact you."

Trisha didn't respond. Her face lost what little color it had, and her eyelids fluttered. Mitchell caught her just before she hit her head on the marble floor.

———

At six o'clock Saturday morning, Jessica returned from her drive to Branson—she had gone back to the theater, hoping desperately that Archer might have decided to meet her after the show and then developed car trouble.

She'd found nothing. Not a single sign of Archer's Kia.

She had even called the state highway patrol to see if there had been an accident in the area. Nothing.

She slowed down at the parsonage, saw no lights. She'd left three messages on the recorder and checked for messages all three times.

He wasn't there.

She drove on past the house.

"Oh, Lord, please . . ." Where was Archer? She had alternately shed tears, shouted in anger, and prayed, sometimes in a whisper, sometimes at the top of her voice.

She raised a hand to dash fresh tears from her face and angrily slapped the steering wheel again. "Stop acting like this!" she told herself. "It isn't going to help if you fall apart."

She battled fear with every word to God, but the comfort didn't come. It was as if her prayers weren't reaching Him, as if some thick cloud of oppression kept getting in the way.

Alone. She was alone. She needed a friend.

But who could she call? All her friends lived and worked in Branson, and it was too early in the morning to bother them—most of them had a show today or tonight or both. She couldn't call Heather and dump all this on her.

Jessica had always been the strong one. She couldn't fall apart now.

Dad? Could she call him? He would come if she asked him to, but what could he do once he got here?

Her best friend in Dogwood Springs—and due to her busy schedule and uneasiness with the church, her *only* friend—was Archer.

"Oh, Archer, I need you," she whispered. "Where are you?"

————

At six-thirty, Grant stepped into exam room three to find one of his favorite—and frequent—young patients sitting on the bed, swinging her legs back and forth, smudged with mud, as usual. Her frowning mother stood next to her.

"Haley Cameron, what have you done now?" Grant asked the child as he shook her mother's hand.

"Fell out of a window." The blond-haired twelve-year-old proudly held her left arm up for him to look at. "Think it's broken, or just sprained like last time?"

"I don't know. Do you want it to be broken?"

"Nope. Then I couldn't play baseball for two whole months."

"You should have thought of that before you tried to sneak out of your bedroom window," her mother scolded. She gave Grant a helpless look. "She knew her father was meeting with some buddies to go help sandbag down along the river near Ford Street. I told her she couldn't go, but she tried to slip out and go anyway."

Grant examined the arm. "Does it hurt, Haley?"

"It does when I wiggle my fingers." She did the deed. "Ow. See?"

Mrs. Cameron rolled her eyes toward the ceiling. "Her best friend broke his leg last week, and Haley has been green with jealousy ever since."

"He has a leg cast, though," Haley said. "He can fit more signatures." This child had an impudent grin, mischievous blue eyes, and usually a smudge or two of mud somewhere on her clothing. When she wasn't out riding four-wheelers with her father, she was playing football or baseball or soccer and driving her poor mother mad with worry.

"Think it'll need x-rays?" Haley asked hopefully.

Grant gently examined her left wrist. There was prominent swelling but no obvious deformity. "Yes," he said. "Think you could stand the pain if we have to reset it?"

"Bet I could."

"I bet you could, too. But I'll have to see the x-rays before we can know for sure."

"Can I have a copy of them? I could take them to school with me."

Mrs. Cameron rubbed her eyes wearily. "Why don't we wait and see if it's broken first?"

"We'll have it checked out soon," Grant assured them. From past experience, he knew Haley had high tolerance for pain and fear. She had once rescued her father from two attacking dogs and had driven him to safety on an all-terrain vehicle.

"Your family physician is still Dr. Caine?" he asked, checking Haley's chart.

"Yes," Mrs. Cameron said, "but does he have to be called?"

Grant stifled a smile. Since Haley already had a family orthopedist due to her accident-prone nature, they wouldn't need their family doctor's referral. "Not right away. I'll order the x-rays."

He stepped out of the room and found Muriel Stark coming toward him along the hallway. He glanced at his watch. "I thought you got off at six. What are you still doing here?"

"Emma called in sick. Eugene's due in at eight. I'm glad I caught you. Got a minute?"

"Yes, but first I need you to order an x-ray of Haley Cameron's left wrist."

"The req's already made out."

"Thanks."

"Dr. Sheldon, I know it's nearly seven, and Dr. Jonas will be here any time, but I need you to check out one of our chronic pain patients."

Grant suppressed a groan. "Chronic? Not an emergency?"

"Not this one." The soothing contralto tones of her voice softened. "Ordinarily I'd just let you visit with Haley, but this is a patient who would probably prefer to see you rather than Dr. Jonas."

He waited.

"Dr. Jonas might just blow her off, if you know what I mean."

"This is a chronic pain patient?" Grant knew Dr. Jonas to be a compassionate physician, but he had a reputation of intolerance for obvious drug seekers—and sometimes even those who weren't so obvious.

"Who's the patient?"

"Mimi Peterson, again."

Grant bit his tongue. Hard.

"I know about what happened Monday night, but Dr. Jonas was on duty when she came in Thursday, and he wasn't very nice. She was in tears when he left her exam room."

Grant had learned months ago to trust Muriel's judgment. "What do you think?"

"I think I'd like to wait and see what *you* think." She handed him the chart and he studied it. Same complaints as last time.

"How many times has she been here in the past couple of weeks?" Grant asked.

"This makes her fourth time."

He took the chart and moved to step around her, but she put a hand on his arm, her doe-brown eyes intent. "When Dr. Jonas saw her, he just ordered a pain shot and released her, never asked any questions, never gave her a word of comfort."

"You don't feel a shot was warranted?"

"I think she feels as if she's being shuffled from doctor to doctor because she's a nuisance, and she's frustrated. I get the feeling she's becoming a little emotionally unstable because of it."

Grant nodded. He had picked up on the slight emotional instability.

"Dr. Caine's her family physician."

"I know."

Muriel tapped his arm and lowered her voice. "To be honest with you, Dr. Caine and I have never gotten along, but a few years ago he could've figured out what's wrong with Mimi. I just don't think he cares enough to try anymore."

"This is an emergency department, Muriel," Grant said gently. "What makes you think I can figure out something Dr. Caine can't?"

"Well, it's a sure bet nobody else is going to do it. You might give Lauren a call, too. The patient asked for her when she first came in. Could be Mimi was more forthcoming with Lauren than she was with me."

He looked at his watch. Lauren was probably up by now—she was an early riser, even on her days off.

When he entered the exam room he could see what Muriel meant. Mimi's long narrow face was flushed from crying, and her short brown hair clung moistly to her forehead.

She did not look overjoyed to see him. "You again."

"Yes, sorry, it's me again."

She shrugged and looked away. "It doesn't matter. You can send me back out the door as well as anyone else. Whatever you do, don't call my family doctor."

Muriel entered the room and closed the door. "Mimi, did someone bring you here this morning?"

"No."

"Mimi," Grant said, "I'm sure your husband is a busy man, with the responsibility of the whole manufacturing plant, but have you ever asked him to go with you to the doctor? You could use the moral support."

Mimi's expression didn't change. "You're trying to say I need the mental support."

"No, but I do wish you had someone who could drive you home today in case I need to give you a pain shot."

"I took a taxi last time."

"So your husband works Saturdays?"

Her chin wobbled, and she looked away again. "My husband doesn't even know I'm here. He's dismissed me as a loony for the past year." She covered her face with her hands. "I can't tell him about this. I'm the whole reason we had to move here in the first place."

Grant sat down on the exam stool. "Muriel, would you see about our patient in three? I'll be talking to Mimi for a few moments. I'll call you when I need you." He might not have to talk to Lauren after all. He was off duty in a minute and a half, and he had some time. Maybe he could get a few more answers this time.

"Okay, Mimi," he said after Muriel left, "when you were in here before, we didn't have much interaction, and I believe you were upset about the fact that Dr. Caine didn't come in while you were here." He repeated the events as he understood them, and she agreed.

He asked a few more questions and discovered that one reason her husband had transferred to a smaller community was because of her inability to emotionally handle the stresses of their life in Little Rock. For a while her symptoms seemed improved, but then she started having the pain and nausea, and symptoms of colitis. Tears continued to trickle down her cheeks as she spoke.

Grant was beginning to pick up on some key points, but he wasn't there yet. It didn't sound like a problem with her gallbladder, but he would check it out with ultrasound. It could be appendicitis, but not likely. Chronic pain and illness could fray a person's nerves, but this patient had something else going on.

"How long have you been struggling with this?" he asked.

"Over two years, off and on." She fidgeted with her hair, wiped her brow, turned her head from side to side as if to stretch her neck muscles. "It comes in spurts, like maybe I'm eating something that doesn't agree with me."

"And you don't remember any specific illness or injury that might have precipitated the problem?"

"I was on a diet when I first started getting all antsy and upset, and I was afraid I'd gain my weight back."

"Obviously you didn't."

There was a hint of a smile that barely registered before it was gone. She shook her head. "I lost more weight."

"Mimi, what medications have you taken in the past two years?"

"You name it, I've been on it. One doctor prescribed some green liquid that was supposed to help me, but it just made it worse."

"Green liquid?" He named a popular GI cocktail with barbiturate, and she nodded.

"Dr. Jonas tried to give me the same stuff, and then he got huffy when I told him I was allergic to it, even though I had already told the nurse about it. Don't you people communicate in this place?"

"Sometimes it's difficult, but we try. Tell me about other medications you've been taking lately."

"Antibiotics for a chronic sinus infection," she said. "The pain's real, though, doctor. It hurts. Please don't tell me it's in my head."

"I'm not going to tell you that, but would you please allow me to run some additional tests on you?"

"Do these tests involve needles?"

"I'd like to check a few leads out first, but it will involve one needle, most likely. We'll make it as painless as possible."

She hesitated.

"Isn't the pain you're suffering worse than a little needle prick?"

She nodded.

He stood up and stepped out to get Muriel's attention. He was going to risk the displeasure of her family doctor, but he agreed with Muriel—there was something wrong with Mimi. He'd been fooled by drug seekers before, and he might feel stupid about this later, but he would feel worse if he overlooked a real problem and Mimi suffered because of it.

Jessica listened to the radio announcement as she pulled into the empty garage.

"If you don't have to go somewhere this morning, I would advise you to stay home and stay off the streets in Dogwood Springs," came Floyd Stewart's molasses-slow, gravel-bass voice over the car speakers. "Lines are down and roads are underwater all over the county, and the forecasters tell us we haven't seen the end of it yet. Unseasonably warm temperatures for April—"

Jessica turned off the radio and got out of the car, taking courage from Floyd's words. Of course she knew the roads were flooded in the valleys. She'd expected lines to be down, as well. Archer was stranded somewhere. It was obvious.

So why couldn't she believe that?

She stepped through the kitchen into the living room and sank down on the love seat. Fatigue and worry had subsided into numbness once more, but the numbness wouldn't last. She had given up on prayer about thirty minutes ago. Either God was ignoring her, or someone else was intercepting her words before they reached Him.

She couldn't "keep the faith." She couldn't do anything else on her own.

With a glance at the clock, she picked up the phone and grabbed the church directory. It was time to make some calls.

———

"Strep throat!" the crusty farmer exclaimed, though his voice didn't seem to carry through the whole department the way it usually did. "Doc, I don't have time to be sick, I've got a load of pigs to take to market tomorrow."

"I'm sorry, Mr. Scroggs," Grant said. "You have all the clinical indications for strep—"

"Guess that means you're gonna try to give me a shot in the butt."

Grant chuckled, looking at the patient's chart. "That would start you feeling better faster than the pills. You're not allergic to penicillin?"

"Nope. But I'm not bending over for no nurse. I want it in my arm."

"I'll advise the nurse about your wishes, but after that you're on your own." He jotted *Bicillin CR, 1.2 million units I M* onto the chart and reached for the door. Then he stopped and turned back.

"Mr. Scroggs, may I ask you something?"

"Spit it out."

"How's your neighbor doing?"

"Which one?"

"Mr. Brisco."

The first time Grant had met Brisco and Scroggs, they'd been feuding neighbors, fighting mad because of an automobile accident. Grant couldn't even remember which of them had caused it.

"Not too good." Mr. Scroggs cleared his throat softly. "Since his grandkid died, he's gone downhill."

Mr. Brisco's grandson, Oakley, had died of a methamphetamine overdose last December.

"Don't worry about him, though," Scroggs said. "If he don't snap out of it pretty soon, I'll hike over to his place and stuff some pig poop in his gas tank. That'll give 'im something to fight about."

"You do that, Mr. Scroggs. Meanwhile, I'll get the nurse in here so we can send you on your way."

After giving Muriel the order, Grant checked the x-rays on Haley's wrist, ordered an extra copy for Haley to show off at school, and returned to her exam room.

"We've got good news and bad news, my dear."

Haley scowled. "Is it broken?"

"Yes, but that's the bad news. The good news is that it isn't a displaced fracture, which means you'll get to wear a cast, but we won't have to set it."

He turned to Mrs. Cameron. "The break involves the growth plate. It's what we call a Salter-Harris fracture. We'll splint it today, but it'll have to be referred to Haley's favorite orthopedic surgeon."

"Dr. Bugs?" Haley brightened.

"Bugs?"

"He's weird. He talks like Bugs Bunny when he's trying to make me think he isn't going to hurt me."

"At least we won't have to contact Dr. Caine today," Mrs. Cameron said.

"Technically I should call him as a courtesy," Grant said.

Mrs. Cameron shook her head. "Last time Haley got hurt he called us at home and chewed us out. He doesn't realize Haley has a mind of her own—like a bulldog. I don't feel like getting another lecture."

Yet more evidence of that Mitchell Caine charm. "Since she already has an orthopedic surgeon, I won't call him, but he'll still receive a copy of the report."

"Fine, let them go to him," Mrs. Cameron said, "but I don't want to talk to him today. If he calls and gives us a hard time again, I wouldn't put it past Cam to go to his office and punch him in the nose."

Haley nodded, blue eyes solemn. "Can't I get my cast today? Nobody can sign their name on a splint."

"Well, I'll tell you what, Haley, since you're such a brave patient, I'll tell Dr. Bugs to give you one of those pretty pink casts."

She scowled. "No way! Pink's for geeks. How about bright red?"

He chuckled. "I'll see what I can do when I call him. Muriel will get you fixed up today, and I'll go ahead and write a prescription for pain medication."

"Won't need it," Haley said.

"Write the prescription, Dr. Sheldon," Mrs. Cameron said. "Just in case."

CHAPTER 17

Grant sat down at his desk and pressed Lauren's speed dial number. The phone rang four times before her machine answered. He heard his own voice advising him that he needed to leave a message after the tone.

When the kids gave Lauren a new answering machine for Christmas, Brooke had insisted they record the announcement with Grant's voice in case strangers called. With the drug culture that had seemed to permeate the town this past year, it seemed like a logical suggestion.

"Lauren, this is Grant. If you're asleep, I apologize." He knew that wouldn't be necessary. Lauren awakened at the first light of dawn. The kids teased her that she had a mind link with the fish. "When you get this, give me a call, would you? I'll probably be at the hospital at least until noon finishing up some paper work. I'd like your input on a return patient." He hesitated. He wasn't quite to the point of saying "I love you" on an answering machine that might announce his words to any of the McCaffrey clan who might be visiting and overhear his message. It wouldn't embarrass him, but it might put undue pressure on Lauren with her family.

Right now, for some reason, she wasn't being very communicative.

Ever since his proposal Tuesday night, she'd been unusually quiet, preoccupied. She didn't joke with the staff, didn't tease the patients, didn't take breaks with Gina. It wasn't like Lauren to isolate herself from others.

Still, she had a lot to think about.

Unfortunately, he'd had scarce opportunity to influence her thinking this week, because she'd worked two additional shifts for another nurse on vacation. It was frustrating.

He returned to the central desk. "Vivian, I'm waiting to hear from Lauren. If she happens to call when I'm not here in the department, would you page me? I really need to talk to her."

"Will do, Dr. Sheldon." The secretary didn't look up from her work.

On his way back to talk to Mimi, he passed Muriel in the hallway, rolling a syringe between her palms to warm the penicillin it contained. She grinned at Grant, nodded, opened the door to the examining room.

"Here we go, Mr. Scroggs. Get ready to feel better fast."

There was a grunt. "Guess he told you where to stick it."

"Yep, and I also heard him say it was my decision." Muriel's voice could be as tough as anyone's when she wanted her way. "Better undo that belt, pal. This stuff is the consistency of glue. I'm *not* sticking it in your arm."

Grant reentered the room where Mimi sat slumped on the side of the bed.

"How are you feeling now?" he asked.

"Better," she mumbled. "Thanks for the pain shot. Is that blond-haired nurse here? Lori . . . or Lauren?"

"Sorry, not today." He sat down beside the bed. "Would you like me to talk to your husband or another family member about the problems you've been having?"

She looked up. "Why?"

"Having the support of close friends and family can have a positive impact on your recovery."

"My husband says I'm just trying to get attention."

"Well, you have my attention. Let's see if we can't help you get well." He hesitated. "Mimi, we have a chaplain call system here at the hospital. I believe prayer also makes a big difference in the healing process, not only physical, but emotional. Would you like me to contact—"

"No. I can't stand the thought of some new stranger knowing about my business."

"That's okay, I understand, but if you should change your mind, let me know and I can put you in touch—"

"Does it have to be a minister?"

"For prayer, you mean?"

She hesitated, nodded.

"No, Mimi. I can pray with you. I'd be happy to."

Again, she nodded.

As he bowed his head Grant heard Scroggs' call through the door. "Hey, nurse! You sure you took that needle back *out*?"

———

"He's been missing since *last night*?" Mrs. Boucher, the church secretary, typically had a gentle voice, but this morning it shrilled over the receiver with considerable force. "Have you called the police? Didn't he go to that potluck deacon dinner at the church? Has he been to the hospital?"

"Yes, yes, and yes," Jessica said. "The last ones to see him were hospital personnel. The police have no reports on him, and I haven't tried to call any of the deacons yet."

"Well, those are the ones we need to contact. Jessica, I wish you'd called me last night. I bet you've been pacing the floor all night long."

"No, I really thought he might have been stranded at Mrs. Eddingly's house because of the flooding. Dr. Sheldon thinks so, too, and he still could be. I tried calling there, but her phone line is most likely down. I'm probably overreacting, and he'll either come walking through the back door any moment, or he'll call me—"

"Meanwhile it doesn't hurt us a bit to start praying. I'll start the prayer chain, and if anyone knows anything I'll have them call you directly."

Jessica thanked her and said good-bye, then sank down onto the sofa with an initial wash of relief. She didn't feel so alone now. Why hadn't she called Mrs. Boucher sooner?

The relief lasted for about sixty seconds. As she thought about it, the panic—which she had fought so hard to control during the night— threatened to overwhelm her. Mrs. Boucher had taken this so seriously. All the excuses, the possible reasons for Archer's absence, were beginning to weaken. She clung to the hope that he was stranded some-where, safe from the flooding.

But what if he wasn't safe?

She punched in the prefix of the next number on her list, then fal-tered, battling the effects of an extended overdose of adrenaline as nau-sea and dizziness attacked her. She replaced the receiver, forced herself to stand up and walk to the bathroom, splashed her face with cold water.

In the mirror she looked drawn, lips pale, eyes shadowed. Looking at her reflection, she could no longer ignore what she had struggled so hard to deny—she was terrified that something bad had happened to Archer. What if something totally unrelated to the storm. . . ?

Patting dry with a towel, she walked into the bedroom, where the bathroom light reflected against a plaque awarded to Archer by the city for providing drug awareness education to the teenagers in Dogwood Springs and the surrounding towns.

The amount of drug activity in this town had dropped with amazing speed since the drug bust at Christmas—and since Simon Royce's death. Because of the drug war, Sergeant Tony Dalton had been blinded in a booby trap last year.

What if someone had chosen last night to retaliate for Archer's role in the battle?

Jessica tried to dismiss the unreasonable fear, but at this point her imagination was attacking her with increasingly vicious intensity.

She picked up the bedroom telephone and punched the church num-ber for at least the tenth time over the past six hours. After the first ring the recorder picked up, and she heard her husband's deep, gentle voice relating information about office schedule, service times, and emergency phone numbers. The same old spiel.

She hung up, and her gaze fell to the silver-framed photograph of Archer on the nightstand on her side of the bed. She never tired of look-ing at those beautiful deep blue eyes, so filled with . . . life.

A knot moved from her chest to her throat. Archer would never leave her to agonize this way if he could help it.

She picked up the telephone and dialed Tony Dalton's home number. He was one of Archer's closest friends. She would remain calm. She would simply explain to Tony that she was an overreacting newlywed and would like to know if she could have her husband arrested for abandonment. Keep it light. Don't let him know how many times she'd thought the worst over the past few hours.

But then he answered with a sleepy voice after the first ring, and for a moment Jessica couldn't speak.

"Hello?" he repeated. The grogginess in his voice dissipated.

"Tony. It's Jessica."

"Jess? Is something wrong?"

She took a deep breath. "I need help."

There was a sound of movement, a surge of tension over the line. "What's wrong?" Tony became a police officer.

Mental visions Jessica had tried so hard to battle all night now thrust toward her with overwhelming force. Archer in trouble. Archer hurt . . . maybe even dead! Life without him. Her head suddenly felt too light for her body. She couldn't fight the fear any longer, not even for a few seconds.

"Please, God," she whispered. "Please, God, don't let this be happening." She was going to lose control.

"Jess, what's wrong?"

"Archer didn't come home last night." She paused, took a breath, forced herself past a wave of dizziness. She could no longer convince herself everything would be okay. As tears ran unchecked from her eyes, she spilled out her fears over the telephone.

———

Mitchell fried eggs and made toast and tried, time after time, to talk through a terminally dry throat. So far their conversation had been stilted. What was he supposed to say? Welcome home?

This wasted young woman slumped at his dining room table wasn't the beautiful child who had grown up under this roof.

Trisha had refused to step foot in this house for three and a half years. The drug addiction, the pregnancy, possibly even countless abortions had transformed his daughter into a wasted skeleton with track marks instead of jewelry on her arms. Instead of looking like a young woman nearing her twenty-first birthday, she looked . . . old.

He placed the toast on the table. The bread had been in the freezer for weeks. Since Darla left, he ate out most of the time. "You're probably hungry," he said. "I can cook more eggs." He put a glass of milk in front of the silent wraith and returned to the stove.

"No."

He looked back at her. After she fainted, he had revived her, checked her over physically, forced her to drink some orange juice. Then he had carried her to the guest bedroom and let her sleep. She had wandered into the kitchen only moments ago, bleary-eyed and silent.

Now she just stared at the food in front of her. "My bedroom . . . isn't mine anymore."

He nodded and pulled a chair out, then hesitated, unwilling to sit down across from her and endure that dead stare. "Your mother took the furniture when she moved out."

Trisha winced and hunched down further in her chair, not moving to pick up a fork or knife, ignoring the food. "She took my stuff?"

"She didn't tell you?"

"I don't even know where she is."

He sat down then. "Trisha, how long has it been since you spoke with her?"

She gave a one-shoulder shrug. "I don't know . . . a few months."

"Did she know where you were? I can't believe she would leave you to wonder where she was, not after—"

"You think I'm lying?" Trisha snapped.

Steel met stiletto and clashed. She definitely had his sharp tongue and icy stare. What father wouldn't be proud?

He waited until Trisha looked away. "What I'm saying," he replied quietly, "is that your mother made you the focus of her life for twenty years. When I refused to allow her to drain our bank account dry—"

A snort from Trisha pricked his temper, and he waited until she was acceptably silent for several seconds before continuing. "All I'm saying is that your mother sold some of her good jewelry in order to send you money every month."

"She shouldn't have had to do that!"

"You're right for once. At the age of twenty, if you hadn't destroyed the last four years of your life, you might be in college, focusing on your future—in whatever career you might have chosen." He felt another rush of frustrated rage at the rebellion that had destroyed her.

He needed to calm himself. It would do no good to fight her. She might even be under the influence of some illegal drug right at this moment. This wasn't the right time.

"And since I didn't finish school like a good little girl, you cut me off," she said.

Pricked again, he snapped, "I didn't cut my daughter off. I cut off a drain of drug money that went straight into my daughter's destruction in the form of methamphetamine. I tried to cut off the flow of poison that murdered my own *granddaughter*."

She sucked in a hard breath.

He bit back the angry flow of words, wincing at the look of shock on her face. He must calm down, find some kindness somewhere, or he would destroy any chance he would ever have to repair the damage that had shattered this family years ago.

Trisha hugged her frail arms around her skeletal body.

Mitchell forced himself to breathe deeply, to look away from the sad specter of what could have been. He could at least try to prevent further fractures. Until Trisha arrived, he hadn't even expected this opportunity.

"Your mother—" How he hated the woman right now. He deeply resented the necessity of repairing Darla's reputation for her own daughter's sake. But *for* Trisha's sake it was a necessary evil. "Misguided as she was, your mother went to a great deal of trouble to see that you received money every month."

Tricia gave a garbled snort. "Sure. To keep me out of her hair, stifle her conscience."

"You can't have it both ways, Trisha. Are you telling me you resent your mother for sending you support money every month, and that you also resent me for withholding what I knew to be your drug money?"

"That's right, stick me in the middle of your little tug-of-war with Mom."

Mitchell grasped the table edge. Darla's preoccupation with and sick attention she had paid to their daughter were what had caused this whole mess in the first place, and all the brat could do was blow her mother off? And him? She'd never grown up, in spite of the years that had passed. She was still that spoiled child whose only concern was for her own—

"Where will I sleep?" Trisha asked.

Mitchell studied a worn hole in the shoulder of her T-shirt. She belonged on the doorstep, like the beggar she had become. "You can use the guest room. Forgive me if I sound like your mother, but your food is getting cold." He heard the emptiness of his own words, and yet he knew nothing else to say right now. There were so many questions he wanted to ask her, but if he did, wouldn't she just grab her grocery bag and flounce back out the front door?

Yet, how could he possibly say, "Trisha, I've missed you. Our lives flew apart when you left with that drug pusher, and nothing has been the same since." She would accuse him of trying to put her on a guilt trip.

He knew things had been wrong in their lives long before that.

He pushed back the wave of regrets and watched his daughter's shaking hand as she picked up her fork and smashed the yolk into a runny mush. She mashed it again and again, then dropped the fork with a clatter and pushed back from the table with her hand over her mouth. She ran from the dining room to the bathroom down the hall, slammed the door. Through the heavy wood he could hear her retch.

He hesitated, then followed, knowing his presence would not be welcomed, but knowing, also, that if he didn't go his silence would convince her he didn't care.

For too many years, he'd cared too much, until he realized that his love for his daughter, and his indulgence of her every request, had done nothing to induce her to love him. Paradoxically, when he attempted to apply discipline it only fostered her anger, even hatred. He'd long ago run out of ideas about how to be an effective parent.

As he walked down the hallway he caught sight of a streak of mud, in the shape of a footstep, coming from the garage. The incongruity of it dislodged all other thoughts for a brief moment, brought to the surface some shadowed memory . . . a nightmare? When Trisha had arrived first thing this morning he had been awakened from the grip of a horrible dream of confused images and sounds.

Such things weren't unusual, unfortunately. Even as the medication produced temporary amnesia, it also induced nightmares. One thing that pricked his conscience lately was the fact that he often didn't wait till he got home before he ingested his first small tablet. In fact, he had done the same last night—he even remembered taking two tablets before he left the hospital, which hadn't been advisable considering the concentration he had known he would need to drive safely home.

He vaguely remembered a brief surge of irritation at . . . someone.

Grant Sheldon? No, wait, it had been Archer Pierce going through his prayer routine in one of the exam rooms with a patient.

Archer Pierce . . . yes, and they'd spoken afterward, but Mitchell couldn't recall what had been said. Most likely one of their typical arguments about the sufficiency of Archer's God. From there, everything grew fuzzy.

At the sound of the flushing toilet, Mitchell returned his attention to his daughter. The least he could do was make sure she was physically okay.

———

Dad and Heather had driven to Dogwood Springs as soon as Jessica called them—although in separate cars—Dad from the farm near Kimberling City and Heather from Branson. Dad had gone immediately to comb the town for signs of Archer.

That was Daddy, always burying himself in work and always doing what needed to be done. He had never been comfortable around a lot of people, but he really liked Archer. Who didn't?

He had just driven away in his old pickup truck when Heather pulled her five-year-old Camaro into the driveway like a jet on a short landing strip. She jumped from the car and came running up the sidewalk, golden blond hair flying behind her.

When she reached Jessica on the porch she grabbed her in a hug. "Oh, Jess, I can't believe this! Have you heard anything more?"

"Nothing." Jessica relished the strength of her sister's embrace. "Thanks for coming."

"Was that Dad's truck I saw driving away?" Heather glanced down the street, now empty of traffic.

"Yes, he's going to drive through town, then take a couple of routes

Archer might have taken to get to Mrs. Eddingly's. He's got those old binoculars he uses to check the cattle."

"Just like Dad to think of something like that."

Jessica heard the tone of grudging admiration in her sister's voice. "Why don't you tell him that next time you see him?"

"Sure, sis, we'll talk about that later. Right now you don't have time to worry about my feud with Dad."

Jessica took her sister's hands and drew her to the wicker chairs at the far end of the porch. "Have a seat. I need to ask you something, and I didn't want to ask you over the telephone."

"Okay, sis, shoot. I'm here for you."

"Do you think I should cancel tonight's show, or can you do it by yourself if Archer doesn't come home?"

Heather's hazel eyes widened. "You're not kidding?"

"I'm not in a kidding mood."

Heather stood up and shoved her hands into the rear pockets of her jeans. She paced the length of the porch, then turned back and nodded. "I'll do it for you."

"I know you'd love to have your own show. This might give you an opportunity to see what it's like without having to commit."

"I wouldn't want my own show like this, Jessie. Never like this."

"I know that."

"And I want to see Archer come walking up the sidewalk."

"It's what I'm praying for." Jessica's voice caught. *Don't fall apart in front of Heather.*

"Do you really think I can do it?"

"You know all the songs, and the audience loves you."

"But it's you they come to see."

"It's our music, Heather, and we do that together."

Heather crossed the porch again and hugged her. "Then don't you worry about a thing, Jess."

"Could you call Lawrence and James at the theater and let them know about the change? Explain the situation to them?"

"Sure. What are you going to do now?"

"I'm going to go look for Archer myself."

"Not without me."

The telephone in the house interrupted, and at the same time Jessica's cell phone chirped.

"You grab one; I'll get the other," Heather said. "And then I'm going to spend some time with you, at least for a little while. I'm not leaving you alone until I have to."

Jessica was surprised by the relief she felt at her sister's words.

CHAPTER | 18

L auren drew back her pole and cast the line far out to the center of Rock River the same way she'd been casting for the past thirty years. It was right here on this rocky ledge, under Grandpa's gentle tutelage, that she'd first learned to catch her own dinner. She loved the feeling of tranquility that bathed her with renewal every time she glimpsed the beauty of God's early springtime handiwork set against a backdrop of a milky blue Missouri sky.

Today, the solitude of this place had drawn her all the way from Dogwood Springs, an hour's drive. It had drawn her past the turnoff to Knolls, which had been home to her for 35 years. She desperately needed this peace, away from old and new friends, away from family.

Away from Brooke. Lately, on an average of two Saturdays a month when the weather allowed, Lauren and Brooke actually went fishing together, and except for Brooke's complaints about the cold, the heat, the slimy fish, and the gross bait Lauren used, she could be a lot of fun. Lauren enjoyed her company, and the two of them had grown very close, talking "girl talk."

Today, however, Lauren had chosen to come alone, because if she knew Brooke, the conversation would have focused on marriage. Of course, that was all Lauren thought about lately, but she did not need to spend a morning debating Brooke about it. She only hoped it didn't hurt Brooke's feelings too much when she discovered she had been intentionally excluded from this fishing expedition.

Solitude was not a word Brooke understood.

The need for some quiet time alone, out of reach of a growing list of people who made demands on Lauren's time and her heart, had made her irritable lately, and she didn't like being that way.

She recalled her last argument with Mom.

"Lauren, they're looking for a nurse director at the hospital emergency department right here in Knolls."

"That's nice, Mom. They shouldn't have any trouble filling the position."

"It sure would be good to see you more often. I told Dr. Bower I'd let you know about the opening, just in case."

Lauren scowled at the heavy hint. "Lukas doesn't do the hiring there, and—"

"No, but I'm sure he'd put in a good word for you if—"

"Mom, I'm not a nurse director, and I don't want to be." Lauren regretted her sharp tone, but sometimes she found herself reverting to adolescence when Mom pushed too hard. "I love my job at Dogwood Springs." Most of the time.

There was a short period of disappointed silence, then, "So how's it going with Grant Sheldon?"

Lauren reeled in her line and cast again, chuckling as she recalled Mom's frustration with lack of details about the romance. Mom was only the leader of the pack. Every single member of the McCaffrey clan had high expectations for Lauren and Grant.

How could anyone miss the hints they had dropped lately, like sledgehammers into the middle of conversations: *"Lauren, those teenagers need a mother before they run wild, and you're so good with them." "Lauren, you're not getting any younger." "Lauren, your mother keeps talking about how she'd like another grandchild."*

She refused to allow others to dictate her future, but she needed to be able to separate their wishes from her own, and from God's will. Too many clamoring voices tended to make her rebel in the wrong direction.

She loved the Sheldons—not just Grant, but Brooke and Beau, too. For the past few months she had worked to ignore an inner voice that reminded her that she would never be Grant's first love and the children would never be her own. In all the years she'd spent dreaming about love and marriage, she hadn't envisioned herself marrying someone who already had half a lifetime of family memories.

She knew it was selfish of her to think that way.

She knew she could never take Annette's place in the lives of her children, and she didn't want to. Annette had left a wonderful heritage for Brooke and Beau to follow.

But if I couldn't be a mother to them, what would I be? Just a friend? A buddy? If she married Grant and moved in with them, would she feel like an interloper?

She'd heard enough horror stories about the difficulties of learning to live with a new spouse; how many times would that difficulty be multiplied connecting with three people instead of just one? And at her age . . .

But she loved them. Didn't that count for something?

The internal argument hadn't let up since Grant proposed, and Lauren knew she had to get everything settled in her own heart before she committed herself to the decision.

The Sheldons had suffered a horrible tragedy with Annette's death three years ago, and they deserved the best. Yes, they needed someone in their lives. Was she that person?

Too many questions had combined with the voices of a strong-willed family to create chaos in Lauren's ordinarily peaceful life.

She leaned back on the stump and focused on the line where it entered the water. Even the weather here had been peaceful recently—nothing like the storms at Dogwood Springs. She was going to enjoy this tranquility for as long as it lasted.

Grant leaned back in his comfortable office chair and closed his eyes for a moment as the words and numbers on the page in the center of the desk gathered into a jumble. He listened to the chatter of a nurse and secretary with Dr. Jonas out in the ER workstation.

After fifteen hours in this place he was getting sick of it, but he needed to catch up on some administrative duties that had come to his attention: there was a problem with a chart and with the doctor who had signed it. Unfortunately, he'd seen the name Mitchell Caine on too much disorganized documentation lately. Mitchell needed to be warned or he could set himself and this hospital up for a malpractice suit.

Grant was only too aware, from recent experience, that all it took to be sued was a bad patient outcome, no matter how excellent the medical care had been. If a physician or nurse didn't document every word, every treatment, every observation with meticulous caution, they could all be in trouble.

It had become glaringly obvious recently that several of Mitchell's late-night handwritten notes were practically unreadable, and although that wasn't a rarity in the medical profession by any means, Mitchell had a reputation for precise record keeping—unless something was bothering him again.

The last time Grant contacted Mitchell about a sloppy report, Mitchell brushed it off, ignoring written requests in his mail slot to discuss the situation. Grant had no reason to believe this time would be any different.

He picked up the phone and punched Mitchell's home number, got a recording—which almost always happened on weekends lately—and left a message for Mitchell to contact him. He disconnected the line and hit the speed dial number for Lauren's home phone, since she had been on duty at the time this patient came in.

Answering machine again.

He could already tell this was going to be one of those Saturdays when he got very little accomplished. He left a message for Lauren to call as soon as she got home, then dialed Archer Pierce's number. As it rang, he glanced out the window and saw William Butler walking with Muriel Stark toward her car, parked in the employee parking lot.

Someone other than Jessica answered the telephone. "Hello?"

"Hello, this is Grant Sheldon. I just wanted to call and see if anyone has heard anything from Archer yet."

A heavy sigh. "Not yet, Grant. This is Heather. I'm just trying to keep Jessica from traipsing out into the countryside all alone looking for him. From the looks of her car, she already drove it everywhere short of the river itself last night. Right now we're fielding calls from church members. Nobody's seen or heard anything yet, but apparently several members have lost telephone service. You know—some of those people out in the deep boonies. Our father's the same way—oops, Jessica's taking the phone away from me. Nice talking to you!"

Outside, Will kissed Muriel briefly on the cheek, held her car door for her, and closed it when she got in.

Jessica came on the line. "Grant? Nothing yet. I don't suppose you've heard from Lauren? I tried to call her earlier and—"

"I know, I just tried her house. I think she would have let me know if she'd planned to be gone long, so I'll try her again later."

"I doubt she knows anything, but I just thought, since they've been friends forever, she or her brother might have some ideas I haven't thought of yet. If she knew Archer was going to be delayed getting home, she would have called me. In fact, *he* would have called, unless . . . Oh, Grant, I'm really worried."

"I know, but it isn't time to panic yet. Tony Dalton called me. He and I agree that Archer is probably stranded out in the 'boonies,' as Heather calls it, and you know he's notorious for letting his cell phone battery get low."

"You're right. I know you're right. It's just that I keep thinking the worst one minute, and then the next minute I find myself expecting him to come walking in the door, full of apologies and explaining the whole thing."

"I understand that," Grant said. "Archer has quite a few friends on the police force, and maybe they'll have some ideas. That way, if he doesn't turn up in the next few hours, the search wheels will already be in unofficial motion. Tony says he has some men out scouring the town already."

"Some people from the church have already started searching for him, too," Jessica said. "Actually, we're received word of fourteen people, but until the floods recede there's no way to reach Mrs. Eddingly's."

"Make that sixteen searchers. Brooke and Beau will want to help, and they'll probably contact some of their friends."

There was a thoughtful silence. "I have a friend in Branson who flies a helicopter for tourist rides," Jessica said. "I think I'll give him a call. Thanks, Grant. I'll let you know when we hear something."

"I'll stay in touch."

When Grant hung up, he noticed that William Butler continued to stand in the employee parking lot, hands in the pockets of his jacket, staring toward the road as if deep in thought. Grant thought he knew what might be going through Will's mind, as the same thoughts had gone through his own more and more lately.

Marriage could be such a wonderful thing.

"I'm not sure I'm cut out for this, Lord," Lauren murmured as she carried tackle box and fishing pole farther down the creek. "Is love enough? Don't I need some kind of special training to even *consider* becoming a stepmom to two seventeen-year-olds?"

Still muttering her prayer half under her breath, as she often did when alone, she sat down on an old favorite tree stump her grandfather had used when he was still alive. "I just don't understand how everyone can take it so casually. 'Oh sure, marry the guy. You can work it out—no problem,'" she said, mimicking what some of her co-workers had been telling her for months. "I don't know how they can think that way."

She settled her carefully organized tackle box at her feet and took her backpack from her shoulders and rested it against the stump. "More important," she continued, "is this your will, or just my want?" She sighed and gazed across the placid surface of this area of the creek, remembering her last solitary creek-side chat with God—no, that hadn't been just a chat, it had been desperate, urgent prayer for her life last summer. She had become suddenly, violently ill, too weak to make it back into the truck and drive for help.

"I need your input now as surely as I needed it last summer, Lord."

These past few months, Grant and his kids had drawn her with increasing insistence and warmth into their hearts, into their lives. With this additional relationship, she didn't feel torn, but she did feel stretched.

Even here, however, in her favorite retreat in the whole world, she couldn't seem to separate herself emotionally from commitments. She'd become overcommitted at church—a habit of hers for years. She loved working in the church, even helping Archer visit and check on people who had been patients in the ER, but she would need to back away from some of those commitments if she married Grant. A family took time and attention.

She also needed to consider the fact that Grant's mother, who was in the beginning stages of Alzheimer's, would need attention. And Lauren's own family, large as it was, put a lot of demands on her time.

She sighed. Though still single at thirty-six, she'd seldom been bored, just lonely for the kind of companionship she and Grant now shared.

To her surprise, it occurred to her that she was enjoying their relationship exactly the way it was right now. She had the best of both worlds. Why change anything?

Because Grant and Brooke and Beau needed more.

Did she have more to give?

Something nibbled at the bait of chicken liver. She gave an expert jerk—not too hard, not too gentle—to set the hook. She could tell before turning the reel that an underwater thief had escaped with her bait.

She shrugged and hauled in the line. No problem. She had a bucket of bait and a whole day to squander. She might even build a fire and cook any fish she caught, enjoy the sunset, and take a leisurely drive back home. This could turn out to be a great day.

———

Grant hung up the phone after still another frustrating attempt to contact someone on a Saturday morning. He would know better next time. Besides, he needed some sleep, because he was getting tired and cranky, and—

"Sounds a little odd to me, that's all I'm saying, and I'm not the only one who thinks it."

The faintly irritating female voice drifted into the office from somewhere nearby, and he recognized the speaker not only by the shrill tone, but also by the typical topic of conversation—someone else. Hospital grapevine. Fiona Perkins was the lifeblood of gossip at this place.

"You know Archer and Lauren are *both* missing, don't you?" Fiona continued. "I knew about them last summer. They had a thing going, I could tell."

Grant cringed at the insinuation. Growing more irritated, he got up from his desk and investigated. The vent between this office and the storage room next door had been redirected at his request, and sound no longer carried between rooms.

" . . . can't find Archer, can't find his car?" the voice continued. "Come on, Vivian, get a clue. He couldn't take the pressure anymore. I heard there was trouble between him and Jessica Lane from the very beginning over Lauren. That's what broke them up last summer, you know."

"No" came the secretary's chilly reply. "I didn't know. And where did you get your information?"

"Hey, where were you last summer? Everybody in the hospital knew about them, and you know how many of our people go to church there."

"And do you really think they'd still be going to that church if this stuff were true?" Vivian's voice held an edge now.

Fiona snorted. "Why not? Everybody does it—why not the preacher?"

Grant caught sight of the culprit. Plump, black-haired Fiona stood leaning against the counter of the central desk, her phlebotomy tray beside her. She had her back turned to him.

"It happens all the time," she continued happily. "Those preachers are the worst. Remember that guy in Springfield a couple years ago? You know, the one who made the news?"

Vivian's gaze barely flicked to Grant as he stepped out the door, and then she turned her focus back to Fiona. "Do you have any idea how many preachers there are in all of Springfield?" Vivian's voice was a little snippier now, and a little louder—a tech and a nurse paused to look at her. "Hundreds. But do their long years of service and fidelity make the news? Very seldom. People are always eager to point fingers, but when you start talking about people I know and care about, you'd better get your facts straight, missy." She turned her attention to Grant. "Heard enough, Dr. Sheldon?"

Fiona stiffened and turned, her blue eyes wide with surprise. "Oh. Hi, Dr. Sheldon. I thought Dr. Jonas was on duty today."

"He is." Grant covered his irritation with a tight smile. "Did you have a patient to see, Fiona?"

She took the hint and picked up her tray. "No, but I guess I could get back to the lab."

She turned to go, and Grant escorted her to the door. He could feel the attention of several of the staff, and he saw Vivian nod with approval. He didn't want to humiliate this young woman in front of a crowd, but he couldn't let her get by with this. Mitchell Caine had complained about her in the past and had nearly gotten her fired when he was chief of staff last year.

Grant held the door for her as she stepped out into the hallway, then continued to walk beside her. "Fiona, I believe you've been an employee here long enough to understand the code of personal respect medical personnel should have for their patients and co-workers."

"Sorry, Dr. Sheldon. I didn't know you were—"

"It doesn't matter whether you thought I was listening or not. What matters is the disregard you showed for someone else's privacy. Whether it's regarding staff or simply citizens of this town, confidentiality is vital because at any moment one of those people could become a patient, and then confidentiality is the law." He stopped at the lab entrance.

Fiona escaped into the lab and didn't look back.

———

Jessica drove the circumference of Dogwood Springs, watching for her husband's tall athletic frame wherever she saw people working to clean up after the flood. Her sister rode shotgun and was presently in the middle of a call to the helicopter pilot who was searching for Archer's car from the air.

"I see." Heather sounded disappointed, and Jessica's fingers automatically clenched the steering wheel. "Well, thanks for looking, Tom. Yes, if you see anything would you please call this number?"

She disconnected, sighed. "Archer never made it to Mrs. Eddingly's."

"Did Tom see anything as he flew over?"

"He said no, but he's going to search a little longer. Another storm front's coming in, he said, so he'll have to go back in soon."

Jessica let a tiny groan escape.

"Mrs. Eddingly is doing fine, by the way. Tom took her the inhaler. He said she refused to let him fly her out. She didn't want to leave her animals."

For a moment, Jessica couldn't force herself to respond. She could barely concentrate enough to continue driving. She shoved the frightening thoughts away. *Don't go there.*

As she neared the bottom of the hillside, she saw a group of men stacking sandbags around a house at the end of Ford Street. Among them was muscle-bound Kent Eckard. If Archer were here, he would stop and help.

Archer. *Oh, Archer.*

"Jess?" Heather said softly. "You need me to drive?"

"No."

"Are you okay?"

A deep breath. "No, I'm not." He had to be out there somewhere. Alive.

Jessica turned onto Highway Z and drove uphill once more, to the section of land for which the city had been named. Atop this ridge, dogwoods bloomed on both sides of the road. Archer loved this spot.

"This is his most likely route," Jessica said. "Unfortunately, the bridge is washed out three miles ahead, so we can't go past that. If Archer's stranded between the bridge and Mrs. Eddingly's, it'll be hard to search right now because so much of the valley is flooded. He could be—" Her voice caught. Again, she clenched the steering wheel. Hard. "He could be anywhere."

"Exactly, sis, and that's what you need to remember. Maybe he took a different route to try to get to her house."

"I'm glad she's okay." *If she'd remembered to take her inhaler in the first place, Archer wouldn't have been out in the storm trying to get it to her.*

Immediately, Jessica regretted her unkind thoughts.

Still . . . if Archer hadn't been out in the storm running another of the millions of errands his church expected of him . . .

His church.

Two vehicles were parked alongside the road up ahead—one a

pickup truck with a volunteer fire department siren light mounted on its dash.

"Looks like there's some people searching for Archer," Heather said.

The Black Oak River had overflowed its banks sometime last night. Jessica slowed as she neared the vehicles.

"But I thought the bridge was farther up the road," Heather said.

"It is, but the river surrounds Dogwood Ridge on three sides. The ridge is shaped like a peninsula, with the road curving down into the valley at the tip. We could park anywhere along here and walk to the river."

"Then let's do it," Heather said. "I know you won't be satisfied unless we at least check it out. Park here, Jessie." Heather indicated the roadside in front of the truck.

Jessica parked. As soon as they stepped from the car they heard the roar past the line of trees. They followed a trail of footprints in the mud and descended down the side of the ridge through a thicket of cedars.

When they emerged at the other side of the thicket, they stopped. Jessica stared in horrified awe.

Heather whistled softly. "That isn't a river, it's a lake."

Jessica stared across the surface of muddy, debris-filled water that mingled with the reflection of ever-darkening clouds. *Oh, Archer. If you got trapped in that . . .*

She scrambled down a gentle slope toward the river's edge. Voices reached her from upriver.

" . . . not gonna find anybody in this mess, specially with the water level rising so fast."

"Just keep on looking. You never know."

"Nobody here anyway, you ask me."

"Didn't ask."

"Think he just couldn't take the pressure and ran off with that pretty blond nurse? Heard stuff about them last summer. Know what I mean?"

Jessica stopped. Behind her, Heather caught her breath. Audibly.

"*What?*" Heather exclaimed. "That *jerk!*" She started to move past Jessica. "Hey!" she shouted, loudly enough for the whole hillside to hear. "Watch your dirty—"

Jessica grasped her arm. "No, honey, don't say anything to them. At least they're looking. Come on, let's walk the other way."

"But that's—"

"Please, Heather. Let's just go upriver. You've got to watch your voice, you know. You're on by yourself tonight."

Her sister relented at last and fell into step behind Jessica. "They were talking about Lauren, weren't they?"

"They don't know *what* they're talking about. It's nothing but silly small-town rumors."

"What rumors?"

"It's nothing." But where was Lauren?

"You'd think they'd be a little more respectful of the—" Heather caught herself.

Jessica stopped.

"Oh, sis, I'm sorry. I didn't mean I thought he was dead, I meant—"

"I know what you meant."

A rumble of thunder startled her. Lightning divided gray thunderheads to the west, much closer now. One of the men downriver muttered something about more flooding.

Jessica pressed through a thicket of weeds and stopped at the shoreline.

"Hey!" called someone from above them. "You down there! Better get back to the road."

Jessica looked up to see a man in hunter-orange rain gear.

He gestured to the sky when he saw he had her attention. "Gonna hit us any time."

She nodded and waited for him to disappear over the hill, then turned and resumed her search. "Heather, you should go back up to the car."

"Not without you.'"

Jessica paused and studied the surface of the water. Three logs floated past, followed by a hubcap and a half-submerged barrel.

Thunder echoed more closely, and the first drops of rain fell.

"Won't do Archer any good for you to get soaked out here," Heather said.

Cold rain struck Jessica's face as she looked up at her sister. "Get to the car, Heather."

"No." Heather took a step toward Jessica, as if she would physically carry her up the hill if she had to, but then she glanced toward the river and caught her breath.

Jessica turned.

"No, don't—"

Jessica stumbled backward at the sight of a dead beagle puppy floating past them only a few feet away.

Heather's arms came around her. "Come on, sis. Let's get out of this."

Jessica relented. She would take Heather home, and then she would come back. She would search until she found him. She couldn't depend on the police department, or volunteers, or family, or church, or God to find her husband for her. She could only depend on herself.

CHAPTER 19

The lights along Olive Street flickered to life as Lauren turned off Highway H, three blocks from her house. It had been a great day of much-needed solitude. Her clothes smelled of fish and smoke from the fire she'd built to cook her dinner. She had avoided guilt about not stopping to see Mom and Daddy by promising herself to make it back to Knolls on Tuesday, when she was scheduled to be off.

She turned from Olive onto Lilac Circle, a block from her house, and frowned when she saw the glow of a porch light . . . *her* porch light. Through the darkness of late twilight she saw the outline of a Ford Bronco—the vehicle Grant had purchased earlier in the year. She smiled and pulled into the drive. Grant wasn't in the Bronco, so he might be waiting for her in the house—he knew where she kept her emergency key to the front door, and he and the kids had used it several times in the past few months. They never abused the privilege, and she enjoyed it when they dropped in.

How would it feel to share a home with them full time?

A flood of warm joy surprised her. Would it be so difficult to come home to this family every night? To have Brooke's witty chatter filling the house as a backdrop for Beau's thoughtful seriousness? To have Grant's steady love and welcoming arms?

She switched off the motor and got out of the truck, feeling more certain with every step that this was right—that the name Lauren Sheldon sounded wonderful.

She saw the outline of a tall form behind the thick lace curtains of her sitting room. She raised her hand and waved, but Grant had already stepped away from the window. Seconds later he came barreling onto the porch and down the front steps.

"Grant, it's so good to—"

"Thank God." He drew her into his arms and buried his face against her neck. "Thank God you're safe."

She felt the first prickling of alarm. This wasn't a social call. "Of course I'm safe. Why would you think—"

He released her and stepped back, cupping her face with his hands. "We've been looking everywhere for you."

"*We?* Why? What's going—" Uh-oh, had she forgotten a fishing date? Brooke had been so excitable lately, and she might have panicked. . . . But Lauren felt sure she hadn't made a date with her for today.

"I've tried calling you every hour all afternoon." Grant pulled her back into his arms.

"Grant, will you please—" She resisted her weak-kneed reaction to the hardness of his arms and pulled out of them. "Please tell me what's going on."

He looked down at the baggy denim bib overalls she wore with an old red-plaid shirt of her brother's. He sniffed, frowned.

"You've been *fishing?*" There was a hint of irritation in his voice.

"Is that a problem? Last time I checked the schedule I wasn't due to work today. What—"

"You haven't seen Archer, then." He sounded disappointed.

What on earth did Archer have to do with anything? "Grant Sheldon, if you don't tell me what you're talking about, I'll—"

"He's been missing since last night."

"*Missing?* What do you mean? Friday's supposed to be his day off. Maybe he and Jessica took off for a little break. They could use—"

"He stopped by the hospital after a deacons' meeting, and I sent him on a mission of mercy to Mrs. Eddingly's. He planned to go home from there. Apparently he never arrived home at all. He never even arrived at Mrs. Eddingly's. The old bridge was washed out."

"The bridge?" Lauren caught her breath and reached for Grant's arm. "What about his car? Is it—"

"Not a sign of it. The storm last night . . . No one's seen him since he left the hospital."

Lauren sank down onto the front porch steps. "Oh, Lord, no."

Grant sat down beside her and put an arm around her shoulders. She allowed him to pull her against him, and she leaned into that comfort, wrestling an attack of overwhelming fear.

Nothing could have happened to Archer. Not Archer! She'd known him since she was ten. He'd been best friends with her younger brothers. He was almost like a brother to her.

"Oh, Lord, no, not Archer." She blinked away tears. "You're thinking he was caught in the flood?"

"It's just one possibility among many at this point. There's no evidence of an accident—although with all the rain we had last night it could have washed away much of the soft evidence. There's been no report of a wreck. . . ." He paused, and his arm tightened around her. "I need to warn you about one more thing, Lauren."

"There's more?"

"Nothing to worry about right now. Some people at the hospital knew I tried to reach you this morning and couldn't find you. They also knew Archer was missing."

Lauren followed the implication of his words. Fiona Perkins was at it again. "So now half the hospital is convinced . . ."

"Not half the hospital. Most of them have more sense than that."

"That old rumor couldn't still be circulating after a year." She narrowed her eyes at Grant. "Could it?"

"You know how things get blown out of pro—"

"What about Jessica? *She* hasn't heard that, has she?"

"I don't think anyone would mention it to her."

"Have you spoken with her?" Lauren asked. "Is she okay? Where is she?"

"I've talked to her several times, and none of them were good. She's frightened, and—"

"Dad, you found her!" came a feminine shout from the direction of the street.

Lauren and Grant turned to find Beau pulling up to the curb in the Volvo, with Brooke hanging half out of the window. Before the car even came to a complete stop Brooke had dislodged herself from the passenger side and was rushing up the driveway.

"Lauren, where have you been? We've looked all over for you." She stopped several yards away, and her nose wrinkled. She glared, hands on hips. "You've been fishing? We've been frantic about you all day, and you've been hiding out somewhere on a creek bank?"

"It wasn't as if I knew something was going to happen, Brooke," Lauren said calmly. "I don't have disaster radar."

"Couldn't you have left a note? You didn't take your cell phone with you, and you couldn't even give anyone a quick call to let us know where you'd be all day. *All day!* How could you—"

"Hold it. Time out." Lauren raised a hand. "Last I heard all was right with the world, and I had the day off."

"And so you went fishing? Alone? All day?" Brooke demanded. The unspoken accusation hung in the air: *Without me?*

"I didn't just go fishing, Brooke, I—"

"You smell like smoke." Brooke stepped closer and sniffed.

"I . . . uh . . . cooked my dinner." Lauren winced at Brooke's expression of hurt.

"I would have gone with you."

"I know, but I needed to get away for a little while—to think about things. Look, can we talk about this later? I need to find out how Archer's—"

Beau emerged from the car at the curb, locked the door, pocketed his keys. "Lauren, you need to call your parents and let them know you're okay," he said as he joined them. "I called them when we were looking for you, and they're probably worried."

Lauren suppressed a groan. "You called my parents?"

Great, they must be frantic. She half expected to turn and see *them* turning into her driveway. "Fine, I'll call them, but as you can all see, I'm in perfect health, no limbs missing." She held her arms out to her sides for emphasis. "And after I've cleaned up I'm going to go see Jessica." She removed herself from Grant's gentle grasp and turned toward the house.

Brooke joined her on the porch. "We'll come with you."

"Not this time, Brooke." The last thing Jessica needed right now was a crowd. And besides, what if someone *had* been obnoxious enough to suggest to Jessica that her husband might have taken off with someone?

"I'm sure she'll need some quiet time," Lauren said. And it was never quiet with the Sheldon family nearby.

Lauren ignored Brooke's feminine sputter of offended pride. "Y'all can come into the kitchen and have a soda while I clean up if you want," she called over her shoulder as she stepped through the front door. "I didn't catch enough fish to save, but there's some chips in the cabinet—"

"I think we'll take off now" came Grant's quiet reply from the sidewalk.

Lauren turned to find the three of them standing together, watching her in silence. Brooke's expression was one of hurt confusion. Even Grant's brows drew together in concern.

"I'm sorry, I didn't mean to imply that you aren't welcome here," she said. "You always are. But if I was in Jessica's position, I think I'd need a friend to hold on to about now, and if I can be that friend, I will. First, however, we might need to clear the air about a few things, and she isn't going to feel comfortable about that in . . . um . . . mixed company." How much had Grant told the kids about the rumor at the hospital?

Jessica had only been in the Dogwood Springs community since Christmas, when she and Archer were married. There'd been little time for her to make friends here. Behind that dazzling public image was a woman who had not grown up in church. She didn't seem to know what Dogwood Springs Baptist expected of their pastor's wife. Would she even feel comfortable asking the church for emotional support?

For a few moments the night of the tornado, Lauren had noticed a bond between the two of them—a sort of silent communication and a link to friendship.

"I think we'll go grab a bite to eat," Grant said at last. "We could wait for you if you want to go with us after you see Jessica."

"Thanks, but I had my fill." Lauren patted her stomach.

There was a feminine snort, the hurt still obvious on Brooke's face

"I may even go prepared to stay the night if Jessica needs me,"

Lauren said, then hesitated, watching them, suddenly feeling guilty for something, though she couldn't quite put her finger on the cause. She would love to go with them to eat, would love to spend time with them, even though she did feel a little crowded all of a sudden, after the day of peaceful solitude. "I'll . . . uh . . . talk to you all later, okay?"

"Of course, Lauren," Grant said. He didn't quite pull off the casual reply. "I'll see you in the morning at work." He and Brooke turned and walked away.

Beau hesitated. "Be sure to tell Jessica we're praying for her."

"I will, Beau."

He looked over his shoulder at Grant and Brooke, then back at Lauren. "I guess you know you'll have some fences to mend with Brooke."

"It looks that way. Maybe with your dad, too."

He nodded and turned to leave, then hesitated, turned back. "You're still thinking about marrying Dad?"

Lauren smiled. Sometimes Beau could be as bold as his sister. "Yes, I'm still thinking."

Grant hadn't seen his daughter this upset since his announcement last spring that they were moving away from St. Louis, and his later announcement that he was thinking about dating again.

"Dad, I don't believe she did that," she said when they reached the Volvo.

He wasn't in the mood to do battle with her emotional roller coaster when he had one of his own to keep in balance. "She didn't do anything wrong." Even if he did feel as if he'd been slapped in the face. An over-reaction, probably. He hoped.

Still, she could have given him a call, or—as Brooke had mentioned—left a note on her door. Anything to keep them from worrying.

"She didn't even want us with her," Brooke said. "She didn't even ask me to go fishing with her. I thought she liked it when we went together. Dad, I don't think she loves us anymore."

Beau joined them at the car. "She's just preoccupied. We should be, too."

"But we've been looking for Archer all day," Brooke said. "It isn't as if we don't care."

"Lauren just found out, though," Grant said. "She's understandably upset, shocked—scared. Don't forget she's been friends with Archer since they were kids."

Brooke leaned her posterior against the front fender of the Volvo, arms crossed. "What if that isn't the only reason—"

"Shut up, Brooke," Beau said. "You know her better than that."

"I'm not saying she's guilty of anything, dummy. I'm saying maybe she really does care more for Archer than—"

"I said shut up." Beau rolled his eyes at his sister and jerked his head in their father's direction.

Brooke crossed her arms and huffed. "She could have at least let *me* go with her. She said she didn't want mixed company. I'm not mixed."

"Yes, you are."

"Beau, I'm not joking."

"Lauren feels that Jessica needs some privacy," Grant said. "Think about it, Brooke. If you were a pastor's wife and—"

"Never."

"But if you *were,* how would you feel if your husband disappeared and some people were less interested in finding him than they were in starting rumors about him?" Grant could identify with Jessica far too well.

"I don't think Jessica would believe that about Archer," Brooke said.

"Why not?" Beau asked. "You seem to."

"I do not! I just—"

Grant put an arm around his daughter's tense shoulders. "Give Lauren some room, Brooke. All of us need to give her some room."

"Fine, let her go by herself." Brooke jerked open the driver's door of the Volvo. "I still don't understand why she couldn't have at least left a note when she left to go fishing *by herself.*"

Beau caught the door, nudged her away, and slid behind the wheel. "Simple. She didn't even think about it. She's lived alone all these years—she's never had to answer to anyone but herself. She's never had anyone but her parents looking out for her."

Grant studied the mature lines of his son's face, saw the faint reflection of the dash light on his glasses, the way his shoulders filled out the thick shirt he wore, and felt a gentle pride. "You're right, Beau. For us, it's a habit."

Brooke stalked around the front of the car, jerked open the door, slumped to the seat. "If she loved us, she'd learn the habit, too."

———

Mitchell studied Trisha's pale skin and haunted eyes while he defrosted frozen dinners from the home delivery service. It amazed him that she would even want to stay in the same room with him, but she was here. Today she had taken two showers and had soaked in the Jacuzzi for nearly an hour before he called her to eat. Her dark hair was still dull and lifeless, but it was clean. She smelled better.

All Mitchell had been able to do today—when Trisha wasn't sleeping or taking a shower—was ask questions. Where had she been? How had she gotten here from Springfield? Had she heard from her mother? The monosyllable replies had served to either frustrate him or scare him.

Hitchhiking?

Why couldn't he just tell her he'd missed her? Why couldn't he show tenderness?

But he couldn't. For so long, he'd wanted to just call and say he loved her but hadn't been able to do it.

The reason Darla gave for leaving him was that he never showed tenderness, that he was to blame for their daughter's drug addiction. Because she had a father who didn't love her.

So where was Darla now if she loved Trisha so much?

She obviously lacked the stamina to stick it out.

"I bet Mom's bled your bank account dry."

He winced at the cynical sound of his daughter's voice, her bitter words, but he refused to let her see how she could shock him. "Your mother has given you enough money this past year to feed you and your lover for ten years. I don't think you need another—"

"My *lover* is *dead*!" Venom cut through her voice.

Mitchell winced again. But at least something still managed to affect her emotions. He studied the pallor of her face, the too-bright eyes, the rigid posture.

Hers was just like the countless other faces he had seen over the years, faces that should be smooth and clear with youth but were hurtling toward death at an accelerated rate.

"Yes, he's dead." Mitchell attempted to contain his satisfaction at that statement. "His drugs killed him. Just like they're killing you."

She crossed her arms over her chest and slouched to the table, where she sat down and stared out the window. "Nobody ever gave him a chance. Nobody ever . . . nobody listened. His parents didn't care about him. Nobody did. Except me. I listened." She sniffed and reached for a napkin.

The timer beeped on the oven, and Mitchell turned from her with relief. At least she was talking. It was better than the short, tense answers of the past few hours.

He watched her wipe her face and nose with the napkin and resisted the urge to tell her to use a facial tissue. How could he be so lacking in human warmth? Had he slipped so far that he didn't even care about his own daughter's despair?

But she didn't seem like his daughter. Had it been too long—too painful—for them ever to reconnect? Why was it that all he could manage to feel right now was . . . distaste?

He took the dinners from the oven and carried them to the table. He set Trisha's in front of her. "Maybe it would be a good idea if we changed the subject so we can at least digest our meal."

She blew her nose on the napkin and looked up. "Sure, change the subject. It's what you do best." She grabbed a fork and stabbed the slice of turkey in its entirety.

"Since we've barely spoken in four years, I don't think you have any idea what I do best."

She nibbled the turkey around the edges, giving Mitchell a look that dared him to call her on her lack of table etiquette. Like a prepubescent child.

He knew better than to say a word about it. She'd used the same ploy fifteen years ago whenever she wanted to rebel. When they had called her on it, her behavior had become more and more immature.

He sat down across the table from her. "Okay, then, suppose I don't change the subject. Suppose we get everything out in the open." He nudged his meal a few inches forward, concentrating on the placement of the plate, on the setting of spoon and knife, neither of which was necessary if they were going to eat like Neanderthals. "Did you know that Oakley Brisco, an eighth grader, dropped dead at school last December after an overdose of methamphetamine?"

She shrugged. "What's that got to do—"

"The police have pictures of an exchange between Simon and Oakley that took place shortly before Oakley's death."

She dropped the turkey back onto her plate and watched him, waiting.

"The point is that Simon killed Oakley by selling him—or giving him—the meth."

She looked at her plate. "The boy didn't . . . he didn't have to take it."

His temper flared at her callousness, but for that brief moment, she sounded like him. Was she just taking after her own father? "Right, and Simon didn't have to become a drug addict just because he didn't get a good start in life. And even if he did, what is your excuse? You had everything you could ever possibly have wanted."

She turned to stare out the window again. He studied her profile—the sharply arched eyebrows that were so much like his own, the hard blue eyes, the shadows beneath them. . . . Yes, she looked a lot like him—except she had her mother's dark hair.

"Trisha." He swallowed and shoved his plate farther away.

She didn't look at him. "What?"

"When did you last see Simon?"

Her lips pressed together for a moment in a forbidding line—that, too, was a habit of his. "I didn't . . . I don't know for sure." This hesitance was a sudden contrast to the tears and belligerence. It was just one more sign of a confused, damaged mind. "It was maybe about a year ago."

Mitchell hid his surprise.

"He wasn't my . . . I didn't know he'd come back down here until . . . until I heard he'd died."

"And still you grieve his death?"

She looked at him then, and the stiletto steel of her eyes pierced deeply enough to touch his conscience. "Somebody has to. I bet nobody else did."

"No." He leaned back from the table and braced himself. Did he want to do this? "So you didn't know that he'd threatened the lives of three teenagers at school on the night he died."

She swallowed. "I read about it in the paper. He held them at gunpoint." If possible, her face grew more pale, her eyes more feverishly bright. "That wasn't the Simon I knew," she murmured. "It was . . . the meth."

"I gather, then, that you had seen him that way in the past, before he left?"

"I saw him that way," she said softly. She hunched forward and stared into her plate.

And the baby. What about the baby? Mitchell felt the flick of a blade in his heart at the memory of that tiny little girl, struggling so hard for life. Had it been two years already? Born prematurely, already affected by the poison Simon had fed Trisha, the baby hadn't been able to endure the fight for long, and she'd died without a name. Except for the one he'd given her. Angela. In his heart she was still his little angel, the only grandchild he would probably ever have.

"You saw the changes in him, Trisha. You knew what was happening. When did you last take the drug?"

She appeared to shrink within herself more deeply. "Been a while."

"Weeks? Months?"

"Months. Maybe three. The last binge was . . . not long after I heard about Simon."

He wanted to believe her. It could be true. She looked like someone who was desperate for another fix. He allowed himself to wonder, briefly, what it might be like to have had a different child—perhaps someone like Beau Sheldon, who was responsible, eager to help out wherever he could when he worked in the emergency department, whose passion for medicine far outdistanced anything Mitchell had ever felt for the profession. Did Grant Sheldon realize how lucky he was to have a son like that?

"I'm trying to stop for good." Trisha's statement brought him back to reality. "You might not believe it, but I tried to quit a couple of times this year."

How badly he wanted to believe her. "As long as you stay clean, you can stay here."

She gave a soft huff of disdain. "Sure, Dad. As long as I'm good, you'll accept me, but as soon as I do something you don't like, I'm out the door."

"You have a problem with the rules?"

She rubbed her arms as if she was cold. "Guess I'll see how long I can be good." She picked up her fork, and without looking at him again she cut the turkey into pieces and devoured the food.

Mitchell put his in the refrigerator for later. He didn't have an appetite.

In the silence after the meal, after Trisha had gone to bed, Mitchell wandered through the dark house. Another memory of this morning's nightmare flashed through his mind—red eyes blinking in darkness. He shuddered the memory away.

But he still had the lump high on his forehead, near his hairline, covered by his hair. How had it happened? For most of the day he'd been so preoccupied by Trisha's arrival that he hadn't taken the time to wonder. Even the slight headache could have been caused by the tension with Trisha. He doubted he would be able to recall what had caused the lump—the amnesia caused by Tranquen was quite impressive, especially after a double dose. Since he had bumped his head, as well, he might even be suffering from a slight concussion.

Once again he saw the mud at the garage door. Where did that come from?

He opened the door and peered into the garage.

The Envoy was parked slightly askew. Mud spattered the shining black finish. The front brush guard was dented in two places.

How had he gotten the dents? Had he damaged the garage door pulling in last night?

He stepped down into the garage and studied the dents, then pressed the garage door opener. He checked the doorframe, the door itself, the concrete planters that Darla had placed on either side of the drive.

He would need to get the dents fixed, of course, but at the moment that wasn't on the top of his list of priorities, and he had the Audi in the other garage. He would just drive the car for a while—after all, he could leave it in the garage at the clinic—he wouldn't have to leave it out in the weather.

Something rocked his memory. Those red eyes he'd seen in the darkness blinked at him again. It had to be an effect of the double doses of Tranquen. He refused to compare his legal drugs to Trisha's dependence, but he needed to get a better handle on the situation and stop depending on those little pills to calm his nerves.

Later. There would be time for all that later. Right now he needed to come to grips with Trisha's arrival, and he had to figure out what to do.

CHAPTER 20

The ghostly sound of moaning awakened Archer, and the torture of pain caught him in its grip once again. The voice was his own, and for a moment he could not stop as he heard it echo back at him. The roar of the river had not abated.

He gritted his teeth and opened his eyes to the same darkness he had left countless hours ago. How long had he been out here? Was this still Friday night?

He didn't see the beam of headlights above him any longer. Had that been his imagination?

Had he imagined the shape of the Envoy behind him, Mitchell's big black SUV?

He closed his eyes again to block out the mocking darkness for a few seconds. His thought processes were clearer than they had been earlier.

Tentatively, moving his head with caution, he glanced around. He remembered hearing his car splash into the water just before everything went black. If Mitchell had been the one who hit him, and if he had suffered a similar fate, then . . .

"Mitchell?" His back shrieked with pain, and he caught his breath at the intensity of it. His head throbbed in response to his effort. Calling did no good anyway. He could barely hear his own voice over the rush of floodwaters that seemed to encompass him.

Cool night air pricked his exposed flesh and crept beneath his wool suit coat. He shivered, and the pain attacked. In agony, he cried out again, losing his concentration, losing control of his thoughts completely as the torture took over his body as surely as if someone were beating him to death.

He could not endure the pain, and he allowed it to take him.

———

"No. Thanks anyway, Helen . . ."

Jessica's voice drifted through the screen door onto the front porch of the parsonage, where Lauren stepped into the light that streamed across the welcome mat. Lauren had just raised her hand to knock when Jessica strolled into the living room from the kitchen, caught sight of her, and gestured enthusiastically for her to enter while she continued to talk on the phone.

"I think it's wonderful that you want to call a prayer meeting, and I'm sure Archer will appreciate it, too." She pushed the screen door open for Lauren. "But I need to stay here at home in case he shows up or tries to contact me. . . . Yes, I know he could just as easily turn up at the church, but I'll take my chan—" She signaled for Lauren to wait and then paced back toward the kitchen with the cordless phone. "Thanks for the offer, Helen, but someone is already here with me. If you and Mr. Netz want to open the church for prayer, feel free."

As Jessica continued to reassure her caller that everything was fine here on the home front, Lauren tried hard not to eavesdrop. She stood at the open door, staring out through the screen at the pools of light that spilled down from the streetlamps.

"Yes, and thanks again, Helen. I'd better see to my company." Jessica hung up and gave a weary sigh as she reentered the living room. "Hi, Lauren. I guess you got my messages?"

"Actually, no. Grant was at my house when I arrived home tonight, and he told me about Archer."

Jessica gave a quiet sigh and joined Lauren at the screen door to stare out into the night. "Grant was worried about you, too."

"I was fishing all day. I never dreamed anything like this was happening."

For a moment, as if in unspoken agreement, they stood side by side, watching the silent street out front. A moment later Jessica sniffed, and Lauren realized she was crying.

Tentatively, Lauren squeezed her arm.

"I don't know how they do it," Jessica whispered.

"What's that?"

Jessica dashed a hand across her face. "How do pastors' wives keep their Sunday school faces? I can't do it. I'm an awful pastor's wife."

"According to whom?"

Jessica made a face. "It doesn't matter anyway. I just want to see Archer come walking in that front door. All day today, when I haven't been out searching for him or on the telephone, I've been standing here, desperately praying that the next car I see will be Archer's, and that he'll come leaping up onto the front porch with a perfectly logical explanation about why—" her voice faltered—"about what happened to him last night."

"I'm praying for that to happen," Lauren said. "He might just be stranded somewhere. I think that's very possible, especially with the flooding."

Jessica sighed. "It's what I've been telling myself. The phone's been ringing all afternoon—people offering to search, offering to come and sit with me, mostly church members. Most people would want company in a situation like this. But for me it's like being on stage constantly."

"Maybe I shouldn't have just come barging in like this," Lauren said, "but I thought you might need some moral support, and when I tried to call you the line was busy."

"I'm glad you came."

"Well, you're not on stage with me, and if you don't want company I'll bar the door for you." She took Jessica's hand and squeezed gently. "Just remember you're not alone. Have your father and sister been in touch?"

"Yes. Dad and Heather both helped search this afternoon, but Heather's taking the show for me tonight, and Dad went home to take care of the livestock." Jessica brushed fresh tears from her face. She got up and closed the heavy oak door and locked it. "Lauren, this afternoon Heather and I overheard some people talking."

"About what?"

Jessica sank back onto the sofa, picked up the pillow, fingered the lace edging.

"Did they try to drag my name into it?"

Jessica closed her eyes, nodded.

"Honey, your husband has never in our adult years shown any interest in me whatsoever, except as a friend and a member of his congregation."

Jessica slid her gaze toward Lauren, gave her a tentative smile. "*Adult* years?"

"Boyhood crush. He got over it in a hurry when I caught him and my brothers, Roger and Hardy, swinging on a rope from the barn loft into a pile of hay like Tarzan when I was thirteen and Archer was eleven. I gave them all Dutch rubs and grounded them until my parents got home."

Some of the tautness eased from Jessica's face. "What's a Dutch rub?"

"Well, to give an effective one, you catch the little criminal's head in a half nelson, then scrub his scalp with your knuckles. I always gave the best, and I have the callouses to prove it." Lauren held her hands up and wiggled her fingers. "Don't worry; it never left a scar. I don't think it would constitute child abuse."

Jessica relaxed a little more, then turned to gaze out the window, as if afraid to stop watching for Archer. "As the hours go by I have more and more trouble convincing myself Archer's okay."

"Give it more time. The flooding is pretty widespread right now. I've heard stories about some folks out in the country who will be stranded for days."

"Others have told me the same stories," Jessica said. "I'm depending on it."

"Good. Now, I came prepared to spend the night, and I can help you answer the front door and the phone, but if my company's going to bother you, just let me know and I'll—"

"Oh, thank you. I didn't know if I was going to be able to face another night alone."

"How long since you ate?"

"It's been . . . I don't know. I haven't had an appetite."

"Why don't you come with me to the kitchen while I raid your fridge and see what I can find."

"I can fix something if you're—"

"Jess, you need to get your mind off this nightmare for a while, and watching me try to cook could be a great distraction. Let's go see what you've got. Meanwhile, we can keep on praying."

A sigh of warm air touched Archer's face, and he awoke suddenly, eyes wide, his heart pumping so hard he could hear the rhythm of it in his breathing.

"Who's there?" he croaked.

No answer, of course—only the river. But was it just a little less noisy than it had been earlier?

The darkness enveloped him. "Oh, Lord, help me." *Keep praying. Stay connected.* If he didn't, he would panic, and that wouldn't help anything.

Pain still radiated across his back, and thirst overwhelmed him. He raised his arms and tried to push himself up, but the pain stopped him before he could raise his head.

Broken back? He couldn't take the chance by forcing movement, at least not yet. But he needed water. With an excruciating sense of helplessness he focused on the rush of water only a few yards away. Flood water. Filthy, contaminated water.

"Please, Lord, don't take me now." He drew the words out slowly, desperate for that extended connection to God.

He had to face the distinct possibility—even probability—that he might never make it home again. He could die right here.

The image of the man in the SUV flashed through his mind once more. Mitchell. But Mitchell would never do something like this.

"Jessica," he whispered. "Lord, be with her."

He continued to pray for her, to surrender her to God. And then he prayed for the church, naming as many members as he could think of. Maybe if he did die, his death would do for them what he couldn't—it would force them to start depending more on God and less on one insignificant pastor to carry the weight of their spiritual and emotional needs.

His thoughts were once again on Jessica as he sank into oblivion.

———

Lauren figured she couldn't go wrong heating the contents of a can of soup on the stove, and Jessica devoured it as if it were a sumptuous feast.

She spread peanut butter over a cracker and gave it to Lauren. "So you heard the rumors about you and Archer last summer."

"Yes. I was devastated." Lauren broke a corner from the cracker and put it in her mouth.

"It's one thing I have against small towns. Sometimes it seems as if everyone knows everyone else."

"They do."

"And they're willing to believe the worst." Jessica made another peanut-butter-and-cracker sandwich. She had mixed strawberry-flavored Nesquik for both of them. She took a sip of hers. "Even people who should know better."

"That's one of the drawbacks, I guess. But that familiarity is also one of the blessings."

"I didn't think much of the blessing last summer when Mr. Netz called and asked me point-blank why I'd broken the engagement with Archer." Jessica stirred her milk with the straw until it foamed. "Turns out he'd heard the same stupid rumor, and he was pumping me for details."

Lauren took a long swallow of the strawberry milk and wiped her mouth with a napkin. "I almost quit the church over it until I realized that would make things look even worse."

"Can I make a confession?" Jessica asked.

"Sure."

"I was so jealous of you last summer I could have strangled you a few times."

Lauren thought about that for a moment, then smiled. "Wow. I wish I'd known."

"You're kidding."

"You see, for a very short time last summer," Lauren said, "I did develop a sort of crush on Archer. Please believe me it wasn't reciprocal, and at the time I didn't think anyone knew, except Gina."

"A crush?" Jessica asked.

"That's all it was. It had a lot to do with the fact that I was longing for a husband and family, and my biological clock was ticking down. I was so humiliated by the rumor and by the implication that several people were willing to think that of me, and of Archer, that I just wanted to go crawl in a hole somewhere and die. It really hurt my feelings."

"And if you'd known I was jealous of you, *that* would have made you feel better?"

"That someone as beautiful and talented as you would consider someone like me to be a rival?" Lauren shrugged. "I wouldn't have wanted you hurt, but in a way, yeah, it probably would've soothed my ego."

Jessica finished her milk and pushed away from the table. "Well, then, you'll be glad to know that it was probably my jealousy of you, more than any other single factor, that made me realize how much I loved Archer."

"I hope you also realize how much he loves you."

Jessica twirled the straw around and around in the empty glass. "Tell me something, Lauren. . . . How do you feel about Grant?"

"I'm crazy about him."

"And Brooke and Beau?"

"Them, too."

"Does that mean you love them? That you're ready to become a part of the Sheldon family?"

"Funny you should ask. I've been thinking about that same question all day. All week, actually."

"Want to know what I think?"

Lauren nodded.

"Don't put it off. Loving someone, and knowing he loves you, is one of the most wonderful experiences in the world. I didn't realize quite how wonderful until today. Now I'm terrified that it may be too late to tell Archer."

"Oh, Jess, don't think like—"

Jessica raised a hand to stop her. "I was afraid to marry Archer because I knew how devoted he was to his church, and I was afraid I'd come in last in a contest for his time and attention."

"I know he's been busy lately."

"Yes, and all this time I've felt as if it were a competition—me against the church. Everything I feared before I agreed to marry him has happened, but I'm still so glad I married him, and . . ." Her voice cracked, and she looked down at the table. "I don't know what I'll do if he doesn't come home, Lauren."

"Why don't we do some more praying," Lauren suggested. "Have you ever heard about the 'Please God' prayer?"

Jessica shook her head.

Lauren reached for a napkin and handed it to her. "A friend of mine, Dr. Mercy Bower, explained it to me once. She said if all you can say is, 'Please God, please God, please God,' then say it. He knows. And He answers. He's right here with us, and he's right there with Archer, wherever that is."

Jessica scooted her chair closer to Lauren's and reached across the table, holding out her hands for Lauren's. "Would you pray it with me?"

Lauren took her hands in a firm grip.

Archer opened his eyes in the darkness and listened to the chatter of water nearby. There was a tiny rivulet trickling about a foot from his head. He reached out to it, allowed some of the water to trickle into his palm, and brought it to his lips. He slurped at it thirstily, then reached for more. It could be contaminated, but it shouldn't be as bad as the river. If he got sick, he got sick. He had to have fluids or he would die for sure.

At least the rivulet wasn't trickling over *him*. In fact, he was protected here from the wind, which seemed to attack the treetops with a roar from time to time. He was also partially protected from the rain by the cliff ledge and by the trees overhead. After the storm Friday night, the temperature had risen. Although Archer felt chilled from time to time, it could have been worse.

It frustrated him that he couldn't at least shuffle his way up the cliff side to the road, where he would quickly be found, but he decided not to concentrate on that.

He would just concentrate on trying to stay alive.

CHAPTER 21

Early Sunday morning Jessica walked into the dining room to find Lauren dressed in her purple print scrubs for work, zipping a small denim backpack that served as her purse-carryall.

"Lauren, if you ever need a place to stay, a shoulder to cry on . . . If you ever need a friend, you've got one."

Lauren flashed that typical broad McCaffrey grin and drew her into a hearty embrace. "Thanks, so've you. Take care of yourself today, will you? And call me at work if you hear anything. Even if I'm busy at the time, I'll return the call as soon as possible."

Jessica wished she could hold on to Lauren and keep her eyes closed and imagine that they were high-school buddies after a sleepover. "I promise."

"If you want someone to come and stay with you today we can call the church—"

"No." Jessica stepped back. "Thanks, Lauren. I'll be okay. I'll be in and out today, probably looking for Archer every second I'm awake."

"I know you haven't learned to trust the church," Lauren said gently, "but I think you'd be surprised at what you discovered if you opened up to them a little." She picked up her backpack and draped it over her shoulder. "I've found that most people have good hearts around here. Maybe they're not always the ones who try hardest to control the church, and maybe they aren't the most outspoken, but they're out there—you just have to find them."

"I'll remember that."

"Do you need someone to stay with you tonight?"

Jessica hesitated. She didn't want to impose on Lauren again. "I'll be fine."

"When are your in-laws planning to arrive?" Lauren asked.

"They're on their way, but they're flying home and then here, so they might not get here until tomorrow. Last I heard they were still working on a flight out of Mexico City."

"I'll come straight here when I get off work tonight."

Jessica knew she should refuse, of course. Lauren had a life of her own, and she didn't need to baby-sit. "Thank you. I would . . . really appreciate it."

Lauren put a hand on her shoulder, bowed her head. "Lord, please protect Archer today and bring him home safely. Please be with Jessica—lift her in your love, and never let her go."

That was it. No *amen*. No typical closing. It was as if those two sentences were just a small section of ongoing prayer with Lauren.

Another hug. Another pat on the shoulder, and Lauren left, promising to be back that night.

———

For the second morning in a row, Mitchell completed the unfamiliar tasks of cooking breakfast for his daughter, checking the hallway every few minutes as he waited for her to come in. She'd kept to herself in her room after that disaster of a meal last night, and he was relieved. How was he supposed to converse with her?

He patted the bacon to keep it crunchy—whether that worked or not he didn't know, because he never cooked bacon for himself. Darla had done so from time to time—it seemed like centuries ago.

Mitchell glanced outside and saw bright blue skies and sunshine—not a threat of rain. He laid his paper towels down and stepped to the dining room window, caught in the confusion that had nagged at him last night.

Pink dogwood blossoms trailed over his neighbor's privacy fence, teasing a vague memory. . . . But why? From where?

He touched the knot on his forehead. Though tender, it wasn't as

swollen as it had been yesterday. A concussion might have caused some
amnesia, but the Tranquen could easily be the culprit.

Wasn't it always? They should market the stuff as an alternative to
Versed for painful medical procedures.

He shrugged away a shiver of unease, blinked, and shook himself.
This worry about the Envoy was most likely for nothing. Surely last
night's insomnia was only another sign of the paranoia that had
attacked him at unexpected times the past couple of weeks—maybe even
a backlash from his conflict with Trisha at dinner.

He had increased his dosage of the Tranquen steadily in the past few
weeks—an extra avenue of peace for those times he needed them. Now
he wondered if he would ever be able to sleep again if he tried to cut
back.

He heard a door close somewhere in the house and turned in time
to see the stranger who was his daughter drift into the room. She wore
a pair of faded jeans so filled with holes she might as well have worn a
swimsuit. Her T-shirt was black, with red paint spattered all over her
chest to look like a gash and bloodstains.

He nearly asked her if that had been her Halloween costume last
year.

"Hungry?" he asked instead.

She nodded and sat in her chair, not looking him in the eye.

"Bacon, eggs, toast, hashbrowns." He caught himself watching her
face for some sign of life, some vestige of interest. Her skin was so pale,
so bloodless, her eyes so empty of hope.

She drank her juice, then grimaced. He had noticed that yesterday,
as well. She ate as if she were hungry, but she showed no enjoyment in
the food. It could be she didn't like his cooking, or his menu choice.

"Maybe I need to get a list of things you like to eat," he suggested.
"I don't do a lot of cooking."

She gave him a brief glance and shook her head. "That looks good.
I like bacon." As if to justify her point, she reached for a piece of bacon
and stuck half of the slice into her mouth. "Better than I've had in a
long time." But she still chewed and swallowed as if she were eating
sawdust.

He filled a dinner plate with the food and set it before her. "Not to nag, but you could stand to gain some weight."

She looked up at him again, and this time held his gaze. Her expression was filled with a shadow of resentment. "Funny, Dad, but you know before I ran away from here with Simon. . . ?"

He stiffened at the sound of that monster's name on her lips. He nodded.

"I always wanted to be this thin."

"You were perfectly healthy before you started dating him. You were . . . pretty." *Until Simon Royce stole your youth and beauty.*

"So you're saying I'm a dog now?" For a breath of a second there was a spark of her old humor in those pale blue eyes.

He watched it fade as quickly as it had come, and he pushed the plate closer to her. "I'm saying I'd like to make an attempt at fleshing you out." He filled his own plate and sat down across from her. "Are you planning to stay for a while?" So proper, so awkward. Why couldn't he show a little more emotion?

"Would I be allowed to stay?"

"I thought we had already discussed that." Still the stiffness. "We might even find some clothing for you to wear to the table that wouldn't make me lose my breakfast." He gestured to the imitation blood spattered on her T-shirt, and he smiled at her.

Once again, that spark of humor, and then Trisha picked up her fork and speared a square of crunchy hashbrowns.

Mitchell did likewise, but he couldn't stop watching her. He hadn't felt this hopeful in years.

———

A little later Sunday morning Jessica caught a glimpse of sunlight as it scattered in dappled beams through the overhanging tree branches, freshly touched with spring green. The brightness nearly blinded her, and she was glad this particular road leading out of Dogwood Springs was deserted at this time of morning.

She had pulled on her hiking boots and filled a canteen with water as soon as Lauren drove off. She had already eaten breakfast, so she wouldn't need anything else for a while—not that she expected to be hungry.

Now she shaded her eyes and drove slowly, studying the roadsides.

"Was I mistaken all this time, Lord?" she asked as she pressed the brake and pulled into the skimpy shade of a pink dogwood in full bloom. "I thought Archer and I were doing exactly what you wanted us to do. I thought you meant for us to be together." Some of the raw anger she had felt toward God yesterday had dwindled this morning. While she wasn't sure He heard her, she continued to talk to Him.

She had been talking to Him practically nonstop ever since Lauren left this morning. Maybe it had been the way Lauren left her prayer open-ended, as if she expected Jessica to continue it. Or maybe it was just that she had discovered that the connection kept the fear at bay.

Whatever it was, she needed this link to God so desperately that every word she thought, she spoke aloud to Him. Every time she thought of someone in the church who needed prayer, she welcomed it. And every time she thought of something else to confess about herself, she did so eagerly.

Even if He wasn't listening.

"I'm so scared right now, and I can't go spilling all this to people in the church, not when there are people like Helen Netz who analyze every little thing I do. . . . But I'm so scared right now." A tremor shook her voice. "Help me, please. Oh, please, help me find Archer."

There was no time for tears right now, and if she found Archer this morning there would be no need. Who was better equipped to know what he might have done Friday night? Who better to understand his heart and know what might have been on his mind when he left the hospital? Something had either happened on his way to Mrs. Eddingly's, or . . . maybe Archer had picked up a hitchhiker, and this time the stranger had been a nutcase and held a knife to his throat or a gun to his head. Maybe someone had attacked him—

"No, stop it," she said aloud. Her imagination had been doing this to her for the past twenty-four hours. It was one reason she'd been so glad to see Lauren last night—and it was why she'd been so frightened this morning to see her leave.

Maybe she *should* go to the church and ask for help, for someone to pray with her. Mrs. Boucher, Archer's long-suffering secretary, was such an encourager.

But Mrs. Boucher had other things to worry about, answering constant calls and questions at the church. She would be buried by now.

Jessica drove to the roadblock on Highway Z, then made a U-turn and drove back into town, past the convenience store on the corner of Z and Hawthorne Street. She had driven all these streets several times already, but somehow just being on them seemed to bring her closer to Archer. She saw a familiar muscular young man restacking sandbags along the side of some houses on Ford Street.

Hadn't she seen him at a different house yesterday?

On impulse, she pulled to the side of the road and parked, got out, squished through a marshy lawn to where Kent worked. He settled a bag into place and turned to her, wiping sweat from his forehead with the back of his wrist.

"Hey," he said.

"Hi, Kent. Did your co-workers take off on you?"

"Gone to church, but I heard more rain's on the way. Thought I'd better keep an eye on things."

She'd heard the same forecast. Looking up at the sky, she wanted to believe the rain would stay away. "I guess you've heard about Archer."

"Sure have. Been out looking for him, too—yesterday afternoon. You not goin' to church?"

"I'm still looking for my husband."

"Guess I'll be headed out that way, too—soon as I check on my little brother. Mom says he's sick, and she might need me to drive them in to see the doc if he doesn't get better. You think you could . . . you know . . ." He shrugged. "Could you pray for him?"

"Oh, Kent, of course I will." Why was it she felt so much more comfortable with this near stranger, this eighteen-year-old lawbreaker, than she did with the upstanding members of the church? "Do you want to pray with me now?"

He looked away, obviously uncomfortable. "Nah, I know you'll do it. I guess I could, uh, pray for Archer, too, while I'm stacking."

She thanked him and returned to her car. The distinction had something to do with expectations. Kent Eckard expected nothing from her, because he hadn't been raised with all those high concepts of a traditional church.

She pressed the brake when she came to Dogwood Avenue, which curved through the center of town, past the church. They would be congregating in the auditorium now. She glanced in the direction of the church and prayed that they wouldn't forget Archer during their services.

She slowed at the intersection. If she went in, they would welcome her, of course. They would pray. Surely nobody at the church would even consider that nasty rumor about him and Lauren. . . . But if they did, could she endure their looks? What if someone even had the audacity to question her about the possibility?

Crazy. Nobody would dare.

But last summer, while Archer was in pain over their broken engagement, John Netz and two of his buddies had dared to suggest that Archer should resign from the church because of that stupid rumor.

She pressed the accelerator and drove past the intersection. Obviously, she wasn't in any shape to endure that kind of attention today.

She would continue the search alone.

About an hour after breakfast Mitchell bundled some of the clothing Darla had discarded when she left. There was a pair of silk pajamas with a button missing, and some underwear that looked as if it might wrap around Trisha twice. He also included some of his T-shirts and a pair of jeans Trisha had worn when she was fifteen. He hadn't realized how much time had passed.

He knocked on the door of the guest bedroom. "Trisha?"

"Yeah." The sound of her voice continued to chill him. Where had all the life and laughter gone?

"I brought some things you might be able to wear."

No answer.

"Trisha?"

The door opened and she appeared, engulfed in an old tattered robe she must have found in the back of her mother's closet. She looked at the bundle he carried, pushed the door open wide, turned back toward the bed, and plopped down onto it, as if she didn't have the energy to stand erect.

He placed the clothes on the dresser. He hadn't expected a thank-you, but he did expect some kind of acknowledgment of his presence.

"Are you still feeling ill?" he asked. Yesterday when he had suggested that she might need his medical attention, she'd rebuffed him solidly.

She shook her head and turned to look out the window toward the unkempt flower garden that her mother had abandoned for more interesting pursuits.

He started to walk out the door.

"Is it true you and Mom had to get married because she was pregnant with me?"

He stopped. Where had that come from? "It's true that we married earlier than we would have otherwise. Did your mother tell you about this?"

"So you would have gotten married anyway?"

"Yes, I believe so."

"Whose idea was it to get a divorce?"

He studied the waif slouched on the side of the bed. Was it necessary for her to drag all this up? "Initially, I think it was a mutual decision. She says I ran her off because of my financial concepts."

"Meaning she left you because you wouldn't support me."

"I think that was one of her general excuses, but there were many factors involved."

"Do you miss her?"

He thought about that for a moment, surprised that she cared and weighing the pros and cons of telling the truth—that by the time her mother had left he was glad to see her go, that the marriage had been going downhill for years.

He sat down on the window seat. "I get lonely," he admitted. Not lonely for Darla, just lonely. It was a big admission for him to make to another living being.

Trisha remained silent. So did he.

"I still miss Simon," she said at last.

He didn't reply. Anything he said about that would ignite another argument.

"He wasn't always a drug pusher, you know."

"I was never formally introduced to him. You never brought him home with you."

"He was a customer at the Dairy Creme when I worked there."

"Why did you go out with him in the first place?"

She shrugged. "He had a hot car."

As if that explained everything.

"All the girls in my class wanted to go out with him. When he asked me, I nearly fainted."

Mitchell became nauseated. "Why? Trisha, you were barely sixteen. He was almost twenty, a high-school dropout. Was he doing the meth then?"

"Some. But it was, like, not such a horrible thing, you know?"

No, he didn't. Anyone with a brain knew the dangers of meth. Which proved his daughter took after her mother. No brain.

"I knew he wasn't good for me," she said. "Maybe that's why I wanted to go out with him."

"That and his 'hot' car." Mitchell couldn't keep the revulsion from his voice.

She didn't seem to notice. "It's just that he was dangerous. My friends always teased me because I was a good girl. I never went out and got drunk, never did drugs, always got good grades. I was so boring."

"But all that changed, of course, when meth came into your life."

He saw the immediate hurt in her eyes. "I loved Simon."

"No. I will *not* accept that. You loved what you thought he could do for you, and you got caught in the same self-destructive trap that held him." Mitchell looked down to find his hands clenched so tightly his knuckles were white.

It was at that moment, as the fury coursed through him, that he made a discovery. He wouldn't feel this kind of frustrated fury if he didn't care deeply. He wouldn't feel a father's rage unless he had first felt a father's love.

He reminded himself that she'd been through a lot these past years, and her brain wasn't healthy. "That man is dead, Trisha." He tried to keep his voice gentle. "He didn't deserve your loyalty, he didn't deserve your love, he didn't even deserve the medication he received for pain before he died."

She caught her breath and turned to look at him. "You were his doctor?"

"I was on duty when they brought him in. I was the one who pronounced him when he died."

"How did he . . . Was it an overdose?"

"I thought you said you read about it."

"I didn't . . . I wasn't exactly at my best then."

"He died of internal injuries from a fall."

She slumped onto the bed and buried her face in her pillow.

"I don't want the same thing to happen to you."

"Why not?" came her muffled voice.

"Because you're my daughter, no matter what. I care about what happens to you." He was such a coward! Why couldn't he say the words?

"No matter what? You mean even if I am a drug addict, you're stuck with me?"

"I would never disown you, if that's what you mean."

She raised her head and looked up at him. "I guess that'll have to work, Dad. I think I'll take a nap now. I'll talk to you after a while."

He took his cue and left the room, closing the door behind him.

Yes, he loved her. Someday he would find the courage to actually say so. There'd been so much time lost. . . . Could he do it this time? Could he build a relationship with this daughter he barely knew?

Jessica checked her watch as she returned to the car after her third foray along the dirt road to check a clump of brush and limbs in the ditch. She had been chased by dogs twice and mooed at by a cow. She had stopped and talked to five people with no results. Four of those five people knew who Archer Pierce was, and one had been a member of the Baptist church years ago, when his father was the pastor.

She had driven to the opposite bank of the Black Oak River, parked at the roadblock, walked through the mud to the river, and scanned its banks. She saw where the high water had flattened the brush. Clumps of last year's leaves hung in the lowest tree branches.

The sight upset her more than she wanted to admit. She left the river, drove the long way around the ridge, crossed the new bridge south of town, and took Highway Z up onto the ridge. She stopped at the farmhouse set back from the southwest corner of the intersection of Highway Z and County 22.

When she knocked on the door a man in his seventies, dressed in overalls and covered in mud, stepped around the side of the house.

"Hello, my name's Jessica Pierce." She met him halfway across the yard, her feet once more sinking into wet grass. "I'm checking to see if you might have noticed any unusual activity on the road late Friday night—perhaps an accident or someone walking along the highway." The same question she'd asked all the others.

"Pierce," he said, self-consciously wiping his muddy hands on the sides of his overalls. "Now that's a familiar name around these parts." He squinted closely at her. "You that feller's wife? The preacher they're all looking for? I read about that in the paper this morning."

"Yes, that's my husband."

He frowned, shaking his head sadly. "Awful. Just awful. I was sorry to hear it."

"Thank you. I wonder if you might have noticed something during the storm Friday? Did you see any cars come this way?"

"Well, now, there's been all kinds of people been by here, some asking and some just searching. It wasn't until this morning when I was reading the paper when I remembered something I didn't think to mention to the others."

Jessica held her breath.

"You want a cup of tea or something? The wife baked some hot rolls—"

"Thank you, no, I've already eaten. Please, would you tell me what you saw?"

"Well, you see, I didn't think much about it at the time, but I got up a little after eleven o'clock or so that night for a drink of water, and I was standing at the window looking out at the rain when a couple of vehicles drove past."

"Could you tell if one was a tan—"

"Couldn't tell no color. I'm not even saying one of them was him, but it struck me odd when I thought about it this morning, 'cause we

don't get much traffic through here at night except for the party crowd."
He jerked his head toward County 22. "Get tired of them bozos screeching their tires."

"These vehicles you saw," she said, "did you notice anything else about them?"

"Just that it looked like a truck followin' too close behind a car. In fact, I didn't even think about the crash I heard till just now."

"A crash?" *No, Lord, no.*

"I was just gettin' back into bed when I heard it."

"Didn't you investigate?"

"Sure did. I went right to the garage, where we have some loose pieces of tin against the outside wall—they make an awful racket when it's windy. I just figured one of the dogs or cats had knocked 'em sidewise." He shrugged. "I went back to bed and went to sleep."

Jessica couldn't move, and for a few seconds she couldn't speak. This man was suggesting Archer might have been involved in an accident. Could that have been what happened? But there was no evidence of an accident, no damaged cars.

"Excuse me, sir. I think I'll be going now, but I'd like to tell the police about this. If you remember anything else, would you please call them?" She should ask more questions, but she didn't know what to ask. Except, "Were you home alone when you saw this?"

"Nope. Wife was with me, but she was snorin' like a freight train by then."

"Are you sure? Didn't the crash wake her up?"

"No chance there. She'd sleep through a tornado. Sleeps through storms all the time, and if I didn't wake her up and get her to the basement she'd be none the wiser in the morning if she woke up in the river."

Jessica thanked him, turned around, and stumbled a few steps, battling a wave of dizziness.

"You going to be okay?" the man asked.

"Yes. Thanks. I'll be fine." She had to tell Tony. She could be on to something.

CHAPTER 22

T he heavy fragrance of moist earth tugged Archer to consciousness. Fine mist sprayed the left side of his face and his left hand, and a deep growl of thunder—or was that just swift water?—vibrated the ground.

He opened his eyes to thick fog rising from the water's surface as rain splashed into it with windblown gusts.

Grateful for the protection of the cliff, Archer took advantage of the light to study his surroundings. Raising his head with hesitant caution, he saw the black cliff rise abruptly about ten feet to his right. About fifteen feet above him a boulder loomed from the hillside, like a lurking troll. The river rushed by to his left.

He needed to get to help. Why had no one found him yet? Wouldn't Mitchell have done something?

Archer tried again to lift his legs, and again the knives attacked his spine. He cried out, his fingers digging into the mud on which he lay.

He felt the earth shift, and he caught his breath, biting back another cry.

"Oh, no. God, please, no. Don't let it dump me into the river." It could easily happen, with the river level so high, eroding the foundation of earth below this ledge.

He lay still for countless moments, listening to the water roar, feeling the rain on his face, barely daring to breathe lest the movement cause a shift.

"Oh, Lord, help me," he whispered.

As he continued to watch the sky, he realized it must be close to noon. The sun streaked from the east through clotted skies in one burst of light, then lost the battle and hid again behind the clouds.

Maybe this little storm wouldn't last long. The northern shore of the river had already disappeared into the forest at the edge of the flood-plain, and more rain would only make it worse.

From past experience he knew the creeks and drainages could raise the level within a short time. The steep hills and canyons above the valley caught water and siphoned it into the Black Oak with efficiency and speed.

And he was stuck here, unable to move. His back was probably broken.

If he were to rely solely on human intellect, he would give up hope now.

"Keep Jessica safe, Lord," he whispered. Then more loudly, "Please, God, I don't know what's happening here, but you can get me out of this mess. I know you're in control."

In times past, he had said those words almost as a dare to God, as if to say, "I'm trusting you, God, so don't let me down, or I won't trust you anymore."

He was in no shape to try to manipulate God. He was helpless, defenseless against the forces around him.

He didn't know how long this heightened sense of assurance would prevail over his fear, but for now he clung with desperation to the powerful feeling that God's hand was on him with purpose.

But did that divine purpose include his own death?

The ground beneath him shifted again, like the beginning tremors of an earthquake.

He remained still. The ground stopped shaking.

Yes, he could die here.

———

Jessica pulled into her driveway to see Tony and Caryn Dalton's car parked at the curb. She jumped out and rushed up to the porch, where she saw them standing at the front door, Tony in his police uniform, wearing dark glasses and carrying a white cane.

"Tony! Caryn! I was just getting ready to call you. I spoke with a man who lives out by the road near the bridge, and he said he heard a crash Friday night. Do you think it might have something to do with Archer?"

Tony shook his head. "It was probably the bridge itself, Jessica."

Caryn stepped forward and put an arm over Jessica's shoulders. "Honey, we came to tell you something."

"What is it? Have you found him? Have you found Archer?"

Caryn looked at her husband. "Why don't we go inside and sit down."

Jessica's breath caught with panic. "Why? What's happened? Tell me."

"Let's go inside, Jess," suggested Caryn.

Jessica unlocked the door and the group went in. Tony held a hand out, palm up, unable to see to reach for her.

Jessica took his hand. She felt the strength of his grip.

"I'm sorry, Jessica," he said. "We found his car."

"Okay. Where?"

"Down in a farmer's bottom field, by the river."

She looked from him to Caryn in confusion. "That doesn't sound so bad. He's always making house calls. Maybe—"

Tony shook his head. "It was in the water, Jessica. That bottom field is a flood-plain area for the river."

She felt the dizziness creep around her again. "But what about Archer? Did you—"

"We didn't find any sign that he was in the car when it entered the water," Tony said.

"Then that could mean he got out and walked . . ." She focused on Tony's face, imagined the steady, unseeing gaze behind the dark lenses.

"Anything's possible at this point, Jess," he said. His voice betrayed him. Jessica heard a gut-wrenched sadness there, a tone of finality and horror. Tony and Archer were so close, such good friends. . . .

The dizziness crept closer. Jessica saw blackness around the edges of her vision. She felt weak. Her grip slid from his, and her body seemed to surge forward.

"Honey, catch her, she's fainting!" Caryn's arms tightened around her to keep her from falling, and Tony grabbed her awkwardly. Together they helped her to the love seat.

Jessica heard the clatter of footsteps entering her kitchen and the swish of water from the tap. She felt Tony's hovering presence as he continued to steady her, to pat her shoulder.

Caryn knew the Pierce kitchen from several visits and dinners together, and she returned quickly to the living room and placed a wet towel over Jessica's face and neck. "Jess? You okay, honey?"

The cool moisture revived her. She looked at Caryn. "Who . . . found the car?"

"Some fishermen found it earlier this morning, about a mile south of the washed-out bridge. SAR has been called in, now that they know for sure he didn't leave the area."

Jessica took the wet towel from Caryn and sat up. *SAR—search and rescue.* "The bridge. Yes. That was one of the places I searched this morning. I thought he might have . . ." Again, the darkness. The nausea. She had to concentrate to control her shaking. "Does the car look like it might have been caught in a flash flood?"

"We don't have any way to tell right now," Tony said gently. "We do know the wooden railing of the bridge was knocked off, but that could have been from a passing tree limb when the river overflowed the bridge. The driver door is missing from the car. Judging by the time Archer was seen leaving the hospital, it's possible he reached the bridge sometime past the point of the initial flood, but we just don't know."

Jessica leaned back and closed her eyes again. The nausea threatened to overwhelm her. "Oh, Archer, where are you? Please, please be safe."

Caryn pressed the back of her hand against Jessica's forehead. "Honey, are you still feeling faint?"

"I feel sick."

"We need to get you checked out by a doctor."

Jessica shook her head. "I'll be okay. I just want to get back out and look for Archer." *He can't be dead. Oh, God, don't let him be dead.*

"When's the last time you ate?" Caryn asked.

"This morning. Don't worry, Lauren McCaffrey slept over last night, and she made sure I ate before she left for work."

"In that case," Tony said, "we're taking you to see a doctor right now. It's probably just a reaction to the stress, but if you've eaten, there might be something else going on here."

––––––––

Voices came gradually through the heavy mist that surrounded Archer.

"Nothin' out here this morning. Didn't think there would be. Everybody says he probably went off the bridge. That's where we oughta be lookin.' "

"Lots farther down, too, if you ask me."

There was the gentle whir of a trolling motor, and the voices drifted away. "We'll go on down a couple miles."

"Yep, always been a strong pull south of the bend . . ."

The voices echoed over Archer's head as if in a dream. They sounded remote, as if they came from the far end of a long pipe.

He realized, at last, that they weren't just more characters in one of the nightmares that had tormented him last night.

His eyes flew open to the gray sky. He tried again to sit up, and he winced as pain shot up his spine and exploded in his head.

"Help me! I'm here! I'm up here!" he cried, forcing himself past the pain. "No, please don't leave me here! Oh, God, stop them!"

He called weakly until he no longer heard the engine across the surface of the river. All he heard was a soft ripple of tiny waves slapping the shore and a distant roar of floodwaters, and the blood throbbing through his head. Pain throbbed down his spine, and his vision grew dark, his thoughts unfocused.

He breathed in through his nose and out through his mouth in tight puffs, closing his eyes in wordless prayer to endure the grip of agony.

They hadn't heard him. He hadn't shouted loudly enough.

But he had to stay awake, keep his thoughts clear, in case they came back. Someone could come back this way looking for him. They were searching for him!

Had to stay focused. Had to think . . . concentrate.

He thought about his last conversation with his wife when he met her for lunch Friday, just before she left for Branson. He could close his eyes and imagine her face . . . see her smile . . . feel her kisses.

"Awake. Stay awake," he whispered to himself, forcing his eyes open once more. He recalled the annoying discussion with the deacons Friday night—how long ago had that been? Hours? Days? He had no way of knowing.

He thought of his talk with Mitchell at the hospital. . . . "Mitchell. Why? What's happened to you?"

His eyelids felt weighted with lead, and he had to force them open again. "Lord, please keep me awake. Please send help. . . . Please help me out of this mess. There's . . . so much left to do . . . so much more. . . ."

The line of the cliff swam out of focus.

Again, he forced himself awake. "Still suffering the effects of the concussion," he muttered. "Can't let it happen. They could come back."

And if they didn't?

He had to get out of here. He pulled his arms to his sides, then tried to push himself up on his elbows. The pain stopped him.

But if he could just endure the pain, if he could drag himself into view, where someone might be able to see him if they came by this way again . . .

"Oh, God, help me!" he cried as he slumped back to the ground, blackness pressing around the circle of his vision.

The earth shifted beneath him. He heard the splash of rocks hitting the river's surface, and the ground continued to shift, then gave way completely in a miniature mudslide. His mouth flew open in a cry of shock as he plunged, head first, into the river.

Water invaded his nose and throat. He tried to kick his way up, but streaks of fire moved up his spine until the agony became too much. His arms fought the water as if in slow motion. He felt himself floating up and thrust his face toward the air. He broke the surface as his mouth opened in a gasp.

Choking, spitting out water, fighting for breath, he allowed the current to carry him downriver, praying he wouldn't be crushed between a log and the rocky cliffs along the shore, praying he wouldn't drown.

Jessica lay her head against the pillow and caught a flash of purple in the periphery of her vision as Lauren stepped into the room with her chart.

"Jessica Pierce, are those muddy hiking boots I see? And look at you, your hair is wet."

"Guilty as charged."

Lauren grabbed a blanket from a nearby cabinet and spread it over Jessica's shoulders. "Went looking for Archer? I guess I'd have done—"

"They found his car."

Lauren's movements halted. Shocked silence hovered for only a moment before she shifted the blanket and patted Jessica's shoulder. "Where?"

"Down in a bottom field, washed there by the flooded river."

"Was it . . . empty?"

"No sign of Archer," Jessica said. "They've called the search-and-rescue people in."

Lauren gave a soft whistle. "Had me going there for a minute."

"Lauren, you know what this means, don't you?"

"Sure do. It means they're narrowing the search."

"It means Archer could have been caught in the flood and washed downstream with his car," Jessica said. "He could be—" She couldn't say it.

"It *means* they're narrowing the search, Jessica Pierce."

Jessica felt the chill deep in her gut, felt it wash outward with a wave of trembling.

Lauren took Jessica's hands. "Remember what I told you? God's in control. Now, I know what Archer would do if he were here. He'd tell me to get you checked out, and that's what I'm going to do. I want to get your vital signs, get your blood pressure lying, sitting, and standing, and then I want to get you on a monitor."

Jessica allowed Lauren to give her a complete nursing exam, and the human touch, human concern, and very Lauren-like human warmth and constant chatter soothed the jagged edges that had begun to fray out there on the lonely search this morning. Maybe there was something, after all, about calling on others in time of need.

Grant joined them as soon as Lauren completed her exam. He

ordered an EKG, had Lauren establish an IV, and had her draw blood for a chemistry panel, a complete blood count, and a serum pregnancy test.

"Pregnancy?" Jessica asked weakly. "You think I could be—"

"It's just routine, Jessica," Grant said. He, too, had a comforting bedside manner. "With the stress you've been under, I know you don't need anything else to worry about right now, but I'd like to check you out and make sure you're okay before we send you home. Lauren told me the news about the car, and that's probably what caused you to faint. Can you tell me if you had been feeling dizzy or nauseated before this happened Friday night?"

Jessica couldn't think, couldn't concentrate. Friday night seemed a whole lifetime ago. "Maybe a little."

"Any new medications, either prescription or over-the-counter?"

"None."

"Have you been near someone who was sick?"

"I talk to people from the audience all the time, so I probably come into contact with a lot of sick people. Grant, are you sure we have to do all this? I really think I'll be okay, and if Archer does come home and I'm not there—"

"If he arrives home and you're not there, you can be sure he'll find you here, Jessica." Grant placed a hand on her shoulder and gently guided her back against the pillow. "You relax and let us take care of you, because if we don't, Archer is going to have our hides when he does get home."

———

Grant called Lauren into his office barely twenty minutes after Jessica's initial tests had been taken. He held the results up for her to see.

Her lips parted and her green eyes widened. "Pregnant?"

"Don't say anything yet. I've asked Lab to run a quantitative before we tell her, so I can let her know immediately that the baby's okay and how far along she is."

"You have doubts about the viability?"

"Just because she fainted, that's all. I want to rule out a tubal. She's had a bad enough time of it—I don't want her to have to wait for more test results. I've put a stat order on this one, but wait for a few minutes before you go back in to see her."

"Why?"

"Because she'll take one look at you and know something's up. Besides, I can tell you're upset about them finding Archer's car."

"Jessica thinks he could be dead." There was a catch in her voice, and Grant could identify with her emotion.

"Forgive me, Lauren, but we can't afford to think about that right now."

She nodded, looking at the results again. "You know, I can't imagine being in Jessica's situation."

"Nobody wants to think it could happen to them."

"But it could. It's a scary thought."

He watched her for a moment. Was she implying that she didn't want to take a chance on the same type of thing happening to her?

"I'm also wondering how it must feel to be pregnant."

"Excuse me for saying it, but I think you should consider being married first."

To his surprise, she gave him a teasing grin. "Is that an offer?"

"That depends. It would make my *second* proposal in less than a week."

"I'm thinking about it, Grant. Believe me, it's all that's been on my mind."

"You could've fooled me." He heard the churlishness in his own voice.

She frowned at him. "This isn't like you. Are you still upset because I went to Jessica's last night?"

"Actually, I'm trying not to be upset at all. I just never realized the decision would be such a struggle for you." In fact, he couldn't help wondering if she'd already decided and was waiting for the right time to let him down gently. His daughter's paranoia was affecting him, big time. He should listen to Beau more often, and to Brooke less.

"Look, I'm sorry, I shouldn't have said anything, okay?" Lauren said. "It's just that I thought you knew how . . . how I felt about having children."

"I do understand about wanting them." Grant knew it was best to keep his mouth shut. He recognized his own growing irritability for what it really was—hurt feelings left over from yesterday's conflict. Still . . . "What I don't understand is, if you really wanted children as badly as you say you do, I'd think you would enjoy the children you would already have. I realize you'd never dreamed of starting a marriage with a ready-made family with two teenagers, but—"

"Two wonderful seventeen-year-olds whom I love, you know that, but loving someone and living with them on a full-time basis are two entirely different things, Grant. Completely. I'm talking major impact here—"

"Okay, okay, I get the picture."

"If you were honest with yourself, and with me, you could be a little more compassionate about how daunting that would be to you if you were in *my* position," she said.

"You're thinking about my mother, aren't you? I know the possibility of living with someone with Alzheimer's can be daunting, but we would have round-the-clock care for her. I wouldn't expect you to be her stay-at-home caretaker."

"You're kidding, right? If I marry you, not only will I be gaining two teenagers, but I'll also be competing with the very real memory of *their* mother. Your wife."

He frowned at her. "Why bring Annette into it? She's been gone for three years."

Lauren shook her head. "Not really." Her voice softened. "She's still alive in your hearts, Grant. I'm sorry. Right now I'm asking myself if I have the strength to compete with a ghost who still has that much power over you. The kids talk about her all the time, and until recently I loved hearing them talk, because I truly have always admired Annette, simply from the stories her family cherishes about her."

"Then what's changed?"

She turned away, but not before he saw the sheen in her eyes. She stepped to the window that overlooked the broad hospital lawn. "I got possessive. I started wanting that family for myself, and I realize I could never have them, not completely. I couldn't live up to that reputation."

Oh, Lauren. He didn't know what to say, because in a way she was right. Annette had been the love of his life for over twenty-one years, counting the years of grief after her death. Every time he looked at Brooke or Beau he saw their mother's vivacious, generous spirit. He, too, had always enjoyed being able to talk to Lauren about Annette.

Would that change?

He should have been more sensitive to Lauren's feelings, but . . . "Lauren, you always encouraged us to talk about her. It was one of the things that has helped all three of us heal. Your compassion was also one of the things that drew us to you."

"Have you considered the possibility that you *haven't* healed completely?" she asked.

An overhead announcement blared through the speaker with a page that didn't concern them, and Grant saw Lauren's shoulders straighten. He knew, without seeing her face, that she was reminding herself sternly about where they were. When she turned around, her professional demeanor was back in place.

"Joanne Bonus is in four with both her sons."

"Both?"

"That's right. Last I saw, Kent was holding the baby. I can't believe the change in that kid. I'll go check with the lab about Jessica's blood test." She brushed past Grant and out the door before he could say anything. And he didn't know what to say.

He followed her out. They had patients to see.

CHAPTER 23

With charmed surprise, Grant studied the chart for Clayton Grant Bonus. Joanne had named her baby after the two doctors who had delivered him—Clayton was Mitchell's middle name, if Grant wasn't mistaken. It would be interesting to see Mitchell's reaction.

Grant noticed the chief complaint was merely "Fussy, won't eat." At least the baby didn't have a fever.

He entered the exam room and greeted Joanne, who sat on the bed alone, and Kent, who sat in the chair in the corner, thick arms cradling the infant as if they had been fashioned for one another. Joanne gave Grant a distracted smile.

"Joanne, you say Clayton is fussy, but I see he's content while he's being held. When does he fuss?" Grant asked, settling into the other chair with his chart.

"Well, he acts like he's hungry, but then when I try to feed him—I'm breast-feeding, you know—he can't quite get ahold. Get my drift?"

"Are you saying he has difficulty with suction?"

"There you go." She gestured to her older son. "See there, Kent, I knew the doctor'd know what I meant."

Kent rocked the baby in his arms, face reddening madly. "Uh, sure, Mom."

Grant made some notations on his T-sheet. "How long has he been this way?"

"Just the last day or so. I didn't want to wait until tomorrow and take a chance he'd get worse."

"Of course, I understand. The nurse has noted that he doesn't have a fever now. Do you know if he's had one in the past day or so?"

"Not that I could find. I didn't try it but once. He hates that rectal thing."

Clayton's cry of protest had been strong and healthy when his temperature had been taken during triage. Everyone in the department must have heard it. Grant wasn't worried about his lungs, and stimulation was good.

Grant performed the evaluation. Clayton's fontanel, heart, lungs, and abdomen looked normal. He had good grips and a good startle reflex. His skin was pink, warm, dry. Other checks were okay.

It wasn't until Grant checked the baby's mouth that he found something questionable. He gently scraped the tongue with the tongue blade to check if the whitish coating scraped off easily. It didn't. The baby squirmed and cried.

Grant removed the blade and otoscope. "Joanne, when were you last able to feed him?"

"Haven't tried for a few hours. He acts hungry, but won't latch on."

"He isn't on any antibiotics, is he?"

"No, why? What's wrong?"

"How about you?"

"Yeah, Mom," Kent said. "You are. You know—for that sinus infection."

"That's right. I forgot to tell the nurse about it, but it's just stuff left over from a bladder infection I had when I was carrying Clayton. They okayed it for pregnancy. I needed the pills for an awful old sinus infection that just keeps hanging on."

Grant was relieved. He hadn't looked forward to being forced to stick the little infant with needles for blood work, and he especially hated the thought of doing a spinal tap looking for meningitis. All these would be deemed necessary for the evaluation of a fussy neonate if there was no good reason for the fussiness.

"I'm pretty sure I know what the problem is, and it isn't serious," he said.

"You won't have to give him a shot will you?" Kent asked.

"Not if this is what I think. Have you ever heard of thrush?"

Blank stares.

"Normally there's a balance in our mouths between good bacteria and a type of fungus called *Candida albicans*. When something happens to kill off the bacteria, such as taking an antibiotic, the fungus grows unchecked and causes a painful white coating over the mouth and gums. Commonly, we call it a yeast infection."

"So he got it from my antibiotics?"

"That's right."

Obviously relieved, Joanne chuckled. "Wait'll he grows up and I tell him the first problem he had was a yeast infection."

"Mom," Kent muttered, still red in the face.

"So you're gonna give us some cream to stick on his tongue?"

"Not exactly, but you've got the right idea. It's nystatin suspension, which you'll give him with a dropper. I've known of some women who eat yogurt, which has the good bacteria they need to replace what was lost. I'm not sure if it would work as well coming through you, but it wouldn't hurt. Just make sure the yogurt you eat has the active cultures."

"I'll do both," Joanne said. "By the time Clayton's a year old, Kent's gonna know the *real* facts of life, right, Dr. Sheldon?"

"You need to know that although I'm comfortable with my diagnosis, many of my colleagues would feel that at least some blood work is indicated for a baby this young."

"Stick him with a needle?" Kent shook his head. "Forget those other guys right now, okay? You're the man."

"I trust you, Dr. Sheldon," Joanne agreed.

"You *will* need to see his regular doctor in a couple of days. Since it's Sunday and no pharmacies are open, we'll dispense the medicine you need. If you have any problems before you get in to see his doctor, come right back here, okay?"

"Gotcha," Kent said. "Thanks, Dr. Sheldon."

Jessica watched her friend check the chart for the third time. "You know, Lauren, I didn't even want to come in. I'm just upset—that's the only thing that's wrong with me. I'd really rather be out there looking for Archer."

"Why don't we sit tight until the test results come back?" Lauren stepped over to the bed and adjusted the monitor.

Jessica studied her expression carefully. "Does Grant think there's a problem? I've been here for forty-five minutes. I feel okay. Really."

Lauren hesitated. "He's just being thorough."

"About what? What does he think this—"

Lauren chuckled, but it sounded forced, and the smile didn't reach her eyes. "Would you please relax and let us take care of you?"

"You're a terrible bluffer—you know that?"

Lauren grinned at her and started to speak, but Grant entered the room. Lauren gave an intentionally obvious sigh of relief.

"Just in time, Dr. Sheldon. The patient is getting hostile."

"And the nurse is withholding information from me."

Grant nodded, distracted, and Jessica's concern turned to worry. "Have you heard something about Archer? Please—"

"No, not at all, Jessica. I've been delaying because I wanted to double check the results on one of the tests we took on you."

She waited for him to continue.

He pulled a chair over to her bedside and sat down. "You knew we took a pregnancy test."

"You told me that was just routine procedure for something like this."

"And there's a good reason for that, because if the symptoms you experienced were due to pregnancy, it would be vital to find any problem as quickly as possible to protect your baby."

"And . . . so . . . you waited. . . ?"

"I wanted to make sure the positive results weren't false."

"You're saying I . . . It can't be possible. I couldn't have tested positive."

"Yes."

"But I haven't missed a monthly."

"You told me your last one was lighter than normal," Lauren said. "That isn't unusual."

"I'm sorry for the delay," Grant said, leaning forward, gray eyes calm. "We did a quantitative test to make sure. The lab numbers look good, and according to them you're about six to seven weeks along."

If Jessica hadn't been lying down she was sure she would have fainted again. "I'm *pregnant*!"

"Congratulations, Jessica," he said gently, taking her hand. "Yes, you're pregnant."

For a few seconds, she couldn't catch her breath. She caught his hand in both of hers and held tightly while the news registered like a shockwave throughout her whole body. The room shifted around her. Grant's hand tightened, and she felt herself engulfed in someone's arms, heard Lauren's voice next to her ear.

"It's okay, honey. It'll be okay."

The growing fear . . . joy . . . bittersweet pain left her feeling breathless. "I just can't . . . It's such a surprise. I mean, I've been so focused on Archer—"

"Of course you have," Lauren said. "It's only normal."

"I want you to have an ultrasound," Grant said, allowing her to lean back as he released her hands. "I'm probably being overly cautious, because it isn't unusual for a woman who is pregnant to pass out, especially in your situation. I just want to make sure the baby looks as good as the lab report indicates. The ultrasound tech should be in here at any time to take you to Radiology. It won't take long, because this isn't a regular outpatient day."

"There's a . . . a problem?"

"Not at all. We're just being thorough."

"Then why do I have this gut feeling that you're not telling me something?" Jessica asked.

Grant smiled at her. "Relax, Jess. This is just routine procedure when an expectant mother faints. We want to make sure the baby is in the right place, and that this isn't a tubal pregnancy." He hesitated. "There's one more thing I need to mention."

"What's that?"

"It is a generally accepted practice that a pelvic exam should be performed prior to the ultrasound."

"A *what*? Oh, no, Grant, you've got to be . . . I can't . . . please . . . is it necessary?"

"I thought you might feel that way. Do you have a family physician here in town?"

"No. I go to Dr. Grace in Springfield."

"Why don't we wait until we get the results of the ultrasound, and then we'll see what we need to do next."

There was a knock at the doorway, and the secretary, Vivian, stuck her head inside. "Heads up, all. Looks like the Dogwood Springs Baptist Church has decided to hold an afternoon service out in the waiting room."

"They're *here*?" Jessica exclaimed.

"Caryn Dalton told me when they brought you in that she was going to call the church for immediate prayer," Vivian told them. "You know Caryn doesn't waste any time. Someone said she interrupted the prayer service they were having for Archer. Now they're converging on you, Jessica. Better get ready."

"They want to *see* me?" She was both touched and alarmed. "Oh, please, Grant, Lauren, please don't tell them what this is all about."

"Don't worry," Grant said. "Your records are confidential. We won't say a word."

"I'll talk to the staff and make sure no one else lets anything slip," Lauren assured her.

"So, do you want company or not?" Vivian asked.

"Not right now, Vivian," Grant said. "We need to do some more tests, and in case anyone asks—"

"I know, Dr. Sheldon. They'll get nothing out of me, even under threat of death."

"Let's hope it doesn't get that drastic."

"You don't know our church very well," Jessica said. Then more softly she added, "Apparently, neither do I."

Archer spat water and choked and fought back scream after scream of pain. He had become a prisoner and the river his jailer, torturing him with every ripple as it whirled him past submerged trees and trash that had caught and piled up like scattered dams.

He felt the jolt of his right foot hitting the root of a giant sycamore as he paddled against the muddy water. His legs were useless.

The river shoved him toward a small ledge that jutted from the rocky terrain of the cliff. The ledge barely rose above the surface of the river, and it formed a small, hollow depression that might hold him. He could go no farther. He forced his arms to move out and grasp a rocky outcropping as he floated by.

With a cry of agony, he pulled himself the mere six inches into the depression. He rested his torso for a moment, then heaved himself forward on his elbows and dragged his legs from the water. Rocks bit through his wool coat.

He collapsed with his head in the crook of his arm, breathing hard against the pain. "God, help me," he panted. His body felt as if it had been ripped in half. Incessant shivers made the pain worse.

And yet the cold water had taken the edge off the sharpest pain.

He concentrated on his breathing, thankful to find this muddy haven from the flooding river, thankful for the jacket—even though it was soaked through. This small, cavelike mud hollow could conserve some of his body heat. If he could endure the pain long enough, maybe it would go away.

He pulled himself into the depression and used the ledge as a lever to turn himself onto his back to give it better support.

Would they find him in time?

Or was he going to die here, alone?

———

Jessica lay with her eyes closed, still overwhelmed by the test results. Archer would be ecstatic.

"Oh, Lord, where is he? Please don't let him be dead. He has a child—a baby! Please, Lord, please don't take him from me now. Don't take him from *us*."

The very thought of losing him hurt so badly she knew she would be willing to die with him. Except now she couldn't just consider herself.

She placed her hand over her stomach and closed her eyes—felt the hot burn of tears on her eyelids. She was vaguely aware of the sound of movement in the exam room and then felt hands on her shoulders. She looked up into Lauren's gentle green eyes and saw her own pain reflected there.

"I feel so lost, Lauren."

"I imagine you do, honey. You don't have to do anything right now, and you've got to remember you're not alone. Never alone." Lauren handed her some tissues and waited patiently while Jessica wiped still more tears from her eyes and blew her nose.

Once again, Jessica allowed Lauren's presence to instill some peace in her. "I'm sorry," she murmured. "I don't know why I'm such a basket case whenever you're around."

"Hey, don't start with me on that," Lauren said. "Remember the tornado warning? Who was the strong one then? That's what friends are for."

"Since you're my friend, would you tell me something?" Jessica asked. "Why aren't my prayers getting through?"

"Oh, honey, God doesn't have any trouble hearing your prayers, but you know as well as I do that there's safety in numbers. I think it's one reason He put us together as churches. Ever read that verse in Ecclesiastes that reminds us about two being able to resist an attack better than one, and a cord of three strands isn't easily torn apart? The more you've got praying for you and *with* you, the better you'll feel."

"Thank you for praying."

"You've got more people out there in the waiting room praying for you and Archer. I think it'd help if you trusted them enough to confide in them just a little more. That way they'd have a better idea about how to pray."

"Helen Netz had a little talk with me about that a few weeks ago."

"Oh, really?" Lauren drawled. "This should be interesting. What did she say?"

"That a pastor and his family shouldn't confide too much in their church family. They should have their own group of ministers to help them share the burdens, and that's what ministerial conferences are for."

"Ministerial conferences!" Lauren exclaimed. "And you attend how many of those a year? One or two?"

"I've been to one with Archer since we got married."

"Well, excuse me, Jessica, but if I wasn't such a wonderful Christian I'd smack that woman silly for telling you such trash."

Jessica gasped aloud before she caught the glint of mischief in Lauren's eyes. Then, in spite of herself, she giggled.

Lauren hugged her tightly. "I don't think you should pay much attention to what she says."

"According to Helen, my mother-in-law never expected the church to carry her burdens, and she was always ready to help someone else, and—"

Lauren clucked her tongue and shook her head as she sat back. "Helen Netz needs her mouth washed out with Lava soap. I was practically born in a church pew. My daddy's been a deacon for forty years, and a church has to be a living, breathing organism if it's going to be the body of Christ. That means give and take, share burdens when they come, and pray for those in need of it—pastors and their families includ—"

Grant knocked and entered the room. "Excuse me for interrupting the sermon, Jessica, but how would you feel about being admitted for an overnight stay on the floor?"

She sat up. "Admitted? Why? What did the ultrasound show?"

"It isn't an ectopic pregnancy, but I would like you to have an exam. Dr. Campbell has a shift here tonight, so she can do it."

"What was wrong with the ultrasound?"

"Nothing at all, but since you're right on the borderline for showing fetal heart activity, an exam would relieve my mind just a little more, and we could watch you for other problems, since you've had a fainting episode. I'm also ordering a serum progesterone level test done as a double check. No more needles, though. We'll run this test on the blood that's already been drawn." He checked his watch. "There are some people from your church who want to see you."

Jessica gave Lauren a quick glance.

Lauren nodded.

"Okay," Jessica said. "I'd like to see some of them. Thanks, Grant."

He stepped out, and Lauren squeezed Jessica's arm. "You've got to trust me on this one, Jessica. You're as much a part of this church as any other member, and you need our support now. You've got to learn to accept it. You let me deal with Helen Netz."

Jessica breathed a silent sigh of relief when the two "representatives" from the church that came into her exam room were Caryn Dalton and the church secretary, Mrs. Boucher.

"Jess, you look a lot better now than you did a couple hours ago." Caryn pulled a chair around beside the bed. "Go ahead and have a seat, Mrs. Boucher. I'm too wired with nervous energy. Tony's using Henry for his eyes today, to help him coordinate the search. They've got SAR driving in from West Plains. He couldn't get the dogs yet, because they're out on another search."

"If it's any consolation, though," Mrs. Boucher said, "judging by all the prayers going up on Archer's behalf, he's covered every minute." She dabbed at her eyes with a tissue. "Every minute, let me tell you, by my prayers alone. You know I love that young man like my own. Have you heard when his parents are coming in? There's lots of people asking, wanting to see them."

"Maybe tomorrow," Jessica said.

Caryn touched her arm. "Jess, I hope you don't mind that I went to the church as soon as we brought you in. I knew you were in good hands with Grant and Lauren, and I felt they needed to know about your situation so they could be praying for you, too."

"Yes, and we got to work right away, let me tell you," Mrs. Boucher said. "We had volunteers for a round-the-clock prayer team and search teams to hit the hollers and roadsides as soon as they get the go-ahead from the police. Tony warned us we'd need to be careful about the possibility of messing up any scent the dogs might pick up on later."

"We've had seventy volunteers from the church to help search so far," Caryn said. "Now that the car's been found, they'll have a better idea about where to look."

"*Seventy!*" Jess exclaimed, overwhelmed by the response.

"Yes, and we spent the whole worship time in prayer this morning," Mrs. Boucher said. "Jessica, we all know this must be horrible for you, and we want you to know we're here for you whenever you want us. Several have volunteered to spend the night with you so you won't have to be alone."

"Thanks so much." *Don't cry again.* "Your prayers mean so much to me. I know God's in control, and I can't help feeling Archer will come walking in here any moment." It wasn't a lie. During her good moments, that was exactly what she believed. She just couldn't bring herself to tell them that her bad moments far outnumbered her good ones.

"You can tell everyone they won't need to pack their overnight bags," she said. "I've been offered the hospitality of a room on the patient floor tonight. They want to keep an eye on me after I passed out this morning."

"Oh, honey," Mrs. Boucher leaned forward, the lines around her eyes deepening with compassion. "I think this is the best place for you right now. You're bound to feel as close to Archer here as you would anywhere else, considering the amount of time he spends here. Nobody knows as well as you do how he loves praying with patients, and you've spent a lot of time here with him."

Jessica could have kissed the lady for referring to Archer in the present tense and for offering such a powerful reminder of the impact his loving concern had made on this place.

She hugged the two ladies good-bye and resigned herself to eating hospital food for the next couple of meals. While she waited to be released, she just might see if she could spend some of that time praying with other patients. It was what Archer would do.

―――――

The pain was becoming bearable again, and Archer lay with his eyes closed, listening to the roar of the river. In his fitful episodes of sleep that roar became the growl of some giant monster intent on swallowing him alive, but as he forced himself to think of other things, he noticed once again that a faint trickle of water dripped down next to him.

He was so thirsty. He reached his hand up and cupped his palm, allowed the water to trickle into it, then raised it to his mouth. It tasted wonderful. He drank again and again, until his thirst was quenched.

He looked out across the muddy surface of the river and felt a quiver of panic in his gut. The movement of the current nauseated him. How had he reached this spot alive?

"Thank you, God," he breathed. It had to be a miracle. He should have drowned.

But now he was hidden from view. Unless they came looking in this particular little depression for him—unless someone knew it was here—there was even less chance than before that they would find him.

He closed his eyes, dismayed by his own lack of faith. In one breath he was thanking God for the miracle, and then his next thought was one of faithless fear.

"Lord, are you here? Are you listening? Am I being punished for something?"

He waited, attempting to block out that devilish roar, but it grew louder. "Lord!" he shouted, then waited.

Nothing.

"Can't you hear me? All I'm asking for is a touch, some acknowledgment that you're here!"

He closed his eyes and waited a few minutes more, and he tried to quote Scripture out loud. The only Scripture that would come to mind at the moment was, "My God, my God, why have you forsaken me?"

Giving in to the fear, he gave another long, agonized cry.

———

Grant walked into his office during a Sunday afternoon slump to find Beau seated at his desk, expertly operating the keyboard.

"I guess you know you're not supposed to be accessing the records of the ER director." Grant pulled out a cushioned ladder-back chair from beneath the front lip of the desk and sank down into it.

Beau nodded and continued typing, his fingers racing across the keys. "I found another free program for your Pocket PC, Dad. It's great. I'm downloading it for you."

"I don't even know how to use all that other stuff you downloaded for me the other day, Beau. Give it a rest. I'll never be a techie—I'm an old-fashioned man who isn't getting any younger."

Beau looked up at Grant. "It's almost done. I can show you how it works whenever you have time."

Grant nodded. "There's the rub. How am I going to find the time?"

Amusement gleamed from Beau's eyes and barely lifted the corners of his mouth—the right side more pronounced than the left. At the sight of that smile, Grant felt a warm glow of joy in spite of his worry about Archer and his continued concerns about his proposal to Lauren.

Beau was mature beyond his age because of the emotional and physical damage he had endured three years ago in the automobile accident that had killed his mother. His special insight and thoughtfulness had given him privileges here at the hospital that few seventeen-year-olds were ever allowed, and Grant couldn't prevent the pride that occasionally caught him unaware.

"Speaking of time, Dad, you need to spend some of it with Brooke." Beau turned from his computer project.

"Is she still moping?" Brooke. Another special blessing—even when she didn't behave.

"She's worse than moping," Beau said. "She's miserable. She wasn't going to go to church this morning until I told her Lauren wouldn't be there because she's working today."

"Sounds to me like she's pouting. I thought we'd already discussed this subject."

"It wasn't a discussion, Dad, it was a lecture. You told her she needed to take a step back from the situation and see it from Lauren's point of view."

"I thought it was a good idea."

"But to Brooke it felt like you were siding with Lauren against her."

"I wasn't siding with anyone." He thought about the argument he'd had with Lauren earlier. She probably thought he was siding with *Brooke* against *her*. What a mess.

"I told her that," Beau said, "but I don't think it sunk in. At least it hadn't when I talked to her last."

"Maybe I just need to give her more time to think about it."

That was definitely disapproval Grant saw in his son's expression. "Remember how Mom used to react when you tried to do that with her."

"I know, I'm sorry, but maybe you and I should both leave it alone, give them a little space."

"And meanwhile act as if it doesn't concern you? Bad idea, Dad."

"No, I don't think it is. Lauren needs some space right now."

"But Brooke thinks it's all her fault that Lauren doesn't want to marry you."

That stung. "What makes you think Lauren doesn't want to—"

"It's just what Brooke thinks, Dad." The computer beeped, and Beau turned back to the screen. "Suit yourself. If you don't want to talk to Brooke about it, you'd better get her and Lauren together pretty soon. You know how Brooke gets emotional and jumps to conclusions. She's blaming herself for being so pushy with Lauren the other night."

"She said that?"

"She didn't have to, Dad, I can read her mind." He got up from the chair. "Your new program's downloaded."

CHAPTER 24

E arlier than usual on Monday morning, Mitchell Caine stood in front of his dressing room mirror, knotting his gray silk tie for the second time. His fingers didn't seem to want to work this morning.

Last night, he and Trisha had spent some strange "bonding" time together, though they had said less than fifteen words apiece during the three-and-a-half hours it had taken to watch two movies in the media room upstairs. She had even popped some popcorn in the microwave and put it into one bowl, which they had actually shared.

Amazing. In the four years preceding yesterday they had exchanged, at most, a dozen civil words.

It was the closest Mitchell had ever expected to come to restoring any kind of relationship with his daughter. Because of their shared time together last night, and because he'd reminded himself repeatedly that he must set a good example for her, he had not taken a Tranquen. Sweating and shaking in bed hours later, he'd given in and swallowed one pill. One innocuous benzodiazepine derivative for the peace he craved.

Now he still felt the effects of the drug taken too recently, with too little sleep. Down in the kitchen he drank espresso in sizable gulps and grimaced at the taste. He had to wash away the effects of the drug before seeing his first patient.

He sat down at the breakfast bar with his toaster pastry and another cup of strong brew, and decided to turn on the radio—a morning ritual in which he hadn't indulged since last Friday. He kept it low enough that it wouldn't awaken Trisha. He felt himself relaxing at the deep bass tones of the local radio announcer sharing tidbits of gossip and humorous vignettes in a segment called *About Dogwood Springs*.

The announcement came as he was swallowing his final bit of pastry, and he nearly choked.

"Efforts are still underway to upgrade the search for Archer Pierce, pastor of the Dogwood Springs Baptist Church. Reverend Pierce was last seen leaving the Dogwood Springs Hospital on Friday night, and was reputed to be en route to visit a sick—"

"Got any more of that?"

The sudden unexpected voice startled Mitchell. He dropped his espresso cup and it shattered on the counter. He stifled a quick curse and glared at his bleary-eyed daughter.

"Hey, sorry," she grumbled. "I didn't mean to interrupt—"

"Shh!" He held up his hand, straining to catch the rest of the news broadcast, but the announcer had gone on to other things.

Mitchell's stomach threatened to rebel against his breakfast. *Calm down. It isn't her fault.*

Archer's missing? He forced a tight smile and a shrug. "Sorry. I didn't expect you up yet. There's orange juice and milk in the refrigerator, but I . . ." He swallowed and cleared his throat. *It can't be.*

"I'm afraid you're on your own for solid food. You could scramble yourself some—"

"I'm not fifteen anymore, Dad," she said in that irritating monotone. "I know how to cook." She fingered a few short strands of dark hair from her forehead and watched him with bleak indifference. "Guess I'll see you tonight?"

"Yes. I'll make my rounds at the hospital during the day if I can get away from the clinic." If he even had rounds to make. As of last Friday afternoon, he had no patients in the hospital.

"Whatever," she said. "You don't have to come home early just for me, you know. It isn't as if we'll have anything to talk about."

He hated the lack of expression on her face, as if life was only to be endured—as if daughter had somehow inherited her father's outlook on life. "I'll see you tonight, then."

"Sure."

For a moment he thought he saw disappointment in the strange-familiar eyes of his daughter, but she turned away with a characteristic one-shoulder shrug and slouched back along the hallway to the guest bedroom.

He walked out the back door to the detached garage, where his Audi and Darla's Ferrari had been housed side by side until Darla moved out. The silver lines of his Audi Infiniti gleamed in the glow of cloudy morning light, and he hesitated.

During one of Darla's many periods of obsessive searching for a life-fulfilling hobby, she had insisted they turn half of their attached garage into a garden room, complete with skylights and a private garden she promised to personally tend. This meant that two of their three automobiles went to the two-car detached garage. Of course, Darla's interest in gardening had lasted about three months, until she realized that the desire of her life was to take courses to become an interior decorator. He had heard recently that she was managing a restaurant in Springfield, and he couldn't help wondering how long it would take for that place to fold.

He backed the Audi out into rain-washed morning light, then switched on the radio—something he rarely did on his way to work.

Today, however, he was leaving a little early, and the announcement was just being made when he turned up the sound.

" . . . Dwight Hahnfeld, a deacon in the pastor's church, told a reporter this morning that Reverend Pierce may have been caught in the flash flood that washed out the old bridge on the Black Oak River late Friday evening. His car was discovered in the early morning hours Sunday. . . ."

Mitchell drove past the hospital, past his clinic, and turned onto Highway Z. It was still a little early for his first patient. Maybe he was being paranoid—most likely so.

But what if he wasn't?

Grant sat down in his office and glanced out the open door toward the central desk of the emergency department. He had discovered years ago that he had a knack for administrative work, but today administration was more than he wanted to handle. He would gladly have traded duties with Dr. Jonas, who was only responsible for patient care this shift.

This was one of those catch-up days, which Grant had planned for when making out the schedule. Trying to play phone tag and conduct a crisis-team meeting while juggling himself through the hoops of ten exam rooms was too much for any ER director to ask of himself or of the people who worked with him. Consequently, he had reduced his shift hours, added another part-time physician and a physician assistant, even included some split shifts so he could make better use of the local family-practice physicians who couldn't pull all-nighters. It worked well, and though he didn't see as many patients now as he would like, his clinical skills were in no danger of getting rusty.

This morning, telephone tag was the game. He had just picked up the receiver to hit William Butler's speed dial number when he saw, to his surprised joy, Lauren McCaffrey approaching his open office door from the employee entrance.

She was dressed for the unseasonably warm spring weather in knee-length cut-off jeans and a T-shirt the color of watermelon. Her thick blond hair was pulled away from her face with clips and lay across her shoulders in loose waves.

She looked wonderful, and her smile was filled with pleasure at the sight of him as she stepped into the office. "A person would think I'd try to stay away from here on my days off," she said. "You busy?"

"Just getting started." He walked around the desk and drew her against him. He caught sight of the secretary grinning at him from the front desk, and with a smile he pushed the office door shut. Since a window graced the door, it offered no privacy, but it would muffle their voices. "How did you know I was just thinking about you?" he asked.

"Because I was thinking of you." She released him and sank down into the nearest chair. "I came to check on Jessica, and I wanted to apologize for—"

"No, I'm the one who needs to do that." He sat down across from her. "Sometimes we Sheldons can get a little self-absorbed. I should've realized long before Saturday that you would need some space, some time to think."

"And I should have understood that my actions might seem like rejection to you."

"I'm not the one we need to worry about."

She leaned forward, elbows on knees. "Brooke's still upset?"

"You know she's practically idolized you for months. I just didn't realize until Saturday evening how attached she'd grown and how deeply this perceived threat to our relationship would affect her."

Lauren looked down and hesitated. That hesitation concerned Grant. A lot.

"Lauren?"

She nodded, still not looking at him.

"I know it must be a little frightening to become emotionally involved with not just one but three strong-willed Sheldons." Lauren's continued lack of response was making him more and more uncomfortable.

She looked up at him. "If you're fishing for a denial, you're not going to get one from me, Grant. You're absolutely right, but it's more than just 'a little frightening.'"

"Good." It really was good. He just had to keep telling himself that, and apparently Lauren, as well.

"Oh, yeah, just wonderful." McCaffrey sarcasm. "It's the romance I've always dreamed of having—afraid to commit to a relationship because I'm such a coward."

"Which means you don't give your heart lightly. It means that when you do finally commit, I will always be able to trust you with my own heart, and my kids'. It means a lot, Lauren."

She looked down again.

He really did *not* like the implication of her silence.

"Look," he said, "what are your plans for the day?"

"I want to spend some time helping search for Archer."

"Would you be able to stop by the house tonight for dinner? Then maybe we could clear the air and let the dust settle."

"I'd like that. But don't go to too much trouble. I'm afraid I won't have an appetite if I'm expecting a conflict."

"Well, then, how about lunch? Just the two of us."

"Can't. Gina's off today, and I promised to have an early lunch with her."

"Okay, but I'd like to spend some quality time with you very soon, away from this place and away from my kids." They needed to iron out some of their recent misunderstandings, and that hadn't happened yesterday. He knew Lauren wasn't one to hold a grudge, but they did need to learn how to speak the same language so days like yesterday and Saturday didn't happen again.

"I barely got to talk to Jessica for a few minutes this morning," Lauren said. "Visitors from church were practically three deep in line to see her in the hallway, and some of them had mud on their shoes, so they'd either been helping in the search for Archer or they were helping some of the farmers dig out of the flooded area."

"No news about Archer yet, then," he said.

"Not yet. Jessica hasn't told anyone about the baby, and I don't blame her. She wants Archer to be the first to know he's going to be a fath—" Her voice faltered, and her eyes closed over the sudden pain betrayed in them. "Oh, Grant, what if they don't find him?"

He could see the struggle on her face. "I'm sorry, Lauren. This is the wrong time for me to be pressuring you about our relationship. You do know, don't you, that above all else, I am your friend? That's something you can depend on no matter what else happens." Not that he'd been proving that very well lately.

"Thanks," she said. "That means a lot. And you understand that I love Archer like a brother? I know there was a time last summer when my emotions became confused, but they aren't now. This has just hit me a lot harder than I would have expected."

"Especially since you lost your own brother so recently. Give yourself a break, Lauren, and I'll give you one, too." He leaned forward and kissed her forehead. "So are we on for dinner tonight?"

"I'll be there."

Mitchell continued to listen to the car radio as he took the final curve on Highway Z out of town. This led to the old bridge that crossed the Black Oak.

The plaintive country-western song ended on a note of steel guitar, and the heavy twang of the next singer's voice jarred on him. Mitchell preferred classical, but folks around here were heavily influenced by Branson, and he wanted to catch any updates about Archer.

He drove for another mile along the flat ridge until he came to the edge of a forest of dogwoods and cedar watered generously by the Black Oak River.

He slowed the car and studied the trees more closely. Dogwoods . . . What was it about the impression of dogwood blooms that stirred his memory?

But those trees were thick in their namesake city, and he would have had no reason to be on this road Friday night.

A car came up behind him, and he waved it around.

The news of Archer's disappearance had struck Mitchell with a sense of loss he would never have expected until a few months ago. Archer Pierce, of all people, had shown Mitchell compassion and kindness when others had spread rumors and stared at him in the hallways of the hospital after Darla left.

It had to be the shock of the news that also triggered this fear that Mitchell should know more than he remembered from Friday night. He'd spoken with Archer, but for how long? Mitchell had taken his Tranquen while he was still at the hospital. Judging from past experience, he most likely would never be able to remember more.

He came to a dip in the road and then a banked curve lined with dogwoods and cedars. He stopped several yards behind a line of pickup trucks and cars—this was the spot for which the town had been named in the first place. Beautiful dogwood trees, in full white-and-pink bloom, covered nearly an acre of land.

Settlers had come here more than a century ago and staked their claim. Mitchell knew this because the town reveled in its history—and Mitchell's great-great grandfather had been one of the founding fathers. He remembered squirming with discomfort in class when the teacher reminded the students of this piece of information.

Mitchell knew the cars belonged to searchers, and he watched as two more cars pulled over and the passengers got out and walked down-hill toward the forest, where the river flowed south of the bridge.

They're in the wrong place.

The thought startled him. He couldn't know that.

He drove another mile, studying the roadside, pressing his brake from time to time, as if staring long enough at the long-familiar land-scape would dredge up some new memory.

He was acting silly.

He blinked and once again saw the flash of red eyes imprinted on his lids.

On impulse, he pulled off the pavement and parked in the mud. In spite of his spotless dress clothes and shoes he got out of the car and treaded cautiously over the mud-laden grass toward the cliff he knew to be several yards past the loosely packed stand of cedar trees to the right side of the road. At the bottom of the cliff the Black Oak River encircled the ridge on three sides.

He knew this place because it had been a favorite party road when he was in high school—not that he came here much. There hadn't been time for that, and he had thought it pretty foolish to drink a six-pack of beer and then come to the cliffs to see who could dive from the highest cliff ledge without injuring himself in the process.

Impatient with himself, he turned from the river. There wasn't time for this trip down memory lane.

He glanced at his watch and trekked back to the car.

Highway Z had suddenly become far too public a place for him, and the radio announcer reminded him of the time. He was due at the clinic for his first appointment in ten minutes.

———

Grant didn't look forward to his next task. He picked up the tele-phone receiver and dialed Mitchell Caine's office number. It was answered on the first ring by a well-modulated female voice.

When he asked for Dr. Caine, he was informed that the doctor wasn't in yet. Reluctant to put this off, Grant left a message for Mitchell to call, then dialed Mitchell's home number and was taken aback when he heard a female voice.

"Hello?"

From what Grant knew of Mitchell's home life, the man was going through a nasty divorce, and his daughter was out of the picture entirely. "Hello, I hope I have the right number. I was looking for Dr. Mitchell Caine. Is this—"

"He already left for work."

"Thank you. I would like to leave a message, if I may. If you would tell him Dr. Grant Sheldon needs to speak with him, I would appreciate it."

"Sure, I'll make a note, but you might want to reach him at his office. I don't know what the number is." She sounded young, perhaps around Brooke's age or a little older, and Grant made a quick guess.

"Is this Trisha?"

A pause, then, "Yeah."

This could only be a good thing, considering all the stories Grant had heard about Mitchell's daughter. "Mitchell must be overjoyed to have you home with him."

There was a soft "Yeah, right."

Grant couldn't believe he'd just opened his mouth and nosed into someone else's business. Dogwood Springs mentality must be rubbing off on him. He smiled. "I'll try to reach him at the clinic."

"Okay. Bye."

Grant replaced the receiver slowly, unable to put a lid on his curiosity. . . . But he had other things to do.

He stepped out of his office and paused in the hallway. He heard Dr. Jonas talking to a patient in the nearest exam room, and then he heard another familiar voice—one he hadn't expected to hear in this department this morning.

"Would you like me to pray with you, Mrs. Normandy? I know it's frightening, but we've got excellent doctors here, and you don't have to do this all by yourself. We can take this case directly to the Great Physician."

The voice came from exam room three. He casually strolled past the open entryway and caught sight of Jessica Pierce standing beside the raised exam bed, holding the hand of an older woman with heart-monitor wires attached to her chest. Jessica's head was bowed in prayer, and she spoke softly, gently.

Grant smiled and returned to his office.

A few moments later, when Jessica stepped past his open doorway, he called to her.

"I thought you were a patient here," he said.

"Dr. Campbell checked me last night, and I'm fine."

"Yes, I know. She called me. I was hoping you would be able to rest some while you were here."

"I can't rest, Grant." She strolled over to a chair in front of his desk and sat down. "I need to get back out there and keep looking for Archer, but if I can't do that, I can at least help comfort others. It's what he'd be doing right now if he could."

"I understand how you must feel, Jessica. You're welcome to hang around and pray as long as you wish."

"Thanks. Archer's parents will be here to take me home this afternoon. In the meantime I'll check in periodically with the nurses on the patient floor." She grimaced. "Last night I had so many visitors from the church the nurses had to shoo them out to get anything done, and I caught Mrs. Netz questioning one of the aides about my condition. Do you think there's any chance that we'll be able to keep the—" she glanced over her shoulder toward the open doorway, then looked back at him—"my situation a secret?"

Grant thought about all the times in the past year that he'd made heroic efforts to ensure patient confidentiality in the emergency department. "It's possible, Jessica, but to be honest, you know how thin these walls are. One consolation I can offer you is that if word does get out, you still don't have to tell them anything. It will only be rumor, and everybody knows they can't count on rumors to be factual."

She gave a distracted nod. "It might seem silly to some people that I'm determined that Archer be the very next person to know about his baby. I think he has that right."

"And I think he's very fortunate to have a wife who loves him the way you do." Grant thought about that final conversation he'd had with Archer Friday night. "He knows it, too, Jessica. When we spoke together, he was making arrangements to lighten his chaplain call time so he could spend more time with you."

She nodded, then looked down at her hands in her lap. "I'm still trying to convince myself that I'll even see him again this side of heaven. I overheard two of the deacons guessing how far Archer might have been washed downriver."

Grant swallowed a sharp remark about the carelessness of those deacons. "What makes them think he was even in the river?"

"The car—"

"No, Jessica, they're making too many assumptions. All we know is that he didn't make it to Mrs. Eddingly's house Friday night, and that the car went in the river at some point. For the rest of the story, we'll have to depend on Archer to tell us about it when he gets home."

"You know, Grant, you're beginning to sound a lot like Lauren."

"Thank you." He stopped short of apologizing to her for sending Archer out on that errand in the first place. There would be time for apologies later.

"Do you feel like praying with another patient?" he asked instead.

"I'd love to."

───────

The smoky aroma of sausage permeated the air as Lauren carried her tray to the far window table in the hospital cafeteria.

Gina Drake's bright hair glowed red-gold in the light that streamed in. Leave it to Gina to find a table as far away from other diners as possible—the two of them seldom had time to eat together lately, and Gina was particularly paranoid about the hospital rumor mill.

Gina shoved a chair back for Lauren, toe tapping impatiently. "Gotta eat fast today." She tossed some fries onto Lauren's plate. "You keep living on lettuce, you'll lose all those great curves."

"I am not living on lettuce."

"I only have thirty minutes today. I'm telling you, we need more help in Respiratory Therapy. We barely get breaks anymore. Want to blow off the ER and join us?"

"Why, sure, Gina. You make it sound so appealing."

Gina tossed another fry at her. "It isn't usually this bad."

Lauren leaned back and looked around the dining area. It was typically busy at this time of day. Hospital personnel scheduled their breaks around the needs of the patients. Like Gina, if they didn't eat quickly, sometimes they missed a meal.

After a quick prayer, Lauren poured dressing over her salad while Gina picked up her steak burger.

"Okay, what's bugging you?" Gina asked. "Or to put it bluntly, give me the latest details in the saga of the Sheldons."

Lauren chuckled. "They haven't changed."

"How's it going with them? Seriously."

Lauren opened a packet of crackers and waved at Becky as she walked by. "Maybe a little uncomfortable right now."

"But I thought you and Grant—"

"Oh, don't get me wrong, I love them. It's just an adjustment trying to fulfill the expectations of so many people at once—and believe me, every one of them has different expectations."

"It's amazing how members of the same family can be so different." Gina doused a fry with mustard—her latest concession to weight management. "Are you implying that you might not mind being a part of that family?"

Lauren nodded.

"Permanently?"

"I'm still in internal argument mode."

"Well, take my advice and keep arguing until you've got it all straight in your head. You don't want to end up like me. You do *not* want to try raising two little kids without any help."

Lauren knew that wouldn't happen with Grant.

"But if you want my *opinion*," Gina said, "I think you've got a big enough heart to love Grant and those kids the way they need to be loved."

"How do you know that?"

"You love me and my kids. You stood by me when I needed a friend."

"That isn't the same."

"Love is love." Gina shrugged. "When you're in church with Brooke and Beau, it's like they're connected to you by remote. Either I hear Brooke talking about something you said, or Beau mentions working with you. Those are some pretty special kids, and they think you're pretty special."

"I still don't think I have what it takes to be their mother."

"Why should you expect to be their mother? You're already their friend."

Lauren thought about that for a moment. "There was a time I thought I would have enjoyed being Annette Sheldon's friend. Just listening to Grant and Brooke and Beau talk about her, I couldn't help admiring her."

"It sounds as if she'd be in good company," Gina said.

"I love it when Brooke comes to my house and plops down on my couch like she lives there, and yet there are times I feel threatened. My whole life is being taken over by these people, but I am growing to love them more with each passing day."

"Take my word for it, you're hooked." Gina's gaze focused on the cafeteria entrance. She put her half-finished burger on the plate.

Lauren looked. Todd Lennard entered with an attractive young tech from radiology. They appeared to be a little more than friendly.

Gina sighed, closing her eyes. "I'm so glad you stopped me before I made a fool of myself over him, Lauren."

"You made the right decision, but I thought he went back to his wife and kids."

"Sure he did, but being married didn't stop him before—why start now?"

Todd glanced toward them, and Gina looked away. "Maybe I won't get another chance, but you have one staring straight at you. Just make sure it's right for you, and for them, and then go for it."

"I will." Lauren reached for Gina's hand and squeezed it, then withdrew. "Your day will come."

CHAPTER 25

Monday evening, when Grant drove past the front of Mitchell Caine's clinic, the building seemed to hover in the shadows between pools of light from the street lamps on either side of it. He turned at the next intersection and circled back around the clinic property. The security system, which ordinarily illuminated the entire building to discourage would-be miscreants, had apparently not been engaged yet. As he slowed and turned the corner, light spilled from the windows of Mitchell's private office.

Willing away his own misgivings, Grant pulled into the deserted staff parking area; Mitchell had a private garage, and a private entrance, at the back of the building.

Soon after coming to Dogwood Springs, Grant had discovered that Dr. Mitchell Caine had a hang-up about authority. When Grant made a few changes in staffing and scheduling, Mitchell had been very unhappy, and since he was chief of medical staff for the hospital at the time, what might have ordinarily been minor conflicts escalated into small-scale wars on a couple of occasions.

The last time had been in December, when the hospital administrator was ill, and Grant was forced to be out of town for a week and a half. During that time Mitchell had attempted to fire Muriel, had alienated most of the hospital staff, including doctors, and had nearly toppled the clergy call program.

Everyone was relieved when the year ended and the mantle of chief of staff rested on the shoulders of another doctor. Grant suspected that even Mitchell had been glad, although he would never have admitted it to anyone.

Grant never needed to guess where he stood with Mitchell, because if the man was unhappy he would express his displeasure immediately and at length. Sadly, Grant had seldom heard him express joy, although Beau had commented a time or two that Dr. Caine had complimented him on his work as a tech in the emergency department.

Difficult to imagine.

To Grant's surprise, however, in spite of Mitchell's detached demeanor and abrasive attempts to gain authority, the man had occasionally revealed signs of tenderness. Unfortunately, he seemed ashamed of that tenderness. He had a particular soft spot for unwed teenaged mothers.

Grant went to the main clinic entrance and tried the door. It was locked, of course. He stepped through the shadows around to the back entrance. Through a gap in the vertical blinds he saw Mitchell seated at his elegant mahogany desk.

He just sat there, staring at the wall across from him. His silver blond hair looked slightly ruffled, the winged arch of his eyebrows drawn low over brooding eyes. He wore the standard uniform of a gray-and-white striped dress shirt with tie and slacks. His broad shoulders were slumped.

Grant knocked on the door. Mitchell didn't even look around.

Grant knocked again, this time harder and longer. "Dr. Caine, I need to speak with you, please," he called through the window.

At last, Mitchell turned and saw him. He got up and stepped out of view of the window.

Lately Grant had sensed something wrong with Mitchell—something more wrong than usual. They had never been the best of friends, but for the past few weeks Mitchell had barely looked him in the eyes. There was no animosity that Grant could see. Just avoidance. Mitchell avoided him entirely except when they were forced to interact on a patient case.

Grant felt uncomfortable about this visit. Who was *he* to pass judgment on someone else's reaction to personal problems? And yet, maybe it was specifically because of his own experience that he could do this with a clear conscience—because he had been through the bad times, and he knew how inappropriate behavior might affect a patient.

Also, as emergency department director, Grant was responsible for the welfare of the patients Mitchell treated when on duty there. He could be liable for any mistakes Mitchell made if he knew something was wrong with him and didn't take steps to make things right.

There was the sound of a lock turning, and then Mitchell pulled open the door. His expression was one of detached interest. "Dr. Sheldon? What can I do for you?"

"I need to speak with you, Mitchell. May I come inside?"

Mitchell hesitated. "Is it necessary at this moment? I'd like to get home."

"I'm sorry. I have no other choice. I attempted to reach you earlier but didn't have a lot of luck."

With obvious reluctance, Mitchell stood back and allowed Grant to enter. He gestured for Grant to be seated in an elegant Victorian chair.

"I'll try not to keep you long," Grant said as he seated himself in the surprisingly comfortable cushion. "When I attempted to contact you at home this morning I spoke with your daughter."

Mitchell's gaze flicked to him in surprise, which he quickly covered by circling the desk and seating himself behind it, as if to allow the expanse of it to separate them. "What can I do for you?"

Obviously, he wasn't interested in talking about Trisha. "First, I'd like to discuss your patient Mimi Peterson."

"Don't tell me she's suing me," Mitchell drawled.

"No, but I think her case could use further research."

"I've seen the reports generated to this office at least three times recently, and I saw nothing outstanding," Mitchell said. "It seems as if you and others have already taken it upon yourselves to do that research, so why should I duplicate what you've done?"

"Because unless you've released her from your service or she's requested a transfer of her medical records, you're still her primary physician. I'm telling you, as one professional to another, that further scrutiny is warranted. There's more going on here than simple drug seeking."

"Are you sure about that, or are you allowing her to manipulate you?" Mitchell asked.

Grant pulled his folded copies of the lab reports out of his shirt pocket and got up to hand them to Mitchell. "How many cases have you seen of acute intermittent porphyria?"

"Not a lot. It's a very rare condition. Don't you think you might be stretching things a little?"

"Read the results of the test."

Mitchell frowned and looked at the report. "You tested her blood PBG levels?"

"I've been doing some research on the condition, and if you'll notice in her records she has had sulfonamide antibiotics prescribed to her in the recent past, and has also had considerable weight loss, and has taken barbiturates, all of which can precipitate the disorder. I've also found that since the disorder affects the hemoglobin, the treatment for it is IV heme."

Grant waited while Mitchell studied the sheets.

Mitchell looked up then, and Grant saw a barely detectable change in the doctor's expression. Was that a spark of professional interest in those steel-hardened eyes?

"If you'll excuse me, I'd like to pull her file." Mitchell strode from the room.

Grant sat back, satisfied that Mimi might now have a better chance of successful treatment. That was the bright side of this visit. The dark side was still to come.

Archer listened to the spatter of rain on the surface of the river inches from his crumbling shelter. He no longer had much concept of time, but he estimated that he'd been without food for two or three days. Thank goodness he'd eaten so heartily Friday night before the deacons' meeting.

If the river continued to rise, his shelter would collapse completely. Even if he could move his legs without excruciating pain, he couldn't swim in the maelstrom that he heard by him in the darkness.

It would take another miracle for him to escape this alive. He had never felt so helpless.

The earth continued to crumble slowly down on top of him, and he lay in an ever-rising pool of river water. He could do nothing about it.

"God, I know you can get me out of this. Strengthen my faith, because right now, it's draining away faster than this cave is filling up."

His mother once told him that the secret to having faith was to stay in constant connection with God through prayer. She had said that she found herself spending more time in prayer for others at those times when she was the most troubled about something in her own life. She had learned the importance of establishing and maintaining constant interaction with the One who could answer her prayers and could ease her fears.

Archer had often followed her advice, but since this accident his prayer connection had been broken and faulty at best.

"I don't want to die yet, but if I do, comfort Jessica." She must be thinking he was dead by now.

His eyes stung with tears. "Jessica . . . Mom and Dad . . . the church. They must all think I'm dead. Give them peace, Lord. Please don't let Jessica carry this burden alone. Remind her that she belongs to you."

He continued to pray, desperate for that connection with God. Talking faster and faster, he named his family members and his friends. He named everyone he could think of in the church and patients with whom he had prayed in the recent past.

He named his friend Tony Dalton, who was preparing to undergo an experimental corneal transplant to regain his vision after being attacked with an ammonia booby trap in the middle of the drug wars. Tony's wife, Caryn, suffered alongside him.

The image of Mitchell Caine rose up in his mind—another victim of the meth influence in Dogwood Springs.

At the moment, Archer wasn't having very kind thoughts toward the man who had caused the accident in the first place.

Was Mitchell caught out in the storm with an injured back, unable to get to help? Had *he* been rammed from the road and left for dead? And yet, Archer knew the man was injured in other ways.

"Show yourself to him, Lord. Somehow take those stammering

words I've spoken to him and help them make sense. Help him to realize that just because I might die, you haven't let me down."

He heard the tone of sarcasm in his own voice.

"I know you haven't let me down, Lord. Just show Mitchell the truth, and dismantle all those barriers he hides behind to avoid you."

The wind picked up, screaming through the forest like a living thing.

The impulse to pray for Mitchell became even stronger.

"Lord, I don't know what else to say. Only you know. Touch his heart and open it to your love, your strength. Deliver him from his broken life. Heal him, Lord."

How ironic that Mitchell Caine would probably be offended if he knew someone was praying for him.

The wind grew louder; the water surged, chilling Archer as it drenched his clothing.

Another wave struck. More dirt crumbled down into his face. He might soon be buried here. Another wave splashed in, filling the space where he lay, trying to drag him from his place of safety into the dark Black Oak. With a cry of pain, he tried to brace himself in the cave, but water rushed over him, pulling him like an ocean tide.

He had to let go.

Whitecaps smacked his arms and legs, tossing him up then submerging him, moving too swiftly for him to catch a breath.

He choked and gasped, splashing ineffectually at the water with his arms. Knives of torture threatened to sever his spine. The river submerged him, rolling him sideways, twisting his body until he lost all sense of direction.

His hand smacked against a piece of debris. He grabbed it and pulled himself toward it until his face broke the surface. He gulped in huge breaths of air, unable to see anything through the blackness. No light struck the water as he battled the waves. He couldn't see either shore, couldn't even see the cliff.

He paddled toward his right, and his arm impacted with something solid. As he reached out to anchor himself, he discovered it was a floating log.

Something long and cold slithered across his hand. He gasped and cringed away from it.

A snake? A lizard?

He swallowed hard and tried not to move. He couldn't waste his time fearing something that probably wouldn't hurt him. Probably. Unless it was a cottonmouth . . . or a copperhead.

Could their venom be any more deadly than this river?

Though the air temperature was warm, he wouldn't last long in the frigid water. Whatever it was, tonight it would have to share this makeshift lifeboat with him. He swallowed his panic and with only the faltering strength of his arms dragged his resistant body to a precarious position on the log.

Still praying, for himself, for Jessica, and for others, he wrapped his arms around the log and held on as the current carried him with floodgorged speed down the river.

———————

"It's a rare condition," Grant said. "You shouldn't fault yourself for not picking up on it."

"I don't." Mitchell's voice held no animosity, but it wasn't exactly chummy. "It's a good diagnosis, I'll give you that, but as you said, hers is a rare condition. We'll begin treatment as soon as possible."

Grant leaned back in his chair and intentionally relaxed his posture. "Remember the baby we delivered the night of the tornado?"

Mitchell raised a cautious eyebrow. Nodded.

"His name is Clayton Grant Bonus."

No response, although Grant thought he saw a very slight softening of the man's features.

"I thought I remembered that your middle name was Clayton."

"I feel sorry for any baby named after me."

And yet Grant heard a faint note of tenderness in that controlled voice.

Grant stood up and stepped over to the highly polished credenza, on which rested a framed photograph of a man and woman, probably husband and wife. The man had many of Mitchell's features.

"Your parents?" he guessed.

"Yes. They died in a boating accident soon after that photograph was taken. I was in my residency at the time."

"I'm sorry. It must have been difficult for you."

"It was a surprise," Mitchell admitted. "My father had planned to have me join him in his practice when I completed my residency."

"I'd heard your father was a doctor."

"Did you also hear that my doctor father gave me no choice about my career?" He grimaced. "I nearly humiliated my whole family when I attempted to change my major from pre-med to physical education. I wanted to be a basketball coach." He shrugged. "Silly of me, I know, but my father was able to convince me of my error almost immediately. My decision was, of course, all financial. Where would I be now if I'd been allowed to follow that silly dream?"

"Maybe you would be happy."

Mitchell shifted in his chair and cleared his throat, as if realizing he'd revealed too much. "I don't think that's something you need to be concerned about, Grant. You didn't come here to commiserate about something that happened nearly a generation ago."

"One more thing and I'll be on my way. You know about the automobile accident that killed my wife and injured Beau. . . ."

"Yes?" Not a hint of compassion in that sharply spoken word, only an unspoken question.

"You also are aware, I believe, that I was injured, as well. So badly, in fact, that I could not attend my own wife's funeral." Grant didn't wait for a reply but continued. "I had thought, until that time, that I had recovered completely from the drug dependency that caught me in my youth. Unfortunately, that wasn't the case. I developed a dependency on my pain medication and was still hooked six months later."

"Dr. Sheldon, this isn't a confessional, and I'm not a priest."

"I know the signs, and I see those signs in you."

Mitchell stood up. "I don't think taking a sleep aid at night constitutes a drug addiction, and I don't have time for this conversa—"

"Why don't I tell you what I see." Grant knew he was taking a great risk confronting Mitchell without strong proof. This wasn't the way the intervention process was ordinarily done. "The first thing I've noticed was a change in the quality of your handwriting. Sometimes I have trouble reading patient charts when you've worked late at night, and when

I first came to Dogwood Springs I was jealous of your precise penmanship."

"You're basing this accusation on handwrit—"

"Mimi Peterson wasn't the first patient you kept waiting an inordinate amount of time after you said you would come in. We've had several complaints. You and I have discussed this problem."

Mitchell stalked to the window. "Complaints." He spat the word over his shoulder. "Since when do physicians get anything but complaints these days?"

"How often do we have babies named after us?" Grant asked softly. No reply.

"I'm wondering if you've been having some difficulty keeping up with your busy schedule lately," Grant said.

"Maybe I should devote myself to my patients at all hours of the day and night, through every weekend, until I drop dead from exhaustion." He swung around and returned to his desk.

"I shouldn't take time to sleep—oh, no! That would be selfish of me. I should come running in here like a good little doctor every single time one of my patients speaks my name, because anything less and I wouldn't be meeting standard of care!"

Grant waited for a few seconds as the harshness of those words hovered in the atmosphere of the office. "Mitchell, your anger has gotten out of control on at least two occasions, according to patients and staff."

"You've been collecting evidence against me?"

"No, I haven't, and after nearly a year of working with me, you should know better. I've tried several times to help you. I know about the difficulties you've been having in your personal life, and—"

"As I said, my personal life is not your busi—"

"It is my business when it affects patient care and when it reflects on our hospital."

"My clinical skills are as good as—"

"No, they aren't as good as they ever were," Grant heard his own voice rising to match Mitchell's, and he lowered it. "Did you even read the review I left in your box? I've tried time after time to contact you by telephone. You're avoiding me."

"Amazing that I should do so, don't you think?" Mitchell said dryly. "Considering the fact that I knew I would most likely be castigated like a schoolboy."

"I'm not treating you like a schoolboy, Mitchell. I'm coming to you with reasonable concerns and an offer to help in any way I can, but I can't help you if you won't let me."

"What makes you think *you* can help *me*? And please don't preach to me about your church ethics."

Church ethics? That was a term Grant had never heard before. "I think I already explained that. I've been in a similar situation."

Mitchell gave no response.

"When I was struggling with prescription-drug dependency, I never noticed my own clinical skills slipping until afterward. If I had allowed myself to continue as I was until I made a serious error in judgment, it might have been too late for one of my patients. I'm sure you don't want that to happen." He paused and then used the argument he knew would most grab Mitchell's attention. "You wouldn't want to be sued."

"I *am* being sued. For divorce."

"Mitchell, you have been observed, from time to time, taking medication while you were on duty in the ER."

"And who would tell you such a thing?"

"More than one person has expressed concern."

"They saw me taking a *pill*? Come on, Grant, even you can see the stupidity in that pitiful attempt to incriminate me. I could have been taking an aspirin or a vitamin, and last I read on the subject, aspirin is not—"

"Do you keep your aspirin in a prescription bottle?"

Mitchell's winged brows lowered and his face darkened with anger. "You're intruding on my privacy. I am *not* a drug addict."

"It is my responsibility to make sure you aren't. I'm sorry, Mitchell, but until further notice, I'm going to have to remove your name from the schedules. Both of them."

The anger drained suddenly from Mitchell's face and was replaced by surprised shock. "Have you spoken with the administrator about—"

"Mr. Butler wanted to spare you the pain of a confrontation with both of us or with the medical staff if at all possible. Please, Mitchell, don't fight me on this."

Mitchell's mouth worked silently and then, "I'm telling you I'm not an addict. I take a sleep aid, that's all."

"But do you take it before you go home in the evening?"

"Only on rare . . . only on occasion, when I know I'm going home before the drug takes effect."

"But you have been observed—"

"Yes, I know, but there have been times lately when I was inordinately delayed after taking the medication."

Grant leaned forward. "Tell me why you would even *want* to take a sleep aid before you get home at night."

"If you had the trouble sleeping that I—"

"Nothing takes that long to take effect, and I *have* had trouble sleeping. Unless you're using the drug for something besides sleep, there would be no need to use it here or at the hospital."

Mitchell said nothing.

"I'm sorry to have to do this," Grant said as he stood up. "Believe me, I want to help you break the cycle before it affects your practice. Would you like to get together over coffee a couple of mornings a week, or maybe come to my house for dinner? I make a mean barbecue, and you could bring Trish—"

"I fail to see how sharing coffee or a meal is going to ease the schedule crunch you'll have if you take me off the schedule."

Not a surprising response, but disappointing. "If you decide to talk with me about it, you know how to reach me. The change in schedule will take place tomorrow."

Grant arrived home to find Brooke, Beau, and Evan Webster congregated around his computer, arguing about an article Evan had written for *The Dogwood*.

Evan had recently won a nationwide competition for high school students in journalism. Grant couldn't help wondering how well Evan would do if he didn't have Brooke and Beau editing him to pieces, correcting his punctuation, cutting his purple prose. It was a moot point, however, since the three of them were inseparable.

"Heads up, you three, we have a dinner guest coming."

Brooke looked up from her post at the keyboard. "Who's that?" she asked warily.

"Guess."

"When's she going to be here?"

He could tell from the tone of his daughter's voice she still hadn't forgiven Lauren for Saturday, but he didn't want to get into it when Evan was within range, or their little disagreement might find its way into the town paper—or maybe the school paper.

"Okay, editing session's over," Beau said, pushing his chair back from the worktable. "Can Evan stay for dinner?"

"Of course," Grant said. "Evan, you know you're always welcome here."

"Thanks, Grant, but Dad's still feeling a little cranky now that he's healing. And Jade's coming to dinner tonight. Dad wants me to help cook." Evan stacked his papers and stood. "Know what I think?"

"Yeah, yeah, we know," Brooke said. "You've told us at least sixteen times in the past week."

"You haven't told me," Grant said.

"He thinks Jade's going to pop the question tonight," Brooke said.

"I didn't say that, Brooke, I said Dad was going to—"

"Well, it'll have to be Jade, because your dad'll never do it. When it comes to women, Norville Webster is as backward as Beau."

"Which goes to show you really *don't* know everything, Brooke," Evan said. "Want to work on this more tomorrow, guys?"

"What don't I know?" Brooke asked.

Ignoring her, Evan stacked his papers and stuffed them into the new leather book bag his stepdad had given him. He winked at Beau and hurried out the front door.

"Evan Webster!" Brooke called after him.

"Let him go," Beau said. "How about barbecue tonight?"

"Lauren likes your apple-honey sauce on chicken, Beau," Brooke said grudgingly, arms crossed over her chest as she strolled to a barstool and perched on it. "But don't make the chocolate cake like you did last time. Chocolate keeps her awake."

Grant and Beau looked at each other. Beau nodded and whispered, "I think she's getting over it, Dad."

"Beau, what was Evan talking about?" Brooke asked.

"Might as well tell her," Grant told his son. "She'll make life miserable for all of us until you do."

"I have a date for the prom," Beau said. "With Dru Stanton."

"You're kidding."

"Am not."

"*You're* going to the prom with her? Do you know how many guys have asked her?"

Beau leaned back in his chair, clasping his hands behind his head, looking smug. "*She* asked *me*."

"Does her grandmother know? She thinks you're a masher."

Grant smiled to himself as his children continued their good-natured insults. Maybe there really was something about springtime inspiring romance. He just hoped everything went well with Lauren tonight, because he was ready for the next step.

So were his kids.

CHAPTER 26

Jessica squirmed in the recliner. Before she could shift her weight Mom Pierce was at her right side. "Honey, do you need something? Can I get you a drink of water?"

"I'm fine, Mom. Thanks." Jessica couldn't imagine the heartache Eileen was going through herself. Her kindness and hospitality put Jessica to shame.

"How about a bite to eat? Can't have you getting sick on us again."

"Thanks, maybe after a while."

"Just let us know. We want you up to snuff when Archer gets here." Mom turned back to her conversation with Mrs. Boucher.

Jessica thanked God silently for her mother-in-law's graciousness. As if to attest to her merits, the living room held some of her closest friends from her many years of service beside her husband in the ministry of Dogwood Springs Baptist Church.

How did she do it?

Each of the visitors had brought food and then stayed for a visit, and Jessica knew it was her mother-in-law's presence that made them feel so welcome. It made Jessica feel that much worse, because she wanted to be alone.

To her left sat Helen Netz, ostensibly visiting to make sure Jessica was feeling better, but in reality everyone knew she wanted a nice long visit with Eileen. She seemed frustrated that others were taking so much of Eileen's attention.

Earlier that afternoon, when Mom and Dad Pierce brought Jessica home from the hospital, she had felt faint at the sight of so many cars parked in the driveway and along the street. She'd recognized those cars—most belonged to church members. One pickup truck belonged to Roger McCaffrey, Lauren's brother, who had been good friends with Archer. The one vehicle she'd been relieved to see was her father's old farm truck.

At this moment, it seemed about half the congregation was either crowded into the parsonage or out combing the riverbanks in search of Archer. Charles Lane had elected to mow the yard for her—an obvious sign of his discomfort around so many strangers in spite of his need to be there for his daughter.

As Jessica sat listening to bits and pieces of at least three sets of conversations around her she felt overwhelmed.

" . . . can't think what's going to happen if the mayor does marry that Webster fella. She's a bit headstrong, if you ask me. . . ."

" . . . that little redhead who works in the Respiratory Department at the hospital? I'm thinkin' about settin' her up with my nephew. . . ."

" . . . don't know why she hasn't put that uncle of hers in a home. He'll get himself killed one day. . . ."

" . . . things seem to've cooled off between Dr. Sheldon and Lauren after she turned up missing all day Saturday. You don't suppose . . ." Several sets of gazes turned in Jessica's direction.

Jessica pretended not to hear. She wished she hadn't. She also wished they would take their gossipy minds out of this house.

Home had always been her haven, where she didn't have to be "Jessica Lane Pierce, Branson entertainer," or "Jessica Pierce, pastor's wife," but just plain Jess, who was far from perfect, who still struggled to have enough faith to get her through this crisis, and who was tired of smiling for the public.

"So, Jessica," Helen Netz said, scooting closer to the recliner and lowering her voice. "We missed you at church yesterday morning." Her birdlike eyes studied Jessica from behind bifocal lenses. "We held a prayer meeting instead of a regular service."

"Thank you, Helen."

"You know, you don't need to be carrying this whole burden on your own shoulders, when God is right there to help you."

Don't start with me, Helen. "I was out searching for Archer."

"We were, too, right in that church on our knees. There's no better way to reach God."

"Thank you," Jessica said. "I appreciate your prayers."

"We want to get our Archer back home. Did the doctor say what was wrong with you yesterday? Did you have the flu or something?" Her attention seemed to focus just a little more intently.

Jessica would not lie, and she would try hard not to be rude. "I don't seem to be handling the stress very well right now."

"Oh?" Helen waited, expectant, as if hoping for further explanation. When none was forthcoming, she put a hand on Jessica's arm and rubbed it, patted it, took her hand and squeezed it. "You're going to have to put all your trust in God to bring Archer back home again."

Jessica couldn't swallow her irritation. "Are you trying to tell me I can't trust God and still keep looking for my husband? If I have to comb the whole countryside myself, I'll do it."

"But why do you feel as if you have to do it yourself?" Helen asked, her voice no longer as soft as it had been. "If you could just put all your trust in God and let Him—"

"You make it sound so easy, Helen," Jessica snapped. "Are you saying that the reason we haven't found my husband yet is directly linked to my lack of faith?"

There was a hush in the room. Jessica felt the chill of humiliation.

Helen looked stunned, and Jessica remembered what Archer had said about the Netzes losing two children years ago. Did Helen feel that her own lack of faith had somehow caused those deaths?

Mom Pierce turned to Jessica. "Honey, that's a question I've asked myself and God from time to time over the years. It's a horrible thought and in my opinion very destructive. I'm sure that isn't what Helen meant at all, is it, dear?"

"I . . ."

"Of course it isn't," Mom continued. "For me, faith isn't something I do, it's something God gives me when I ask, and when I keep the communication lines open to Him. Over the years, especially through the hard times, I've found that all the faith I need is the faith to pray. I give voice to my needs and let God take it from there."

"I've been doing that constantly," Jessica said softly.

"Of course you have," Mom said. "But you know what? When you're struggling, I need to know how to pray for you. When I'm struggling, you need to know how to pray for me."

"Are you struggling, Mom Pierce?"

Those beautiful eyes filmed with tears. "You'd better believe it," she whispered. "I have to keep giving it to God every few seconds."

The doorbell rang. One of the neighbors came in carrying a pot roast. Mom got up to take the roast and thank the neighbor and invite her to have some tea and a piece of pie that someone had brought to the house sometime during the afternoon.

Jessica had lost track of the number of people who had come through the front door in the past few hours bringing food and offering help, loving hugs, a prayer or two. Mom Pierce had taken it upon herself to keep a list of visitors.

The house smelled richly of fried chicken and baked ham and liver and onions and apple cobbler. Any other time, Jessica would have tasted a little of everything. Today she had to force the bites down, reminding herself she was feeding the baby.

The baby . . . Archer should be here right now to share the joy with me.

She wanted to go into their bedroom and look at his picture and smell the scent of him in the room. If she could just open the closet door and inhale and close her eyes, she could imagine, for a few seconds, that he was nearby, and if she didn't have all these witnesses in the house, she would talk out loud to him and give him the news and imagine his response.

Oh, Archer, where are you?

And yet, she knew these dear people also felt the impact of the horror. They needed to feel as if they were doing something. She couldn't turn them away. She could, however, escape for a few minutes—if Mom Pierce and Mrs. Netz and the rest of the visitors would let her get out of the chair. How did *they* spell overprotective?

The front door opened once again. Jessica looked up expectantly, as she did every time someone new arrived; Archer could be the very next one to cross the threshold.

This time it was her father, his jeans and chambray shirt and well-worn work boots covered with grass from mowing the lawn—he'd obviously finished the job in the dark.

He looked straight at her over the heads of the company. "Heard anything, punkin?"

She took comfort from the earnest compassion in those shy hazel eyes. Her father hadn't always known how to express his gentler feelings when she was growing up, but lately she had been able to understand the meaning behind his awkward gestures. "Not yet, Daddy. Why don't you come on in and—"

"Mr. Lane, why don't I get you a tall glass of tea?" Mom Pierce strode across the room and placed a hand on his shoulder. "I know you must be hot and tired after chopping down that forest out there."

Daddy looked down at his clothes again, dusted his hands off on his jeans. "Naw, I can get a drink from the spigot out back. Don't want to track grass all through—"

"Nonsense, this house has had plenty of grass tracked through it." Eileen gently drew him toward the kitchen archway. "I tell you, lawn mowing was almost a full-time job when we lived here. I like living in a townhouse and letting someone else do the yard work for us."

"And how about some cake." Helen Netz jumped up and followed her friend, obviously eager to be of service to somebody. She turned to include the rest of the visitors in her invitation. "The Amish family down the road from us brought a gallon of their rich whole milk, straight from the cow. I swear that's the best stuff I've ever tasted, like pure cream, and if someone else doesn't drink it I'll have to take it home with me and down the whole gallon myself, and then John'll make me go with him on his exercise excursions all over town. . . ."

While Dad protested about leaving grass stains on the carpet and Helen and Eileen assured him they would clean it up, the majority of the visitors either made their farewells or drifted toward the kitchen and dining room for an evening snack.

Jessica sat back in relief. Mom Pierce had easily settled into the role of hostess once again.

Mitchell made a small detour and drove past Archer Pierce's house on his way home from the clinic. He counted seven cars parked along the street and two more in the driveway. He drove past without stopping, frowning at the incongruity. A local pastor turns up missing, and everyone in town—probably everyone in the Ozarks—knows about it. A local physician's daughter comes home after being gone for years, and no one even knows.

Would anyone care if they did know?

It was possible that the one person who might have cared was the person they were searching for.

Irritated by his own thoughts, Mitchell made a U-turn. Time to get home.

Still, he wondered how Archer's wife was taking the pressure. Was she experiencing that perfect peace that he'd heard Christians claim to have?

He doubted it. Nothing could ease the pain of loss he had felt when Trisha ran away from home. Both times.

Perhaps if he were to speak with Jessica, maybe let her know he understood what she was going through. . . . He touched the brake pedal as he thought about it, but when he passed the house again and saw those cars parked along the curb, he hit the accelerator and drove past.

Not tonight.

If Archer was right and there was a physical hell, then today had been a prime example of it at the office. Not only had the news of Archer's disappearance been announced at least ten times over the course of the day on the radio—the secretary insisted on keeping it on all day—but the announcer who came on at noon kept referring to the search for "the body" of Archer Pierce

As if he were already dead.

Something about that enraged Mitchell. How dare they assume such a thing?

And then tonight Grant comes by the clinic to ruin the day completely. It must take a special type of self-control to be so polite when you're thrusting a knife blade into someone's back.

Would the hospital try to alienate his own patients from him? Would they even call him if one of his patients needed treatment for any reason? He'd had no experience with this kind of thing before. Of *course* he'd had no experience—it wasn't as if he were an alcoholic or a drug addict!

He pulled the Audi into the rear garage and pressed the remote to close the overhead door.

He walked from one garage to the other and switched on the light. He had not removed the dented, muddy brush guard from the Envoy, and as he looked at the SUV he felt a subtle tightening along his neck and shoulder muscles, as if a weight were pressing down on him.

What was he missing?

When he walked into the rear foyer of the house from the garage, the lights were on in the kitchen and great room, but all was silent. No radio. No television.

"Trisha?"

He checked the guest bedroom, which would, he hoped, be her bedroom for quite some time. The door was open, the room empty.

After a few minutes of searching he realized Trisha wasn't in the house. But what did it matter? The girl was past the age of accountability, even if she did look like a starving waif. If she stayed home long enough, he hoped to feed her back to health.

What he didn't want to think about was where she had gone. Was she meeting someone? Was she looking for a meth fix?

If not, then how long would it be before she did so? He knew the statistics. Every time a meth addict took the drug, he was making it infinitely more difficult for himself to break the cycle. If he continued, he could expect the habit to last about eight years. Then he died. She'd been at this for how long? Nearly four years? He didn't know for sure.

He didn't know how to help her. She wouldn't stay home long without her mother. Without Darla here, he didn't even know how to pretend to be a family.

He sank down onto a living room chair and cradled his forehead in his hands, feeling as if his own life were being stolen from him. He'd been taken off the call list. He'd been taken off the ER schedule.

Perhaps if he called Grant at home . . . Perhaps if he made another attempt at a better explanation . . . Or maybe he should put out some feelers to see exactly what Grant meant by "help."

Or maybe, if he kept his mouth shut and stayed away from the hospital for a while except to make rounds, all this would blow over. All he had to do was make sure he always waited until he got home to take the Tranquen. Simple. Any brainless idiot could figure that out.

So why couldn't he wait?

Maybe he should stop taking the medication altogether.

Perhaps a few sleepless nights would be preferable to this nightmare.

———

"I'm gonna take off now, punkin."

Jessica looked up to see her father pulling on his bill cap and hunkering down beside her chair. "Okay, Dad. I guess you've got some animals to feed at home."

"Got a couple of cows getting ready to calve. Hounds'll be hungry." He looked down at his work boots, his weathered face lined with worry. "Guess you got plenty of people here to watch out for you. Everything looks up to snuff outside, I think."

She eased down the footrest of the recliner. "I'll be okay, Daddy." Daddy. She longed to be able to tell him he would be a granddaddy in a few months. There would be time—later, after they found Archer.

She eased up from the chair and stood. She didn't feel dizzy. She felt strong enough to go searching for Archer again.

"Guess I'll be back up tomorrow," Dad said. "I'd like to help more with the search. Don't know what good I'll be, but I've hunted down a few cows in my time. Might be an extra pair of eyes when they're needed." He paused. "Besides, I need to make sure my girl's okay."

"Oh, Daddy." Jessica laid her head against his shoulder and let the tears come while he patted her awkwardly on the arm. "I know he's out there somewhere, and I don't believe he's . . . dead. I can't believe that."

"Well, might be you oughta keep believin' he's hangin' on. I might bring Coot with me tomorrow. He'd be more likely to sniff Archer out than those other dogs. He already knows the scent."

"Thanks, Daddy." She gave him a final hug and let him go. As she watched him drive away, she placed a hand over her abdomen.

Under cover of the chatter in the kitchen, she stepped down the hallway into the master bedroom, switched on the lamp, and closed the door behind her. Their wedding picture graced the bureau beneath the mirror on the far side of the room. She walked over to it and picked it up, and reverently caressing the carved wood frame, she gazed into those precious blue eyes of her husband for a long moment.

"How I love you, Archer," she whispered. "Now more than ever. I can't wait to tell you about the baby. When they find you . . . when *we* find you . . . I hope no one lets the news slip before I have the chance to tell you about it. I want to see your reaction, to watch your face, to see your happiness."

Holding the picture against her chest with one arm, she strolled over to the framed miniaturized sheet music of a song she had written a few months after she first met Archer. "Diamond in the Rough." She sang it in her show. She had never won an award for it, as she had some of the others. It had never hit the charts. But it was one of her favorite songs and one of Archer's, as well. For her birthday last year he had surprised her with this framed copy of the complete song. He was always doing things like that. It was one reason she loved him so much.

She closed her eyes and softly whispered a few lines from the song. *"Don't forget, when times are tough, you're a diamond in the rough. He wants you to reflect His light, like a jewel glowing in the night."* Archer had been the one to convince her that God had all the power necessary to use the pain in life for goodness when His people allowed it.

She opened the closet door and allowed the familiar scents to waft across her. She could almost feel his presence.

There was a knock at the door. "Jessica?" The familiar female voice startled her from the bittersweet drift of imagination.

"Yes, Helen?"

"You okay in there?"

"Yes, I'm fine." *Keep the voice pleasant.* "What can I do for you?" *You grumpy old busybody.*

"I was just checking on you."

Jessica knew the lady was hovering at the other side of the door, and she finally relented and opened it. Helen stood there with her hands clasped together in front of her.

Jessica swallowed her annoyance. But, really, she was a grown woman. Why did Mrs. Netz have to continually treat her like a disobedient child?

Patience, Jess. Got to have patience. "Thank you for your concern, Mrs. Netz, but I'm fine. Really."

"Oh, good, because I certainly didn't intend to be hurtful earlier. I just felt I might be able to help you see the importance of faith and faithfulness, the way I see it, anyway."

"Thank you for wanting to help," Jessica said. "I agree that I probably have a lot to learn about faith in God, because I haven't been a Christian for very many years. But I don't feel that my doubts, or my fear for Archer's life, will *end* his life." *Just as you didn't cause your children's deaths because you couldn't work up enough faith to protect them, Helen.*

"Yes, but the Bible says if we don't have faith—"

"Jessica?" Eileen came walking down the hallway toward them. Her face had lost its healthy color. Her steps were unsteady.

"Mom? What is it?"

Eileen reached for her, gripped her hands hard, drew her into a tight embrace. "Oh, honey, Dwight just arrived. They're pulling a body from—"

"No!" Jessica screamed the word. "Oh, God, no, no. Please!"

L auren covered her right ear with her free hand and placed the receiver over her left, waiting for someone at the Sheldon household to pick up, while trying to ignore the tension behind her in the Pierce kitchen. She would have used the extension in the den, but there were people in there, as well. Her cell phone was at home where she usually left it.

Word had obviously spread that Archer's parents were in town— some twenty visitors were congregated in tearful prayer groups around the house.

Eileen Pierce sat with both arms around Jessica at the kitchen table while John Netz prayed aloud, voice broken with tears. Helen cried with heartbroken sobs.

All they could do was wait for further word. The rescuers were having a difficult time getting the body out of the water, according to Dwight, who was pacing in front of the living room door with his cell phone in his hand, as if his diligence would prevent more bad news from entering the house.

Nobody knew the identity of the victim yet.

"Hello?" Brooke answered the phone.

"Hi, Brooke, this is Lauren." She spoke as softly as possible. "Is your dad there?"

"He's outside tending the barbecue grill. When are you coming over?

We thought you'd be here an hour ago. Beau's fixed your favorite barbecue sauce."

"Well, something has come—"

"I told Beau specifically not to fix chocolate cake, but he's making
your favorite fruit salad."

"Oh, Brooke, I'm so sorry about this, but—"

"Lauren, don't you *dare* tell me you're going to stand us up."

At the table behind her, William Butler took up the thread of prayer.

"Lauren?" Brooke said.

"I'm sorry, honey, I'll explain later. Why don't you go ahead and
start without me."

There was a long silence.

Lauren cleared her throat. "Brooke, I—"

"You're not coming, are you?"

"Probably not tonight. I'll have to talk to you later, okay?"

A long silence, then a heavy sigh. "Oh." There was definitely hurt in
Brooke's voice. Until they knew for sure the identity of the victim, she
didn't want to say any more, and she was secretly furious at Dwight for
barging in with the awful news without waiting to see if it was Archer.

"Thanks for at least calling," Brooke said.

"I'll talk to you soon."

"Yeah. Sure. Bye." The line disconnected.

Lauren joined the others at the table as Muriel Stark's quiet entreaty
to God filled the silence.

———

Mitchell was waiting at the front door when Trisha unlocked it and
peered inside.

"Where have you been?"

"I didn't think you'd be home so soon," she said, her voice a little
too bright, "so I went out for a walk, thought I'd get something for
dinner." She picked up a pizza box from the wrought-iron bench on the
porch and carried it inside.

He glanced at the jeans that hung down around her hips and one of
his shirts he'd given her to wear, with the tails tied around her stomach
to reveal her navel and far too much of her abdomen.

"Where did you get the money?"

"I raided the cash you always leave on your dresser. You know, you've done that forever, Dad. And you don't have a lot of food in the house."

He could smell the sharp, smoky scents of tomato sauce and cheese, and the mellow aroma of freshly baked bread. For just a moment, he allowed himself to be relieved. She was home. And she was hungry.

But as he followed her into the kitchen his relief ebbed. Something about the way she behaved—a little too quick to explain where she'd been, unwilling to meet his gaze . . .

"I don't suppose you happened to run into any of your old friends while you were out walking." He pulled some plates from the cabinet and set them on the table.

"No." None of the defensiveness he would have expected from her.

He gave her a quick look as he took napkins from another counter. "You might not have heard about the major meth house raid we had a week before Simon died. Tony Dalton organized it, and they took down some major players. They've caught a few more since then. Even blind, Tony is very vigilant, and the drug trade has dwindled a great deal recently."

She gave that one-shoulder shrug. "So why are you telling me this?"

The effort to appear nonchalant didn't fool him. "Because I don't want you to waste your time looking for something that isn't there."

A flush rose to her face. She didn't reply.

It almost confirmed his suspicions, and it frightened him. "Tell me something, Trisha. Why did you really come back to Dogwood Springs?"

She opened the box of pizza, fumbling with the cardboard. "Because I was kicked out of my apartment and didn't have anyplace else to go."

"Any other reason?"

She shot him an irritated glance and grabbed one of the plates from the table, shoved a slice of pizza onto it, slapped it onto the table at his place. "Why don't *you* tell *me*, since you seem to know so much."

"I think your source ran dry in Springfield, and you thought you could con your parents out of more money if you came home and played the contrite daughter."

She glared at him. "Did I try to con you out of money?"

He gestured toward the pizza. "If you could find enough of my cash lying around to buy that, you had enough to buy a hit of meth if you could find the right person. You knew exactly where to look." He needed to be more careful about where he put his money from now on. He'd never lived with a junkie before.

Her gaze narrowed, iced over, plunged through him. "I don't know how Mother stayed with you for twenty years," she spat. "I'm grown now. I can leave anytime I want."

Spoken like a rebellious adolescent. "You've already told me you don't have a place to stay. Home was your last resort." He swallowed his bitterness at this nasty fact. "You don't even have a car you can sleep in, and obviously you have no money. What are you going to do to earn it? Steal the ingredients and cook up a batch of meth yourself? Sell your body on the street?"

Surprise flashed for a moment, and then her icy gaze darkened. She looked down at her plate.

He would have preferred it if she'd thrown the pizza in his face and flounced out of the kitchen. It frightened him that she didn't. What else *had* she done?

"You can stay here and let me help you through this," he said, "or you can go out there and take your chances. I have a feeling that as mean as I am, your drug buddies can be meaner."

As she continued to stare at her plate, his own thoughts mocked him. What made him think he could help her now? He couldn't even help himself.

———

"It wasn't Archer!" Dwight's cry shot through the house, interrupting prayers and tears and bringing a loud gasp from Helen.

He came dancing into the kitchen, holding his cell phone above his head as if it were proof of his words. "Said it wasn't him!"

"You sure?" John asked.

"Yep. Said it was some older guy with gray hair. They're trying to find some ID now, but it wasn't our Archer!"

The house erupted. John Netz shouted a hallelujah and hugged his wife. Eileen caught Jessica in a choking grip, tears streaming down her face. Over Eileen's shoulder, Jessica saw Lauren cover her face with her hands.

"Thank you, God," Jessica whispered as her mother-in-law released her and turned to the others. "Thank you."

"But who was the poor man?" Helen asked softly.

"Guess we'll wait and find out," Dwight said.

Archer awakened shivering, teeth chattering. He found himself lying in a tangle of leaves and vines with water trickling nearby. The pain was gone. For a moment, he allowed himself time to appreciate the relief. Maybe the soak in river water had reduced some of the swelling in his back.

At any rate he welcomed the respite, and for a moment he lay still, with his forehead resting in the cold, clammy leaves and pine needles. Amazingly, he was alive after his tumultuous ride. As rotten a swimmer as he'd always been, that in itself was another miracle.

"Thank you, Lord," he whispered through chattering teeth. "Now can I go home?"

Still shivering, he reached through the darkness for the log that had carried him here. The scent of pine wafted over him, and his hand came into contact with the lower branch of an evergreen of some kind. He tried to bend his knees, test his legs, see if he could at least move them beneath him for leverage. A branch must have snagged on his slacks, because he couldn't jerk free.

He angled for a firmer hold on the branch with both hands and tried again to bend his knees.

Nothing.

He reached down with his left hand and felt around to discover where he was caught. He couldn't feel his own hand touching his leg.

The cold shock of awful knowledge took his breath.

He couldn't feel anything below his waist.

The litany of prayer that he had continued in his heart, even through the black unconsciousness, now drifted into silence as the discovery surged through him like knives of ice. He was paralyzed.

"No!" he cried. "God, no!" He gritted his teeth and heaved a cry into the damp earth. "I'm going to die here, crippled and helpless, after all this. . . . Oh, God, no!"

An overwhelming sense of defeat paralyzed his mind, just as the river had done to his legs. He hated this river that had wrenched him into its depths like a black demon tide. It seemed as if the storms that had attacked Dogwood Springs lately had narrowed their focus to him, personally.

"My faith lies in you, Lord. Protect me in death's shadow," he murmured under his breath in desperation. " '. . . by which the rising sun will come to us from heaven to shine on those living in darkness and in the shadow of death, to guide our feet into the path of peace.' Oh, God, help!"

Panic screamed through him with such violence that for a moment he couldn't breathe. He could only grit his teeth and try to still the racing, black ugliness of his deepest fears. He clenched his hands and screamed into the night for help, heard the echo of his voice from the cliffs, screamed again.

No one was there to hear him.

He grasped the lower branches of the tree and pulled himself, inch by inch, away from the water's edge. He rested his head on a cluster of pine needles, fighting despair, shivering, teeth chattering.

"Lord, I can't do this anymore. Oh, please, help me."

He'd never been this helpless before.

And yet . . . he had to remember what he had told countless patients he'd counseled in the hospital—they were never alone. Their helplessness, their weakness, would be God's strength. They could trust that, and they could depend on Him.

Pulling his jacket more closely around him, Archer collapsed, still shivering, lips still moving silently.

———

Jessica climbed into Lauren's truck, pulled the seat belt snugly around her, and leaned back. "I'll never forget this, Lauren. You should be with the Sheldons tonight—I heard you on the phone."

"They'll understand once they know. You obviously needed some time alone, especially after that awful scare. I can't believe Dwight did that. Couldn't he have waited a few more minutes, until they knew who the victim was? Or at least who he wasn't?"

"It wasn't just Dwight that had me upset. I've never been this weepy and emotional, and you should have heard me with poor Mrs. Netz before Dwight even came to the house. I nearly snapped her head off."

"Hormones."

"Hormones?"

Lauren took Jessica's arm and squeezed it. She still hadn't started the truck. "Get used to it. You're pregnant. Add to that the fact that you're nearly out of your mind with worry—"

"Which is a sin, as I've been reminded tonight—"

"Which is a *human emotion*. Would you lighten up on yourself a little bit?"

"Sorry. Helen knows how to push my buttons."

"She does seem to have some kind of a hang-up about you. Guess you'll have to deal with her the way I deal with my mom when she starts interfering a little too much."

"How's that?"

"Kill her with kindness, and pray really hard for her."

Jessica smiled. "I'll try both."

"So I bet you're dying to talk about babies, right?" Lauren said. "Did you know twins run in Archer's family? I think he said once that his mother was a twin, and he had twin cousins."

It was the right thing to say. Jessica chuckled. "They run in mine, too. Can you imagine if we had quadruplets?"

"I wouldn't want to think about it."

Jessica placed a hand over her abdomen. "Oh, Lauren, a *baby*."

"You'll be a great mom."

"Half of me wants to run out tomorrow and buy baby clothes and redecorate a bedroom for a nursery. I'm ready to start wearing maternity dresses right now." She stopped and stared out the window. "And part of me wants to scream at God for taking Archer away at a time like this, when he would be the most happy father in the world." She was quiet for a moment, then whispered, "Tell me, Lauren, what am I going to do if he's really dead?"

"I don't even want to think about that possibility."

"But we both know the statistics. The longer he's missing the less likely it'll be for him to be found alive. I need to be prepared in case the worst does happen. That little scare might have been just a precursor for worse to come."

Lauren glanced toward her through the dim glow of the streetlight. "If the worst happens, you're going to depend on friends and family and nurture that baby and get through it. You know you won't be alone, no matter what."

"Someone told me the other day that they hoped we would quickly find out one way or the other what had happened to Archer, because they thought waiting was the worst part."

"Is that how you feel?"

"No. They're wrong. Knowing for sure that Archer is dead would be the worst part. I realized that the hard way tonight when Dwight dropped his little bombshell on us."

"I agree, so let's just keep praying that God will protect Archer and keep him alive and well wherever he is."

"Would you take me to the river?" Jessica asked.

"At night? The sun's already—"

Jess placed a hand on Lauren's arm. "Since Archer's car was found there . . . if he did get forced off the bridge . . . I don't know. . . . I think I'll feel closer to him there, or at least closer to finding him there. If he was conscious he would have done all he could to fight his way to shore."

Lauren started the truck, put it into gear, pulled away from the curb. "In that case, why don't we drive to the river?"

Jessica sat back in her seat. "Thanks."

CHAPTER | **28**

Tuesday morning Mitchell jerked upright with a gasp.

Eyes. Those same glowing red eyes had been staring at him through the darkness.

Nightmares.

He dabbed perspiration from his forehead with the back of his hand.

As he tossed the comforter aside, his alarm went off suddenly, startling him beyond reason. He snapped it off and got out of bed, shuddering inwardly at the feel of those red eyes watching him.

He'd heard stories about people who thought they were being haunted in their dreams and who lost their sanity when those dreams began to follow them when they were awake.

He was not one of those people. And he wanted to know the source of that fragmented, confusing dream. But it was unlikely he would find it.

Still, for it to recur this often . . .

He went to the attached garage and switched on the overhead lights. Since Saturday he'd avoided this garage, preferring, instead, to drive the Audi and try to push his little brush-guard bender from his mind during working hours. He had too many other more important things to worry about.

But in spite of everything else, he couldn't stop wondering exactly what had caused the accident, and where he had been when it happened. He had obviously hit his head, but that wouldn't have happened if the air bags had deployed. That could mean he had fallen afterward, possibly during a completely unrelated event. He could have tripped on the nightstand Friday night.

He couldn't stop wondering why those red eyes continued to haunt him. Other nightmares vanished as soon as he opened his eyes. This one had more substance.

He also couldn't stop thinking about Archer Pierce.

He studied the Envoy. Dried mud caked the guard and tires, and made splash patterns on the black body of the vehicle.

He descended the steps and bent over to examine the guard, dented in two places. What was the connection?

He brushed away some of the dried mud on the dented grill. Where had it come from? He wouldn't have picked this up between here and the hospital, because the roads were paved.

He closed his eyes. *Focus, Mitchell.*

All he saw were those devilish red eyes flashing at him, taunting him—sometimes bright, sometimes dim, sometimes winking slyly.

Tranquen hallucinations? Even overdoing the dosage lately, he doubted it would carry over into the next morning like this. Tranquen had a fairly short half-life.

Postconcussion syndrome? That was a possibility. Those symptoms were fatigue, dizziness, headache, and difficulty concentrating after mild head injury.

Fingering the tender spot high on his forehead, he climbed into the cab of the SUV. It was quite a sight, with both the side and the front air bags hanging and powder everywhere.

Focus.

The last time he had sat behind this wheel, he had just arrived home from . . . where? The hospital? He must have driven somewhere else to have picked up the mud.

But why?

Friday night, soon after taking the first pill, he'd had a conversation with Archer. Much of it about God, he could be sure, knowing Archer's penchant for the subject. Funny how many of Mitchell's thoughts turned to the supernatural when the drugs first began to kick in, almost as if his grip on reality tried to slip a few notches.

So this meant that he might have been one of the last people to see Archer before he disappeared that night.

Experts had decided that Archer had almost certainly lost control of his vehicle, either getting hit by a tide of flash-flood water as he tried to cross the bridge, or farther up the hill, possibly hydroplaning on the road above the Black Oak River.

It was the hydroplaning that concerned Mitchell.

Was it possible that he, too, had encountered difficulty that night? Not as likely, of course, with this heavy SUV, compared to Archer's little car.

Still, with the flooding Friday, it was likely half the cars on the road in Dogwood Springs that night had encountered mud.

He switched on the headlights and got out of the vehicle to make sure everything was in working order. He would have to get the brush guard repaired—or purchase a new one—and get the air bags repaired, but he could find no damage otherwise. He must not have been traveling very fast.

He circled the back of the Envoy and found that the taillights worked perfectly. He frowned and stepped backward. Something about those lights . . .

He completed the circle around the SUV, checked the headlights, nodded, satisfied there was no electrical damage. He was stepping into the vehicle once more when he hesitated, frowned, and got back out again. Something about the taillights . . . Had he missed some evidence of damage?

As soon as he reached the back of the vehicle the second time, and saw the red glow, and closed his eyes, another memory slipped into place—a very vital piece of the puzzle. Those "demon" eyes that had haunted him for the past few days—they were taillights.

Someone *else's* taillights?

Archer's taillights?

Mitchell felt energy drain from him. He saw the flash of red imprinted on his lids. "What have I done?"

He climbed back into the Envoy and switched off the lights. Then he leaned his head back against the headrest and closed his eyes once more. He focused on those "eyes." It was so hard to focus on anything lately for a very long period of time . . . but the pictures matched and merged into one. Taillights reflecting against a rain-washed road—it was exactly the vision that continued to trouble him.

Had he passed Archer on the road for some reason? And if so, what possible reason could he have had to be on that road at that time in the storm?

Crazy. Especially since he always tried to be conscientious about getting home before the drug could affect his reaction time.

Of course, there was that evening when he had caught the side of the garage door with the grill—barely nicked the metal frame, barely smudged the grill. He'd told no one. And there had been the time he'd fallen asleep at his desk at the clinic.

Had he somehow caused Archer's accident?

If he was having luck with recall, this might be the time to drive back out and try again to find the place where he had found himself Friday night. Maybe now he would recognize something.

He checked on Trisha and found her still asleep. She knew he would be home tonight. He would drive the Envoy this time, after a quick cleanup.

———

Archer awakened to the sound of beautiful music. Were those angels? It was the most heavenly singing . . . and the whisper of a gentle breeze on his skin . . . like heaven.

He opened his eyes and stared past a lacing of pine branches into the bluest Missouri sky he had ever seen. Not heaven. He saw the flutter of bird wings in the branches of a nearby oak tree that was sprigged with the leaves of spring green.

Golden butterflies flicked around the upper branches, and the gentle rush of the river accompanied the birdsong instead of thundering through his head as it had done the past few days. Maybe the storms were over.

He frowned and turned his head to glance toward the river that had carried him here, and his breath caught in surprise. The flooding had indeed gone down overnight, but unless he was hallucinating, that was not the Black Oak River directly below.

He squinted toward the sun again and then turned his head and studied the surrounding terrain. Using the sun on the eastern horizon as a gauge, he located Dogwood Ridge about a quarter of a mile south of him, its cliffs rising nearly a hundred feet above the Black Oak River in one spot.

He wasn't even *close* to the main river! Apparently, the log that served as his watery transportation last night had somehow been thrust down the north fork of the river. No wonder he had hit shallow water. This was Shadow Branch. He had hiked this area countless times.

If he could travel straight north about a mile and a half—uphill most of the way—he would come to an old farm road.

He closed his eyes and rested. The prickly needles of the pine branches scratched his head, neck, and shoulders. At least *that* part of his body wasn't paralyzed.

The ache in his temples had receded. The roaring in his ears had stopped. Maybe he could drag himself to help.

But a mile and a half? In his condition, he might as well be halfway to the moon. He hadn't been able to even pull himself forward without the leverage of the tree branches overhead.

And yet, if the unseasonably warm weather were to change suddenly, he could die from hypothermia.

That would be too easy.

He reached for a pine branch and strained to pull himself forward. Inch by hard-earned inch.

He collapsed again. He didn't have the strength.

"Oh, Lord, please."

He closed his eyes and listened to the birdsong once more. How long had it been since he'd taken time to listen? How long since he'd taken more than a few seconds to enjoy the beauty of the spring blossoms? How long since he'd taken time just to *be*?

He shuffled up on his elbows and tried to roll over onto his side. His lower body lay there like a lump of concrete.

"God, please," he murmured. "Don't take me now. I can't do this, Lord. I can't just wait here helplessly to die."

He thought about that for a moment, then grimaced at such a stupid remark. He had no choice. It was all he *could* do.

A verse he had memorized years ago came to him: "Those who hope in the Lord will renew their strength. They will soar on wings like eagles; they will run and not grow weary, they will walk and not be faint."

He looked up into the sky, past the branches again. "Lord, can this possibly be your will?"

Had something gone horribly wrong? All these years he thought he'd been doing God's will. He'd tried so hard, ministering to the members of Dogwood Springs Baptist Church with a true servant's heart, going far above the call of duty, answering every cry for help. After the struggle last summer with doubts about his calling, he'd felt confirmed, renewed, and so sure. His faith in God had grown, strengthening his life and the lives of those to whom he ministered. His ministry had grown and—

He closed his eyes and laid his head back. *His* ministry.

"Is that it?"

The constant activity, the constant scramble to meet the needs and requests of so many people . . . had overwhelmed him.

And yet . . . what else did God expect him to do? Ignore the requests? Let those people sit alone in their hospital beds or isolated in their homes?

The special ministry to which he'd felt most led these past months did not take place within the church building. It had taken place within the hospital building and in the homes of patients as they recovered.

More often recently he'd been drawn to patients. He'd thought of that as another calling.

Could that be his true calling? His *only* calling?

And was it too late now to answer?

Until now, Archer thought one of his spiritual gifts was faith. But as this awareness of his mortality attacked him with frightening intensity, he had to face something he had never faced before—at least not to this extent: Had he ever learned to trust God perfectly? Or even to trust Him at all?

He recalled something his mother believed about faith—that it wasn't something you automatically *did*; it was something God gave you when you asked. What a person really needed was enough faith to pray, and then they had to let God take it from there.

"Oh, God, help me, please. I have no faith at all."

———

The deep, warm molasses voice of Floyd Stewart, the local radio announcer, spilled from Mitchell's speakers. "Although efforts are still underway to find the body, a spokesman for the search-and-rescue operation has informed us that the more time that elapses, the less chance they have of finding the pastor alive."

Mitchell snapped the radio off. "The body," he muttered. "What makes you think he's already dead?" And how would Archer's wife feel if she heard those words?

He glanced into his rearview mirror and glared at the bumper-hungry driver behind him. He pulled to the side of Highway Z and motioned angrily for the moron to pass, then checked to make sure some other speed demon wasn't racing up behind him.

He steered back onto the road and continued to drive slowly for another mile. Nothing tugged at his memory, and he began to question his own sanity. What made him think he could find evidence about where Archer was, when well over a hundred people had already combed the area below the bridge where Archer's car had allegedly gone off?

He tapped his brake when he saw cars parked up ahead. Instead of driving past them, he started to pull onto the side of the road again, but then he caught sight of the marker for County Road 22.

The county road circled back along the edge of this ridge into town. It had been a favorite parking spot for lovers back when he was a teenager, both for its beautiful view across the Black Oak River and for its privacy.

There would have been no reason for Archer to use it Friday night.

It was no use. If Archer was anywhere to be found, the searchers would have found him. They must have combed every inch of those riverbanks in the past couple of days.

Mitchell checked his time. He was late for his first appointment. He made a U-turn, gunned the motor, drove back toward town. He had no time to follow rabbit trails.

And yet . . . was he missing something?

———

"Hello! Is anyone out there? Can anyone hear me?"

Archer's throat burned from overuse. His elbows, forearms, and hands were bruised and scraped.

He had managed to drag himself perhaps twenty-five feet from Shadow Branch before collapsing with exhaustion.

He thought of a lady who had belonged to their church years ago. She'd been bound to a wheelchair for twenty years before her death. Though physically weak and as frail and helpless as Archer was now, Annabelle Jordan had been one of the greatest prayer warriors Archer had ever known.

Oftentimes, when something went wrong with the life of a church family or citizen of Dogwood Springs, Dad would call Annabelle immediately. Her serene faith had struck Archer with an awareness of God's power, even back then. Annabelle had never had to take a step, never had to climb out of bed when she received a call during the night. She prayed. It was something he'd remembered well when she died. Her example had taught him a lot about the power of prayer.

Now he found himself wondering if he'd forgotten all he'd ever learned. After all this time, how could he doubt God's presence and power in his life?

"Lord, if I'm finished here on earth, I'm ready to come home to you." Tears of sorrow burned his eyes. He didn't want to die yet. He didn't want to leave Jessica. He wanted the experience of raising a family.

He wanted . . . *he* wanted.

And that was the whole problem, wasn't it? What he wanted didn't matter. He needed what *God* wanted for his life.

He took a deep breath and could almost taste the dank, moldy leaves that surrounded him. He looked around for a small puddle of water—anything—but found nothing.

Rivulets of water trickled down toward the river somewhere in the distance, but where he lay, as far as he could tell, the ground was nothing but mud. Oak, cedar, and sycamore trees formed a light canopy overhead.

He couldn't remember how he'd gotten here, because so much of that horrible float trip had been filled with pain and fear, and he'd been overwhelmed by the struggle to hold on to the log. He had a vague recollection of the log drifting with the current of the river, and of other logs and debris colliding with him or his mode of transportation. He remembered the other passenger on the log. A snake.

It hadn't touched him after that first contact.

A passage from Isaiah struck Archer's heart, "When you pass through the waters, I will be with you; and when you pass through the rivers, they will not sweep over you."

He needed to focus on those words. He needed to allow the peace to carry him, no matter what happened.

Don't listen to the whispers of fear. Sometimes faith had as much to do with what you *didn't* believe as what you *did*.

He thought of Mitchell Caine, who didn't believe, period. The seeking, angry, struggling doctor had no prayer to fall back on, no hope of a future past the boundaries of his lonely life.

"Watch over him, Lord. Protect him. He's in so much more peril than I am."

Archer still couldn't move his legs, but he was more aware than ever before that God had all the strength necessary to see him through . . . whatever his fate may be.

After a short rest, he checked his bearings and reached for the base of a sapling to pull himself forward.

CHAPTER 29

Mitchell could not get Archer out of his mind. Every time he closed his eyes he saw those taillights. Every time he thought about his earlier drive along Dogwood Ridge, he thought again about that other road—County 22.

Common sense told him there would be no reason for Archer to have taken that road. But common sense also told Mitchell that if Archer was on the north side of Dogwood Ridge, anywhere near the river, especially since the flooding had gone down, someone would have found him. There were too many people looking for him. And so, unless Archer was buried somewhere in the bottom of the river, he would have been found.

After the final patient of the day walked out of the office, Mitchell swiveled around to stare out the window. Was he obsessing? Why this sudden overwhelming concern for a man with whom he seldom agreed and who irritated him beyond measure with his presence in the ER, supposedly "helping" patients to heal with his prayer talk?

A flicker of pastel caught his attention from the corner of the clinic building—pink-and-white dogwood blooms, side by side, gracing the dark brown brick with delicate beauty.

He leaned back in his chair, closed his eyes, took a deep breath.

The shape of those blooms flicked through his mind. Red eyes replaced them.

He sat up abruptly, eyes open wide. With fuzzy inaccuracy, he remembered a visual of pink-and-white dogwood blossoms glaring in the headlights.

Friday night? Early Saturday morning? He had awakened to that vision.

In less than ten minutes he was driving along Dogwood Ridge.

He still could not recall anything that might have placed him here on Friday night, except for the dogwood blooms. Could he have hydroplaned and gone off the road and collided with trees?

Was there a second collision?

He bypassed the cars parked alongside the road and studied the dogwood trees for signs of damage. When he came to County 22 he stopped. It wouldn't be logical to search that road for him.

But was it logical to cover the same area that had already been covered many times?

He turned west on the loop back toward town, watching for a copse of pink-and-white dogwoods together. About a mile from the turnoff he found them. He pulled off the pavement and parked. The trees stood about five yards from the edge of the curved asphalt. Mitchell got out of the Envoy.

He found nothing. No scarred bark that might have been damaged by his vehicle. No uprooted dirt. No marks in the mud indicating recent activity.

He strolled to the edge of the overlook and gazed down into the river valley below.

Mitchell had developed a heightened sense of responsibility early in life, and until the past few months he would never have dreamed of driving under the influence of drugs or alcohol. And yet, he was forced to admit that Grant Sheldon had been right when he confronted him.

"What if I killed Archer?" he whispered. He held his hands up and stared at them. These hands that had always been used to help the sick might well have been used to steer this vehicle into Archer Pierce.

If that turned out to be true, he wasn't sure he could bear the guilt of it.

He turned and walked along the rim of the cliff, studying the river's edge. From here he could see the deposits of mud along the bank caused by the flood. Trash and uprooted trees had collected at the curve, where the river forked. Typically, the left fork became a shallow creek called Shadow Branch, which flowed into Honey Creek a few miles down.

While the Black Oak River followed the curve of Dogwood Ridge, the creek meandered through a forest of pine and oak.

Mitchell studied the watermarks along the river's edge. The flattened grass and line of waterlogged trash showed that the valley had, indeed, been a veritable lake when the flood reached its zenith sometime this past weekend. No wonder they were having trouble finding Archer. If he'd been caught by the current as his car had been, he might be anywhere by now.

But what if he hadn't been caught by the current?

Mitchell realized that he'd been subconsciously searching for a human form down there amidst the rubble. Archer's form.

He swung away and covered his face in a wash of unaccustomed grief. "He can't be dead," he whispered to himself. "Not Archer. Of all people, not Archer."

He recalled sitting in church and listening to Aaron Pierce's sermons week after week, desperately wishing he could speak to this God Archer's father had believed in so completely.

Then he remembered something Archer told him late last December.

"How can an intelligent man continue to believe after so many unanswered prayers?" Mitchell had demanded. "Your God is a tyrant without a heart. He does what He wants, and the devil take the rest of us."

And Archer had responded with some inane words about God's love and about how He truly did answer prayers.

Mitchell had paced around the desk in Grant's office and leaned over Archer with a glare. "Are you trying to tell me my daughter's drug addiction is part of His will? Are you trying to tell me that Oakley Brisco's death was God's will? What a vindictive god you serve."

"Those were results of free human choice, not God's will. But, Mitchell, I can tell you that what is happening now, no matter what it might be or how horrible it might seem to you, is something that can have a better ending if the right choices are made and if you ask Him for help."

Mitchell glared at the dogwood trees, then turned back to the river.

"Help," he muttered under his breath. "Is He helping you *now,* Archer?"

Still . . . what if . . .

"Maybe you really are there." His mutter softened to a hushed whisper. "Maybe you just choose to hate certain people. Maybe I'm at the top of your hate list." The words came as a hard taunt. "But why do this to Pierce? He's been your staunchest supporter in this town. If he was right about you, why did you let him be hurt?"

He stopped and swallowed, and focused his glare over the river that rushed past. "Where is he now? Why didn't you save *him,* of all people?"

He felt the rush of familiar confusion.

What a fool to even try.

"He's dead and rotting in some washed-out mud bank." He felt dark laughter catch in his throat, and he raised his hands in front of him, studying them. They were all that held power over life and death. These hands. No greater power was out there.

He lowered his hands to his sides and closed his eyes.

Pierce had never hurt him. Pierce had been one of the few people who had almost convinced him to listen when he spoke about his God.

The love of God. What a joke.

Of course, maybe Archer Pierce's foolishness had, in reality, harmed a lot more people than the pusher had. How many people had his sermons reached every week? How many patients had listened to his misrepresentations about his so-called God?

"You are worthless to him," he hissed at the sky, then retreated to the SUV, turning his back on whatever gods or sentient beings might have been eavesdropping on his questions. Crazy to open himself to such stupidity. If he had any sense at all, it would never happen again.

He was halfway back to town, observing that it was just as well this road was not heavily traveled, since the high shoulders made it so slick during wet weather. Another memory hit him, and he slammed on his brakes.

Hydroplaning! Those red eyes, dim-bright-dim-bright, then winking slyly . . . sliding across his field of vision like a taunting spirit . . .

Archer's taillights slid back and forth because he was hydroplaning.

Mitchell caught his breath and made a U-turn. He'd remembered one more thing—the river that night. For one brief second, in a flare of lightning, Mitchell remembered wresting his gaze from the sight of those glaring red eyes and catching a glimpse of the valley below in a flare of lightning. He'd seen the flooded river that had overwhelmed its banks.

And then those eyes blinked at him—the taillights attacking his front bumper with a jolt as he stomped the brakes and tried to avoid them.

No, *they* had not attacked *him*. With a welling of nausea he realized *he* had attacked *them*. His tires had wavered and he'd swerved, most likely losing traction, and he'd felt the jolt again. And then the brakes had caught and held, and the taillights went on without him, into the trees, over the . . . cliff. All had gone black for Mitchell then.

It made sense. His air bags had deployed upon impact with Archer's car. They had deflated by the time he hit the trees.

He stopped at another copse of blooming pink-and-white dogwoods and cedars, where the view of the river was best. He parked and got out.

He was about thirty feet from the trees when he saw the damage on the bark of the two dogwoods closest to him. He ran to them and knelt to study them more closely. He looked back at the brush guard of the Envoy. Exact match. This was it. This was the place!

They were slightly bent, barely scraped, where his guard had rested. From the look of it, they had apparently kept him from going over the cliff.

And Archer?

Mitchell ran to the cliff and peered over the side. The car would not have had a straight shot into the river from here, because about ten feet down the side of the cliff was an outcropping of rock. About twenty feet below that was a ledge of dirt about four feet wide that looked as if part of it had collapsed into the water. Could the car have done the damage?

Mitchell grabbed a tree root and swung over the edge of the cliff. He wasn't dressed for rock climbing, but he could scramble down this cliff easily enough if he was cautious.

He reached the boulder and found a small sprinkling of glass that looked as if it might match the shattered windshield of a car. It could be the car had hit this boulder on the way down—or it could be the remains of some long-ago accident.

He scrambled down to the ledge below the boulder, cautious not to collapse it further. He peered over the edge and saw that Archer could have dropped directly into the water. The surface was about twenty feet farther down right now, but might have been much closer a couple of days ago, during the worst of the flood.

A thorough search of the ledge showed him nothing until he turned to start the climb back up. There, embedded in the cliff, was the titanium-colored cell phone he had seen Archer using in the hospital.

Archer had gone over this cliff.

Mitchell rushed back up the side of the cliff and called Tony Dalton from his car phone.

"Sergeant Dalton," he said when Tony answered. "This is Dr. Mitchell Caine. You're looking for Archer Pierce in the wrong place."

Mitchell pulled back into his own driveway at home about seven-thirty Tuesday evening, after successfully convincing Tony Dalton to move the search upriver. Of course, the searchers had been thorough, but they hadn't thought about that stretch of County Road 22 as a possibility.

Why would they? Everyone expected Archer to be on his way out of town on Highway Z, which would have been a direct shot across the bridge. But if, for some reason, the highway had been blocked closer to town, Archer would have taken County 22 to intersect with the highway above the bridge.

Mitchell knew the river well. He'd explored its banks when he was a kid. If his estimates were correct—if Archer had gone into the river—he might have floated down the other branch of the river, which divided from the main branch above the bridge. No one had considered this before. But they were doing it now.

When Mitchell pulled into his garage he found Trisha standing in the doorway, her painfully slender form outlined in the light from the kitchen pantry. He parked and got out, trying to decide what to tell her about his discovery.

He held his arms out to his sides, indicating the mud that covered him from shirt collar to shoes. "I've been searching for a friend."

"Dad?" Her voice was soft and tremulous, and she stood hugging herself as if chilled. She paid no attention to his words or to his appearance.

"Trisha? I hope I didn't frighten you. Did you see my note?" He pressed the button to lower the garage door.

"I saw it." Her lashes were spiked with moisture.

"Trisha, is something wrong?"

She turned and preceded him into the house, then stopped and turned back to him. Tears poured down her cheeks. "Dad, I'm in trouble. I need help."

———

Tuesday night at eight-fifteen, Grant wielded his spatula and wok with expert ease. The smell of grilled steak, onions, and peppers filled the large great room of the Sheldon home with its smoky aroma.

"I'm really sorry about last night," Lauren said. "I just didn't see how I could leave Jessica—"

"Would you stop it?" Grant sliced three avocados in half. "You make me feel like some hardhearted ogre. Of course I was disappointed, but if there had been something for me to do to help Jessica right then, I'd have done it just as you did."

Lauren perched on the stool at the end of the breakfast bar to watch Grant cook. She loved cooking—she could watch it for hours. That was another thing she didn't have in common with this family. She could grill a mess of white bass over live coals that would please the most discerning camper, but she'd never been much of an indoor cook. Of course, neither was Brooke most of the time.

"You know you can come over any time," Grant said.

"I don't think she wants to get that comfy with us, Dad" came a feminine voice from the hallway at the far end of the living room.

Lauren and Grant turned to see Brooke sauntering toward them, arms crossed over her chest, the edge in her expression as sharp as the prick of a needle.

"You know that isn't true," Lauren said. "Don't I keep root beer in the fridge for you all the time? And those gross sweet-potato chips you love so much?"

Brooke shrugged. Her cool gaze slid from Lauren's face.

Lauren scrutinized Brooke's behavior more closely—the way her thumb rubbed the knuckles on her right hand, the frown line between her brows.

Lauren looked at Grant, who kept his attention focused on his culinary efforts. This must be some kind of test, to see if she and Brooke could work out their differences without him as go-between. Now if she could just remember those books she had read years ago about handling interpersonal conflict with teenagers in a healthy way.

If it had been one of Lauren's brothers or sisters, they would have shouted it out and recovered quickly. Ordinarily, Brooke would have done the same. Something else was going on here—had been going on for the past few days. Had Brooke suddenly realized she was jealous of her father's affection for Lauren? Did she feel threatened?

"Brooke, I didn't want to stand you up last night," Lauren said.

Brooke slid her gaze back to Lauren in her typical "Oh, sure" expression.

Again, Lauren curbed her impatience. "You know about the scare Jessica had last night."

"I heard. But I also know it didn't take them all night to discover the poor guy they found was an ATVer from Jefferson City. I think you just used that as an excuse not to come over."

"That isn't true, and you know it. Jessica needed—"

"Don't even say it," Brooke snapped. "Jessica needed solitude," she mimicked. "Jessica needed reassurance. You know what I think? Maybe you're just trying to cut us out of your life, and you're using Jessica as an excuse."

"That isn't true, Brooke," Lauren said gently. "I don't want to cut you out of my life."

Brooke's eyes suddenly filled with tears. She crossed her arms and looked down at the floor, as if the pattern of the wood grain fascinated her.

Lauren moved a stool out from beneath the bar with her foot and gestured for Brooke to have a seat beside her. "You're not still mad about my fishing trip, are you?"

Brooke didn't make a move toward the stool. "Who said I was mad?"

"Honey, you didn't have to say a word—your expression says it for you." Lauren hesitated. How far should she push it? Especially with Grant listening to every word across the kitchen, and Beau most likely somewhere nearby doing the same thing. She should have made it a point to spend some time alone with Brooke before this.

She hadn't. Maybe that was the whole problem.

"So if you're not mad about the fishing trip, what are you mad about?"

Brooke gave a shrug and sauntered across the kitchen, sidled up beside her dad. She reached for a fresh slice of avocado and slid it into her mouth.

"You'll ruin your appetite for fajitas," Grant warned her.

"I'm not that hungry, Dad." She gave Lauren a pointed look. "Maybe you two'll want to eat alone."

Lauren gave a quiet sigh. "I wouldn't have come over here if I'd wanted to be alone, Brooke." She tried to keep the sharp edges from her voice, but she didn't quite get the job done.

"Well, maybe I don't feel like eating tonight."

"Brooke." Grant slid the wok off the burner.

"Dad, I'm just saying—"

"Maybe we should save it until after we eat. Then, if Lauren is agreeable, we'll have a family discussion and clear the air."

Lauren's appetite did a death plunge. Oh, yeah, give this discussion even more significance, as if their whole future together hinged on this dinner and her ability to make amends with Brooke, who might be rightly accused of behaving like a spoiled brat if there weren't so much more involved.

In reality, Lauren knew Brooke was behaving like any healthy, strong-willed seventeen-year-old coming to terms, once again, with the permanence of her own mother's death and the possibility of a future stepmom coming to take Annette's place.

"Dad, I don't think she wants—"

"As I said, save it until after we eat. Where's your brother?"

"In here, Dad," Beau called from the other room, in the vicinity of the office. "Out of the danger zone."

"Get washed up for dinner. You, too, Brooke."

After Brooke left the room, Lauren swallowed, took a deep breath, and avoided looking at Grant. What a joyous occasion, their first big family fight. And she hadn't even told him she wanted to be a *part* of this family.

Yet.

But she did.

———

After changing from his muddy clothes, Mitchell sat beside his daughter on the love seat in front of the unlit fireplace, and all other thoughts, all fears about his responsibility for Archer's disappearance, receded from his mind at the broken sound of Trisha's crying.

She sat huddled against the overstuffed arm, wearing a pair of black silk pajamas her mother had left behind. The V of the neckline plunged deeply, and Mitchell was shocked by the sharp outline of her collarbone. He should have insisted she get on the scale as soon as she arrived Saturday morning.

She continued to hug her shaking shoulders, and her face shone with tears. In her right hand she clasped a handful of tissues Mitchell had given her.

"Trisha, just tell me what's wrong. If I know what it is, maybe I can do something—"

"There's nothing anybody can do." Another tightly controlled sob. "I've spent so much time online reading about this stuff . . . and they say the damage is permanent."

"Who are *they*?"

"The *experts*! It's the meth. You were right all the time, Dad. I didn't listen because I didn't want to think about what's going to happen to me."

"What damage are you talking about?" he asked quietly.

"You know. Even if I can stay off the drugs, they've already damaged my system. I'm more prone to heart attacks and strokes, and I'll always struggle with depression. It's right there on your computer if you want to pull it up. And that's just if I never do drugs again. But, Dad, the temptation to go out and find another hit—just to get rid of this awful feeling that I'd be better off dead—is almost too strong to resist sometimes."

He carefully controlled his own panicked reaction. "You wouldn't be better off dead."

"No? Look at what I've done to you and Mom."

"You haven't done anything to us. If anything, this is what we've done to you. It's what a drug pusher did to you."

She nudged away more tears.

"Trisha, when did he convince you to start doing the meth?"

"About six months after we met, and even then it was just the pills." She dabbed at her face with the tissues, blew her nose, leaned her head against the cushion. "I lost the weight, remember?"

"I remember."

"Simon was so friendly, so fun, so hot."

"Tell me more about your experiences with the meth." He needed to know how long she'd been shooting up or snorting.

"Like I said, I just did the pills at first, but then Simon convinced me to try the injection. He said it would feel so much better."

Mitchell truly did hope there was a real hell, so he could know for sure that Simon Royce was burning in it. "How long after you first started did you go to injections?"

"I'm not sure. It was after I left the second time."

"Several months, then."

"Yeah. A few months, I think. The high was so extreme," she said. "It felt so great at first."

"Those times you left were two of the worst of my life."

"Why?"

"That should be evident. My only child runs away from home with a drug pusher who is ruining her life?"

"Mom told me last year that you were just upset because it would hurt your practice."

Her loathsome mother had stooped to new lows. "And you believed her?"

Trisha looked away, and Mitchell swallowed his own pain. "If that had been the case, I wouldn't have brought you back home with you protesting at the top of your lungs to anyone who would listen. What happened after you left us the second time?"

She blew her nose and dabbed at her tears again. "Everything just got worse. The highs were good at first, but not for long." She buried her face in her tissue-padded hands.

"Trisha," he said gently, "tell me about the baby."

Her eyes squeezed shut. Her shoulders rocked with silent sobs.

Mitchell ached to comfort her, to put his arms around her like a real father would do for his daughter. "It's okay, you don't have to talk about it right now."

She sniffed and nodded, looked up at him. "I want to. Mom was still sending me money, but Simon took it before I could use it for visits to the doctor. When I was about seven and a half months pregnant, he moved out for a while, told me I looked repulsive."

"You could never be repulsive," Mitchell said. "He was the repulsive one."

"He said I was used up and worthless. He injected me one more time before he left, saying it was a good-bye present. I had the baby two weeks later. She died. That was when I gave up."

Mitchell felt the overwhelming wash of his own grief at the child's death. "What did you name her, Trisha?"

She shook her head. "She never had a name. I wasn't even in my right mind long enough to think about anything like that."

"Then her name is Angela," he said. "My granddaughter, Angela."

Trisha looked up at him. "You're naming her?"

"I named her in the hospital, when she was still alive."

Trisha looked away, face crumpling again. "I was too ashamed to tell you what was happening."

"A friend of mine called me. I tried to see you when you were in the hospital. Don't you remember?"

"No." She blinked at him. "I guess I don't remember much of anything."

"I spent as much time with Angela as I could."

Again, Trisha cried. It was as if the well of tears had no end. As Mitchell endured the sound of her suffering, he felt the final supports of his carefully planned life give way beneath him.

There was no hope, nothing left. His family lay in ruins, and his own daughter sat broken before him. The one person whom he had thought, for a brief period of time, might actually have some kind of tenuous grasp on hope had disappeared in a storm.

And yet.

Mitchell remembered sitting on a love seat one day years ago—a seat not nearly as padded and comfortable as this one—while Darla Miller confided to him that she was pregnant with his child. He remembered, even now, the horror and the joy that flooded and confused him. Horrified by the overwhelming sense of responsibility, he had still reveled with excitement at the knowledge of life he had helped create.

"Trisha, you can't give up," he said. "Those Web sites don't take everything into consideration."

She didn't raise her head. "What?"

"You're not alone. You will always have a place with me, and I'll help you with this."

She looked up at him. "But look at what I've done, Dad. I've ruined it all. You know those plans you had for me? College and a career? I can barely concentrate on anything now. Get it, Dad? I'm used up, burned out."

She sounded too much like him.

"You're Trisha Caine. You still bear my name, and you will always be a part of me. You will always have a part of my heart. All those plans I had for you were because I loved you. That hasn't changed, and it never will." He felt his own tears and watched the blurred lines of Trisha's face, a face that reddened and crumpled as she leaned forward into his outstretched arms.

She clung to him, staining his fresh shirt with her tears, those precious tears. His child had come home broken and needy, and once again, just like when he first heard about her conception, he felt the heaviness of his own responsibility, and now he felt the renewed joy of their connection.

As he held her and rocked her, he wished so badly he could talk to Archer. But Archer wasn't there. One other person had offered to talk with him.

It went against his nature. How could he possibly confide in the one man who had done the most damage to his professional career in the past year?

Or maybe Mitchell had done it to himself.

He would call Grant.

t's almost ready," Grant announced.

Lauren looked across the kitchen in time to see him spill a slice of grilled onion on the counter and burn his hand on the stove-top grill.

He gave her a sheepish grin. "Even expert chefs have their off days."

"Nervous, huh?" she taunted.

"Maybe a little. Hungry?"

"Not a bit."

He grinned at her, and she grinned back, and she realized again that she desperately wanted to be able to work things out with this family. She owed them that, and she owed it to herself, in spite of the doubts and inner conflicts.

Yes, one of the reasons she had moved away from Knolls was to get away from the over-involved influence of her parents and siblings. This was different in every way.

Marriage was something she'd dreamed about for years. If she were to marry Grant and become Brooke and Beau's stepmother, the McCaffreys would be ecstatic. That old, uncomfortable feeling of disconnection from the rest of the world—of being a misfit single in a society of couples—would be gone.

But she refused to use that as a reason to get married. The real reason she wanted to marry Grant was because she loved him and she loved his kids.

The stool beside her shuffled backward, and she heard Grant groan softly as he sat down next to her.

"I know my family can be . . . a little challenging," he said in a tone of frustrated amusement.

Challenging? Is that your term for it? "These past few days I've spent a lot of time trying to imagine what my life would be like if your family suddenly vanished," she said. "I hated the way it made me feel." Although it wouldn't hurt if Brooke would quietly get out of her face on occasion, just not permanently.

"And yet, you don't think feelings should be the basis for a permanent relationship," he said.

"That wasn't exactly what I said. I just didn't want to get all caught up in some emotional moment, make all kinds of promises, and then realize later that I couldn't keep those promises."

"So you don't want to get married." There was no inflection in his voice.

She studied his face carefully. She couldn't tell by his expression if that would disappoint him or relieve him or break his heart. "You know, you could be a great poker player."

"I know."

"I love you."

He nodded, smiled, looked at her. "Um-hmm."

"I love Brooke and Beau."

"Especially when Brooke keeps her mouth shut?"

"I heard that!" came a voice from behind them—a voice a little less irritable than it had been a few minutes ago.

Lauren continued as if Brooke hadn't interrupted. "I believe that if it's true love, it must be unconditional, which means Brooke can talk a blue streak, and I'd still love her." She turned to find the twins standing side by side beneath the archway at the far side of the great room.

Beau had an enigmatic smile on his face—which for Beau translated into a broad grin.

Brooke still had her arms crossed, still wouldn't look Lauren in the eye.

Beau walked to Lauren and put his arms around her. "We love you, too, don't we, Brooke?"

Brooke remained conspicuously silent.

Lauren returned Beau's hug with enthusiasm.

Chair legs scraped noisily against the hardwood floor. "I'm not into the group hug thing yet," Brooke snapped. "Keep it up and we'll all lose our appetites."

Reluctantly, Lauren released Beau and turned to find that the typically blunt Brooke Sheldon veneer was safely in place. Lips in a grim line. Gaze directed toward the window at the far side of the room.

"Please, can't we just clear the air so we can have a meal in peace?" Lauren asked. Without waiting for Grant's reply, she said, "Brooke, I know you're still upset with me about Saturday. I'm sorry you felt that I stood you up. I did need to get away by myself and think about things, but I'll check with you next time I do that, okay?" *Oops. Watch the sarcasm.*

"Brooke the probation officer," Beau muttered.

"Shut up, Beau," Brooke said. "Dad wanted us to drop the subject until after dinner."

"Too bad," Lauren said. "He isn't the only one who gets a vote." She risked a look at Grant and found him calmly spooning the food into serving dishes.

She looked back at Brooke, who had taken her seat at the table. "I don't feel like sitting down and pretending to have a peaceful family dinner while you continue to make your snide comments."

"It never bothered you before," Brooke said.

Lauren sat down directly across from Brooke. "You've never roasted Lauren McCaffrey for dinner before, and it sure isn't going to start now." They might as well focus on the basics. "So, as for our little problem, no one's kept tabs on my daily whereabouts since I moved out on my own in my twenties. Frankly, I was insulted by the implication last Saturday that I might have been with Archer on some tryst just because I didn't check in here when I left."

"I never implied that," Brooke said. "But you were so upset when we told you about him, and you just raced off to his house to—"

"To comfort Jessica, because I knew—"

"It was like our feelings didn't even matter."

"They did, Brooke, but at that moment Jessica's feelings mattered more," Lauren said. "I felt Jessica needed reassurance more than you did at the moment." It seemed she might have been wrong about that.

Brooke looked down at her empty plate. No one else spoke. The silence became oppressive.

"You always matter to me," Lauren said more gently. "But there will be times when I'll act without consulting you. I've always been that way, and at my age I doubt that's going to change."

Brooke pressed her lips together and stared at her clasped hands—hands so tense their nail beds were white.

"I agree with Lauren," Beau said. "At her age, she's pretty set in her—"

"Watch it," Grant warned. "You're not helping."

"A true family wants to spend time together, not avoid each other," Brooke said.

"That isn't fair, either," Beau said. "You never feel the need to be alone. Lauren's the kind of person who needs time by herself."

"Want to know what I think," Brooke asked. "I think that if Dad didn't have kids, he and Lauren would already be married."

"No, we wouldn't," Lauren said.

Grant paused as he transferred a platter to the table. "We wouldn't?"

Lauren narrowed her eyes. He didn't seem to be taking this conversation as seriously as the rest of them.

"Mom never took a day just to get away from us," Brooke said.

Lauren felt the sting of those words. "Brooke, I'm not your mother."

Brooke flinched as if she'd been slapped.

"I'm sorry," Lauren said. "That obviously didn't come out the way I meant it to. It makes me feel inadequate as a person when you continue to compare me to Annette Sheldon. I am Lauren McCaffrey—"

"But we're talking about you becoming Lauren *Sheldon*," Beau said. "We *would* be upset if Lauren Sheldon ever left for a whole day without telling anyone."

Lauren Sheldon. "If I was your stepmom, I would never do that."

The telephone rang, and Grant picked it up. He listened for a moment, frowned, then switched the call to his office and excused himself, muttering something about a confidential conversation.

"Go ahead and eat, you three," he said over his shoulder as he walked from the room. "And cool your jets until I get back. I don't want to miss a single word of this fascinating conversation."

Sarcasm again. Lauren sighed. The world was filled with sarcastic people.

Grant felt like the turkey wishbone after Thanksgiving dinner. The last thing he wanted to do was walk out of the dining room and leave Lauren, Brooke, and Beau discussing the whole future of this family— *his* future!—without his helpful input.

It was insanity.

Not that he'd been contributing much. But he hadn't intended to. He had no desire to play referee between Lauren and his kids for the rest of his life. He had a feeling that if he did, that position would become a barrier between them.

Lauren might not have any experience as a mother, but she would soon discover that she had a lot more influence over his kids than she realized. They were both crazy about her, and appearances to the contrary, Brooke had attached to Lauren emotionally months ago.

He closed the office door, picked up the phone, and punched the button to release the hold. "Mitchell, I'm back with you. Do you want me to come over to your place?"

For a moment there was no answer.

"Mitchell?"

"Yes. I'm still here." Another pause. "I . . . need to know what you meant when you offered to help me with my . . . drug problem."

Grant sat down heavily on the edge of the desk. "I would help set you up for professional treatment—and the hospital's insurance would pay for it. I would help you find someone to take over your practice while you're gone."

"And if I'm in prison?"

"Prison! I seriously doubt you would go to prison for this."

"Evidence seems to suggest that I had an accident Friday night. At the time, I would have been under the influence of Tranquen."

Grant collapsed into his chair. "*Evidence?* Mitchell, don't you remember?"

"No. Tranquen has an amnesic effect, especially in doses higher than prescribed. I woke up Saturday morning with a knot on my head, as well. It wasn't until today that a few indications led me to suspect that I might have been involved in an accident that Archer—"

"Hold it. You only had a *few* indications? What makes you think—"

"I found his cell phone on the cliff," Mitchell said. "I've already called Tony Dalton, and the search has been redirected."

Grant caught his breath. *Oh, Mitchell, what have you done?*

"My daughter is here," Mitchell continued. "She is the reason I called."

"Trisha? Is she okay?"

"She's—" Mitchell's voice broke, fell silent.

Grant waited.

"She is addicted to methamphetamine. She needs my help, and I don't know how to give it."

"We can help her." Grant was still scrambling to comprehend the situation. He cleared his throat. "Of course we'll help her. You tell me what you need, and I'll see that it happens."

Lauren had no appetite. Obviously, neither did the twins. "Do you two remember when we had this little talk before? On our way back from Knolls when my brother died?"

"We said a lot of things that night," Beau said. "It's an hour's drive, and Brooke talked most of the way."

"I did not."

"Yes, you did. I remember, because—"

"Okay." Lauren raised a hand for silence. "But remember when I told you that the adjustment to a stepmom would be a hard one for you, and that you couldn't expect her to take your mother's place?"

"That was when Brooke was nagging you to go out on a date with Dad," Beau said. "It worked, too. You two went out on your first date soon after that."

"I remember," Brooke said softly. She reached for a napkin, unfolded it, then instead of laying it on her lap she wrapped the end of it around her left forefinger. She watched her own hands instead of looking at Lauren. "You said it would be difficult for us to adjust to someone else in our lives because we would have different habits, a different family history, stuff like that."

"So you did listen," Lauren said. "So you can't say I didn't warn you."

Brooke shrugged and unwrapped her finger, twisted the napkin into a rope.

"I took your father's marriage proposal last week seriously," Lauren said. "And I have *not* been looking for an excuse to reject it. Maybe I would have married your father without quite so much thought if he didn't have children, but that isn't because I don't want those children."

"Oh, yeah?" Brooke challenged. "Then why?"

"I think partly because I've heard so much about Annette Sheldon that she seems almost too wonderful, too perfect. I can't live up to the expectations of a family who's lived with a woman like that. I can't be what she was. I think part of my problem has been fear of disappointing you."

"But I already love you because of who you are," Brooke said quietly. The twisted rope tautened, and some of the edges started to fray.

Lauren put her hands over Brooke's. "Honey, I think we've gotten to know each other pretty well this past year."

The fingers continued to twitch, as if Brooke couldn't prevent the nervous tic.

"In all that time, have I ever lied to you or done anything that would make you believe you couldn't trust me for some reason?"

The hands grew still. Brooke cleared her throat. "No."

"Then would you please trust me now?"

She hesitated, cleared her throat again. "If you were already my stepmom I would trust you. Even if you agreed to marry Dad, I'd trust you then. But right now I just can't take the stress, okay? If you're not looking for an excuse to ditch us, then what are you waiting for?"

"I'm not waiting."

"What?"

In her peripheral vision, Lauren saw Grant walk into the dining room. She didn't turn. "You know that porch swing you got me for my birthday? Do you think you could put it up for me on your back deck?"

Brooke screamed.

Beau shouted, "Yes!"

Lauren turned to Grant, who rushed across the dining room and grabbed her up into his arms and swung her around, laughing out loud.

"Does this mean you'll marry me?"

Beau tackled them from Lauren's right side.

"Yes, it means I'll marry you."

Brooke tackled them from Lauren's left side.

So much for the tender romantic moment. Lauren decided this suited her better.

———

Mitchell sat alone in his kitchen, staring out into the night through the plate-glass window of the dining room. Trisha slept peacefully at last, hopefully feeling more secure than she had when she first came home.

Could he continue to provide that security?

After talking to Grant he had begun to believe that there was hope.

He stared at the stars and the sliver of moon that crept over the eastern horizon. "I may have made a hasty judgment earlier—maybe you are out there and you do care," he said to whomever was listening. "And if that's the case, I apologize. I sincerely apologize." His voice cracked.

"I plead for Archer Pierce's life. I know it won't ease the guilt I feel over what I've done, but because Archer believed in you with such determination, I beg you to save his life for his sake, for the sake of his wife, and for the sake of the people he touches."

He stared into the night for another moment. "My daughter . . . She needs another chance. If you can work in Archer Pierce's life, you can work in Trisha's."

Mitchell felt he hadn't yet done enough. He picked up the telephone and dialed Jessica Pierce's number. Before it could ring he hung up, realizing that he would be calling her out of a need to assuage his own guilt. It wouldn't help her right now.

Later. He would speak with her later.

CHAPTER | 31

Archer heard the trickle of water in the distance and felt the burning thirst. He opened his eyes to sunlight filtering through the cedar branches. He still felt no pain in his back. His biggest discomfort was thirst, and it attacked him with a vengeance.

His throat was raw from shouting for help, his shoulder muscles tight and achy from overuse after pulling himself through the mud after the water receded, elbows stiff and sore from scrapes. He reached up and touched his face, and felt the heat.

Fever.

He tried again to wiggle his toes, flex his ankles, bend his knees.

Nothing. No pain. Nothing at all.

He looked around him at the sea of mud and debris. Last night, as he'd dragged himself over the rocks and brush and trash, he hadn't been able to find a single puddle in the sandy soil from which to drink. He was already weak from hunger, but now quenching his thirst took top priority, especially if he was running a fever.

He reached for the trunk of the pine tree to which he had pulled himself before collapsing for the night.

Time to start the shuffle again. He drew his bearings from the cliffs that rose above Black Oak River, about two hundred yards south of him now. He would go directly north from here, in the direction of the road, and pray he came upon a rivulet of water before he ran out of strength.

The telephone awakened Jessica Wednesday morning, and she rushed to pick it up before it could awaken her in-laws.

"Yes?"

"Jessie, it's me."

She sat up and glanced at the clock. Seven in the morning. "Heather? What's wrong? Is everything okay?"

"Everything's fine on this end. Have you had any leads on Archer?"

"Actually, yes. I received a call last night from Tony Dalton. They've broadened the parameters of the search because of new information. Someone found his cell phone upriver from the bridge, buried in the mud of a cliff bank."

"Good. You'll let me know if you hear more?"

"Of course I will. How did the show go last night?"

"It went." There was a hint of hesitation in her voice. "Same as Saturday and Sunday."

"Did something go wrong?"

"Not a thing, but, Jessie, it's just not the same without you. That's why I called Garth Hammerstain and told him I didn't want the solo show."

Thank you, Lord. "You turned him down?"

"Sure did. He gave me the whole spiel. I knew you'd die of embarrassment if you saw some of those outfits he wanted me to wear. Whoa, talk about cleavage city. And the songs were brainless."

"You're staying with me at the theater?"

"Yep. I don't want to have my own show. We're a team. It isn't the same unless we do it together."

"Sis, that's the best news I've heard . . . in a while." She thought about the baby and decided not to say anything yet. She still wanted Archer to be the first person she told.

"Dad there yet?" Heather asked.

"I haven't seen him."

"He's probably already out searching. He called me last night—you believe that? I'm surprised he knew my number."

"He needs to know about the change in search location."

"I'll see if I can get in touch with him."

"Thanks. I'll see you soon?"

"Sure you will. Talk to you later."

As Jessica hung up, she recalled a dream she'd had last night. She had never put much stock in the portent of dreams, but she knew immediately that something had changed for her.

The dream, which even now threatened to disappear from her last wisps of memory, had been more of an impression, really. In it she had been in Eureka Springs, Arkansas, where she and Archer had spent their honeymoon. She'd been standing before the seven-story-tall statue that depicted Christ. Impressed into the shape of that open-armed statue had been many familiar faces. Archer. Mom and Dad Pierce. Shirley Boucher. John and Helen Netz. Jade Myers. Lauren. Grant and Brooke and Beau.

Together, with many others from the church and others from Jessica's life, they had formed the body. Together, she knew, they truly formed the body of Christ, not just some statue.

Of course, intellectually, she had grasped that concept long ago, but ever since she joined the Dogwood Springs Baptist Church, she had been so overwhelmed by her attempts to be a "pastor's wife" that she'd been unable to interact with the church the way she needed to—simply as another church member. Part of the problem was that she still didn't fit into this tightly knit community. Another part of it had been her relationship with Helen Netz.

That had changed. Somewhere along the way she had come to understand Helen, a woman who had been lost in despair since the death of her children, and who, apparently, continued to blame herself for their deaths. She was an injured part of that same body of Christ, and she would need extra attention and kindness.

Jessica left the house quietly, allowing her in-laws to sleep in. They had been up late last night, and she knew they were tired.

When she pulled into the upper parking lot of the church a few minutes later, she saw three other cars parked there, none of which belonged to John and Helen Netz. She had known that the church was being kept open for a round-the-clock prayer vigil until they found Archer—Helen had reminded her of it several times.

She walked silently through the carpeted foyer and entered the sanctuary, then stopped. She had never been in this place without feeling Archer's presence here.

His presence.

Not God's presence. Archer's.

Oh, Lord, is that what I've been doing?

Five people sat together at the far right front of the sanctuary, and someone spoke in a deep prayer voice that didn't carry clearly to the back. It sounded like Leo Latshaw. Jessica crept down the aisle as she listened to Leo's voice grow more distinct.

Not wanting to disrupt them, Jessica crept to the steps beside the Lord's Supper table and knelt silently. When that prayer ended, another began, and she felt a soothing presence steal over her. This was her church now. Lauren was right; she needed them. They also needed her.

"Jessica?" someone whispered beside her and placed a hand on her arm.

She looked up to find Jade Myers kneeling down next to her.

Dwight and Anne Hahnfeld and Leo Latshaw came to join them.

Without comment they knelt around her and placed their hands on her shoulders and began, once more, to pray.

———

No more sweat.

Archer collapsed into the mud, panting. The muscles in his arms and shoulders screamed with pain. He was no longer sweating. The heat was building up in his body. His heartbeat pounded in his ears. The world went dark.

In that darkness someone smacked his head between two river rocks, harder and harder, with devilish glee. He felt himself fade in and out of consciousness, unable to get a grip long enough to open his eyes.

Gradually, his heart rhythm slowed, and his breathing regulated. His tormentor lost interest and faded away.

A warm wind riffled his hair. He waited another few seconds and opened his eyes. The sky spun around him sickeningly. He retched with a dry heave.

A moment later he raised his head.

Prickles of pain showered down his neck. Slowly, cautiously, he levered himself up to look behind him.

"Fifty feet," he muttered hoarsely. He'd come no more than fifty feet. He felt as if he'd just run a marathon, dragging himself forward from sapling to tree to bush, using them as anchors to pull himself forward a few inches at a time.

Without water.

Throbbing pain streaked across his head and down his neck once more. He collapsed, pressing his forehead into the cool mud.

He'd spent all these months hanging out in the ER, and he had no idea what kind of damage he might be doing to his back, or to his brain after that concussion.

As he rested, however, the pain subsided in his head. He became aware, once more, of birdsong harmonizing with the whisper of wind through the branches above his head.

It was beautiful music. Why had he never heard it this way before?

If he got out alive, he would be sure to listen.

Maybe he'd be able to hear this in heaven.

Or if he lived, maybe he would have more time to listen from a wheelchair.

He closed his eyes and felt his lids burn, felt the dryness of his mouth. He could barely swallow, could hear the wheeze in his throat.

The fever was definitely getting worse.

The harmony changed slightly, and he tried to place it. Strange, it sounded like a dog baying. He'd heard of catbirds but never dogbirds. Auditory hallucinations? The hounds of hell?

In the past twenty-four hours—was that how long it had been since the roar of the river had dissipated?—he'd been the audience to this musical concert. Every time he'd slowed to rest after dragging himself inch by inch over the rough terrain, he had heard the singing. At times he still suspected that the angels must be hovering nearby, listening, maybe even prompting the birds when they missed a note.

He closed his eyes, and he could almost imagine the ethereal beauty of his wife's voice reaching him from somewhere in the distance. *Jessica . . . Lord, be with her.*

Along with the heavenly music, he'd seen artwork in the sky so supreme it had brought tears to his eyes. The Master Artist knew how to use the stars and the clouds, the moon and the sun to highlight the spring green of the forest.

If not for Jessica, he would gladly die right here, right now.

He might have no choice.

Again the baying inserted an odd dissonance into the music. It came more insistently than before, and Archer frowned. A hound from a nearby farm. He'd heard no sounds of other farm animals—no horses, cows, no roosters crowing. He'd heard an occasional jet fly overhead, and in the distance he'd heard a train whistle or a honking car horn.

Would his body become the prey of hungry dogs . . . maybe coyotes, vultures?

He retreated into darkness, seeking oblivion, but the baying followed him there, chasing him through the heat, stalking him along the trail he had created in the forest—the short yet endless trail.

Maybe there were dogs in heaven. He had always suspected that there were. Had hoped.

Maybe he was there already. He gave up his hold on consciousness as he opened his mouth to whisper, "Just take me, Lo—"

A wet sponge attacked his face, drawing a slimy line down his right cheekbone. He reached up to push it away, and it attacked his hand.

He forced his burning eyes open and found himself looking into the soulful dark eyes of a familiar, long-snouted face.

Coot, Charles Lane's bloodhound.

As if in a dream he heard a shout in the distance, laughter, saw his normally shy father-in-law hollering at the dog to get back while he ran to Archer's side and dropped to his knees.

Coot danced in an excited circle, baying merrily like this was some kind of celebration.

Charles leaned over him. "Archer? Son, can you hear me? Are you hurt?"

"My back," he said. "Dad, I think my back's broken."

———

Jessica held Mimi Peterson's hand as she sat beside the exam bed and listened to Mimi tell about the struggle she'd had with her undi-agnosed disorder.

"It's been so awful, all these months being accused of faking pain just so I could get a shot of that stupid medication that made things even worse."

"It sounds horrible. I wish you could have found help sooner."

"If you ask me, it was Dr. Sheldon who discovered the real problem, even though it was Dr. Caine's office that called me and set me up for treatment."

Archer had been right. Patients desperately needed a listening ear, and Mimi was especially needy right now.

"How is the pain?" Jessica asked.

"It's getting better, but I had another episode this morning, and thought I'd come in and make sure everything's doing what it should. Dr. Caine told me yesterday that the pain should go away soon. I hope so."

"So do I," Jessica said. She smiled at Mimi.

"They gave me blood transfusions . . . something like that. It's the heme in hemoglobin that my body isn't producing right. Dr. Caine explained all about it. I'm hoping this will be my last time in here."

"Jessica?" someone called from behind her.

She turned to see Lauren standing in the doorway, blond hair pulled back in its workday ponytail, a half smile on her face.

"Mimi, do you mind if I borrow your prayer partner for a few minutes?" Lauren asked.

Mimi looked disappointed. "No, that's okay. Jessica, why don't we get together for lunch sometime next week? My treat."

"That sounds good." She said good-bye and followed Lauren out of the room.

"What's up? Do you have another patient for me?"

Lauren's McCaffrey smile shot across her face. "Come with me to Grant's office."

From the corner of her eye, Jessica saw a nurse and a secretary watching her intently.

Lauren ushered her into the office, where Grant stood waiting. Lauren closed the door.

"Jessica," Grant said, "we've got some good news."

Jessica looked from Lauren to Grant, then caught her breath. "Archer."

Lauren burst into delighted laughter.

"It *is* Archer?" Jessica exclaimed.

"They've found him," Grant said. "He's alive."

She cried out and caught him by the shoulders. "Alive! He's alive! Oh, thank you, God!"

"You need to be prepared, though, Jessica." Grant pulled a chair over for her. "Have a seat."

"Why? What's wrong?" She sat down.

Grant sat facing her. "He's unable to walk. At this point we don't know the extent of his injuries, and I wouldn't want to venture a guess. He's conscious and talking, though he isn't making complete sense right now. He has a high fever. They've secured him on a long spine board with c-spine immobilization."

"Talking. He's talking!" Archer was alive! It was the only thing she could grasp. "Has anyone told Mom and Dad Pierce? Do they know yet?"

"I thought you might want to call them." Grant paused. "Jessica, do you understand what I'm saying about Archer? We don't know what condition he might be in when they bring him here."

"How soon before he gets here?"

"Probably about ten minutes."

Jessica reached for Lauren's hands and held them tightly. "Why didn't I listen to you? Archer's coming home! I'm going to see my husband in ten minutes!" She jumped to her feet and caught Lauren in a tight hug. Then she hugged Grant and then hugged Lauren again.

"Oh, thank you, God. Thank you, thank you, thank you!"

Archer heard his wife's voice and saw her face as soon as he was pulled from the ambulance. He looked up to find her accompanying the gurney through the automatic entrance doors at the ambulance bay. Her face was streaked with tears, and she wore the broadest smile he had ever seen.

"Oh, honey, you're alive!" She laid a hand on his face, and more tears fell down her cheeks as she walked beside him toward the trauma room.

He had never been so relieved. He was alive. His wife was right beside him. He wouldn't worry about his back and legs, wouldn't worry about anything. Right now, all he wanted to do was revel in the fact that he was alive. God had answered his prayers—and those of his wife, his family, his friends, and most likely every single member of his church.

Thank you, God!

Jessica didn't leave Archer's side until Grant and Lauren shooed her out of the room.

"It's just for a few minutes," Lauren explained, giving Jessica's arm a reassuring squeeze. "I'll call you as soon as we get him checked out."

Jessica nodded, unable to speak, keeping her gaze fixed on that wonderful muddy face until the door blocked the view of her living, breathing husband.

She turned to pace the hallway of the place that had become so familiar to her. This ER was where she had discovered she was pregnant and where she had discovered the strength of friendship and church kinship. After learning, in this very place just moments ago, that her husband was still alive, the ER had become sacred to her.

She glanced through the reception window to the waiting room as a bedraggled man with broad shoulders stepped through the entry door.

"Dad?"

Her father caught sight of her and rushed across the tile floor, unconcerned about the muddy tracks or the stares from two ladies seated at the far end of the room. "Did they bring him in?" he asked as he reached the reception window and tried to peer around the partition into the ER proper. "He here yet?"

"Yes, he's here. Dad, he's alive!"

He nodded.

She opened the door for him to join her. "You know they found him?"

A pleased grin broadened his face by half. "I know the fella who did."

She caught her breath. "You?"

"Coot did it. Knew he could. Didn't even need that jacket of Archer's. All I had to do was say his name. You know how Coot wallers all over him when you two are down at the farm."

"Oh, Daddy." She flung her arms around him and squeezed, mud and all. "Oh, Daddy, thank you."

CHAPTER 32

On Thursday morning Mitchell Caine walked down the busy hallway of the orthopedics floor of Cox South Hospital in Springfield, avoiding the gazes of staff members. He knew several of the physicians, nurses, and technicians here from residency training as well as years of practice, during which he referred regularly to colleagues at this facility. He had also met many others at regional conferences and social functions.

The medical community was a tight one. When word spread about what he had done, he might well be ostracized at future events. He tried to tell himself that it wouldn't matter, but he knew better.

So many memories . . . Too much to think about right now.

He stopped at the room number the volunteer in the downstairs lobby had given him and took a moment to breathe deeply.

He hesitated at the open door, then stepped into the room. To his relief, Archer was alone. The other hospital bed had no patient.

Archer opened his eyes as Mitchell stepped to the bedside.

To Mitchell's amazement, Archer welcomed him with one of his typical smiles and an outstretched hand.

"Hello, Mitchell, I was hoping to see you."

Mitchell took the hand and held it gently. The skin was scraped and raw-looking.

"Archer, I . . . I can't find the words to express how very sorry . . . I can't—"

"Tony already filled me in on some details," Archer said. "I understand you were the one who called and told him what happened. It was because of that call that my father-in-law found me yesterday."

"It's so hard to believe . . . to imagine . . . that I actually would have done something so despicable, and yet the evidence . . ."

Archer hesitated. "You don't remember?"

"No. I have a . . . a problem with prescription drugs." The humiliation of those words . . . "I was under the influence Friday night. Didn't Tony tell you?"

"He didn't give me all the details, only the important information. I was a little out of it yesterday." Archer watched Mitchell as if trying to decide whether or not he was emotionally stable enough to hear this.

"Tell me what happened," Mitchell said.

"You were behind me, and your SUV hydroplaned. My car had already begun to slide, and it didn't take much force from your front bumper to push me over the edge."

Mitchell winced. "I'm so sorry."

"But surely you've heard the prognosis," Archer said. "I have a broken back." He reached for the bed rail and repositioned himself slightly. "But there was no displacement—I think that's what you docs like to call it—and no permanent damage. I have what you physicians like to refer to as spinal shock. I should regain the use of my legs in a few days. Meanwhile, I'm going to take it easy and make the most of my downtime."

"Tony also said you weren't pressing charges."

"Why would I do that?"

"Because of me you nearly died. Your wife and your family, your church . . . all of them endured a great deal of agony. There is such a thing as justice."

"Over an accident?"

"An unnecessary accident. One that would not have happened if I had been behaving responsibly."

"I'm safe now, Mitchell. I've had a life-changing experience that I wouldn't trade for anything."

Mitchell didn't understand this man. He never had.

"I don't know if I can explain this well enough for you to understand it," Archer said. "My mind's still a little foggy from the fever, but I discovered a lot about myself while I was out there. I realized that I had a problem with faith and with wanting my own way. While I was out there I had to struggle to forgive you, because I had seen your face in the glow of my headlights just before I went over the side. I knew you had been the one to hit me, and I couldn't understand why you hadn't come to help me."

"So why forgive me?"

"Because I realized that you could well have been injured, too. In fact, you've been among the walking injured for years. And so instead of blaming you I prayed for you."

"I don't—"

"I know you don't want my prayers, Mitchell, but—"

"I don't *deserve* your prayers," Mitchell said softly. "I've come to realize that I do need them. Very much."

Any other time he would have been amused by the expression of surprise that crossed Archer's features. Now he was only gratified that Archer had brought up a subject Mitchell very much wanted to discuss.

"Why don't we talk about it?" Archer asked. "My schedule looks pretty clear for the next hour or so."

Mitchell pulled a chair to the bedside and sat down. "Go ahead and talk, Archer, I'm listening."

———

Lauren sat in the sunlight of the brilliant April morning and watched the antics of Brooke and Beau Sheldon as they worked to put the porch swing together.

"Oh, *duh*, not that way," Brooke said. "You've got the ratchy thingy turned backward."

"It's a ratchet, not a thingy, and it isn't backward, it's just the wrong size."

"You know, Beau, you could use a shop class next year."

"*You* could use another class or two in home ec. I'm still burping that meatless wonder you tried to pass off as meatloaf last night."

"Would you just give me those instructions and shut up?"

Lauren sat back and closed her eyes as she listened to them.

"Do you think that thing will be safe once they get the swing up?" came a deep, beloved voice beside her.

She opened her eyes to find Grant placing a lawn chair beside hers. He held out a cup of tea for her.

She took it and sipped. "Mmm, vanilla. I love it. Thanks. I think I'll let Brooke test the swing first. If she doesn't fall and break something, I'd be willing to give it a try."

"I heard that!"

Lauren chuckled. Yes, she could definitely get accustomed to this. Grant sank down into the chair and leaned toward her for a kiss. She loved the feel of him, the smell of him, and the gleam of attraction she saw in those gray eyes.

She couldn't imagine, now, why she'd had any doubts at all. This was going to be a wonderful life.

———

Jessica closed the door to Archer's room and leaned against it, giving a satisfied sigh. "Finally! Some time alone."

He took her hand as she leaned over his bed. "You handled all the visitors wonderfully, Jessica. You're a natural."

"Ha. That's what you think."

"You are, you just don't know it yet. I need to talk to you about something."

Her expression froze. "What, Archer? Has the doctor been in? Is there a problem with—"

"There's no problem with my back. Would you please relax? Remember last summer, when I told you my work wasn't finished at Dogwood Springs Baptist Church?"

"Sure do. It was during the mercury scare—"

"When you proposed to me," Archer teased.

"Oh, yes, and you tried to use the church as an excuse to keep from accepting my proposal."

"That isn't how I remember it," Archer said. "Anyway, things have changed since then." He paused and looked out the window, his heart sending up a quick prayer for strength and wisdom. Was he sure about this? Enough to tell Jessica?

Yes, he was.

Jessica leaned forward and laid her hand on his cheek. "Honey? What is it?"

"I believe my work at the church *is* finished now."

She continued to hover over him, waiting, as if she expected a punch line.

"I'm serious," he said. "Our church needs someone besides me to be the administrative pastor. I might take the youth, or we might eventually take another much smaller church, but I don't belong in this particular position. I think that's what this whole thing might have been about."

"You think God dumped you in the river to get your attention?" she teased.

"I don't think it's that simple, but something occurred to me forcibly while I lay there in the darkness all those hours. That whole accident became a metaphor depicting my out-of-control life."

Jessica sat down in the chair beside his bed. "Interesting, because for me it became a depiction of our marriage and my fear of losing you to the church. But when I realized I might lose you for good, it was the very same church that supported me through it."

"I love our church," Archer said. "But I allowed my work there to take the place of God as the focus of my life. Just as my tires lost contact with the surface of the road and spun out of control because of the depth of the water, my life—our lives—were out of control. Up until this accident, the frantic pace of life had become so overwhelming that some mornings I hit the floor at a run and didn't slow down until my head hit the pillow late at night. I had my meals on the run, said my prayers on the run, and only brought out my Bible when I needed to share a comforting Scripture with a church member or a patient at the hospital. I've been going about it all the wrong way."

"And so you think it took this to get your priorities back into line?" Jessica asked.

"Seems like it to me. Do you think I could get a full-time job as a hospital chaplain?"

"I think you could do anything God calls you to do." Her smile widened. "He's called you to do one more thing."

Archer shifted in the bed, mystified that she didn't seem to be getting what he was trying to tell her. "Jess, I'm resigning as church pastor."

She laughed. "Hallelujah! Perfect timing, Daddy."

He chuckled at her. She'd finally gotten . . . *"Daddy?"*

She kissed him on the cheek, her soft breath warm on his skin. "One of the worst days of my life turned out to be one of *our* best. Sunday morning, when Tony and Caryn broke the news to me that a farmer had found the Kia in his bottom field by the river, I fainted. Tony and Caryn took me to the ER. Grant ran tests, and I'm pregnant."

She wasn't kidding . . . She was serious.

"Oh, Jessica! *Yes!*" He shouted it so loudly he was afraid a nurse might open the door and come rushing in.

"I'm about seven weeks along now," Jessica said. "So I want you to start healing so you'll be in perfect shape to help me with diapers when the time comes."

"Diapers! Yes! Anything you want. Hey, you know those bubble gum cigars they used to sell in the stores? They came in pink and blue. Is it too soon—"

"Archer! Cigars?"

"We're having a baby!"

Jessica chuckled. "Now we can spread the news to our families and to the church. I wanted you to be the first person I told." Her gaze sobered. "How do you think the church will handle both our announcements at once?"

"They handled the tornado, and they handled the flood. They can handle a new baby and a new pastor."

"And you've thought it all through? You're sure this is God's will?"

He took her hands and kissed them. "Jess, I thought you'd be ecstatic about the prospect of actually seeing me every day."

"Oh, I will. I think it's wonderful. But I don't want you to feel pressured into it because of my demands."

"It's almost as if God gave me a word picture—a very literal one."

"And so you decided you aren't a pastor? Archer, you're wonderful with—"

"That's just it, Jess. I'm a pastor, I'm not a church administrator, and that's what our growing church needs now, someone who can manage a large number of people without killing himself—and his marriage—in the process."

She smiled down at him. "So you feel at peace with the decision?"

"Yes. Do you?"

Her smile widened. "I'm trying not to get too excited about this. I don't want to get my hopes up and then—"

"Then you want me to do it?"

"More than anything, especially with a baby coming."

"We'll lose my salary," he warned.

"We'll keep mine. If God's directing you to do this, then He'll take care of us. Besides, He might just be directing you to a smaller congregation."

"You think?"

"You're a healer. You have to be able to give that personal touch, that personal, individualized compassion."

"Have I told you lately how much I love you?" he said softly.

"Sounds like a country-western song."

"Come here and kiss me."

Thanks again to the Bethany House staff, whose kind wisdom and encouragement have kept us going. Dave Horton, your friendship and guidance have been priceless to us. Karen Schurrer, how do you manage to read our minds so clearly? Thank you for always being there. Jolene Steffer, thank you for your tight attention to detail. You've saved us from embarrassment several times. Alex Fane, thank you for your computer expertise and understanding with all the questions from the computer-challenged. Gary and Carol Johnson, Jeanne Mikkelson, Jill Parker, Brett Benson, Teresa Fogarty, Alison Curtis, you've been a joyful part of our lives.

As always, without the love and support of family we would never have attempted this book. Lorene Cook, thank you for your selfless giving, for unconditional love and support all these years. We love you, Mom. Mother and Pa, Vera and Ray Overall, thank you for always encouraging, always accepting.

Thank you, Angie Hunt, who can do more things in one day than I can do in a year. Thank you for starting ChiLibris. And thank you, dear friends of ChiLibris, for the cord of loving friendship that binds us together.

Thanks to Harry Lee Kraus, Jr., fellow writer, physician, and friend, who was kind enough to give us a consult on a medical case.

Thank you, Ellie Schroder, for selflessly sharing your world of fiction from New Zealand. Thank you, friends and sisters in WritingChambers, who touch my soul, and whose laughter echoes around the world.

Lori Copeland, B. J. Hoff, Brenda Minton, Robin Lee Hatcher, Terri Blackstock, Jack Cavanaugh, Deb Raney, Colleen Coble, Steph Whitson, Jim Bell, Lisa Samson, Janelle Schneider, Nancy Moser, Eric Wiggin . . . your encouragement keeps us breathing through the inevitable hurts and disappointments.

Thanks, Barbara Warren of the Blue Mountain Editing Service. You're a writing coach of the toughest kind, and we love you for it.

Jackie Bolton, teacher, editor, and friend, thank you for all the years of knowing us well and loving us anyway.

Grant, Bonnie, Jessica, and Megan Schmidt, you provided us with enough inspiration to people countless books with talented and wonderful characters. The best is yet to come.

Thanks to John Stubblefield, who helped us with mechanical specifics for the electrical difficulties in a hospital attacked by a storm's fury.

The list should go on, because we've received so much help for this book and this series, from so many people, so many friends. May God fill you with purpose, and may your kindnesses to us be repaid a hundred times over.